CHANDELIER

CHANDELIER

CHANDELIER

DAVID O'MEARA

NIGHTWOOD EDITIONS

2024

Copyright © David O'Meara, 2024

1 2 3 4 5 — 28 27 26 25 24

ALL RIGHTS RESERVED. No part of this publication may be reproduced, stored in a retrieval system or transmitted, in any form or by any means, without prior permission of the publisher or, in the case of photocopying or other reprographic copying, a licence from Access Copyright, the Canadian Copyright Licensing Agency, www.accesscopyright.ca, info@accesscopyright.ca.

Nightwood Editions
P.O. Box 1779
Gibsons, BC VON 1V0
Canada
www.nightwoodeditions.com

COVER DESIGN AND TYPOGRAPHY: Rafael Chimicatti
COVER IMAGE: Maryna Yazbeck

Nightwood Editions acknowledges the support of the Canada Council for the Arts, the Government of Canada, and the Province of British Columbia through the BC Arts Council.

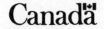 

This book has been printed on 100% post-consumer recycled paper.

Printed and bound in Canada.

LIBRARY AND ARCHIVES CANADA CATALOGUING IN PUBLICATION

Title: Chandelier / David O'Meara.
Names: O'Meara, David, 1968- author.
Identifiers: Canadiana (print) 20240380800 | Canadiana (ebook) 20240384989 | ISBN 9780889714762 (softcover) | ISBN 9780889714779 (EPUB)
Subjects: LCGFT: Novels.
Classification: LCC PS8579.M359 C43 2024 | DDC C813/.54—dc23

For Dorothy

Part 1
GEORGIA AT SEA

1

BREAKFAST WAS A BUFFET exhibition of fish and vegetables. Sugary pastries. Orange juice and coffee. Georgia managed to eat some rice, persimmons and the spicy kimchi, flushing it all down with three cups of instant coffee. She felt fuzzy and whacked-out. She felt like her head had been wrapped in a bulky towel and thumped with a rubber mallet several times. Everyone milled about the conference tables clutching paper plates. There was a lot of hushed chatter, suspicion and speculation, as if they were part of some social experiment. Blended with jetlag, it drove her spinning. She was having trouble keeping track of everything; the people she met and their countries of origin: England, Ireland, Australia. A woman from Jamaica. She met Phil, a middle-aged guy from Atlanta. James from San Francisco. The conversations were all the same. *When did you get here? What is going to happen next? Where will they send us?*

She took out the journal she'd bought at the airport bookstore. Its thick red cover was still in plastic wrap. Her therapist had suggested she write down her thoughts if she was feeling overwhelmed, if the information was arriving too fast. So, Georgia started a list of names. She could cross any of them out later.

Eve, another Canadian, located Georgia and sauntered over. She was wearing some kind of spandex jogging ensemble, complaining about thrombosis and fretting over her chances of finding peanut butter in South Korea. "I can't understand a word the instructors are saying, can you? Their English is terrible. I don't know how I'm going to make it through this year without my sweetie-pie."

"Who is that?"

Eve showed Georgia a picture of her white terrier.

Eve would be the first to be purged from Georgia's list.

At the education centre, they had orientation classes. Lectures on Korean culture, language and history. A lot of the presenters just handed out sheets that they read from, so Georgia decided to skip the second half and suntan on some grass by the river. A few others joined her. Phil and James. Ita from Dublin. Ray, who was from Birmingham, England, via Tanzania. He had rolled up his pant legs and waded into the water. Georgia was bumming smokes.

Phil and James tossed a baseball back and forth.

"Where did you get the gloves?" Georgia shouted.

"We brought them," James said.

"Isn't that cute. You found each other," she said, slathering her shoulders with sunscreen. She was a basement dweller and consistently turned lobster in the sun.

"The water seems pretty clean. Anyone want to swim?" Ray said.

"You first," Georgia challenged.

He considered the dare and stood looking at the water. Georgia leapt up and charged past him down the rough beach, exploded into the shallows before plunging into a deeper area beyond.

Ray hurdled after her, kicking up chaotic torrents of water.

"You idiots," Phil shouted from the grass.

They splashed around laughing, soaked in their clothes, the water a refuge from the naked pulse of the afternoon sun. Georgia waded toward a sandbar. The anvil of her jetlag had lifted. "That's kind of gross, isn't it?" she said to Ray as their ripples grew calmer, the silt dispersing. Mud was sucking at her foot. There were pop cans. A dead fish. Rotting branches. Screaming and cackling, Georgia chased Ray off the beach.

They'd posted the list of their teaching placements. Everyone crowded around the pinned display of results. Beside Georgia's name was "Gwangju."

She checked with Ita. "Where are you going?"

"Chinju. No idea where that is," she said.

James was going to Busan.

They found a map. It didn't help with any reality, only general scale, gazing over their life from a projected height, the roads into pink cities, the coastlines and green summits marked with a cross. They hardly knew where they were going even then. Just into mysterious streets and rooms, away from these two-day friendships. Buses would be arriving in the morning. There was nothing left to do but wander about and say goodbye. They chatted in the sun, waiting for the closing ceremony. Dragon dancers performed for them in the university square. The air shook with drums. People found other participants assigned to the same city as theirs. Ray was going to Gwangju too. Georgia squealed and laughed and hugged him.

Someone suggested they all get a drink and a group headed to a corner store with a makeshift tented patio. There was a yard to the side, with trampled dirt between high grass and a water tank. Several plastic chairs and stools were placed around tables. They'd go inside for beers and carry them back. Soon, the owner was serving everyone, clearing empty bottles, selling cigarettes and some phone cards. He was making a killing.

"Do you want a beer?" James asked Georgia.

"I don't drink."

He raised an eyebrow.

"I'd murder for some weed though," she said. "I wonder if I can find a hook-up in Gwangju."

"Good luck," he said.

The intel seemed to be true: you couldn't find marijuana in Korea. There were seismic fines and jail time. Georgia had heard a rumour that there was some distribution through the internet. Seemed risky. She figured she might have to go without.

When the smiling store owner returned, grappling three big beer bottles in each hand, Georgia watched as the group passed the drinks around, jealous of the available exit routes out of their heads. Everyone had been given an envelope of advance Korean cash and was throwing it around like it wasn't real. No one knew the value of the change they got back. No one cared. They were getting drunk in the sun in the waning afternoon, cooking up plans to visit each other, sharing cell numbers, posting selfies on their Instagram feeds and wandering off to piss behind some crates.

"Escape or adventure?" Phil asked as he shared another cigarette with Ray and Georgia.

She filled her lungs and let the smoke roll lazily out between her lips. "What do you mean?"

Phil's theory was that the people who came to teach overseas fell into two categories: those looking for an adventure or those trying to escape.

"I've met a whole bunch of people these past few days," he said. "A lot of us want to travel, maybe work off a debt while we're doing it. But a number of people are just trying to get away from a problem they want to leave behind."

"Example," Georgia stated.

"Barbara over there," Phil said, pointing to a grassy side of the patio a few tables away. Barbara was in her forties, wore retro sixties glasses, was tanned with a black tumbleweed head of hair. She had a smoker's rasp and a guilty laugh. Georgia had only talked to her briefly over the last two days.

"Messy divorce," Phil said. "Police. Lots of legal shit."

Georgia watched her puff at her cigarette, imagining some frenzied argument with a nasty spouse.

"I talked to this guy—David?—yesterday. Did you meet him? Short dude with the tribal tattoo?" Phil pointed to his forearm.

"Says he did time for theft. Mostly electronics. TVs. But he tapped a few cars too. Loves to talk about it. Just ask him. His father made him apply here just to keep him out of jail. He did the ESL teaching course and got a certificate two months ago."

"He's better qualified than me." Georgia laughed.

They glanced around to see if David was nearby.

"He's probably going through all our luggage now," Ray said.

"*Where's* your *car*?!" Georgia said with fake alarm.

They were laughing, smoking. Phil. Ray and James. They ripped through more beers. Georgia was enjoying the nicotine buzz and the cool evening air. Talking empty talk without any meaning to it. There was no connection to her life. She felt untouched. She'd slipped off her old skin and left it in the grass. The abandoned trajectories. She hadn't laughed like this for months.

Months and months.

"What about you," Ray said to her. "Escape or adventure?"

She looked at him. "Neither," she said. "This was my friend's idea."

"She here?"

Georgia watched the crowd of half-inebriated westerners, trying to imagine Natalie among them; what she'd say, what she'd think, if she could have come all this way. Georgia kept conjuring her friend's scissoring stare, the radiance of her sardonic grin. Nothing had weakened her contours. What madness they could have had. It would have been a sight.

It would have been a whole different world.

"No," Georgia finally said. "She couldn't make it."

"Where you coming from, Ray? What's your story?" James mumbled, handing him a beer.

"I was just trying to get away from all you white people."

2

IN THE LATE AFTERNOON the bus left for Gwangju with a dozen ESL teachers scattered toward the back. She didn't recognize the other westerners, other than Ray, who joined her in a seat and listened while the organizer described the next day's itinerary. The sun dropped and disappeared across the low hills and it was dark highways and concrete apartment blocks, the traffic signs lit up by headlights, the driver's serious face studying the road in the glow of his console as they drove south. Exhausted and humbled by the midday farewell drinks session, other participants nodded off, or stared quietly through windows, overwhelmed by the transitions. Two hours passed. Darkness hid the new marvels Georgia had travelled to find. She was grateful for the silence and time, not wanting to arrive, or go back, only to be suspended between, erased for now from who she was, there in a capsule of nightfall and fibreglass and steel. She adjusted her overhead light and opened the red journal. The first time her therapist recommended buying a notebook, Georgia had filled one with black stars, those satisfying five-pointed doodles of obliteration, adrift in a self-annulling void she felt everything had become then.

"Are you using the journal?" the therapist had asked.

"Yes."

"What are you writing?"

Georgia showed her.

The therapist looked blankly at the barbed scribbles.

"Have you shown this to anyone?" she asked.

"Like who?"

"Anyone. Your parents . . ."

"No."

"Well, it's progress. I think that's good. But try to express different views."

On the bus now, she began to stroke black marks across James and Phil and Ita, ferried to other destinations in the South Korean landscape. No one left but Ray. The list was pointless now. She tore the sheet along the margin and exposed a fresh white one. A start needed to be made. She resisted thinking too much and moved the pen over the top of the page, trying to keep it legible in the shaking from the bus:

I'm going to tell you about what I did and how I felt about it. But what with all the stupidity and hurt feelings and pain and regret, I don't know if I'm up for the job.

She got no further. The variations of possibility stopped her. She watched a fan oscillating above the driver, blowing the sluggish air around. Fields and the lights of towns danced past. When they steered into a hotel parking lot, Georgia wished she'd slept like the others. Outside, a reception waited for them, with various officials, members of the school board and persons assigned to be co-teachers. Georgia met Mr. Yung. Bowing, he introduced himself and informed everyone they'd be driven to have blood tests and eye exams tomorrow, for insurance purposes.

"I'd like a haircut too," Georgia said.

Mr. Yung looked at her with confusion. Then he saw her start to laugh.

"I think I am very lucky to meet you," he said.

Mr. Yung was an English grammar teacher at Georgia's assigned school. He was fifty-eight, wore thick glasses and had the distracted look of being constantly harassed.

At the welcome dinner, they were given maps of the city. Georgia looked at hers. The city core was ringed by expressways. Neighbourhoods of crosshatch streets. An airport to the southwest. A river.

"Where are we?" she asked, her hand hovering over the map.

Mr. Yung reached across the table, pointing.

"Here."

Teachers and school officials stuffed themselves with marinated beef, fish and vegetables in an array of small metal bowls. At a long table close to the floor, they knelt or sat cross-legged on little pillows. Bottles were passed around. Beer and soju. Georgia felt waves of exhaustion and picked at the cabbage and beans, apologizing mournfully as she declined the alcohol.

Now the westerners decamped to a bar. Despite spending the day together, they'd hardly spoken, between the official speeches and tours.

Georgia eyed the group, her assorted colleagues randomly conjoined to a shared orbit for the future. Jean, from Vancouver, struck her as uptight, controlling and maybe a bit severe. She kept labelled folders to organize her things, with different coloured pens, seemingly task-coded for priority. Likewise, Ron from Massachusetts set off alarms with his faded Hawaiian shirts and fleeing eye contact.

There were two Australians, Mick and Becca. Mick was older, pushing forty, but she knew she'd like him the first time they met.

"Where you from?" he asked Georgia.

"Canada."

"Snowy bastards."

Ray snorted.

"Any word on where anyone is living?" Becca said to the air.

"Board said they're looking for apartments," Ray said.

"Look," Mick said. "We talked to my co-teacher, Mr. Shin, and he said that maybe a few of us could get something together."

GEORGIA AT SEA

The bar they'd chosen was dark and empty. Mirrors, bannisters and vinyl. More bottles of beer arrived. Georgia watched everyone getting leisurely stewed. She was smoking like a forest fire.

"Are you straight-edge?" Ron asked, noticing her untouched tumbler.

"I gave it up."

Becca, the Australian, threw her hand over Georgia's shoulder and hugged her conspiratorially. "We'll have to fix that. Won't we, mate?"

Outside, later, she was still sober and exhausted.

"You want to share one?" Georgia said to Ray. She shook the cigarette pack. It was a Korean brand. They'd run out of American Lucky Strikes. They lifted themselves onto a concrete wall and lit up.

"You're going through a lot of these," he said, holding the cigarette awkwardly, like a specimen.

"I'm used to doing a lot of dumb things."

"Issues, is it?"

"I collect them. Start a list."

"Are you doing okay?"

"Of course. Look at me."

Georgia struck a pose, the cigarette dangling from the side of her mouth, her eyes crossed. They sat there laughing. A moped buzzed past, the driver looking at them like they'd just landed from Mars.

"I don't know what I'm doing here," Georgia said. "I'm not a teacher."

She told Ray how teaching overseas had been her friend's idea. This was Natalie's adventure, not Georgia's. She felt like she'd stolen the blueprint. The chaos was rented; she was a fraud. These last days were beautiful and wild but Georgia had no idea what she was doing here. Maybe she should pack it in while there was still time. She was talking, her mind headlong with indecision.

"Sorry," she said.

They sat there.

"Don't go, love," Ray said. "You'll see. It's going to be brilliant."

"I feel fucking lost."

"You can't be lost. You're right here, aren't you?"

3

SHE'D BEEN ASSIGNED to a middle school of burgeoning teenagers. Georgia felt like an imposter. She foresaw disruption, chaos and hormones. Only a few years older than her students, she was still affiliated with teenage rebellion. The universe was reversing its rule already. There would be eighteen different classes with fifty students, each class once a week. Nine hundred students. It should have been a cinch: prep one lesson each week, teach it eighteen times. But the reality was that every class was different and the lesson needed to be adjusted for each class's capabilities, maturity and interest. It took some time for her to figure this out and make it work. Over the first weeks, she made a new list. The best classes. The worst. The keeners and the clowns.

On Georgia's second day of teaching, Mrs. Kim, who taught English grammar, walked toward her, waving.

"We can show you your apartment now."

It was just before lunch. They got into Mr. Yung's car. He drove them through the school gates, turning right, then right again. They were soon walking down an alley between low, two-storey houses. Georgia could hear the physical education students cheering their teams in a baseball game back in the schoolyard. At the end of the alley was a metal gate, painted powder blue and solid except for a prohibition-style sliding peephole. It was surrounded by a concrete arch. Mr. Yung pressed a buzzer. Immediately there were loud barks and vicious snarls from the opposite side. They exchanged looks.

"It's a dog," Mr. Yung said.

The gate emitted a series of metallic scrapes, and a short, elderly woman appeared. Mr. Yung talked to her. She scrutinized Georgia up and down as if Georgia were a head of cabbage she was thinking of buying, nodding as they talked, the deep wrinkles rippling along her mouth like a river delta.

On the second storey was a rooftop deck and a separate apartment. Two small rooms with linoleum floors. A makeshift kitchen was attached to a lean-to where the house's oil tank was stored under corrugated metal. Past a sundeck with sliding doors the bathroom held a western toilet and a shower head jutting from the tiled wall. It seemed more like a converted shack than an apartment but Georgia felt relieved. The September sun was bathing her in its hopeful glow.

"You have to buy furniture," Mrs. Kim said. She had a mother's worry on her face. The worry made Georgia worry.

"There is a cheap place," Mr. Yung said. "They have many old things."

"Used," Mrs. Kim corrected him.

They drove to some junkyard garage stacked with torn, dusty couches, wooden chairs and tables. Mrs. Kim looked over the furniture reluctantly, poking her fingers into the tired upholstery. The junkman was showing Mr. Yung a few of the more stable options.

"I like that table," Georgia said, pointing to one near the entrance. It was made of light wood, with narrow lines carved near its edges and down the legs.

The junkman laughed and said something.

"He eats his lunch there," Mr. Yung said.

But the man was happy to sell it, and to prove that he didn't care, he grabbed another table from the stack and pushed it into place beside the current one. Its legs were uneven, so he folded a square of cardboard three times and fitted it below the shortest leg. He moved a bottle of hot sauce onto the substituted table and

GEORGIA AT SEA

stood there admiring the new set-up as if he'd done some major renovation. They picked out two chairs and a small, yellow sofa. Mrs. Kim found a decent mattress. The man produced a metal gas cooker with two elements, practically new.

Mr. Yung haggled. The man groaned in shocked tones. Their heads took turns shaking with reluctance. Georgia heard the words for "hundred" and "thousand" and a few other numbers she'd been coached on at the university, but they were trading too fast for her to understand.

Mr. Yung beamed.

"It's a good price," he said.

The man went into the back to write a receipt.

Georgia touched her pockets.

"The school will pay," Mr. Yung said. "Don't worry."

Georgia was happy. They would be her own things. A couch and chairs. A table.

She had things.

But Mrs. Kim wasn't happy. She'd hardly said a word since they'd arrived. She'd been meandering through the makeshift jumble with an anxious expression, like they were in a submarine struck by a torpedo.

"Are you sure you don't want a homestay?" she asked. "You will miss your family. You'll be all alone. How will you cook?"

Georgia lifted the gas cooker. She couldn't guess how it even worked.

"I'm going to be fine."

4

THE PHONE RANG SIX TIMES before her mother answered. "George. I've been worried." No hello. Her voice brisk, concerned, scolding. The usual passive-aggressive flim-flam. Guilt and care, onslaught and restraint.

"I'm calling from the school," Georgia said. "Still trying to sort cellphone service. I can give you this number for an emergency. A friend's too. I just wanted to say everything's fine. You don't need to freak out. I'm fine. I'm swamped. They've kept us going non-stop."

"Where are you living?"

She told her about the school, the rooftop apartment, the used furniture. Silence. "I love it," Georgia felt the need to add.

"There are some letters here for you, a T4 from the coffee shop . . . What do you want me to do with them?"

Georgia could hear tapping on computer keys.

"Sorry," her mother said. "I'm just getting this note off to a client. Those boxes in the hall? You just left them there."

The faraway clutter made Georgia panic. It was the same dread and guilt and feeling of failure choking out her oxygen, her breath wrapped in dust.

"I don't know. Throw them out."

"Don't you need to look at them? There could be something important. Do you want me to look at them?"

"Sure. Whatever."

"Did you bring enough meds?"

"I don't take those anymore."

"You don't? Since when? Do you think that's a good idea?"

"What's a good idea?"

She could hear her mother thinking, transforming the paused seconds into onus and disappointment, even while she tapped away on her client's note. "Oh, Georgia," she produced through distraction.

"I'm giving you numbers," Georgia said. "Do you have a pen?"

Georgia plugged in the used refrigerator they'd delivered, another artifact from the appliance junkyard. It whirred and clicked to life, like an animal shifting inside a sleeping bag. She needed to spray it down. The sculpted plastic smelled of mould and vinegar and obscure fermentation. After fifteen minutes, she placed her hand on the middle rack. Its tiny engines were circulating cold air already. She'd get some milk and inaugurate it with groceries. A grocery. Putting something on a shelf would lift her resolve.

The gas cooker was hooked up as well, but she stalled at trying it. There were hurdles. Georgia couldn't cook a thing. Her parents had been keenly dedicated to restaurant-going. She was a child of the take-out container and the deli box. The fridge in Ottawa was sporadically stocked with expensive foods more for display than enjoyment. Wasabi mayo and lobster sandwiches. Shepherd's pie with Kobe ground beef, seasoned with Cornish sea salt and Tellicherry black pepper. It was a form of rebellion to leave a Burger King wrapper on the counter.

Ray dropped by after his classes. "I'm fucking exhausted," he said. Then he looked around. "Nice place."

"Is that sarcasm?"

"Do you prefer passive aggression?"

"Versatile, aren't you?"

"You're just getting to know me."

Georgia glanced at the room. "The floors heat up, you know."

"Well, that's good," he said. "You'll need all the help you can get once the wind starts blowing through those cracks."

He pointed at the gap between the wall and the sunroom. The apartment seemed to have been constructed in stages. It was originally an attic with additions slapped into place to make it rentable. The toilet and shower were just a corrugated shed fixed to the side of the building. It had no insulation. But it was solid and snug.

"At least I have a home," Georgia said. "Where do I drop by to visit *you*? The hotel?"

"It's sorted. There's a flat near my school. I move in Friday. And looks like Mick and Becca are sharing a place."

Ray had brought a bag of bottled beer from the corner store. The brands were Hite and OB.

"Groceries! I just plugged the fridge in."

They opened it. Ray placed the beer on the shelves. He'd bought juices too. There was mango and plum. He shook one at Georgia, who had started to tally the things she'd still need—some plates, bowls, pots, spoons and knives—for a functional kitchen. She sighed heavily.

"Maybe give me a beer," she said.

"You sure? It's not regulation."

Using her lighter, she popped the tops off two bottles and handed one to Ray.

They sat on the rooftop, which doubled as a balcony with a low concrete balustrade along its walls. There was enough room for fifteen people up there. Georgia's landlady had a few ochre porcelain jars on one end to ferment her kimchi. There was a clothesline wired from the eaves to a metal post. A large quince tree with wide, emerald leaves rose up from the yard below, its canopy spreading out at roof level.

"I want to have a party," she said. "It's so nice up here."

"Tomorrow?"

"We don't know anyone. Who are we going to invite?"

"There's the Australian lot. Mick's co-teacher, Mr. Shin, is good for a laugh. He could bring a few mates."

"There's only two chairs! I don't have any glasses. I should've bought glasses. I need a nice lamp. I need a list! But I'm flat broke until the thirty-first."

She'd been worrying about her finances the whole week. Her bank account was a windy badlands. The program had paid for her flight; she'd arrived with nothing and the school advance was quickly drying up. There was no Plan B now. But at the bottom of two large beers, she didn't care. The alcohol had hit her fast after so long without. It opened a wobbly space in all the tightness. Reality's towering obstructions seemed to teeter and shift. The temptation was to test their direction. Give a good shove.

They had finished the bottles and it was early yet. It was decided to find more beer. The evening was beautiful. Orange light. A warm, silky breeze. They just kept walking. Georgia was glad to have someone to explore the neighbourhood with her. She had been suffering from an information shift, rattled by the newness of everything, relying on images instead of language to steer through the city.

"Ray, did you escape something?"

"Nothing that dramatic. Compromise mostly. Just practical shit. Patience and money."

His girlfriend was finishing her PhD in the States and they'd agreed it would be a good idea for him to make some money in the meantime. A little stockpile against the costs of education. Korea seemed the best option. The accommodation was covered, the pay good. But he said it would be hard for him.

"Being apart?"

"Distance. Time."

They waited to cross the street in the waning light.

"Why didn't your friend come?" Ray asked.

"My—?"

"Your friend Natalie. You said Korea was her idea."

"It was. She had it all planned out." Ray sensed a glitch in Georgia's repose. Her face seemed to harden.

"She died," Georgia said.

"Died? Really? What happened?"

"Car accident. Plunged into a ditch. The car rolled a bunch of times."

"Fuck," Ray said. "I'm so sorry. Were you with her?"

"No."

They saw a sign with a beer mug on it. A door led down some stairs. After a few steps, it was immediately gloomy. Ray wanted to ask more about Natalie, but Georgia's face told him the topic had moved on.

Fringed tablecloths and red lamps decorated seven separate booths. Korean muzak with shrill synthesizers overlapped with western muzak with shrill synthesizers. But there was no sign of anyone until they took a seat. A woman with a pile of eyeliner appeared and looked at them with alarm, not expecting two westerners, a white woman and a black man, to arrive in her bar at 7:30 on a Thursday evening. They said hello and ordered two beers. She returned with the bottles and some plates of appetizers. Pretzel sticks and nuts mixed with seaweed. She'd recovered from her surprise and displayed an affected boredom. Then she sat down beside them, smiling awkwardly. They smiled back. They thought she would leave but she stayed sitting with them.

"What do you reckon is going on?" Georgia said to Ray.

She'd just started to employ the word "reckon." She'd picked it up from Becca.

"Maybe she's bored," Ray said without looking at the woman, smiling and scooping up some pretzels. They tried to talk about work and plans for the weekend but it was impossible. It was like trying to decide on shoes while the salesperson is standing beside you looking at each shoe you pick up.

"I think she's *hosting* us," Ray said.

"What?"

"I think she's being a host. I think this is some kind of place where you come for company."

"Company?" Georgia air-quoted.

"Not sex. Maybe just to talk."

The woman's eyes shifted and looked at Ray. Sex was one of those English words. Everyone knew it. Ray was immediately embarrassed. He asked for the bill, very formally. The woman returned through some beaded fringes past the counter. The bill was on a little plastic tray with two chocolates on top.

"Can this be right?" Georgia said. The Korean total was thousands of won. She did the conversion. Each beer was close to thirty Canadian dollars.

The woman had taken their empty snack bowls to the kitchen.

"C'mon!" Georgia said.

She grabbed Ray's hand, dragging him past a spot-lit aquarium and up the narrow stairs into the dusk-heated street. He was both running and resisting, trailing Georgia's lead by a few feet up the uneven sidewalk. Seconds later they heard an angry cry pealing through the air. The woman had reached street-level but was hindered from pursuit by her spiky heels. She protested, in scolding tones, down the sidewalk. Whatever she was saying, it increased with fury. They gasped as they rounded the corner onto a busier road. Walking quickly for another block, they risked a look behind them. Ray shook his head.

"What the fuck was that?"

"Door dash. She was trying to fleece us," Georgia said.

They were still striding as fast as they could, out of breath, exposed with each glance over their shoulders.

"That was really daft," Ray said between breaths. "We're not exactly anonymous here. You only live a few blocks from the bloody place."

"What? She's going to hunt us down? For the price of two beers?"

5

GEORGIA FLOPPED AGAINST the terrace wall, puffing out smoke from a dwindling cigarette. She whirred with dark energy and couldn't sleep. Times like this she needed a co-conspirator. Ray had stayed downtown for two more drinks but went home before eleven. Did she imagine how moody he'd become?

Was it too late to call someone? Was Becca, the Australian girl, up for it?

The drink-and-dash had raised memories. How Natalie would run inside an apartment foyer and press all the buzzers and then run off. Or in Ottawa's downtown core, they'd dial a random room code at four in the morning until someone answered, and say, "Hi, did you order the calamari platter?"

It seemed hilarious back then.

One night they discovered the "secret pool." After a punk show in the ByWard Market, drenched in sweat and stumbling the streets home, they'd ducked behind a parked car to pee. They noticed a ramp. They climbed it and squatted by a thin hedge. Georgia could see a flat glowing surface on the other side.

"Nat," she whispered, her faux leopard-skin skirt bunched around her waist, "there's a swimming pool here." They pushed through the sharp branches. It was a full-size pool for an apartment residence. The L-shaped high-rise wrapped around it, a tall wooden fence framing the other side. Plastic deck chairs. Two picnic tables sat squarely on the grass. Sub-surface lights wobbled below the water.

There was no discussion. They stripped down to bras and underwear and cannonballed the deep end. The water was cool, invigorating. Humidity left behind, they dove and splashed, the waves and ripples smacking the pool's walls. Georgia floated on her back, checking the balconies to see if they'd woken anyone. It felt like they'd escaped the city. Like they'd been transported outside their lives. An hour of anonymity from suffocating normality. In the lambent silence they buoyantly loitered, uninterrupted, then tugged their clothes back on and lit a joint for the walk home.

All during that hot summer, they returned in the middle of the night. It became a reason to stay after shows, past last call. Leaving the club, one of them would say, "Secret pool" and they were giggling, cackling, chasing each other down the sidewalk and squeezing through the hedge.

They shouldn't have told anyone. Did they? But word spread. First there was a small, dedicated group. Beer cans were left, spliffs ground out on the patio tiles. No one had been caught. But every paradise becomes tainted, abused. The following June, a squad of very drunk teenagers converged on the secret pool, shouting and screaming, thundering into the water. Natalie and Georgia had been making out on the picnic table when the cops showed. A flashlight was in Georgia's face.

"Fuck off," she said into the blinding intrusion.

"Put the beer down," a voice said. Rising and stumbling forward, Natalie started laughing hysterically, a high-pitched, respirating cackle from the bottom of her chemical-enhanced mind. She'd taken acid before the dance, washing it down with a PBR.

Georgia heard her beer hit the tile and watched it spill across the poured concrete. She started laughing too, even as she saw the badge on the cop's hat. She leaned back and dropped her joint into the grass.

They were charged with underage possession. They got the lecture about dangers of drug use, respect to private property and the general evil of being young. There'd been several complaints from tenants about noise, the illegal use of their pool and dumped detritus. A stern lecture was issued on the temptation to return. In early September, when they did, an eight-foot-high fence had been erected. "Secret pool" was history.

The incident supplied more evidence to Georgia's parents that Natalie was a bad scene and should be banished from her vicinity. Weeks later, while Georgia and her father had one of their infrequent coffees, he started again.

"It was just some fun," Georgia defended.

"You need to grow up."

"That's what I'm doing. Currently struggling through the late teen phase, by the way."

But "secret pool" had raised the stakes. After its demise, Natalie insisted they really get away, go somewhere real, another place entirely. Global mischief. "We can teach English," she said. She had pamphlets and brochures. Schools were looking for people in Japan and Korea.

"Travel's covered. You live in an apartment and get paid. We can just go," she said, flinging her hand at the dark street like salvation was out there past the trees and suburban neighbourhoods. The next summer, she told Georgia, she was writing an application. "It has to happen."

"What does?"

"*It*. Whatever it *is*. When it starts, we'll find out."

It had been more than three years now since the paramedics had reported no vital signs.

There'd been a house party off Leitrim Road. A fridge full of beer. Vodka. Rye mixed with Pepsi. And shrooms. Celebrations for the end of grade twelve. Or the beginning of summer. It was a party, in any case. No reason was needed. The mixed bag of teenagers convened mostly in the basement. Then the party shifted outside, through sliding doors onto a square deck that faced an undersized backyard. Fields stretched out behind it where a dirt road had been bulldozed. The reflective letters of a developer's notice signalled the fabricated, evolving neighbourhood out in the darkness.

The stereo thundered with pop hits and a plan developed to get some live music going. It was mostly Natalie's idea. She wanted to make some noise but all that was available was a tambourine and an acoustic guitar with dead nylon strings.

"Let's get our gear," she said to Georgia.

Georgia was splayed in a lawn chair balancing a vodka 7 on her thigh.

"Too far. I'm not going anywhere."

She couldn't remember when Natalie left but she never saw her again. When they'd pulled her from the car, she was dead.

Two days later, Georgia went to Natalie's parents' house. Natalie's mother answered the door and held it open emptily. Her face was strained, played out to a pallid zombie state. Red bruises smudged her skin from incessantly wiped tears. She took Georgia to Natalie's room, sitting her on the side of the bed while she went to get some tea. The bed was neatly made. Natalie's clothes were folded on a chair and lined up in the heart-breaking closet. Georgia had never seen it so tidy. A desperate order was being maintained in the chaos of the inexpressible. Georgia sat there, numb. Natalie's "Ramones" comforter was tucked painstakingly over the bed corners, a crocheted shawl spread at the bottom. She looked at Natalie's things. Her desk. Her shelves. A few tattoo magazines, receipts, a beeswax candle shaped like an owl, her studded wristband: the things she touched, treasured and ignored, all saturated with meaning now. A clown nose, red and round, fitted over the head of a Chewbacca action figure. There were the more successful attempts at origami: a few cranes, a star, a marijuana leaf. Natalie's remnants. Her holy junk.

"Be careful, it's hot," Nat's mother said when she handed Georgia the mug.

They were silent, sagging on the saggy bed.

"I'm so sorry," was all Georgia could say. "I can't . . ."

Her eyes searched the ceiling for respite from the pain that surrounded the objects in the room. The window, the yard, the school, the people still going about their lives. How dare it all go on?

"What happened?"

"I don't know. We were at the party and she left."

The police forensics determined she'd skidded once, tried to right herself, and the car went over. Then rolled over twice more. The roof was punched flat.

"Do you want anything?" Natalie's mother asked. "All this stuff."

The question startled her. Georgia studied the woman's face. Blank, raw, washed out.

There was a sock monkey on the nightstand. A button was pinned on its chest that said *The Past Starts Here.*

Georgia picked up a travel guide to Korea lying next to it. She flipped through the pages. There were circles around some entries, and places boxed with blue marker. Georgia took a sip of tea. The heat was a numbing chamomile. She gulped half the cup and looked at Nat's mother, who was staring through the half-opened curtains at a branch with green leaves. When would Georgia come into this room again? Why would she? She watched Nat's mother's face. At their most intimate moment, they were starting to move away from its centre.

She took the leather wristband and put it on, the three snaps making it snug but not tight. Natalie would laugh at her. Crappy sentiment. But she took the clown nose and the button and the travel guide and she slipped them into her messenger bag.

Outside, she dropped her skateboard on the driveway and had just placed her foot on the deck when the door of the family's camping trailer creaked open. Natalie's family had bought it four summers ago, but rarely moved it beyond the property. Mostly it seemed permanently parked on the side of their driveway, used as a summer bedroom or a place to smoke and drink. Georgia and Natalie would have little barbeques, play board games or cards, listen to the shortwave transmissions of new punk and trance music throughout the night. US college stations in Michigan and Vermont, Syracuse and Ithaca. It was necessary to know the bands no one else had heard of, no matter how bad, bland or ridiculous. The music failed or was excellent, but first dibs on discovery was important. Some were not worthy of broadcast. "Sketchy," Nat would say as the chords faded. "Definitely sketchy."

It was Nat's brother who appeared from the trailer door now. He gripped a dustpan and looked at Georgia without expression.

"Hi Matthew," she said. It was all she usually said to him. He was two years younger than her. A lifetime.

"Hi."

"I can't believe it," she said, which was the truth, and the way of saying something.

He clenched his jaw. She could see the muscles move, tighten and shift. He looked down at his hand holding the dustpan, glanced back inside the half-open trailer door, then looked at Georgia again. He picked something off the dustpan and held it out.

"Do you want this?" he said.

It was an old joint, dry and brittle, like ancient papyrus. Probably rolled months ago.

"I found it between some cushions," Matthew said.

Maybe Nat had rolled this one and then lost it. Maybe that's what Matthew was thinking too, though his face showed no trace of his thoughts. He was a quiet kid, Georgia thought, but kind of cool for a younger brother. His hands looked strong. He was on the swim team.

He held it between his fingers, and then he flicked it into the tall grass across the fence. Georgia didn't say anything after that. She didn't know why. She wasn't speechless exactly. But something. Something else. Like embarrassment. There was an edge of exposure to all of it. Vulnerability. Death and youth and pain. The mess or tidying up. And the sudden formality of being alive.

She turned and pushed her board down the driveway.

6

SHE DIDN'T WANT A CELLPHONE. She ditched her laptop. She'd closed her Facebook account and posted a *Gone Fishing* meme on her Instagram. She wanted nothing virtual anymore, just a split from her past and a whirling vacuum ahead. She was here to attend the present. She let her cell service lapse. She would check email at the middle school on a limited basis, send letters and make the occasional call. She wanted to isolate her life and harvest all the loneliness, rage and the fear with it, and that would be a gift too.

And besides, she had no money and the data rates were going to kill her.

But Ray had a point. "That's very romantic, George. But how'm I gonna reach you besides dropping by?"

"Land line, okay? Installed next week."

"Brilliant," he said, like it was innovation. "You're the new old."

She waited another week to give the number to her mother.

"There you are," her mother said. "I thought you'd fallen off the planet. I tried calling you at school but no one understood what I was saying."

"I'm in Korea."

"Yes."

"They speak Korean here."

"Don't be a smartass. It's not attractive."

Weeks passed. Georgia coasted through an economy routine of school and reading. Buses downtown. Lotteria burgers for lunch.

It cost nothing to wander the city, to poke her head through some doors, spelunk the underground intersections. She'd fill herself up on a big lunch at the school cafeteria, free as part of her contract, and then snack on rice and seaweed or soup at night. There were things she still needed—a kettle, some blankets—but it would have to wait until she got paid. Mr. Yung dropped by one morning at eight a.m. with a used iron and an ominous canister of bug spray, shaking it while he raised his eyebrows and positioning it on a nearby eye-level shelf.

She didn't have hot water yet. No pillow either, just rolled-up T-shirts she wrapped in a fuzzy towel. Her bed was a single mattress on the floor. She'd splurged for a fitted sheet, which snapped perfectly into place on the corners. She had the equivalent of thirty-five Canadian dollars in won for the rest of the month.

Mr. Yung arrived unexpectedly the next afternoon, rapping on the door. He explained why there was no hot water and why the stove wouldn't work. "No oil." He pointed to her fuel tank. He said a delivery would be coming in the next thirty minutes, so she should be ready for them.

"It will cost you four hundred thousand won," he said. "Please pay them right away."

She wasn't sure if she heard right. "Mr. Yung, I don't have it."

"Can you go to the bank, please?"

"But I don't have *any* money," she was mortified to admit. There was a frozen, perplexed look behind his thick glasses followed by a series of shallow nods of his head.

"I see," he said. He took out his wallet and counted out a handful of large bills, then gave them to her. "I will lend it to you. The school will reverse the money."

"Reimburse?"

"Yes, exactly," he said, and tapped her on the shoulder. Stepping through the door onto the terrace, he added, "They will deliver soon."

Forty minutes later a buzzer rang. The neighbours' dogs went apeshit, barking and snarling, metal clangs and creaks, crazy growling in crescendos. Her landlady, who she now called "grandmother," came charging up the steps with two men dressed in green trousers and yellow vests. Grandmother was explaining that they'd come to deliver oil for her tank. She pointed to the thick hose the men heaved in their wake. She guided them across the terrace to a small shed attached to Georgia's kitchen. The grandmother kept talking and pointing. Georgia nodded. It was all pretty clear, though the accompanying mime saved her. So far, she'd only mastered "hello," "goodbye," "thank you," and "grandmother."

The delivery guys were using numbers now, but Georgia couldn't follow, so they pulled out some paper and wrote the won sign and seven hundred and forty thousand beside it. Georgia gasped. She showed them the four hundred thousand Mr. Yung had given her and held out her hands in the luckless universal gesture of "I have nothing else; I'm cleaned out." They asked her questions she couldn't understand. Grandmother was telling them something, then told Georgia something. The men were discussing the oil and looking back wistfully at the hose they'd dragged through the gate, up the concrete steps, and along the terrace, as if all was for naught. They looked suspiciously at the inadequate cash Georgia offered them, tsking and head-shaking. They were at a stalemate of incomprehension. The ensuing events were a great mystery to them all. They stared and shifted their feet. They stood around hoping for a solution to the riddle of the oil, fraught with a language barrier and the insufficient payment.

Finally, Georgia motioned to the school, miming herself running over there and returning. So, she ran over and returned empty-handed after finding the classes and offices empty. This seemed deeply baffling to them, but she was on the right track and pointed to the cellphone in the delivery man's hand. She called Mr. Yung.

His wife answered, or maybe it was his daughter, but a woman's voice was either telling Georgia that Mr. Yung wasn't home, or she didn't know what Georgia wanted, or the whole moon landing was a hoax, for that matter, because Georgia couldn't understand a single thing she was saying. The oil guy took the phone. They had a long discussion. Grandmother listened nearby, nodding in concern. The oil man hung up and gestured that they'd be back the next day.

And then they were gone.

Grandmother continued to hurriedly talk to Georgia, pulling her into the kitchen and pointing at the gas stove. While she spoke, the blankets strapped to her back shifted a little and made a tiny noise. Through the swaddle, Georgia realized, a baby was blinking its eyes. Grandmother *was* a grandmother, or more likely a great-grandmother. Georgia guessed she must have been in her eighties or nineties. Georgia looked at her face while the ancient woman gestured and pointed, bombarding her with incomprehensible instructions. Deep, noble wrinkles circled her eyes and contoured her broad forehead. Lines sagged, V-shaped, at the corners of her mouth. She could have lived through the war, Georgia thought. Her mind must have carried countless memories; her steady eyes rinsed with images of pain and hunger Georgia couldn't even imagine.

7

ON THE LAST DAY of the month, the ESL teachers were all summoned to the immigration office to fill out "alien registration" cards. Then they were driven to the education office. There was a speech by the Minister of Something. They were being thanked for their dedication to teaching. Georgia didn't feel dedicated. She still felt disorganized and overwhelmed. She felt like she'd just bungee jumped out of a window and the cord was still unravelling. But she stood in a row and shook hands with the officials, and a secretary handed the teachers thick envelopes after they signed their initials on a columned sheet.

Then they were in the parking lot.

"It's a whack of dosh," Ray said. They all ripped the envelopes open and thumbed the pile of Korean bills arranged neatly inside. The school board had paid their first month in cash because no one had a bank account yet.

Georgia counted out what she owed Ray and handed it to him.

"Lose a bet?" Becca said.

It was the end of September. They stood in the sunshine.

"What now?" Georgia said.

"Dinner?"

"Drinks, definitely."

Mick had already been studying his Korean, so once in a taxi, he started showing off and talking to the driver, asking him questions. The driver understood and was impressed. Georgia felt jealous, inadequate and unconnected.

39

Mick turned to everyone in the taxi with a big grin slathered across his mug.

"Okay kids, the driver's going to take us to a really good Korean restaurant. I asked him for something special. *Special,* yeah?" he said to the driver.

The driver gave them a thumbs-up and said, *"Teuk-byeol-han."*

"That means special."

The restaurant was marked with a wood-carved sign above a bamboo archway. It served bulgogi. The marinated beef came to the table in strips. There were fat cloves of garlic. Everything was grilled at the table, where the group sat on low wooden benches.

The beer and soju went around. Georgia abstained, sipping juice.

"There's close to three million won in there," Ray said, gesturing to his school folder, where he'd put his envelope. He made a quick conversion in his head. "Between the four of us, we're sitting here with something like seven thousand pounds."

"Twelve thousand dollars," Georgia said.

"It's a fucking heist," Mick said. "Dinner's on me. You lot get the beers later."

The bill arrived on a bamboo tray, weighed down by four peppermints. Mick threw down a fistful of cash.

They felt stupid in their work clothes. They were a shabby squad of blazers, dress shirts, heels and matching skirts.

"It's not right," Becca said. "How do I cut loose in this clobber?"

They'd moved on to a hof bar. Georgia walked with Becca. They talked about their first weeks at school. The different classes. The good students. The "little shits" Becca said affectionately.

Georgia could hear Ray telling Mick the story of their drink-and-dash: "And we're legging it down the street, the woman's come outside, screaming at us. I'm looking around like, what just happened...?"

They were all laughing, but she could see Ray was anxious about something. Standing at the bar, Georgia thanked him again for the money he'd lent her.

"Listen, are you pissed at me?" she said.

"Nah, don't worry."

"Don't be so holy. Didn't you ever shoplift when you were a kid?"

"It's different for me." Ray patted the skin on his cheek. "Who do you think that woman will blame when she tells people about it? I've got to work a little harder than you."

"Am I an asshole?" she said by way of apology.

"It's not always about you, love."

"Oi!" Mick was shouting from the table they'd claimed. A J-Lo tune was pumping out of the speakers and he was nerd dancing again.

"That's it. That's it," he said, shaking his ridiculous skinny butt at Becca, who was stretched out in her chair, contorted in laughter with big, shining red cheekbones. Georgia slipped in beside him and shimmied along for a few minutes.

"Do you know the truck driver?" Mick shouted.

"What's that?"

He started a mime of shifting gears and pulling an air cord as a form of dance move. Then turned a big steering wheel in time to the chorus.

The pitcher of beer went around.

"Why are these bars called hofs, anyway?" Becca said.

"Some German was the first to import potatoes to Korea," Ray said. "Read it somewhere."

Becca started chatting about teaching strategies and practicalities. Discipline. Communication. She'd heard of some good bookstores with texts on English acquisition and wanted to hunt them down. Georgia was keen to find some structure to her class. She volunteered for the treasure hunt that weekend.

"And what are you doing about nylons?" Becca said. The other women at Becca's school had wondered why she wasn't wearing them with her skirts. Her legs had become a source of minor fascination in the teachers' room. She sipped from her mug and said, "They're lucky I even shave them."

Georgia thought this was immensely funny and talked about her pits, the shaving dilemma, and the itchiness therein. Laughing, they poked each other's scratchy underarms, rolling in their chairs.

Everyone but Georgia had had a few drinks and it was only 8:30 p.m.

"We're going shopping, mate," Becca said, shaking her envelope of cash in the air. The plan was to meet back at the beer hof at ten, then head to the club.

Georgia and Becca quickly found some party dresses in a shop with ceiling-high glass walls facing the street. Georgia's had bold bands of colour slanting right to left flawlessly to the hemline. Becca's skirt was fire-truck red. In the next shop she found a black long-sleeved top with a pattern of white dots, diaphanous and transparent. Discussion ensued about whether to find a tank top or just go with her black bra.

Ray was having trouble.

"Those are great slacks. We just need to find you a killer shirt," Becca said.

At another store, there was a unisex selection. Lots of bold metro-wear. The women found tank tops but many were covered, Wham!-like, with juxtaposed western words and phrases that were popular in Korea and Japan.

"Too easy," Becca said. She pulled a hanger from the rack, *Funky Nixon* printed across the chest of the shirt. They wondered if wearing the shirts, as westerners, was irony or parody.

Ray suggested it was irony for Koreans too. "It's doubled. Commentary on commentary. It's kitsch. Their western cultural nostalgia has become self-aware. They *totally* know this."

"Those look nice," Georgia said. Ray was holding a few clothes hangers in his hands. One held a fluffy, grey short-sleeve. The other was a dress shirt, neon and yellow, with a high, stiff collar. "The yellow one's super hot."

Ray went into the dressing room. Becca gave Georgia a look.

"What?"

"You just made that sale," Becca said. "Tell a man he'll look super hot in a shirt . . ."

"Hope it fits."

"He'll *make* it fit."

Georgia rattled a few more hangers down the rack but nothing caught her attention.

"You fancy him?" Becca said.

"Geez, Becks. I like his shirt."

"Not what I asked," she said.

"He's got a major-serious girl back home. Or in the States or something. None of my business."

Ray came out of the dressing booth. The shirt fit perfectly and looked very fine. Becca whistled and the two shop girls giggled behind the counter.

They found Mick at the beer hof, already ensconced behind a sweating pitcher of lager, a stupid grin zippered across his face. He'd managed a bit of shopping of his own and was sporting a loud wide-collared thing with blue and silver paisley patterns.

"Fucking hell," Ray said. "What happened to you?"

"Pretty sharp, innit?"

Mick ran his palm down the sleeve and pulled on the collars.

"Disco nightmare, more like," Becca said.

They were laughing.

"What?" Mick said.

"Don't worry, old man. It's totally you," Becca said.

She loved to rib Mick, take the piss out of him, but it was all good fun. Mick was older than the others, in his late thirties. He'd been in banking, then became a trader. But he'd got sick of the suit and the stress and chucked the whole thing to travel and teach. Georgia was still trying to figure him out. He had money. Savings. He loved to buy rounds. He couldn't shake the habit of wearing golf shirts, though they teased him about these too. He didn't mind being teased.

They all took turns catwalking their outfits, making merciless fun of each other.

"You get a discount for those pieces missing?" Mick asked, pointing at the open ovals along the back of Georgia's dress.

Mick was telling them about his former job. How he never slept. How it was like an addiction. He couldn't shut it off. *Everything* related to what to buy or sell. Elections, government policies, natural disasters. He was always thinking: Where is it? Where's the money going? What commodities does it effect? You had to be absolutely on top of it the very second it changed. If something went down, something was going up. He'd lost a marriage over the job. It was far more addictive than love or happiness. It *was* happiness.

"Doesn't sound like happiness," Ray said.

"If happiness is the continuing state of feeling you are in the best possible place, then it was happiness," Mick said. "It's really not though. It's addiction, the hunt for euphoria, right? But euphoria can't last. That's the lie of happiness. Happiness is an event, not a state. So, I buried myself and buried myself trying to find the right formula for keeping it going. And everything fell to shit around me. Absolute shit. Last year I just thought, Fuck it, I gotta get out. This is not life. But what do you do in that situation? If you're on drugs, you go cold turkey, you get away from the stuff, lock yourself away somewhere until you sweat it out. But the numbers were all still around me, going up, down, up. The newspapers, the smart phone..."

"So, you go somewhere that breaks your habits," Becca said.

Mick gave her a smile and air-clinked her drink. "Right. Different world entirely. Another culture. Another language. Completely other routine."

"Escape," Ray said.

"I sometimes feel like a failure," Mick said. "Like I've been left out of something. I'll hear from some jerk-off I used to work with and think, Shit, I could have done that better, I could've made that money. If this was done, and that was done . . ."

He dismissed something invisible with a wave of his hand.

"What's life then?" Ray said.

Mick groaned, "Oh Christ."

"No, come on, mate. You said it's not life. So, what is it? Take a shot then. Any idea?"

"Maybe that world is life for some. Either abundance or oblivion. It's both at the same time, yeah? Some people can balance better than others. Wasn't for me. That's all I'm saying."

"I think it was fucking brave of you to chuck it," Becca said.

Georgia jumped in, preaching how Mick was a more interesting human being because of what he gave up. She said she believed money was a worthless way to think. His choice wasn't a failure. He'd gotten free from the illusion of the quick solution. Unfinished people are the most remarkable, she said. They're still open to being flawed. It's a sign they're still fighting for completion. They're not compromised by being satisfied yet.

"That's a trap though," Ray said. "You're saying that if someone's happy, he's just boring."

"No, happiness is potential on your own terms. Failure is paying for all the things you're expected to have. The fucking mortgages and car payments and a new coffee table."

"Spoken like someone without a house, car or coffee table," Ray said.

"Marxist hippie," Becca said.

"Namaste," Georgia said, cupping her palms solemnly together. She dug her knuckle into Becca's shoulder.

"To square one," Ray toasted and they drained their glasses. In the mirrored lights, Georgia watched him over the bottles and seaweed snacks. He was getting drunk, but seemed to slow down, his gestures more deliberate, his words carefully formed. She recognized a composure, a discipline, she could never possess. Stability. The idea of it. As a choice, it dangled beyond her grasp. While all she managed was dumb chance and abandon.

She'd been trashed at Natalie's funeral. Beforehand, alternating gulps of rum and ginger ale on a bench by the canal, she'd then smoked a pudgy joint as she stumbled down Gladstone in the grey morning. At a Mac's Milk, she bought a pack of orange-flavoured Tic Tacs and pulverized half of them between her molars to hide the skunk waft of her breath. She stumbled through the parking lot. A few smokers were talking quietly in clusters. No one she recognized. The funeral home was grey stone with peaked dormer windows. A gothic house of horrors, Georgia thought.

Everyone seemed to turn and stop when she entered the visitation room. There were other classmates, her school principal and a few teachers milling around a table with broccoli florets, cherry tomatoes and baby carrots beside a bowl of sour cream. The reek of flowers blitzed her nostrils. A thick carpet absorbed the whispers of grief.

One of her teachers, Mrs. Brock, who acted as a guidance counsellor, advanced with a grim stare.

"Are you okay, Georgia?"

"Who cares," Georgia said.

"That's not fair. Don't think that way."

Georgia scanned the room. It all seemed unreal. No one dressed like this. This, it seemed, was only a piece of theatre in Georgia's medicated mind. Death in the round. Her eyes found Christine, who was posing on an overstuffed couch, conspicuous with the heavy cast locked around her right arm, a patch of taped gauze over her cheekbone. Christine had been in the car with Natalie when it rolled. She'd survived. Probably would have been dead if not for her seatbelt. Georgia hadn't seen Christine since the accident. She couldn't bear it. They weren't friends. Christine hardly knew Natalie. She'd just begged for a ride downtown and so became a passenger in the tragic configuration of that night. At a stroke she'd become legendary. The "survivor." Georgia couldn't help but resent her. The last to see Natalie. The one they pulled from the car still alive. It was a power Christine had for eternity.

"Maybe you should sit down," Mrs. Brock suggested.

Georgia looked at her. Mrs. Brock's hand was directing her to a wingback chair by the light of one of the parlour's lampshades. It was an ugly chair, upholstered with Victorian patterns. She did not want to sit there. Instead, she turned and marched toward the back corner where five men stood sombrely in their dark suits. She knew only one of them: Natalie's brother. The rest were uncles and cousins. They were the pallbearers waiting for the director's signal.

"I'll help," Georgia said, stumbling toward Matthew.

His face reddened.

"It's okay," one of the other men said. He lifted his thick fingers in a nullifying gesture, considerate but hindering. Georgia stiffened.

"She was my best friend."

"I'm so sorry," he said. "We've had a great loss. She was my niece."

She looked at him. She looked at the group of them. She didn't like that she was being pushed aside, sidelined from Natalie's being. She didn't like that they were all men chosen to lift the casket. Where were the women? Natalie would need a woman to help carry her. Couldn't they see that? Instead, Georgia was being ushered to an office and told to calm down. They tapped her gently on a shoulder, Mrs. Brock and another man, as if nudging her out of danger and the proximity to loss. They were saying they understood her grief. But did they? Because they could not let it go on, this grief erected with anger. It might shatter the carefully sculpted structure of their ritual.

"Nat needs me," she mumbled.

"You're in no condition," Mrs. Brock said.

Georgia squirmed in the chair they'd tapped her into, searching through a nauseous mist for the trash bin. There was a black plastic cube by the photocopier. It slid around in the chaos of the moment. By the time they helped her to her feet, she'd vomited twice on the recycled paper.

For months, she saw Natalie everywhere.

On the bus, across the street.

Even later, after she'd started working again at Bean There, Georgia would look up and witness an afterimage of her friend's lost face. In someone's eyebrow or mouth, the expression would assemble and fade. It would evaporate around the corner of a street. Natalie would be sitting at tables Georgia was walking toward. Then she wasn't. The cruel reversal of a wish, the mind shaping an irrational demand against its loss. The phantom shred would fragment and Natalie's image would retreat, but the emotional confusion would remain, centred on the contradictory fear that time would usher the feeling away, no matter how vital. She wanted any pain to remain, real against the whiff of oblivion. The pain was evidence of life. It signalled that Natalie was not far and could still be retrieved.

8

THE CLUB WAS SARDINES by the time they arrived, shortly before one. They walked through an alley lined with dumpsters, then down a concrete service ramp. There was a massive garage door and a smaller steel version off to the side. Mick yanked on the handle. A loud heavy beat enveloped them.

A wide, long space with two service islands flanked either end, an ample dance floor in the middle, like a sports field between bleachers. Chrome tables scattered by the sides, booths with black faux leather along back walls. Not many frills. Hip industrial: exposed ductwork, ceiling girders, checkerboard tiles. The only decoration was mirrors and rotating strobes.

It was Eighties Night. A large screen to the side of the club showed vintage videos. Big hair, baggy shirts, pleated pants. Georgia and Becca charged straight to the dance floor, throwing their naked arms in the air. They shouted along to each song, the music so loud it was like they were only lip-synching. "Hey little sister. Shotgun!" They pogo-ed through two songs before they abandoned the floor in search of Ray and Mick, who had found a booth at the very back.

Ray handed Becca a drink. "You guys made an entrance."

"This place is brilliant," Becca said, half-collapsed on the seat.

The other patrons were their age, some younger. The Koreans looked very hip, took the club culture seriously, had moves, and seemed to know all the western hits. The westerners fell into two general categories: English teacher or reps of some Christian group. Missionaries. The Christian types were easy to spot: young, clean-cut in white dress shirts and conservative ties. The other westerners in the club were all teachers, though Georgia didn't cross paths with them often, as they taught at hagwons, the cram schools that were everywhere, official or not. The hagwon teachers came and went. It was easy to find work; you just needed to get to Korea. The only other requirement was you could speak English. And spell it reasonably well. Most cram schools didn't pay well. There was no job security either. Many of them operated at the whim of the owner. Profit was the bottom line. They might close without warning, with teachers owed months of promised back pay. And good luck tracking the owner down.

Georgia and Becca examined the other westerners as they stumbled around, guzzling drinks or dancing.

There were five guys they couldn't figure out, clustered at the corner of the bar watching everyone in a stony, sober, detached way. White, complexions like mushrooms. They had brush cuts and weird suits. One guy wore harem pants with a striped vest. Their shoes had Velcro bands instead of laces. They didn't fit any of the models, not missionaries or teachers or the military types seen in Seoul. Another guy was extremely tall and muscular, another famine thin. One had a black handlebar moustache.

"He's channelling Freddie Mercury," Becca said.

"These dudes *nailed* Eighties Night."

Boy band videos, mostly K-pop, played on the screen. The Korean songs were more contemporary, the videos crisp and HD. The eighties ones looked washed out, fuzzy and vintage cheeseball. Mick, Ray, Becca and Georgia laughed their way through a Howard Jones video. The hair. But all the videos were ridiculous, new or old. In the next Korean one, a boy band was in sailor suits trying to impress the same girl. The lyrics were all Korean except for the chorus, which went "ship of love, ship of love."

"Hey, can anyone name a music video that isn't cheeseball?" Georgia challenged.

Everyone sat around like scientists saying nothing.

A Men at Work song started and Becca and Mick were obligated to cavort across the dance floor. Ray and Georgia watched them for a minute as Mick did his trucker moves and Becca made disgusted faces at them through the spinning light beams.

"Having a good time?" Georgia half-shouted at Ray.

He slid closer in the booth.

"Good to have a laugh, innit?"

"There's lots to laugh at," she said.

"You're pretty cynical, you know that?" Ray said. He smiled. Georgia gave him a skeptical scowl. "You're always taking the piss. Not everything has to be ridiculed."

"It's all fucking stupid anyway."

"That's a pretty inclusive statement."

"You getting all Freud on me?"

Ray shook his head and flicked a finger against his beer glass a couple of times. Then he said, "I think you hide behind it. The disdain, y'know? The scorn. The way you dumb yourself down when you're much much smarter."

"*Thank you,*" she said with generous sarcasm.

"See?"

Georgia shrugged.

Ray smiled. "I just notice, okay?"

The music had changed. "Walk Like an Egyptian." Georgia squinted through the shaking light display where Becca and Mick's heads surfaced above the roiling crowd. Georgia shook her middle finger at them. The laughter and sarcasm. It was all a way of hiding how she felt.

"I went back, you know."

"What?"

"I went back to that restaurant," Georgia said. "And paid the woman for the beer. You were right. I felt badly."

The day after their drink-and-dash Georgia had asked Mr. Yung how to say "I'm very sorry. It is my fault" in Korean. She had him write it down. Once school was over, she went home and changed, then walked down the street and found the café-bar and went down the stairs. The lights were up and there was no music but it was still early. A vacuum cleaner sat abandoned by the fish tank, some rags and a bucket on the bar counter. As she stood there, a small child toddled out of the kitchen and stopped dumbfounded at the sight of Georgia. "*Eomma*," the boy called. The woman came through the doorway. She almost gasped. Without a word, Georgia handed her the note, with sixty thousand won, bowed and dashed out the door again.

"I'm impressed," Ray said.

"I can adapt, you know. I'm evolving."

They were both laughing again. The club had turned on the blacklight and their teeth and eyeballs glowed. Bits of Styrofoam, or some kind of packing material, glimmered through the fabric of her new dress. Ray's synthetic shirt looked like Chernobyl. Georgia grabbed his hand and leaned over and kissed him.

9

WHEN BECCA FOUND GEORGIA, she was slamming glasses down on the bar with the oddball group of westerners.

"Are you drinking?"

"Just some shots." Georgia gestured at the group. "They're Russian," she said.

Becca looked at them. They stood there grinning in a semicircle.

It turned out the five westerners were not teachers or missionaries. They were part of a circus from Moscow. It was finishing a small tour of Korea: a week in Seoul, then two shows in Gwangju before going to Busan for two more, then a ship home. Their English was loose but functional. Alex, a trapeze guy—he had flipped his hands in the air to illustrate—told Georgia they would arrive in Vladivostok, then board the trans-Siberian for two months, stopping to perform along the way, "to make money, and so the elephant is not sick."

"You're shitting me," Becca said when Georgia re-capped.

The circus group all smirked and nodded. Alex bowed.

"He does the trapeze," Georgia said and he somersaulted his hands in the air again, the ends of his left fingers catching the ends of his right fingers above an imaginary net.

"Okay, what's he do?" Becca said, not convinced.

They looked at the reedy guy in the harem pants.

Alex exchanged a few words with him in Russian.

"Contortionist," the man said. Then, while the rest watched, he joined his hands together, stepped through them, snaked them—the hands still joined—up behind his back and over his head so the joints had completed a full circle in their sockets. This drew a few stares from the patrons nearby.

"Fuck. I'm gonna toss," Becca said.

The men explained they'd been looking for a pool hall when they stumbled into the club. Mick joined the discussion and the contortionist went through his whole routine again.

"That's brilliant, mate," Mick said to them collectively. The carny with the moustache had a snakehead tattoo on his neck. A forked tongue licked his earlobe.

"You should see the whole tattoo," Alex said. It apparently wound around his torso and down his leg. The tail was over his ankle. "Boa constrictor. He will show you if you want." Alex smiled. "He likes to take the clothes away."

"Where's Ray?" Becca asked, glancing around the crowded dance floor.

"Out of steam. Went home," Georgia said.

"Chucked it in?" Mick said.

The carny was lifting his shirt to show Georgia more sections of the snake stretched over his ribs and hipbone. She kept busy looking at it, joking about where it was headed.

The group of westerners had collected a small crowd.

Georgia turned to one of the Korean guys near her.

"Do you know where there's a pool room?" She mimed a pool shot, her left fingers and thumb shaped in a cue cradle.

"Yes," he said and turned to his friend to discuss this, their skeptical tone suggesting a debate over location, suitability or existence. "Yes, you can find it . . ." He made gestures of left and right directions. They were the horizontal version of the trapeze movements. His face contorted in frustration. He raised himself on the balls of his feet and scanned for someone else, waving him over through the crowd.

Another guy appeared.

"Hi," he said and shook Georgia's hand. "I'm Jimmy."

"What's your Korean name, mate?" Mick asked. Mick hated the custom of Koreans taking western names for a westerner's convenience.

"Ji-tae," he shouted to Mick through the synthey strains of the Pet Shop Boys. His friend said something to him in Korean. Ji-tae nodded and said, "You are looking for billiards?"

Georgia explained it was the Russians who were looking. She told Alex they were trying to find a pool hall, which surprised him. The Russians didn't seem interested anymore. They were having fun at the club. Ji-tae was confused. But now Mick was game for a change of location. Georgia needed air too. She told Ji-tae they would go to the pool hall. He said he'd show them. And the Russians decided to tag along after all.

All nine of them, with Ji-tae, filed out the door.

A mob of smokers dominated the alley. The heat had worn off from the early autumn sun and the night air was perfect. Plump stars wobbled between the rooftops. Ji-tae turned to Mick. "You are Australian?"

"Yeah, that's right."

"Excellent surfing," Ji-tae said. He told them his parents had taken him to the Gold Coast for a three-week holiday when he was seventeen. He'd tried surfing there for the first time. He was hooked. He'd surfed every day, even on the morning before their flight home. It was his great dream to go back. He kept talking about Snapper Rocks, big waves and "Superbank." "Do you know Snapper Rocks?" he said to Mick with great reverence.

"Heard of it," Mick said.

"Gold Coast. Queensland. Snapper Rocks," Ji-tae insisted.

"Yeah, mate. I know where you're talking about. That's the east coast. I'm from *Perth*," he said. "Other side of the country." He moved his hands from left to right as if crossing an imaginary continent.

"Yes," Ji-tae said. "The west coast is good too. Surfers Point. Margaret River. Do you know it?"

"I'm more of a wine drinker, to be honest."

It seemed inconceivable to Ji-tae that, as an Australian, Mick was not surfing every day. He continued to name popular coastal locations and famous Aussie surfing champions. They stumbled along the uneven paving stones.

"Geez, you're really mad about it, aren't you?" Mick said.

"I'm not mad."

"No, I mean you're really into it. Extremely interested, I mean."

"I am a waxhead," Ji-tae said and started to laugh at the confused looks on their faces. "It's a surfer name for passionate surfers. Now I am teaching you English."

"Is there good surfing in Korea?" Becca asked.

"In Jeju-do. Or on the coast near Busan. Songjeong. Haeundae. It's okay. It's not Gold Coast. I'm going next weekend. As many times as I can. Do you want to try?"

"I'd break my legs," Mick said. "Crack my skull open, mate."

"He fucking would," Becca said.

"It's too bad. He was so young," Ji-tae said, cracking them all up. It was easy to like Ji-tae. He was laid-back, earnest, good-natured.

They had just arrived at the pool hall. A sign above the door showed fifteen coloured circles inside a triangle.

"I'll go with you," Georgia volunteered.

"For surfing!?"

"Yeah, sounds like a blast."

She was shooting her mouth off, buzzed from the shots, but completely earnest, caught up in the idea, as Ji-tae discussed logistics of travel and accommodation. Georgia knew people in Busan and said she could crash with them. Becca had surfed before and agreed to go along. In twenty minutes, they had formed a plan.

The entrance to the second-floor pool hall was between a closed bakery and an electronics store. They walked up. Inside, a dozen pool tables occupied the room. A small bar with stools filled one corner. Posters of sunsets and lush mountains covered the walls between the cue racks. The clientele was a mix of the social and the serious. Amateurs just out for drinks mingled with owners of their own custom-made cues with carrying cases. The Russians had quickly lodged themselves around one table near the bar and were deep into a series of eight ball rivalries, the winner holding the table. They took selfies, mugging for the camera. Georgia saw wads of Russian currency changing hands after each game.

Ji-tae handed his card with his email and cell number to Georgia and Becca, excitedly detailing the surfing expedition. He would reserve some boards for them, give Georgia a lesson, start them on the easier waves. Mick just kept shaking his head, sharing out the big bottles of Hite into their glasses.

Georgia smelled something familiar. Sweet. Earthy.

Fuck.

Was that what she thought it was?

She looked around.

A couple of groups were gathered at the bar, drinking cocktails layered with orange and pink juice, a vein of grenadine threading itself through crushed ice. They didn't look the type Georgia was imagining. But the three guys two tables over did. One of them was a westerner, an unshaven faux nerd wearing horn-rims and a cardigan with the elbows blown out. The two Koreans had some kind of *Wild One* thing going, but more Fonzie than Brando, in pristine black leather and pompadours of hair product. They were in the middle of a pool game. Sort of. The break had happened and the majority of the balls were dispersed across the felt. But the pool game seemed a prop rather than an activity. They looked like a window display of a pool game. They held the cues and chalked them. They circled the table and paused over pockets. They weighed possibilities, squinting at angles, best combinations, sipping their glasses of beer and trading the occasional remark. They just sort of hung around the table, with little action or result. They were like a cloud around an island that never rained. But after a few minutes, two of them headed toward the exit, passing within a few feet of where Georgia was standing.

It was definitely weed.

Georgia told Ji-tae, Becca and Mick that she'd be right back and descended into the night air through the narrow entrance. It was wobbly work on the steps. This was the result of the drinks she shouldn't have had, but also the heels of her new shoes, the steep descent and fatigue from an uninterrupted long day of work and other people. Other people were too much effort. Georgia could only ever manage a few friends at a time, the ragtag recipients of her fickle affection. She didn't have the energy to love beyond a tight-knit circle. There were too many petty, vain, mean, shallow, humourless, soul-draining assholes in the world and she believed she was too petty, vain, mean, selfish, moody and impatient to hitch her burdens to theirs. Other people were a bad marriage she kept cheating on. The only mainstay had been Natalie, and Georgia had let Natalie down. She'd let her go off on her own, drunk and driving, to die beside some creature named Christine.

Once outside, Georgia scanned the street. The usual smokers. Glow from shop signs. In front of one gated entrance, a vendor was stirring something in his portable deep fryer, scooping the product—small, brown—into paper cones. Steam rose in a shapeless cloud around his shoulders. Georgia spotted one of the pool players near a dumpster halfway to the next intersection. She walked over to them, smiling.

"Hi," she said.

They looked her over and nodded. Pompadour made no attempt to hide the joint wedged between his fingers. Faux-nerd westerner returned her greeting with a guarded grunt.

The other Korean was a little down the alley, keeping an eye on the corner.

GEORGIA AT SEA

"I'm sorry to bother you guys but I couldn't help notice your weed and oh my god I haven't had any for over a month which is crazy and I'm just dying for one puff of it and I know it's not super cool of me to be hassling you guys in the street," she babbled.

Pompadour took a hit off the joint. His eyes were black and expressionless.

"Weed?" the westerner said. "What weed?"

She looked at Pompadour. It was definitely weed they were smoking.

The westerner said, "Weed is very illegal here."

He and Pompadour started snickering.

"Can I have a drag of your *cigarette* then?"

Westerner and Pompadour exchanged looks. Pompadour's face was blank, completely cheerless now. But his eyes were working toward a decision. He handed the joint to Georgia.

"Oh my god, thank you, thank you," she said, taking it from him. "This is so amazing you can't imagine how amazing this is." She sucked the smoke through the makeshift filter, the weed crackling inside the paper. Inhaling deeply, she dragged it down into her lungs and felt immediately calm, though it could hardly have started any effect yet. The smoke was musky, with nothing harsh. She took one more short pull and handed it over to the westerner. She didn't want to look greedy or ungrateful.

"You teaching?" he said as he pinched and huffed.

She laughed and hung her thumbs from her pockets. "What else?" she said. It was an embarrassing fact to be so obvious but there was no getting around it. She nodded at him. "You?"

"I did a little hagwon when I got here." He shrugged. "But I wasn't very good at it." The two Koreans shared a subversive laugh with him over this. The non-Pompadour, whose hair was dyed a rust tone, had taken the last drags and dropped the joint, smoked down to a microscopic crumb, onto the ground and toed it into the concrete.

59

"How long have you been here?" she asked.

Westerner said, "A while." The emphasis sounded enough to be two years. Then he answered her next question: "I'm working at a club over there."

He motioned nebulously down the street.

The information made her envious. Working at a club was way out-cooling her teaching job. And he seemed smug with the unconformity. She was jealous of his insider status, immediately wanting to be someone else. That club he worked at was a few blocks farther north, toward the river. He described it as if it was a challenge: below ground, dark, lounge tables, DJ and open until dawn. She said she'd go sometime if she could find it. He said his name was Brad. Georgia watched his jaw grinding away on nothing. Just then, Becca appeared on the corner and waved. Georgia dashed across the street.

10

AT TEN A.M. THE NEXT MORNING, Georgia woke to knocking. She rumbled toward the door with all the grace of a set of rapids, dressed in an oversized T-shirt. Her black hair was flattened, collapsed in a wiry cluster over her shoulders. Ray stood there smiling outside her apartment.

"Morning."

"Oh no. Oh no." Georgia plunged her face into her hands.

"Hi."

"Oh god. Don't even look at me," she said, rolling her eyes and laughing grimly. "I'm a moron."

"You smell bloody awful too."

"Shut up."

Ray leaned against the door, laughing. "Listen up, Dracula," he said. "I'm not going to waste a beautiful Sunday feeling hungover. I'm grabbing the bus to Mokpo to take a look at the sea. Get your kit on and join me."

"I'm so fucked."

"Yeah, well, you look like you got dragged through a leaf shredder. Take a shower and I'll wait outside."

"Mokpo?"

"Right on the coast. Fresh air and seafood."

"Bleh." She made a puking gesture with her finger down her throat.

"Get a move on. The bus is in an hour."

They picked up food and coffee at Shinsegae Department Store next to the terminal and found their gate just before departure. Through the suburbs of Gwangju, Georgia picked at her croissant, unsuccessfully trying not to scatter flakes all over her lap. Then she dropped half of it in the aisle and groaned pitifully as Ray shook his head. It became a bit of theatre between them, her clumsiness and his tolerant mockery, if only to distract from the incident of the previous evening. Because, for Georgia, the kiss was pinned between them like a red banner fluttering with her mortification. It hung there, unspoken, as the bus vibrated down the highway. They talked sporadically as the low hills diminished to flood plain, where rice paddy terraces were being prepped for another cycle of planting season. Georgia tried to muster energies out of her lack of sleep (and reintroduction to weed). She could feel blood pulse through her cheekbones. She sipped at a can of tropical juice and then chugged an energy drink, trying to wash the fur from her tongue.

In Mokpo there was another bus to get to the port, where they eventually found the cable car station Ray's co-teacher had recommended. Massive cables ascended over the bay and dipped between the volcanic outcrops of the coast. They both laughed piteously as the glass-bottomed gondola swung off its platform and they realized how high they were going to climb. Below them, rocks and forest paths, high-rises across the valley and then the sea. "I'll look down if you do," Ray dared. And they did, whimpering comically. They reached a hilltop pagoda with a windy panorama where they disembarked. A sign said *Yudal Mountain*. Ray took a photo with the water far below. The waves sparkled and flashed in the industrial wake of the ships leaving port, their progress so distant toward the horizon, it seemed a kind of languor. Each summit revealed a new angle. "Cool," Georgia would say. Or Ray. "Amazing." Korean families in cheerful hiking gear crowded snack booths and squatted over makeshift picnics in the autumn sun. The trail descended to an extensive boardwalk that shadowed the coast.

GEORGIA AT SEA

Seagulls teamed for scraps overhead, then plunged toward the current, squawky with complaint. Mostly, there was silence, punctuated by their own superlatives, until they retraced their way back to the city centre, where they found a café near the fish market.

The daylight protected them from the pressure of intimacy. Georgia's anxiety waned as the hours passed. There were different people inside her, alert to warring perceptions. What had she felt last night, or today? She was aware of the reckless spills of attraction that could reappear and vex her. They surged like the buzz of an amplifier, the electric shift when a guitar is plugged in, but for the most part, she had managed the free leanings of her unworkable desires.

Ray thumbed through his Mokpo photos between gulps of kimbap.

"Are those for your blog?"

"I don't have a daft *blog*."

Georgia snorted.

"I saw *you* take some pictures," Ray said. "With that archaic camera of yours."

"Point and shoot, baby."

"Phones do that, you know."

"But then I just put it away. I don't post and wait for likes. The photos are for me." Georgia pointed with her chopsticks at the spicy yams covered in sesame seeds. "I just want to eat the experience, not advertise it."

"You keep talking that way, there's going to be a revolution."

"They've done studies, you know. It's fucking us up. All the FOMO. Our GOAT moments and humble brags."

"It's archives. Humans have been doing it forever. All those animal drawings in French caves, right? They were celebrating a presence. Verifying the spirit of who they were."

"Just like posting a picture of new shoes!"

Ray sighed. "You win," he said. He nodded with a weary smile. They munched a few spoonfuls of rice. A truck was delivering baskets of clams to the stand across the street. They watched the exchange of money.

"I don't think I know how to express affection without drama," Georgia said. "I hold off and hold off and then self-sabotage. I throw everything at the wall. It's my nuclear impatience. All or nothing. I wish. . ." She banged her fist against her forehead. Ray swallowed his barley tea and waited for her to finish. They were having the conversation without planning the conversation, the icky dance of it, fraught with misunderstanding.

Georgia made a squeamish face. "Can I just say *I'm sorry*?"

"Yes, you can. But you don't have to. And you're buying dinner." He leaned back in his chair and gestured to the cash register. "Go on then."

"You raging bandit!"

"Georgia," he said. She turned around. "We're all a work in progress, yeah?"

On the ride back to Gwangju, they read, napped, talked about work and watched the evening darken and shimmy along the western skyline. In the darkness of their seats, she watched Ray sleeping and wanted to take his hand. That electric shift. But the energy of it lay within a wider field now, a feeling she couldn't pinpoint as she hovered over herself for a safe place to land. The day had been so easy when it shouldn't have been. Its mutual risk could have veered into more embarrassment, or anger, or complicated affection, and it was romantic that it had not. Still, she wondered at Ray's motivation, and wrestled lingering doubts, fluctuating around the protection of her inner life. They parted on the Gwangju sidewalk and she said, "Thank you for taking me."

When he replied, "It was a beautiful day," her second-guesses seemed petty and were replaced by a comprehension she took the leap to name. Trust is rarer than love.

11

THE FOLLOWING FRIDAY was a designated holiday. Ji-tae planned to surf. He arranged an unholy seven a.m. pickup. Becca agreed to stay over at Georgia's place to save time in the morning. Bonus, Becca had a cellphone. Reliable contact was not proving to be a phrase synonymous with Georgia's name.

They were still struggling to drag their asses from the shared mattress on the floor when Ji-tae rang at the entrance.

"Christ, Ji-tae," Georgia said, squinting through the half-open door. "You're ten minutes early."

"The early bird eats the worm," he said with a big goofy smile.

"Here," Georgia said, handing him a jar of instant coffee. "The bird likes coffee too."

He found her kettle and fired up the gas stove. As the women thundered back and forth to the shower, he made himself busy, avoiding their states of undress, spooning out the freeze-dried crystals of caffeine. The artificial taste was growing on Georgia.

"You're my personal Jesus," she told him as he handed her the hot mug.

They were soon on the Honam Expressway going east. As they entered the on-ramp, the car seemed to lift into the sky above the low-rise apartment blocks. Magpies frisked around water tanks on rooftops. Lines of laundry snatched at the breeze.

When Georgia had woken that morning, she hadn't wanted to go anywhere at all. She'd just hoped to lie there the whole weekend and stare stupidly at the wallpapered ceiling. Now all she wanted was this drive. This day. She was doing something, at least.

As they sped along the road, with the Korean mountains gently fencing the horizon, Ji-tae recited a pop version of surf history, from its origins in Polynesian culture, early modern meccas of Malibu and Hawaii, and its growth in Australia and Asia. The Golden Age of surfing, according to him, was the late fifties and early sixties, when airline travel became widespread and affordable, and the best surfing spots were still under-crowded. He told them when the movie *The Endless Summer* was released in 1966, it drove people to global beaches looking for the perfect wave. That was the idea behind the film's title: that if you travelled in a timed circumnavigation, you could avoid winter infinitely and never stop surfing. Though the best surfing was actually in winter.

"We are lucky," he said, looking up through the windshield. "The forecast is very good for today and tomorrow."

Georgia watched Ji-tae steer around a Hyundai in a rare road pass. The countless hills in Korea made straight stretches rare.

"Endless weekend," Becca said flatly. She was curled up into a sleepy ball in the back seat, hugging her knapsack. She had overdone it at Georgia's place the night before, taking advantage of the warm weather on the terrace to sponge up five or six beers while the sun set.

But Georgia felt great that morning, hungry and happy as they motored along the expressway, a few leaves already turning orange in the trees, the weather still in the twenties. After two hours, Ji-tae pulled into a rest stop of food kiosks and a gas station for a break. Scattered outdoor tables hosted families and groups of seniors on their own road trips. The lineup for food seemed endless but moved quickly. The three of them chowed down on cartons of miniature potatoes rolled in butter and tossed in salt.

"So, where's this beach, Ji-tae?" Becca said. "It's time to get cracking."

An hour later, Ji-tae drove them straight to the coast parking lot so they could get the last of the morning waves. Haeundae, he claimed, was too busy in the summer, but would be better now. The beach was at the end of its season, officially closed, but the ban wasn't enforced. The swimmers were gone. Only the diehards persisted.

"Translation: *fucking cold*," Becca said.

Georgia had emailed James—a brief friend at orientation, now posted in Busan—truffling for a place to crash. He was going to meet them after four for drinks. They parked in a lot and walked to a beach shop. Ji-tae bumped fists with Kyung-chul, a guy sporting a mullet and headband. His wetsuit was stripped to the waist, his chest and stomach lean and hairless. A row of tanned abs linked his ribcage to his navel like pierogies on a tray. He shook their hands and welcomed them, then propped two boards against the counter.

"I reserved them," Ji-tae said. They were called funboards, shorter and more rounded than the advanced ones, but Ji-tae assured Georgia it would be easier to handle. They didn't look very cool, an announcement of amateur talent. She gave them a skeptical look.

"Becca's not a beginner," Georgia protested.

"I lied," Becca said. "I've surfed maybe twice. Total shark biscuit."

They changed into swimsuits. Becca and Georgia had gone shopping for some sporty bikinis with good straps, stylish but solid enough to prevent unintended flashes of boob etc. Becca's was striped blue and white. Georgia's had big sixties polka dots. She could see Becca was fit. She had a swimmer's body with broad shoulders and a strong-looking back. Georgia felt like a white twig next to her. She'd lost a few pounds from the Korean diet and was glad to get some exercise.

"Please don't wear these," Ji-tae said, pointing to Georgia's wrist. "It's dangerous if anything tangles."

She wore a collection of bracelets above her left hand. Skull charms and coral. Natalie's leather wristband. All gathered in a twisted bundle. Georgia untangled them, pulling the bracelets off one by one, unfastening the snaps. She rubbed her wrist, itchy in the exposed air.

When Becca looked over, she saw, in half-comprehending shock, the two raised scars running red and parallel from the bottom of Georgia's palm down her forearm.

The two women caught each other's eye.

Georgia turned and picked up her board.

Ji-tae led them down the beach, boards tucked under their arms. There were only ten, maybe fifteen, surfers riding waves on the horizon ahead. A few swimmers and sunbathers near the shore. Becca sang, "Two girls for eeev-ry boooyy." They ankled the water where it was dark with rough sand. A sandcastle dissolved into its moat. The last edge of a wave slopped over their shins.

"Fuck, that's freezing," Georgia said.

"Don't worry. It's good. You'll like it," Ji-tae reassured. He immediately fanned a few handfuls of water over his torso and arms, waded out farther until his legs disappeared and then dropped entirely below the waves. He bobbed up and dunked himself again. He pushed his hair back off his forehead and laughed maniacally. "See? It's good! Come on."

He showed them how to tie their safety leashes on, strapping one end of the cord to Georgia's ankle with a Velcro cuff.

"Now I'll show you how to paddle," he said.

"Don't we get another coffee first?"

He splashed an icy sprig of sea at her. Becca plunged in and groaned, part primal pleasure, part agony. She carved a dozen exploratory strokes through the shallows, her board drifting on the leash behind her. The water was clear, pleated by playful surges, with clouds of sea kelp spidering above the sand. Small fish fussed about Georgia's ankles. Perfect stillness, then a flash. She dangled her fingers below the surface.

"C'mon, Gee," Becca shouted.

Georgia heaved her knees over the tide and lunged into a breaker.

"Pretty sure I can handle the paddling," she said to Ji-tae. He watched as she steadied the board and put her knee down on the smooth, slippery surface. It wobbled slightly and she shifted her weight, stretching her stomach flat over the middle stripe of the fiberglass. It tipped over and she dropped hard into the waves. When she came up for air, Becca was already cackling. Ji-tae too. She climbed back on and kicked forward but the nose of the funboard dropped into another low wave and upended.

"Not so easy," Ji-tae said.

Becca called from where she was steadying her own board. "We're only twenty feet from the beach."

Soon, Ji-tae gave the lowdown on the best position, on finding a centre where the nose wouldn't ride too high or dig into a wave. They paddled around past the shallows, nudged by the swells, getting dunked and rebalancing. After thirty minutes of this, Georgia was winded. Her heart pinched, her shoulders and biceps strained. Ji-tae dragged patient scans over the horizon. Georgia could see he wanted to go deeper and carve up into some bigger waves. The drama was out there, cresting into a line of white ruff that broke to the beach, several surfers riding down the shifting terraces of water. With each surge, at least a few silhouettes lifted and crashed, others skidding gracefully down into the shallows. It had looked so easy in movies and YouTube clips, like tobogganing a gentle slope of snow. But out there, closer to the tumbling plunges of sea, the challenge of mounting a polished slab of foam and keeping upright for more than three shaky seconds seemed to defy physics.

"You go, Ji-tae." Georgia pointed to the mixed surges. "Let's see your stuff."

He cracked a giant smile, gave a thumbs-up and immediately heaved his board into the tide, paddling it out. Within a few minutes, Georgia and Becca watched him queuing along the bobbing handful of surfers to the left of the main action. There was a lineup in surfing, he'd told them. Like the bus stop, it had its own etiquette. You had to give people space; you had to respect who was waiting, their position and also their ability. "Sounds Korean," Becca had said. Soon, as a southeast swell lifted toward the beach, Ji-tae paddled hard to merge into it. Then he stood up on the board. Georgia and Becca cheered from the waist-deep water. He easily rode the surf into the shallows thirty feet to the left of them. When he jogged back, his board tucked along his forearm, they chanted, "Ji-tae! Ji-tae!"

Embarrassed, he waved his hand and shook his head.

"It was amazing," Georgia said.

"No, it's easy," he said, then corrected himself in case it sounded like boasting. "Haeundae surf is not difficult."

They had the horizon mostly to themselves. Later, they'd stay with James or Ji-tae's friends, or if they went on Sunday, they'd drive back to Gwangju as late as they could, headlights dropping and pitching ahead of them through the mountain passes and seaside roads. They'd be exhausted, emptied, with no energy to talk. Words were superfluous. They were whittled down to the purest, trimmed versions of themselves. Like her late-night taxi returns from the bars, Georgia loved this state best, the passive transfer of her cored-out self. Staring out the window, her thoughts drifting around as the great adventure of the world flashed past, the stands of trees and twinkling lights off the coast, on one side a wall of rock, on the other guardrails and the plunge down to boathouses nestled in an inlet. She wanted to eat better, get her head clear. She wanted the combo of air, water and exercise to flush the dark anxieties out of her.

12

AT MICK AND BECCA'S, weeks later. By ten o'clock, twenty-some people were hanging about. Beer. Soju. Whiskey. Plates of cheezies, pretzels, dried squid and seaweed. Mick introduced Georgia to Woo-jin and So-eun, two servers at a traditional tea house he frequented. There was Calline, an American from Wisconsin, who was visiting from teaching in Suncheon, and Sean, a guy from Hamilton, fresh from Canada and freaked out.

In the kitchen, they were discussing slang. Mick and Becca would revert to Aussie lingo, thickening their accents to incomprehensible levels for a laugh. As Australians, they'd do an impression of Australians. Everyone would do their own country.

Georgia: "How's it going, eh?"

She liked the Australian stuff. Becca would call their swimsuits "bathers" and "cozzies." Sunglasses were "sunnies." Now they were talking slang for drugs. Ji-tae had come across "wacky tobaccy" in a magazine and loved the sound of the phrase.

"Have you ever heard *hippie lettuce*?" Georgia asked. She took a few minutes to explain to Woo-jin what a hippie was.

"*You* know," Mick said. "Smelly, long hair . . ."

Mick weaved side to side in a spacy, drugged-out mime.

Woo-jin watched him, wide-eyed, until the penny dropped.

"Ahh, yes. I know," she said. She pulled her long hair down over her eyes and raised her two fingers. "Peace, man." They all howled.

Mick asked, "What's the word for 'hippie' in Korean?"

"Hippie."

Slang has to be natural, Georgia argued. A challenge for non-native speakers. Mick thought it was helpful to teach it. To understand the play of language. But Georgia thought it was a bad idea. She told them that "hippie lettuce" might exist as slang, but no one she knew ever actually used it in a real conversation. Not "wacky tobaccy" either. Not really. Or the many others: ganja, reefer, cheeba, herbage, pakalolo...

Each use was organic, popular in some places, dropped in others, braided from different languages and cultures. Even a specific crowd has its own secret language. Surfers. Truck drivers. Kitchen workers. For a few months in high school, there was nothing worse you could call someone than a "trout," Georgia said. It was a kind of loser. Where did it come from? And where did it go? Even more complicated, the purpose of drug slang was to actually hide meaning from authority or police. It was coded. For use in a select group. Especially so with drugs. Slang upon slang. Layers. To communicate *only* to those inside the culture.

"Look at ganja," she said. "Everyone thinks it's a Jamaican word. But it's actually Hindi. Just a regular word for hemp. Indian labourers, years back, introduced it to Jamaica. So Jamaican smokers started using it because the cops didn't know what the word meant."

"Pretty scholastic about it," Mick said.

"I got very into it," she said, miming a spliff. She turned to Becca. "What was that expression you use for men's tiny Speedos?"

"Budgie smugglers."

Laughter. But Woo-jin and Ji-tae waited for an explanation. Mick tried *budgies*. "Little birds, yeah?" He raised his hands in a tight fist, fingertips like a beak. Once "smuggling" was established, he put the two together with a number of hand gestures in the vicinity of the crotch area.

"Stop the bird noises, you tosser. It's just confusing," Becca said.

He tromped around the kitchen, his hands clutched near his balls, beaks chirping away.

Clarity was not served.

It was still great fun, Woo-jin a good sport and endlessly interested. Georgia tried a few more drug euphemisms with them. She'd loved all the stupid terms for marijuana. She and Natalie had used them regularly and unexpectantly. They'd look up stuff and try to stump each other and cackle at the answers. Georgia's favourite was "Are you anywhere?"

"What does this mean?" Ji-tae said.

"It means 'Do you smoke marijuana?'"

The inclusive, spacious, unfixed meaning of the phrase impressed Ji-tae, who wandered throughout the party as he got drunker and drunker, leaning in close to people's faces and enthusiastically shouting, "Are you anywhere?"

Ray squeezed past to get to the fridge. He'd arrived moments before, waving and bowing as he hung up his coat. He patted Mick on the shoulder. "Hi."

"Fuck, mate. What took you?"

Ray rolled his eyes tiredly. He scanned for Georgia, caught her eye, and they hugged. His hands on her back.

"Hi," he said.

"You look miserable."

"Thanks. Any more dazzling superlatives you want to share?" He selected a beer, leaning against the kitchen counter.

"Cantankerous? Mysterious? Dim?"

"Perfect."

"Gorgeous."

"Even better. Busy, actually. The school's got me doing extra classes every evening. The kids were cramming for some kind of SATs. I'm fucking exhausted. I shouldn't have come tonight."

"Glad you did," Georgia said.

He snapped open the tab on his beer can. A gush of foam rolled out of the opening, which he quickly covered with his mouth.

"Sexy," Georgia deadpanned.

Ray grabbed a paper towel and wiped at the splotch on his collar. He asked about the last surfing weekends, a regular thing now. They talked about their workloads. Ray was trying to save money; the extra teaching payments didn't hurt. He made no mention of the PhD girlfriend in America. Georgia wanted to ask. Though she didn't want to ask.

"It's so good to get out," Ray said, looking around at the assembled gang, feeling his shoulders relax. "I hear you're making new friends."

"What do you mean?"

"Those punters from the pool hall."

"Them? Supply and demand. That's all. They're just goofs."

"Worse than that. It's criminal. Korea is pretty hard-ass about possession. They could charge you. Throw you in jail. The whole lot, George. You've got to be careful."

"I can take care of myself."

"I know that. But the circumstances aren't always in your control."

"Thanks, Dad."

"I'd have to bust you out. Disguised as a kimchi merchant. I'd hide you in a barrel of spicy cabbage and we'd make for the coast."

"Romantic. You'd do that for me?"

"In a second."

A round of shouts exploded from the kitchen table nearby. Becca, Ji-tae and the others had started some game with wood blocks, trying to remove ones from the bottom and putting them on top without toppling the whole pile. The goal was avoiding the disaster as long as you could. Pieces went missing, fallen somewhere, and couldn't be found. They looked under the couch, in people's shoes.

They tried to invent games. They took out all the cutlery and dumped it on the table in a pile. There were two teams: spoon and fork. Knives were too hard. They all took turns. You had to rescue each of your utensils by picking them up with a pair of chopsticks and returning them to the drawer. You couldn't drop them or let them touch anything else. Ray successfully conveyed two forks across the kitchen under Georgia's barrage of popcorn.

Ji-tae was disqualified for using an extra chopstick.

The reports from Busan had been good lately, he told Georgia from the sidelines. The early winter swell was developing, more vertical than normal, and he was hoping for "tubes," the hollow waves formed when the water, with enough height and forward momentum, create an empty, rolling cavern that's possible to surf through. The chance for tubes had been Ji-tae's passion, back and forth to the east coast, enduring the freezing water in his wetsuit. He was going again.

Georgia was game. They tried to convince Mick and Ray to join them.

"No way am I giving you the pleasure of watching me falling on my head repeatedly," Ray said, adding, "Surfing is not much of an English sport."

"You are an island nation," Georgia informed him.

"Yes, but our coasts are big impenetrable walls of rock. We are a shipwrecker's paradise. Ever heard of the Spanish Armada?"

13

IN LATE OCTOBER, the protests started. There was a standoff up the main street leading to the municipal building. Demonstrators throwing chunks of concrete at police. Police armed with plastic masks, clubs and shields. Hundreds more climbing from vans, marching into formation, performing rituals of shouts then slamming their shields on the ground to a great clatter. The demonstrators shouted back, shook signs, charged forward and crabbed back.

"It's against corruption," Ji-tae said. "The government takes people's money."

He was trying to think of a word.

"Stealing? Bribes?" Becca offered.

"Bribes, yes. The big business gives bribes and the government gives special treatment."

"Sums it up."

"Same as fucking everywhere," Georgia grunted.

They had headed for burgers, only to turn the corner into a full riot. They watched for a few minutes. When the demonstrators began to look tired, the police moved in with coordinated groups, each line taking turns pushing the students back, firing tear gas as they went.

"Fuckers," Georgia said.

Becca took photos, posting them with angry emojis.

"Koreans like to protest, especially in Gwangju," Ji-tae said. "But the month of May is most important, because we remember the massacre."

Georgia told Ji-tae she'd seen the memorial for the Gwangju Massacre. The new teachers had been taken there in their first days in the city. They criss-crossed rows of marble stones exhibiting photos of victims under glass covers. "They are many of the victims," Ji-tae said. The massacre was taught in schools now, but he'd known various details through his family. "My father's uncle was there. It was in 1980." After the South Korean dictator Park Chung-hee was assassinated, Ji-tae explained, he was replaced by a military regime headed by Chun Doo-hwan, an army general. The new government brought martial law, but there was hope once things settled that the country would return to democracy with Park gone. Student unions formed. They demanded minimum wage levels and freedom of the press. There were protests in Seoul, but the army stepped in and broke them up. They banned political activity, arrested pro-democracy politicians and closed the universities. On May 18, Ji-tae's great-uncle and hundreds of students went to the university gate in Gwangju. They shouted slogans against Chun Doo-hwan. Soldiers came. They used their shields to push the students back and the students threw rocks at them. Then the demonstration continued into the downtown core.

"It was there." Ji-tae pointed toward the main road two blocks away. "There, Kumnam-ro, the street to the provincial office. Thousands of people crowded around the fountain in front. Police gathered there but soldiers—Special Forces—came and used bayonets. They beat them and stabbed them. They shot people. Many died. My relatives too."

When they'd finished eating, Ji-tae said, "I can show you."

They walked past the shops toward the rhythm of drums and chants. Exiting the side lane onto Kumnam Street, they looked north. Some groups of demonstrators were gathered in circles ahead, the symbolic centre of civic dissent since 1980.

Beautifully painted portraits of people were clipped on ropes between the trees. One showed a woman in a traditional dress beating a hand drum. There was a close-up of a man's stricken face. Another painting depicted a woman raising a Korean flag, the pole in her fist lifted defiantly toward the viewer. "They are the heroes of May 18," Ji-tae said before Georgia could ask. She looked them over again, those faces, perhaps accurate, perhaps not, changed by the sacrifice they represented. "The fountain is still there," Ji-tae said. He pointed to the top of the street. There was a traffic circle where three roads met. Georgia had walked past it several times without a second thought. The fountain and its basin needed a paint job. There were patches of rust below the spouts. Just before the circle, a police barricade now blocked access to where a stage had been built under scaffolds of lighting equipment. A concert had been planned but cancelled due to unrest.

"Do you think there'll be violence?"

"It will depend on the students and soldiers."

Georgia told him that one protest she'd already witnessed had seemed controlled, acted out, like a rehearsed play. Ji-tae nodded and looked over past the small camps of students and the police barricades beyond.

"Understand, because in Korea, everyone must be a soldier. It is required by law. Mandatory," he said after finding the word.

"Were *you* a soldier?" she asked Ji-tae.

"Yes."

He'd started his five-week training right after high school. He admitted he resented losing two years of his life to drills. Though the exercise got him in good shape. But now he was reluctant to find a permanent job. To go from one strict routine to another. "You are only young once. If you want to finish your studies, you can postpone, but you must go. Everyone must be in the army for two years." He gestured ahead of them. It was dusk, the sky reddish grey. The jutting silhouettes of office buildings made the street look like a narrow canyon. He shook his head.

"It's very strange and difficult. All these students look at the soldiers and know they will become them soon. And all soldiers were those students a short time ago. Behind their shields, they see what they once were."

"How can they even fight?"

"Many times it's like what you say: a play. In 1980 it was different. The paratroopers were brought to Gwangju from the north, near Seoul, because Chun Doo-hwan knew they could use force better. Because they wouldn't have family or friends in the protest. But even now, sometimes, the play becomes real. We forget our identity for a false self. With our public self, we change. Our outside forgets our inside. Something else takes control. In these protests, maybe the students don't understand their future; or sometimes the soldiers forget the past. So, the present is difficult."

Weekly now, there seemed to be more clashes. There was no end to causes and reasons for groups to form and march: government corruption, police brutality, anti-American, anti-Japanese, protests for Korean reunification, protests against Korean reunification.

Then someone was killed in Seoul. A protest against corruption had escalated into riot. A student was hit in the head by a tear gas canister. The police blamed the other protesters for his fatal injuries, citing the trampling and chaos that interfered with medical access to the scene. Another protest became a memorial. It expanded across the country. Everyone at school said the tension was rising. Georgia got used to the smell of tear gas and started to carry a handkerchief to wrap over her mouth and nose. Downtown was eerie. Blocks away from the main protests, she took a shortcut to get to her bus stop and came across twenty riot police waiting in weird silence around the corner in an alley. Some of them were holding their helmets, crouched against walls. An order hissed over a radio and they picked up their gear and marched off.

The story of the Gwangju uprising was deeply personal to the people in her city. As the current protests escalated, the subject became more frequent at her school. Some of the teachers were children in Gwangju when it happened. No one knew what was going to happen. Mr. Yung listened grimly as the art teacher described his mother hiding him in a potato bin in 1980. The soldiers would drag people out of their homes, pull them off buses and beat them.

"They came to our house," Mr. Yung said. "They shot through the window. We ducked below." Sitting at his desk, he lowered his head, shielding it with his hands, as if they were still shooting. "Bang, bang, bang," he said.

Mr. Choi, the technical arts teacher, had rolled the sliding door to the staff room open and walked past to the small kitchen counter. He listened, smiling as he filled an electric kettle with water and plugged it in. After a few moments, he said something in Korean and Mr. Yung responded. This went back and forth. Scolding, nagging tones.

After Mr. Choi left with his tea, Mr. Yung looked at Georgia, guessing her question.

"Mr. Choi thinks we shouldn't talk about this. *Why?* he asks. *It's in the past.*"

"Isn't it important to remember things?"

He shrugged. "Yes. Maybe. But some things are painful," Mr. Yung said. "Mr. Choi was a student then."

14

THE NEWSPAPERS WERE ADVISING people to stay away from the downtown core. But Georgia and Ji-tae convinced Becca to come back to Kumnam-ro to join the memorial and see what would happen. Resolute, Georgia took the bus through the suburbs and over the river, her old anger and sense of injustice increasing. Everyone was told to get out at a makeshift drop-off area near the centre; only authorized vehicles were allowed beyond.

An acidic fog hung in the air.

She walked the next few blocks and found Ji-tae and Becca at a favourite coffee shop.

"We're sticking our noses in it," Becca announced.

It was a new phrase for Ji-tae.

"Your nose," Becca said. "Sticking out too far. Where it shouldn't be. Where you're not invited."

"It's everyone's worry," Ji-tae insisted. "They don't want us here. They say it's trouble. But we must show we can remember."

Ji-tae thought it was good they'd come. In 1980 foreign reporters had been a welcome presence. They provided international confirmation of the brutality of government troops. A few reporters were able to get word of the beatings and shootings to the outside world. One German cameraman smuggled footage of dead bodies and burned-out buildings through the barricades outside the city, and then to Tokyo, disguised as a wedding present, in his luggage.

"Today it won't be dangerous. But it's better if more people see," Ji-tae said.

Bolting down their soup and rice, they headed to Kumnam-ro. It was the same scene as before. At the far end, near the fountain, police lines were formed behind plastic riot shields. In front of them, a silent assembly of protesters squatted to act as the forward edge of resistance. All wore bandanas around their faces. Some had protective goggles. For two blocks farther back, the student groups filled the street: chanting in circles, banging small drums, waiting under protest banners that hung from trees or were strung across the boulevard. But as dusk came and the sky changed colour, something changed. There was a shift of momentum. A few small fires were started, lighter fluid squirted across cardboard and wedges of wood. The police line pushed into the stubborn crowd of students, forcing them back ten metres, knocking a few to the ground. One of the protesters bashed at the police shields with a wooden sign. Three cops broke ranks, shoved the guy to the pavement and dragged him away, his hands tied off with plastic cuffs. Georgia noticed more protesters arrive with metal pipes, their faces hidden by hospital masks. A few garbage cans were set on fire. A column of smoke swelled between the buildings.

They walked around. Ji-tae talked to different union groups. Some students had come by bus from Mokpo, Suncheon or Muan. It was a tradition to protest and they felt it was important to be in Gwangju. Becca and Georgia watched a few students—all wearing the same red T-shirt with a cartoon explosion on it—perform a dance to what they guessed was a protest song. Twice more the police pushed the front of the demonstration back, ten or fifteen metres, where it would stabilize. There would be a puff of smoke and a chorus of shouts, some scrambling back, a few holding their faces. It stank, but the tear gas wasn't as concentrated where they stood. But the more progress the police made, the more determined the students became. There seemed to be an invisible line

GEORGIA AT SEA

they would not surrender. As the front was forced back, the throng got thicker and more focused. The metal pipes and clubs held by many in the crowd stiffened in the air like thorns. There was still a space between the protesters and the police line, a no-man's land, where a few defiantly stood, goading police, poking at their plastic shields with the pipes.

After a few tense moments, the police all shouted in unison and began to move forward again, keeping their line in control. Students wouldn't give any ground and started beating at the plastic shields. The air was full of rattling and banging. The front was getting close to where they now stood. Becca took more pictures. They were shoving some students, knocking them off balance. One student who was stumbling tripped and fell hard, smacking his head on the pavement. He immediately tried to drag himself away to the side of the street, but he looked dazed, attempted three ungainly steps and dropped to the ground again.

Georgia bolted forward and kicked at the shields. *"You fucking assholes,"* she shouted.

"Shit," Becca said and ran forward.

Georgia was screaming into a face behind a police helmet: "What the fuck's the matter with you?!"

Becca rushed up behind her. The student lay there, dazed but propping himself on his elbows. "We need to help him," Becca said.

They both crouched and supported the student's arms as he raised himself.

"Are you okay?" Georgia said. He looked at her. His eyes were bloodshot from tear gas, or likely fatigue. There was a lot of shouting around them. He focused on Georgia's face for a long second. "Yes," he said in English.

With his hand on her shoulder, he steadied himself and they moved toward the sidewalk, only four steps, when Georgia heard *pop, pop, pop* as a tear gas canister arced down from the sky and skittered right to their feet.

The smoke jetted out the top and Georgia caught a blast to her nose and eyes, like a splash of wildfire. The student who she'd been helping now tugged on her sleeve. Within seconds, it was chaos. The police were sprinting, at full charge, their shields strapped around shoulders, waving short black clubs. Everyone was scattering, screaming, tripping over each other. Someone stumbled through a bonfire and kicked sparks off hot, burning wood into the panic. The tear gas billowed and crept. Georgia hadn't had time to pull on her bandana. Her throat stung. She was choking. Her eyes felt scorched. Within seconds of exposure, they'd squeezed up, ducts violently gushing water.

"Becca!" she yelled blindly. "Becca! Ji-tae!"

There was shouting and footfalls and banging. Georgia groped forward, impelled by the direction she'd been going, but everything was jumbled and reversed. Someone tripped over her ankle and she fell, her arm bearing the worst of the impact. She got up. She darted forward again, both hands probing the air until they bumped a surface. A wall. Grainy, poured concrete. Painfully, she forced an eye open and discovered she'd reached the west side of Kumnam, past the sidewalk and at the start of a short alley. It was impossible, too much agony, to keep her eyes open, so she hauled herself along the walls a step at a time. The street was full of gas, searing each inhale. Snot poured from her nostrils. Around the next corner, she found a small alcove so she crouched down inside its hollow to rest, crushing her palms against eye sockets.

"Don't rub your eyes," she heard a male voice say. "It'll just make it worse."

Everything was still blurry, fog-red.

The voice again: "It's Ray."

"Ray. Ray! I need to flush my eyes."

He had a bottle of water on him. She tilted her head and told him to pour the water over her face so the chemicals dripped to the ground, not into her clothes. Two fingers touched her forehead and liquid rolled across her eyes. Her skin was instantly cooler. She could now see the transparent shape of the plastic bottle, tipped just above her. She squinted and assembled Ray's face through the blur.

"How the fuck did you find me?"

15

"IT WAS NUTTERS," Becca said as they drank persimmon tea at Georgia's place.

Georgia, winded, had stripped down and dumped her clothes in a basin of water, then took a cold shower to rinse the chemicals off. Her eyes still smouldered like coals. Ray brought her a cup of barley water while she slumped there in a towel, raw from tear gas and her numerous falls, as they took turns recounting timelines. There'd been a crush of retreating protesters. Becca was knocked over. They'd lost track of Georgia. The smoke and gas and chaos of people. They'd rushed around frantically. The police had broken up the hard-core resistance and sent extra squads down the side streets, targeting anyone with metal pipes and arresting them.

They'd detained Ji-tae for a moment but let him go.

Ray had joined the protests too, further back, when he saw the police move forward.

And there was Georgia screaming and bashing away.

"Not exactly inconspicuous. Figures. Right in the thick of it."

"So much for neutrality," Becca said. She finished her tea and pulled a can of beer from their purchases at the corner store. "You were fucking marvellous, Gee. Absolutely mythic. Like the fucking Medusa. Epic lunacy. Hair all over the place, your eyes like two lava pits, screaming bloody murder at that squirmy cop while kicking away at him. He didn't stand a chance."

Georgia watched them all laughing.

Drinks went round. Georgia ranted, her hands now flapping, flitting like butterflies, voice fired up, raging about control and general oppression and the farce of authority. It was all greed and power and the police state, she spat. Her angry, headlong passion. The general feeling of helplessness, the recognition that the many are all sacrificed to the whims of someone's bloated profit. "All fucking bullshit," she summed up, shaking her hair still wet from the shower.

Georgia looked a sensation, as Becca described it. Her skin had reacted to the tear gas, leaving a red rash on her cheeks and forehead. Her bruised hand and a deep scrape on her forearm were more visible than the pulled muscles in her back. She was so stiff that she moved in Frankenstein strides through the school hallways, rigid and groaning. For the next few weeks, the students regarded her with baffled attention. She was an open mystery to them.

Several times before Christmas, Georgia, Ji-tae and Becca drove back to Busan to try out the surf. "Red sky in the morning," Ji-tae would chime as they started out. Or "When a swallow flies low." He was an avid weather watcher. He kept track of offshore winds on the internet. Obsessed over the south-east swells. Surfing forecasts were a continual fixation. So many variables contributed to the right waves, he enthused. The cyclone season raised the tide's drama but Ji-tae had faith in the winter surf. When it arrived, they'd scream running in. It was cripplingly cold, even with their wetsuits. The breakers could be dramatic, rough and challenging. Ji-tae was in his element. A chance at choppy, unpredictable surges invigorated him. The December waves knocked Becca and Georgia all over the place, ass-flat on their boards, chin-first into bulwarks of water. Georgia, having worked the basics out in past months, now attacked the water with a disjointed hostility. She was lining up well, and finding her balance once she'd stood, but now worked too hard at scaling the swell, as if she could defeat it, as if the waves were a maze she could axe her way through, escape from, rather than ride. She got hungrier, looking for openings to convert her luck into skill, but her newfound fury made her stiff and reckless and accident prone.

"Your mind should be aggressive but your body must relax," Ji-tae counselled after she'd tumbled a countless time.

"Thank you, Yoda," she said.

This time, before they drove back to Gwangju, Ji-tae took them to Beomeosa, the hilltop Buddhist temple in the centre of the city. The car moved through apartment blocks on a gentle rise out of the downtown core. Trees and hilly lanes softened the urban scatter. They inched through a jammed parking lot. The temple was popular on the weekend. Families held impromptu picnics on benches and grass verges leading to the temple gates. There were a few restaurants near the parking area, all mobbed by groups of patrons. Waiters dashed about with side dishes of kimchi, octopus, bowls of red soup bobbing with clams and white fish. They strolled toward the entrance, the path lined with black granite steles, many capped with carved dragons or turtles as their base. The sun was just starting to nudge from shadows onto the west side of the temple buildings.

They stood looking at the first gate. Its beams were painted elaborately with bright blue and crimson swirls and bands.

"This is called *Iljumun*," Ji-tae said. "The first gate. It's very important. A barrier from the world. You must leave your earthly desires behind once you pass."

"Good luck," Georgia mumbled.

Ji-tae gestured to the curves in the beams rising toward and joining at the peak. "You see the wood parts? This shape stops evil from getting inside. People believe that evil only travels through straight lines."

Monks filed from a doorway, marched across the open square and disappeared into another temple. A few of them were women. Their rust-coloured robes shifted over grey beneath. They all had their heads shaved. Cast-iron bells hung from the corners of the roof. The clappers, weighted down by fish made of flattened copper, rang limpidly in the wind.

"This sound," Ji-tae said, "also tells you to stop thinking of the world."

They roamed around with no goal, besieged by yellow leaves scattering to the forest floor. Several buildings and pagodas were arranged around the central temple. A recent rain had left a sensuous line of displaced mud meandering down the compound's open ground. Georgia's arms still ached from the day's vigorous surf.

"All that fucking paddling," she grunted. They climbed some steps to an entrance where three giant gold Buddhas sat between hundreds of candles, incense coiling up into the air. The walls were covered with bright murals of flowers and other seated Buddhas. Pyramids of apples and oranges were set out on miniature platforms. The spiritual bling of it seemed weird to Georgia amidst all the humble structures of stone and wood. But the air hung with lazy serenity. Following Ji-tae's lead, they left their shoes at the top step and moved over the polished floor to a mat made of bamboo, bowing and kneeling down.

The monks chanted.

Becca felt Georgia tapping her knee. She looked at Georgia's face, gone distraught and grey, her breath stifled with heaves.

"You okay, mate? You look absolute shite."

Georgia scrambled from her knees for the exit. Becca followed, winking at Ji-tae. A few other tourists watched them leave, but the monks kept chanting, oblivious of Georgia running past her shoes, along the path and beyond the temple porch in her sock feet.

There was a stone bench to the side of the temple where she collapsed.

Becca arrived a minute behind her and waited for Georgia to get her breath back.

"What's wrong, Gee? You sick?"

She could now see Georgia was sobbing, her cheeks battered red with inner turmoil. Becca pulled her close into her, palms cupping Georgia's shoulders as she gasped and wept.

"It's alright, mate," she said. "The hangover can't be that bad."

They drove home Sunday evening, the east at their backs. Mountainous silhouettes followed their progress. Gaps in trees showed sea. North of Jinju they stopped for coffee and ate the small potatoes rolled in butter. Georgia craved salt while Becca drank water between sips of coffee. Ji-tae needed a few minutes to buy some presents for his parents and disappeared into the display shelves of a shop stacked with gift-wrapped desserts and specialty fish.

The women slouched on a bench facing the parking lot. Through a wide bay window, they watched a family rearranging luggage in their hatchback.

"Sorry I lost it back there," Georgia said.

"No worries," Becca said. "We all deserve a meltdown. You okay?"

"I'm a bit overwhelmed."

"Shit's fucked up," Becca offered.

"Maybe the protest set me off. I've been trying to keep things . . . uncomplicated," Georgia said, struggling to put thoughts into words. "The last couple of years I was staying under the radar. Flat, y'know? Monochrome. Everything neutral. Just coasting. It was my mantra. I stayed out of university. I worked at a coffee shop and tried to avoid imposed social situations and drama. But my mother was driving me nuts. She was either super-worried or pissed at me. I had to get out of there. I needed to fulfill a promise. I thought Korea would bring solitude. And these great kids and work and you and Mick. Ray and Ji-tae. I miss the numbness. I'd actually thought I'd lost interest in being interested in things anymore. I'm not making much sense, am I? I'm starting to feel happy again. The highs and lows are terrifying. It's all freaking me out." She laughed pathetically.

The hatchback family had finished their re-packing and now posed with each other as a passerby took their picture against the sea's reddening skyline.

"I saw your wrist when we were surfing," Becca said.

Georgia nodded. She'd seen Becca noticing, had registered the raw alarm. The subject matter was difficult, the loaded moment difficult to share. Her therapist had said she needed to identify the shadow and comprehend the intensities of her despair and panic. But Georgia had struggled with the process and closed herself off. At what point do you say, *Give me help*? Life was so intimate when it scraped against death.

"What happened?" Becca said.

Georgia leaned forward and rested her left arm across her thigh. She dragged all the bracelets and beaded strings up to her elbow, and unsnapped Natalie's leather wristband. There they were, the naked, dramatic scars. One white slash, several centimetres long, ran from the bottom of Georgia's palm halfway to the inside of her forearm, like a satellite photo of a dried-up riverbed. A second line, much shorter, as if an afterthought, was cut at an angle, like a comma added to sever the scar's main flow. The word FIGHTER, tiny, but in caps, was inscribed there, tattooed across her wrist, perpendicular to the cuts.

Georgia pressed her thumb along the lines, as if to show the danger had passed, the seams were tight, the darkness could be contained, and the pain locked out.

You could see the blood pulsing in an artery nearby.

"A bit cliché, right?" Georgia said.

Becca took her hand and squeezed it.

Ji-tae was waving at them near the exit, clutching gift boxes as he pushed through the doors.

Part 2

HUGO WALSER DURING HIS ILLNESS

16

AS MY TAXI ARRIVES at the Ottawa airport, only a few travellers are loping through the rain toward the entrance. Inside: couples, business types, clusters of small families mill about the uncomfortable seating areas. A bored security officer scans another's revolver with a metal detector. The black wand beeps. They laugh. They reverse roles.

I have time for a haircut, so take a chair. "A number two all around and float it on top," the barber states with certainty, as if I'm a regular. Why not? He pulls hot foam off my neck with a straight razor and dumps the paper collar in the trash. Restaurants and a bookstore are stagnant. Afternoon departure. A lull in the non-time of airports. International flights require you to arrive three hours in advance, leaving you plenty of time to spend your domestic cash. I watch two toddlers stumble back and forth between their mother and a display case of confiscated and stuffed endangered animals. The children screech, dashing about. The rules to their game are few. Run and touch. Shriek. Run and touch. Shriek. The protective glass near the turtle shells is smudged with applesauce. They're soon tiring. It is hours from bedtime. I recognize their parents' strategy. Run the little kiddies on the wheel until fatigued. Though no doubt, when it catches up to them a few hours over the Atlantic, that red glow on their cheekbones will transform into renewed shrills.

Near the departure lounge, there is rescue. A bar is open for business. Darcy McGee's, one of its franchise locations from the downtown Ottawa mother ship. Faux Ireland coziness fitted like a quaint wood drawer into the glass-and-steel efficiency of a contemporary airport. Amid framed prints of James Joyce in that unfortunate hat, amid black-and-whites of turf fields and stone hovels, amid shelves of glass jars, tankards and shillelaghs, we are to be convinced of the modest, rural authenticity of the universal claim to an Irishness. I won't complain. Just a half pint and some Bushmills. I will embrace the imperfect stereotype.

Ich bin ein Irelander.

I am joined by a youth in a Hugo Boss suit. Well, likely he's pushing thirty. He is red-faced, with a military haircut. He's got a class ring and grips a sleek briefcase.

"Hiya," he says, swinging his leg onto the stool next to mine. "Where you heading?"

He doesn't look old enough to shave. But he wants to chat and I'm bored.

"Barcelona," I say. "The 4:15 connection out of Montreal."

He nods like he's done it a few times himself.

The crying has started. One of the racing children, clumsy and breathless, has fallen just short of the glass display, knocking his chin against it. A wizened cobra glares from its trembling container of formaldehyde, its submerged visage warning, *Do not wrench me from my land of origin or I will bring this curse upon you.* The child screeches back toward his mother, a tiny banshee, all heated arms and self-remorse.

My current drinking partner with the class ring offers info. He's on his way to Vienna. Something to do with sales. Office furniture. Austrian-made. Ongoing expansion. Increased orders. The internet culture.

"Furniture, right? You always need somewhere to park your ass," he says.

"Two more is what *I* say." I point to my drained tumbler. Class-ring laughs and puffs his cheeks.

"Boy," he says, "I probably shouldn't."

He's been here three hours already on a stopover from Vancouver. But he takes one and we tap the glasses congenially.

"What do you do?" he asks.

"Architect," I say, though immediately regret it. Should have gone for a story. Chef or sea captain. Ambassador. Tug on his chain for the thirty minutes of our short-lived time together on this earth.

"Oh yeah? You build stuff?"

"No, that's someone else. I imagine the thing. Design it. Somebody else builds," I say. Though that isn't really the truth either. At least not now.

He's already got fourteen questions. Is it business or residential? Anything outside of Ottawa? Barcelona? I can see where this is going on his transparent MBA face. He's mentally placing all his precious, overpriced Austrian furniture on the corporate floors of my buildings in Shanghai, Riyadh and Mexico City while trying to look cucumber-cool with disinterest.

I finish my whiskey. He is still talking, something about environment and productivity and economics.

"Do you like the terminal?" I ask him, nodding at the copper and limestone finishes, the exposed ductwork and panoramic windows.

"You designed it?" he says, his grin half-incredulous. I push my empty glass an inch toward the bartender, the visual cue directed at my furniture salesman. It's his round now, if he has any fucking manners.

"This one's on me," he obeys. The bartender's and my eyes agree. He has slugged back the last nip of Bushmills and, immediately upon receiving the fresh glass, drains that too. "Tell you what," he says, "let me get one more round and then I'd better find the men's before they call my flight." And he slides a platinum Visa card across the wood. He's become tetchily drunk. His mind is on nothing now but a shift in location. I'm impressed. He wasn't working me at all. Or he was but gave up. Maybe he was actually making conversation. Lonely, like the world.

He gets his PIN number right on the second try.

"Christ, I'm gonna sleep," he says, tilting on his bar stool. Profound lines under his eyes seem circled with red crayon. I could almost feel sorry for him, so young, with years of these terminal dialogues ahead. He dredges up a leather carry-on from the base of the stool and places it beside the briefcase.

"So, was this airport yours? Did you design it?" He gestures to the concourse.

"No. Not me at all."

I could look back. I could write entire books about certain days. I could drag out something from the marriage. Sarah and me. One of our fights would be a great chapter. Like that day in Chicago when she threw the ice cream cone at me in the hotel lobby. We thought it was quite funny afterward. Both of us laughing our asses off in the security office, even with the strawberry stain on my grey three-piece. And Sarah with her mad tears. The injustices against me! There's a day there, but which one to choose in all that slow-moving, seemingly eventless accumulation of ruin? How could something with such grandeur be so abused?

It was only a half truth I told back there. I was an architect. Quite successful for a while. Commissions. Decent ones. Not the Royal Library in Denmark, but some business designs. A condominium. A regional gallery. There was even my brief reign as cultural panelist on a weekly TV program.

But then something fell. It was a wall, actually, and the best part of the glass roof. There *had* been an earthquake in the area, it must be mentioned. Ten days prior to the collapse. Nothing Japan-like in scale. One of our cheery, eastern Canadian earthquakes, a few numbers on the Richter. Tilted picture frames and yelping dogs.

HUGO WALSER DURING HIS ILLNESS

That kind of thing. But the foundation of my charming gallery had shifted and the wall came down. And what can you do? This is about media and public perception in the end. Engineers were questioned. The building contractors were put under suspicion too. There had been a lot of Montreal mafia in the news. Public servants had been fired, rumours of hefty bribes. There's big money in development and wherever those dollar signs accumulate there is usually some burly entourage with overseas connections driving very nice cars. For a few weeks it looked like my gallery would be overshadowed by the organized crime circus, one of the tiny tails pinned to their stalwart donkey. But in the age of internet, it's hard to shake the fallout from a collapsing wall, no matter where speculation shifts. One efficient search engine and your name is attached to fallen public galleries and crime bosses for eternity.

Most of the offers dried up. But I didn't care. The money had been good but who wants to piss and moan about possible load-bearing options all his life. My forte had been aesthetics. The Philosophy of the Dwelling. The *Feng Shui* of Glass and Steel. Building these structures was one thing, but the idea of them was far more interesting. I had already been writing architectural reviews for the *Globe and Mail* and *Independent*, lengthier articles for *Architect Today*, so the minor earthquake was a sign. Or a forcible shove.

They call my flight.

I am going to wait until the last possible second. I am going to finish this drink, pay my bill, take a leak and then stroll toward my gate only once they announce my name. They can sweat a bit. They're always making us wait. This business flight is on my dime and I'm going to do it at my own pace.

You would think after the unfortunate wall malfunction that my career would be shit, my reputation rubbish, my credit as ghastly as roadkill. But the opposite happened. I was never so interesting or in demand. My status may have been roadkill, smeared across the asphalt, but the spectators liked the colours, the contours and the spectacle of entrails left by my downfall. Why?

Cheek and insolence.

Refusing to crawl in a hole, I carried on blithely, as if, in fact, it was everyone else who had designed that ridiculous wall and I was just on hand to explain it to them. I turned it all around. Instead of accepting the ripe tomatoes thrown at my face, I blew raspberries into the wind. The public wanted a jester and I was there with my jug ears and air horn. Hasn't it always been that way with me? Criticism is just bait and switch anyway. I have challenged and mocked what others have held dear. The sincerest efforts, when dissected, can become the subject of ridicule and embarrassment. Since no one wants to touch the unpalatable verities, I will.

My cellphone sings a tinny ditty, but I'm looking at it and there's no name, just an unfamiliar number. A million guesses but I'm not going to answer it now. They can leave a message at this point. Who would be calling me at two p.m. on a Saturday afternoon? I could, after all, be on the runway and powered off lest my satellite signal breaches the cockpit's sophisticated instruments and catastrophe reigns. I'll shut it down now, in fact; I'm on vacation. No, that's not true. I'm on a quest for redemption and closure.

There, you see?

They are just calling my name.

17

A LURCH, THEN WE ARE free of the runway. So much rain earlier in the week, there was talk of delays, cancellations. Though grim clouds beckon through the oval windows, my route is clear. I wave off a complimentary newspaper but munch the barbeque peanuts. South Ottawa, its burbs and green spaces, sweep away beneath our fuselage. I'm suddenly thirsty and wave for a second bottle of water. They are shorter, miniature versions of those on sale in the real world. Is our hydration being rationed? Is this some cost-saving strategy, a payload issue? Some hint of future portioning? Oh, the wars to come. There is no alcohol for sale on this forty-minute flight. The seatbelt lights are still aglow, but I unclip mine. The attendant is at me like a vengeful harridan.

"Sir, your seatbelt should remain on until the warning light indicates otherwise."

I provide a withering nod, designed to remind her I will not drift off into outer space should we scud across a stratum of turbulence, but she hardly looks like the indulging type, so I lazily slide the straps back over my lap and couple the metal clips again. Her curt "Thanks" is filled with suspicion.

I have always loved to fly. I suspect it started in my mid-twenties, those stolen weekends in Boston or New Orleans with Sarah when the future was a gold curtain about to be raised on a sunlit stage. Other pleasures would surrender themselves in the hotels, but squeezing onto those DC-10s never failed to buoy my small reserves of contentment and anticipation. I never feared.

I knew enough of engineering to be satisfied with the design and safety features of airplanes. Statistics show we are in far more mortal danger every single time we step inside a car, yet few of us count rosary beads or hyperventilate as we back out of our driveway. My only hesitation, then, was the cost. Back in those days, I resented having to plunk half a grand onto my credit card for an extended weekend of jambalaya and coitus.

Air travel really blossomed for me once it became free. Or more accurately, paid for by the *Globe and Mail* or *Architecture Now*. Writing reviews for them became my open ticket to soar across the Atlantic and Europe on a corporate budget. I'd duly arrive at the inaugural press viewing of some lauded new museum, civic headquarters or private home, and squeeze out my three hundred words of judgement on the aesthetics and applied value of its design. The regional wines would flow. The trays of hors d'oeuvres would drift past, canapés replaced by those ridiculous diminutive burgers that are so in fashion now. What are they called? Sliders.

I wiggle my raised finger at the attendant. She approaches with that saintly touchiness tightened across her mouth.

"More peanuts, please."

She checks her wristwatch. They have already cleared the used paper cups and snack packages.

"We'll be landing in Montreal in a few minutes, sir," she says.

"I'll enjoy them later then."

A moment later she drops two packages into my lap to assure me of Air Canada's unwavering generosity while reminding me to return my seat to its upright position. Soon we are touching the dun tarmac of Trudeau Airport two minutes ahead of schedule.

I've reviewed a few airports in the past. I have always admired them. Most of their designers have judiciously accepted that an airport should be a trouble-free conduit between points of arrival and gates of departure. The experience of them should be nothing more than a transitional flow. When an airport gets in trouble is when its architect wishes to be original and unique. Name all the airports you've become lost in; they are likely the result of some quixotic image of future travel. Passage imagined as organic interplay. But we do not want adventure in our transition points. We don't want interplay. We want ninety-degree turns and clear signage. If travel aspires to be extraordinary, its junctions should be typical. The ones you can't bring clearly to your mind are the ones that served you best. Ottawa's Macdonald-Cartier has its artistic flourishes—a babbling water highlight symbolizing the meeting of three rivers, a hapless inuksuk marking *what* exactly?—but they are kept to a minimum and don't interrupt the natural flow of monotony ushering travellers through duty free and food courts. Here at Trudeau the experience is much the same. I could hardly tell the two apart, including the views of the runway. The same should be said of many airports.

There are exceptions.

Those majestic mountains surrounding Kuala Lumpur's terminal emphasized through soaring cut-out ceilings of glass.

Or Abu Dhabi's curved pillars bursting with Islam-inspired mosaic. Beautiful. But for the traveller: a distraction. Raze them to the ground, says I. Save your panorama for beyond the arrival hall.

You will imagine I'm a functionalist by all this. But that is not exactly the truth. It's much more complicated, though not as convoluted or sordid as Alan Norcock would have you think. But we'll get to Alan Norcock in a moment. Yes, we will. Since Alan Norcock is the reason for this particular journey. I'm going to go over there and I'm going to set the whole story straight. Yes, I am ready to draw some moustaches on the poster boy.

I have barely more than an hour between flights but manage to consume a flaccid panini, a Johnny Walker and half a lager. They announce a delay—twenty-five minutes—so I linger a bit in this cafeteria, which struggles to substitute as an authentic Italian restaurant. The gingham design of the plastic tabletops. The bolted, swivelling chairs are lozenges of primary colour. The orange platters with waxed paper have been reduced to a prodded smudge of ketchup.

I power the cellphone up. Corporate logos pulse and flit across the screen. Three calls. My anonymous caller has tried twice but has left a message only at the second opportunity: *Hello, Mr. Walser. This is Nora Riedy calling. I work for Sarah Trimble at the agency. Can you . . . give me a call as soon as you're able? I'm wondering if you've been in contact with her in the last few days. Yes. The number at the office is 613-231-2071. Okay. If you can call, that would be great. Thanks.*

The second message is from Douglas, her realtor partner, employing that brisk tone he uses to sound busy. He probably is. There is an airy, shouted acoustic sound over the line. Calling while on the expressway, no doubt. A habit he won't break, even with two traffic fines.

Hugo, it's Douglas. Have you talked to your ex lately? She doesn't answer her calls, and I haven't heard from her since Wednesday. She hasn't come in to the office, as far as I can tell, and she's missed a meeting on Friday. It's just not like her, so I thought you might know if she's been . . . you know, if something came up. Could you call me? I'm sure it's fine, but better call. I'm on the road to Mississauga. Okay, bye.

I save the call and roll my head around a few times. Strain has developed across my shoulders, as if the muscles were hoisted by tight hooks to my clavicles. I should have got one of those fifteen-minute massages back at the gate.

Next to me, a couple discuss the addresses on their luggage tags with existential anxiety. Should they have written their home address instead of their Genoa house rental? If lost and recovered quickly, they will have their dining attire and swimsuits for most of the holiday. If the luggage circles the globe for weeks, then it will arrive after they've returned to Canada. Will someone be responsible for sending it on? Will it be abandoned in that scenic part of Italy?

Once, Sarah and I spent the better part of a holiday in Rome without our luggage. Those plastic cases enjoyed a sojourn in Singapore while we bandied about the finer restaurants of the Eternal City in newly purchased linens and silks subsidized by Air Italia. It was a licence to splurge, though a portion of the money was our own. Sarah could spend in those days, and so could I. We could eat and drink as if Christ the Redeemer was bringing down the sky. One hundred euros on breakfast if the croissants looked good and it came with a terrace view. At the drop of a hat. "Go for it," I'd say, as she'd drape a designer sleeveless thing across her imperishable curves and raise her eyebrows in feigned guilt. Then I'd jauntily trundle off to peruse the latest offerings in the Zegna flagship store on Via Condotti.

And why not? We thought we'd have money. We were so sure of ourselves. The market was hot. It wasn't only set to bake; it was on broil. My commissions were starting; the real estate that skipped mercurially through Sarah's new office trays was pricey and competitive. The numbers had taken over. When it's like that you can just let them sit in their accounts and they grow like mould. Some mornings you look at yourself in the mirror and can't help but wink.

We met in our student days. There was an exhibit on at the Canadian Centre for Architecture in Montreal. One Thursday morning I hopped off the metro, slugged back a long espresso in a café near the Faubourg, then strolled down St. Marc to the Centre's glass and steel façade that commandingly overlooked the parish steeples beyond Autoroute Ville Marie. The subject of the exhibit was "The American Lawn." Crossing the square to the main entrance, voices called out "Touch me," "Feel me," "Step on me" from the green grass below my feet. I looked down. Tiny speakers had been placed on the verge, triggered by motion sensors. Inside, the exhibit was quirky. Borderline interesting. Utopian layouts for early community zoning contrasted with diagrams of contemporary urban sprawl. In one room they had squares of

Astroturf—differing examples of density and texture from football, baseball and rugby fields—with their corresponding sport shoe. I got easily bored in those days. I drifted toward the windows in the vestibule and yearned to wander off in the unfamiliar street again. But to the side of the entrance was a bookstore, packed ceiling-high with volumes, the mecca of architecture books. I had begun work on a class paper on prison design a few weeks earlier, inspired by my first reading of Foucault's discussion of Bentham's panopticon. His was a shift in the conception of prison design away from the seclusion of the dungeon fortification. He argued that visibility is the key to incarceration and, ultimately, power. The panopticon contained an array of separated cells observed by a central tower, like a tire spoked on a wheel well. All the prisoners could be viewed by a single supervisor from this central position. Foucault emphasized the effectiveness of unverifiability. Further to the subtle sublimation of the prisoner, the guard's presence, opposed to the prisoners' visibility, would be shielded from view by blinds and zigzag entrances, so the prisoner could never be certain when they were being observed. Blah, blah, blah.

I was thinking of the Minotaur in its labyrinth.

Naturally, as the young so often do, I had convinced myself that Foucault's thoughts on power and confinement had never been truly understood until I alone had read these pages. The idea rivuleted through my grey matter for weeks. Just as Palladio's concepts of uniformity and proportion led to the beauty of Versailles, or the monumentality of the Lincoln Memorial, so too the architecture of incarceration must be the fruit of an elegant mind. I coasted along the bookshelves of the CCA in hopes of finding more literature on the subject. There were sections devoted to individuals: Niemeyer, van der Rohe, Le Corbusier, Gehry, Ando, even Speer. Vitruvius. Hadid. There were historical perspectives of Chicago. Coffee table books on Gothic and Bauhaus. Entire sections devoted to skyscrapers, Arts and Crafts, green design or landscaping.

Follies and ha-has.

Japanese bridges. Palazzi.

A young woman, only a few years older than me, was reorganizing hardbacks for a display island near the entrance. I dallied in her periphery. She glanced up amid the jumble of volumes still in their plastic wrap.

"Can I help you?"

"Do you have any books on prison architecture?"

"I think we do. Let me just see," she said, nudging her hip against the saloon-style door and positioning herself behind the counter as her fingertips trickled across the keyboard of the bookstore's computer. Brisk tappings filled the silence. The soaring ceiling made the room cool and bright. I waited. We were alone. I noticed her hands hovered there above the letters. They were somewhat masculine, despite the graceful typing skills. No colourful polish on her nails, though pared cleanly. Sensible, one could say. Not quite the hands of a shot putter's, but perhaps a volleyball player. The situation felt faintly erotic. But I was young then and drugged by my own hormones.

"Yes," she said. "There should be. Shelved beside leisure." And she pointed to a lower section along the wall closest to us.

The section contained books on resort design. Some were practical examinations of efficient uses of terrain in the all-inclusive sprawl; aesthetic layouts of lodging, swimming pools, exercise spaces and eating areas. Others had lavish, glossy photo spreads of exclusive getaways in the Maldives and the Caribbean. Vacation porn. And next to them were three books on prisons. I selected one called *Rooms for Restraint* and returned to the counter.

"How did you do?" the woman said, rearranging a stack of Fallingwater memo pads to make room for our transaction.

I pushed the book toward her and smiled. She scanned the barcode, running her thumb along the spine.

"Planning on building a prison?" She smiled.

"Why? Do you need to be restrained?"

"Depends by whom," she said, and fitted a bookmark into the pages of my purchase before dropping it in a plastic bag, snapping the corners straight and holding it out to me. I was momentarily tongue-tied. I took the bag. Parked below the distant skylight, I stood there, drained of purpose and wit.

"Uh, thanks," I said.

"Sarah," she said.

"Hugo."

She gripped the hand I must have offered.

"Weird that the prisons are shelved beside resorts," I said.

"I did that," she explained. "Similar functions, really. Efficient use of space, coordinated resemblance to familiar living areas. The delicate balance of imitation comfort and concealed pacification."

"My god," I said. "Are you free for a drink?"

She laughed and winked and said nothing more, returning to her display.

I haunted that part of town for weeks, intending to run into her again. But it was on Saint-Laurent I saw her next, in the grungy chaos of the Copacabana, draining a plastic pitcher of lager with some sartorial suitor in a pinstriped button-down and a gloopy sculpture of black hair. After twenty minutes of being studied in my peripheral vision, she appeared at the counter beside me. She ordered two margaritas and slouched winsomely a few centimetres to my left. I watched her in the bar mirror. Brunette curls poured past her shoulders. Cheekbones you could whittle wood with.

"The architecture centre," I deadpanned.

"How's the prison coming?" she said without a pause. A blender rattled and revved as we waited to resume our banter. The bartender was rimming two glasses with salt.

When I asked her how she was, she shrugged.

"Your companion not entertaining enough?" I suggested and gave him another once-over from my seat. He was watching us while pretending not to watch us. "How about I join you?"

She'd drained her first margarita in two gulps and picked up the second by the stem. I followed her to the table. She introduced me to Gary but had to ask my name again. There was immediate tension. Poor Gary had no inkling why I'd been summoned to their sticky tabletop, nor what status I had. Sarah repeated the whole story of how we met, and the book I was looking for, to which Gary only smiled. A thin, irritated smile. He had two gold chains on his wrist that dropped inside his sleeve each time he lifted his glass to his lips. I didn't ask Gary what he did for work or pleasure. Our mutual lack of interest was palpable. It vetoed any normal course of conversation. I think Sarah was enjoying herself though. I would learn how much she thrived in uncomfortable situations. The threat of conflict or social breakdown invigorated her. Though she hated small talk, this was small talk of the most delicate order, electrified by concentration and precariousness, like carrying a tray of crystal down a winding flight of stairs.

But after fifteen minutes, I thought it was enough. I was tired of looking at Gary's carefully unshaved jaw modelling his contemptuous pout. When he ordered another pitcher, I reached across the table and filled my beer glass from it. This pissed him off acutely. His eyes sort of trembled in their sockets as I slouched back in my chair and drained half the glass. A few minutes later, when I reached toward the handle to extract from the same jug, his big fingers gripped my wrist mid-operation.

"Why don't you get your own beer?" he said.

"I'm enjoying yours, Gerry. You're a very lavish guy."

He looked at Sarah. In that moment, I guess, he decided that his rage was more pressing than looking polite. Through his teeth, he said, "Why don't you fuck off, asshole?"

"Why don't you fuck off, asshole?" I parodied in my best dumb-guy tone.

He hit me. It was a good one. Solid. A real thump in the jaw.

Then I hit him.

Well, I threw a punch that sort of woodchopped his mouth while my full weight landed against the table's edge, knocking it into him, dumping the beer and scattering a few nearby patrons. A short, sloppy exchange of punches followed. He probably got the best of me, if I'd been judging from ringside. The son of a bitch was pretty strong. But I'd managed to cut his cheek and the visuals were convincing. The smear of blood down his neck presented a dramatic accent. He'd popped a button and torn a sleeve. So much for designer shirts. All kinds of unpleasant words issued from his mouth as the bartenders escorted him into the street.

I was sent to the back closet for their mop.

"Hugo, you asshole," Rene said. He was sweeping the broken glass into a dustpan. "If I knew who started this . . ."

"I did."

He looked at me with exasperation. I had been in a few shouting matches with other patrons before but this was the first physical incident. They tolerated me here, if only because I picked on bigger blowhards than myself. He'd collected most of the glass, so I volunteered to mop up while he went to get the bucket. I shifted the chairs around until I'd soaked most of the mess up. My shoulder throbbed from where I'd fallen in the tussle. There were tender patches on my neck where he tried to squeeze off my oxygen with his beefy fingers. Bruised by morning, likely. A grape necklace. I wrung the sodden mop head over the bucket. Rene and I straightened the table and chairs. Displaced patrons re-inhabited adjacent berths under the fake palm tree. Returning from the washroom, I stopped to retrieve my knapsack hung near the bar stool. It was my usual spot, perched opposite the cut lemons and limes, tabasco bottles and celery salt.

Rene placed a tumbler of whiskey on the coaster in front of me. "For your troubles," he said. It was a good sign. We were still going to be friends. "But for Christ's sake, don't pull that shit again."

"Passive aggressive."

Rene waggled a finger at me like I was a naughty dog. The whiskey stung on my lip. Gary had connected there too, sometime during the melee. I touched the rawness down my neck. My face was a constellation of scorched points. He'd made a roadworks of me. It must have been quite the spectacle for everyone. The speakers blared acid jazz, or whatever it was they played there in those days.

The door had opened and there stood Sarah, studying me like a cop through a car window. I'd assumed she'd accompanied Gary to some nursing station up the wrought iron railings of the apartments on Avenue Coloniale, or wherever people like Gary lodged themselves. I remember she placed her tote bag on the other end of the bar and sat on the edge of the stool, very seriously not approaching me yet. It was her *Stay away, I'm thinking* look. I learned in the years ahead that to encroach inside that boundary had its consequences. You would face changed door locks or thrown ice cream. The punishment varied, not always in scale to the misconduct committed. Unverifiability. That word. It was a lesson I never learned and practised only this once, the very first time. I ordered a margarita and asked Rene to send it to her, but I said nothing, made no gesture, staring like the sphinx past the liqueur bottles at my face in the mirror.

"Men are assholes," she said.

I turned my head and looked at her. Being one among the accused, I held my tongue. She still had not met my eyes but raised the margarita with an ironic smirk. She plowed an index finger along the rim crusted with salt, then dipped it into the citrine liquid.

"He was pissed off at *me*, you know," she said and finally looked up.

"What?"

"I guess for letting you sit with us. Or for having an opinion. For not just sitting there and accepting his half-baked theories on everything."

"Boring, was he?"

She nodded. "Very. What about you?"

"Me?"

"Are you boring?"

"Boring and repetitive," I said. "But very honest."

She allowed a friendlier smile at that. I touched my face where the bruising had already started. She was almost finished her drink and sat looking out the window onto Saint-Laurent. Three hippies were kicking a hacky sack expertly into the air between each other. One of them was lighting a joint with a Zippo while keeping the sack in play. Through the open door you could hear the quick shift of the beads as they kicked the fabric sack into the air, Rastafarian with colour.

"Why must men compete? What about grace and communication?" she said. "Whether you two choose to act as human adults or silverback gorillas shouldn't be my problem."

"Were you on a date?"

She scrutinized me with all the suspicion and calm intent of a Bond villain. I could feel her emotional scalpel tracing the incision she was still planning. She dismissed both Gary and my question with directness. "He asked me out for a drink. I had every intention to finish it, or several, then end the evening politely and never answer his calls."

"I guess I just speeded things up."

"Well, you distracted him."

She laughed, a full throat of it, a deep gurgle from the bottom of her soul. I guess I had started to love her then. At that moment, who knew what was in store for us? The future, the depth of our devotion and the breadth of its unravelling.

The queen and her silverback gorilla.

So where has she gone? It isn't like Sarah to just drop everything and disappear. No, that's not entirely true. If there was a good reason, Sarah could do anything. Something pissed her off maybe. Or she unilaterally decided it was vacation time, no matter how many properties she was staging. Though unpredictable, Sarah was headstrong, impetuous and iron-willed.

Is. Sarah *is*.

Nevertheless, I try her cell, as if no one has thought of it yet. Her message centre is full.

There is still fifteen minutes until my connecting flight. Montreal to Barcelona direct. There have been no announcements to my gate yet, so I take a stroll through the duty-free aisles and flick my cellphone awake again and try to make a call. It beeps in delayed speeds and rings eventually. Three sequences of tones, then the message service:

Yoboseyo. Hi, it's me. Georgia. Please leave me a message.

There is a pause again, and the beep arrives.

"Hi George. It's your father," I warble into the cell. "It's been a while, I guess. How's Korea? You need anything? I'm on my way to Barcelona. For a conference. But listen, have you heard from your mother? Let me know, will you? I'll probably kill the phone for the flight. Taking off soon. But you can leave a message and I'll check in when I land. Okay?"

Why do I always seem to adopt that breezy tone with my daughter lately? As if we'd just run into each other in the entrance to a coffee shop. As if we were the best of pals. We're not. She's a puzzle, difficult, always fighting everything. She was just eleven when Sarah and I split up. I tried to keep the gap from widening. Until her early teens I made efforts to join in some form of recreational father and daughter activity. It should have made it easier that she was a tomboy of sorts. She excelled at sports. She worked trees like an orangutan. It made it complicated. I couldn't negotiate the nuance of her. Attempting to connect in that brief contact, at least once a month, I'd truck her out to some park or art gallery, slouching beside her uncomfortably like an ill-suited participant in a Big Brother program. But I never quite got it right. The jigsaw was always a bit hard to fit together. And the pieces kept changing. I'd take her to a baseball game, only to learn in the fourth inning that she loved rock music.

"How about some fishing?" I asked her one early Saturday morning, my voice suggesting that the idea had just occurred to me.

My Volvo idled at her mother's condo entrance where I'd picked her up. The back seat bristled with rods and flies, the trunk funky with a packed container of bait. She looked me over, eyes squinting with sleepy disbelief as she informed me she was a vegetarian.

"Fish aren't animals. Suck it up," I joked. We drove to the lake and rented a canoe anyway. It was a beautiful morning, the sunlight still burning the haze off the trees. We paddled quietly through reeds and snagged branches. At intervals, stout, gleaming and untouched trout broke the tranquil surface.

As she entered her teens, our weekends and summer days ceased to interest her. She'd rejected the pretence, more attentive to her pimply inner circle of malcontents. While I was off skirting the rivals to Petronas Towers, or interviewing engineers about the bridge to P.E.I., she busied herself in growing up.

"Georgia, come and talk to your father," Sarah was often bellowing on the other side of a cupped phone receiver.

"Hi Dad, just going out. I have music camp," Georgia would say impatiently.

"Still playing trumpet?"

"No, that was school band. I'm playing piano. Did I leave my cellphone charger at your place?"

"Haven't seen it."

"K. Here's Mom."

HUGO WALSER DURING HIS ILLNESS

"Georgia's going to Korea," Sarah said one day after I'd lunched with a former colleague in Canary Wharf. I had called her about an old insurance claim on the house.

"What's that noise?" Sarah said.

"People," I told her. "I've just had lunch. Sri Nam on Cabot Square. Remember it?"

"Mmm. The pumpkin curry thing."

"Just had Mongolian lamb with caramelized onions. What do you mean Korea?"

"She applied to teach there. She's going in August."

"Thank you."

"What for?"

"No, that was me talking to the waiter."

"Are you calling me while you're eating?" Sarah always hated my complete disregard for ritual. While I had argued that multi-tasking was the cause of my success, she professed it drained any real achievement of purity. Overlap is diluting your life, she once told me.

"No, a drink. Jim has left and I'm having a drink." It was some house cocktail with mango and a big wheel of lime slotted onto the glass rim. I'd been inspired by the baking sun outside, tropically slathering the polished marble of the square.

"Is Georgia ready to be going to Korea?"

"She's twenty-two, Hugo."

"Yes," I said like a B-movie robot. Because I hadn't done the math, that crucial lifelong exercise of subtracting dates to get to the ages of people, letting its flags alarm you about time and its preservation. "But y'know . . . after all that's happened?"

"She's better. She needs to be out in the world."

"I don't think it's a good idea."

"She's teaching, Hugo. She's going to teach English. It's good money and a good experience."

"It's a long way to go. She's not ready. Did you agree to this?"

"Life, Hugo."

"What?"

"Life. This is life."

"Does she need money?"

"She doesn't want your money. Or your life, for that matter. She wants to do something for herself. I don't have time to argue with you, or her, about this."

I sucked up a mouthful of my cocktail, rolling some ice chips around my gums, and tried to picture Georgia in South Korea. Concrete apartment blocks, brown hills, spicy cabbage. I had been there briefly a few years before to write an article on the new generation of architects. A fluff piece, really. You know, "The Young Turks challenging the complacency of the old. Breathing new forms into the destruction of the past." Blah blah. The centrepiece was the so-called Conan House designed by Moon Hoon for some wealthy figurine collectors. A Mr. Park collected me at the Seoul airport, drove me for a few hours through the hilly countryside, where we cased the residence like a couple of thieves, then sped back to the capital at dusk to eat barbequed beef and get shitfaced on warm beer and soju.

"Tomorrow, we'll go to business district," Mr. Park had said, promising glass-fronted office towers and organic rooftop gardens. He was an enthusiastic magazine intern, with a folder of highlighted maps, farmed out to drag me around to the newest buildings. The next day, my stomach lurching like a tractor in mud, we doorhopped several corporate headquarters while I took notes, most of which I couldn't understand once I returned home via Tokyo.

"How long will she be there?" I asked my ex-wife as the bill for lunch arrived.

"A year. Two or three. I don't know."

18

FOR A BRIEF MOMENT I thought I was a child again. It must have been the dream I was having. I was wading through waist-high clover in a field beside the house where I grew up.

Strange how the mind works. Not like a building at all, with its solid joists, crossbeams, gyprock and plaster. That ordered control of space. In our hours of consciousness, we're also confident of the logic of our actions, the structure of our routine and goals. But the wiring and plumbing have sometimes been installed wrong, or get damaged, or are corroded over time. So, when we reach for the switch, nothing happens. Or suddenly all the lights go on for seemingly no reason. We do things that are perfectly idiotic if we stopped and examined ourselves. And due to circumstance, we allow ramshackle emotions—lust, jealousy—to populate our decisions and tear us down. It's like we aren't living in the house anymore but direct its residents from a distant cot in a crumbling tool shed.

Take this flight, for example. I have been advised against it.

Yet here I am.

I am parting the pale green stalks of clover with my torso, brushing my open palms across the furry tops, when a voice interrupts and I open my eyes. But it's not my mother I see in the curtained daybreak of my bedroom, prodding me with the promise of breakfast if I am to catch my bus on time. No. It's a smart young man in a steward's jacket, gently informing me that the first-class in-flight dinner will be served very shortly. And there is the smell of food. Not toast and apple juice, but something else. Peach and dried fruits. A splash of citrus. The steward is offering champagne, a cuvée from Reims, he explains.

I must have nodded off. We are already ninety minutes into the flight, the green of Nova Scotia shifting below the patchy cloud cover.

"Certainly," I say, and rub at the dry skin around my eyes. I drag myself into an upright position and receive the sparkling flute of fermented bubbly, bottled and then transported over an ocean in order to be enjoyed on the journey back. I ask for water too, and while he's at it, why not another glass of the sparkly stuff? The water is brought to me in an actual glass made of glass with the Air Canada logo frosted into its side. There is an appetizer of crayfish tails with cream cheese, saffron prawn and tabbouleh. I sip the Chilean Sauvignon Blanc from the Maipo Valley as my pan-seared cod fillet arrives, and though the parsley-seasoned rice is dry from reheating, it will certainly have travelled better than the rack of lamb on offer. The stewards carry forth crème brûlée and a selection of cheeses. Coffee and another glass from Chile. They are dimming the lights, a simulation of dusk. The baked glow of entertainment screens now prevails. But I am just waking from my slumber. And though the hijinks of some super spy entices on the movie channel, I'd best get down to my own mission at hand: the safekeeping of my status in the face of extinction.

From the overhead compartment, I pull down my valise and pop the two brass catches. My laptop rests on several paper files, a yellow memo pad and a new toothbrush, still in its packaging. Though my dentist has soberly advised, on more than one occasion, the use of extra-soft bristles for my deteriorating gums, I still purchase a medium. There it is on the label. Anything softer seems emasculating, a rebuff to my vigorous dental pummelling. Flawed logic, I suppose. We all have our strategies. Look at my choice of laptop. No Mac for me. Only the most cut-rate computer available.

HUGO WALSER DURING HIS ILLNESS

To travel as much as I do would be to go always in fear of losing or damaging the overpriced name brands. Few thieves stalk my café tables hoping to snatch a processor in its plastic box so cheap it might be obsolete by the time they return to their criminal squat. In fact, I have started the habit of buying a new laptop each Boxing Day. There is a small corner of a landfill polluted with a stack of my technological excess. It's wasteful I know, this cycle of acquisitions and discards.

But my current subject is Norcock. Alan Norcock. There he is in my mind adjusting his spectacles, dropping his chin to study something across the tops of the rims. He is not one to simply look at you. He *scrutinizes*. I have only met him in the flesh perhaps four, five times, but I experience that bored glance of intelligence each time I have read an article of his. The condescension is in the prose. A study could be done on how he achieves the effect. It's dismissive. World-weary. Reluctantly forgiving of your shortfalls. Even if he's praising a subject, he manages to evoke a tone of disdainful encouragement, as if he admires how we're all operating under the handicap of substandard aptitude.

I have kept a few of these articles in my files. Who knows why I brought them along? To stoke my rage? There won't be time to quote them all back to him. But in the last two weeks, since the moment I chose this course of action, they've steadied me. In those cheerful daylight hours when my resolve wavered, recommending I adopt a live-and-let-live approach to Norcock's superciliousness, I only needed to scan their affected contortions of communication to feel my profound ire toward him renew itself. I have even brought along his book, *Wings of Dwelling*. I quote from the introduction:

Since the dark caves of our homo sapiens relatives, we have sought shelter from the weather in dependable chambers; protective, yes, but binding to our souls and spirits. The Greek columns, the walled cities of Europe, the rafters and buttresses and heavy arches, though useful against thunder's rumble and the sun's heat, have proven stubborn to innovation. In the short history of contemporary architecture, culminating in the twentieth century, a few individuals have endeavoured to rattle the ramparts and rearrange the resident cliché of habitation.

Rattle the ramparts?

Christ. That is Alan Norcock distilled to his oily essence, like a thimbleful of rancid honey. *Wings of Dwelling.* I ask you, What the fuck does it mean? The answer is there in his prose. Norcock is the foreman of posturing, the architectural laureate of asshats. He couldn't put an honest, clear sentence together if he ate *The Elements of Style* methodically for breakfast. I confess I reviewed *Wings of Dwelling* and its hardback manifesto when Norcock released it to the public a few years ago and found it necessary to remind the author that columns, rafters and arches are not merely useful, but by all rules of engineering and physics seem to fall under the category of "essential." By removing the distracting cliché of walls and pillars, we are faced with the unfortunate brainteaser of how to keep rooftops from falling on our heads. I pointed out the contradiction of his arguments by citing Gaudi, one of Norcock's heroes. I noted that Gaudi's unfinished cathedral, which is often praised as a majestic expression of the human desire to touch heaven, does so supported by what look suspiciously like pillars and arches. He responded, of course. How could he keep his mouth shut? He reminded my readership that I was the last person to be lecturing anyone of architectural stability. Ouch. The poisonous exchange between us is well-documented in the "Letters" pages of *Architecture Now.*

He accused me of literalism.

I called him a fantasist.

He defended what he termed "lyrical solutions."

I said, Okay, then I'm an elf in a top hat. I was going to suggest that he, likewise, was a chimp in an ascot, but my lawyer advised against it.

So there our enlightened polemic terminated.

Over time, I've learned, or so others have told me, I am too often given to ridicule as a form of communication. It's my "go-to" emotion. An offence that may enrage someone, or bring sorrow, will inspire me to mockery. I have never employed a short fuse, only a burlesque whip. It's true, this hectoring ridicule, my sarcasm, was not the most effective aid to childcare. In her adolescent stages, my daughter Georgia could break up into laughter just as much as cry and shriek. But she bristled at the banter more and more. It had no legitimacy by the time she was a teen. I was out of the house, unmoored and invalid.

Perhaps it was karma whistling up my trousers.

Perhaps Norcock is too. I have mocked him on more than one occasion. So, it doesn't surprise me that only a couple of weeks ago I received an email from a Spanish colleague tipping me off to the subject of Norcock's keynote address at the Arquitectura Cívica conference: me. This was a bold move. To date we had only taken indirect malicious swipes at each other in the context of larger arguments. If our articles and essays were large garden parties, we used each other like wretched piñatas whenever the opportunity arose. A jab here, a nick there.

But if it were true that he'd taken me on as a central subject, this was a battle of a higher order. A signal we have finished with daggers and unsheathed the broadswords.

I move my materials and laptop aside and fold the adjustable tray back into its slot. I have sudden need of the toilet; my bladder is doing the backstroke. They have closed the curtains between Executive First and the general seating behind, so our twenty little pods of comfort, in muted light, have taken on the look of a gated community in the peace of dusk. A few TVs flicker. Some of my neighbours have already moved their retractable seats into their horizontal positions and settled comfortably into REMs under the thick wool blankets. The fuselage hums. The stewards have returned the dinner trolleys to their niches and chat to each other. What else could they do in these quiet hours of simulated night?

Read a book? Go for a smoke?

I push the latch and half tumble into the washroom. Its cramped space is relatively unabused due to attentive care. My legs ache. I stretch my back for a moment and look into the mirror, rubbing at my temples. The toilet seat is still raised, abandoned to its present position by a recent occupant.

Sarah cured me of this male breach of decorum a year into our marriage. We were travelling in India and had spent two weeks in some of the gorgeous, finer boutique hotels along the coast of Kerala. But on a one-night stopover further inland we were forced to take the best available room of considerably few accommodation options. We were exhausted and paid for one of those places that operates outside of any star-rated system. You know the type. Every country hosts them. Assigning a star to such grim approximations of lodging would be a test of generosity to any Michelin reviewer's definition of comfort. It was stained, unswept, viewless, lightless, not secure and six dollars a night. It was the deep backwoods of what could be termed "hospitality." After inspecting the WC, Sarah emerged looking both angry and in despair, and immediately said to me, "If I get up in the middle of the night and drop my ass into that toilet because you forgot to put the seat down, I will fucking kill you" in such icy tones that I have never forgotten to lower the seat since. Sarah had her faults, but lack of conviction was not one of them. Whatever she said she'd do, she did. Our divorce, when it came, after she made it clear she'd no love for me anymore, dropped with the swift, uncomplicated justice of a guillotine. She laid out the terms of our assets and property, the responsibilities I had for George, the proprietorship of friends and colleagues. The papers were delivered, I signed (no hard feelings) and we became acquaintances again. No great mess at all. I did love that about her.

She may in fact be the inspiration behind my bold resolve to purchase this ticket and fly to Barcelona. The conference is in three days. I have booked a room for five nights in Hotel Colón across the square from the Old Cathedral. With time to entrench and shake my jetlag, I should be fighting fit to attend the keynote address. Norcock will never know what hit him. The anticipated shock of his reaction plays across my imagination. I catch myself squinting at the airplane mirror while I shake the last drops of urine into the toilet. I throw some water over my face and dry off, feeling refreshed and less dehydrated. On the way past the steward, I ask for another drink.

Perhaps one of those dreadful films on the entertainment system might be distracting.

Above my head the non-smoking sign hangs like an eternal porch light. I have dozed off again. I glance to my sides and down the gloomy aisle. No one is moving. The stewards are absent. Their own blue curtain is pulled across the end of the section. What's happened to me? The last I remember I'd been half-heartedly watching some actress—Sandra something—having it off in a mismatched love affair with a colleague half her age. The screen's blank, the film over.

How long was I asleep?

I really do have a terrible headache. My mouth is dry and chalky. I should have drunk that water. There is a teaspoon of it left in the bottle so I tip it into my mouth. God, I feel dreadful. Drained, exhausted, parched and disoriented. How did I end up here, on a hundred-tonne assemblage of plastic and metal over the ocean, steeped in such poisonous arrangements?

Wings of Dwelling.

What's this? The cabin lights are being raised. The glow is gradual, almost serene, blue and then a white effulgence. The stewards are shifting the section drapes and tying them back. Breakfast service is being prepared; a bouquet of coffee and cooked egg wafts past the porthole windows. It's "morning" already. Seven hours have passed in the blink of an eye. We are only a short way to our destination. I should be glad the new day is here. The lights are fully up. Other passengers are stretching. There is a genteel line forming for the washrooms. A quick visit before the food and drink trolleys block the aisles. Through the half-lifted window shutter, I glimpse the very slightest wink of blue, like a trace of silk over the Iberian darkness. It is almost six a.m. if I'm converting the hands on my wristwatch correctly.

They are bringing the trays of food around.

"Good morning, sir," the steward says. He kicks the trolley brake into its locked position. "Did you have a good night? Everything was comfortable?" He is busily screwing caps off bottles and folding back tinfoil on heated breakfasts. He hasn't looked me in the eye just yet. He reaches over and places my breakfast in front of me. "Eggs benedict with asparagus tips," he says. "Would you like coffee or some tea, sir?"

Now that they've cleared the trays and I've had some of that coffee, let me reminisce. Why not? It's less than an hour until we land. What is there to do otherwise but sample the comedy programs as our wings snip through the gauze of clouds and trim a path to the runway? Perhaps I should be writing this down. Keep a record of events. I have my own sitcoms to air, even if the laugh track rings a little bitterly.

The night I took a battering from Gary in the Copacabana had the desired effect. If not a display of gallantry, I had at least got Sarah's attention. Did she take me seriously? Probably not.

But I was there, in front of her, real, more than an anecdote in her bookstore. I was a person with every intention to make a name for myself in the mid-twenties of her life. So, we dated. We skipped the films but walked a lot on those leafy Montreal streets lined with their wrought iron walk-ups. There were the pubs, of course; those dark, smoky (cigarettes were a vocation, not a habit, in those days) brasseries up Saint-Laurent and Saint-Denis and sometimes west of downtown when I met her after work.

"Watch out," she would say as we approached another deposit of dog crap on the sidewalk. "People should be fined."

What did we have in common? Drive. Ambition. I talked incessantly about big projects, plans for my own architectural firm, the houses on several continents. I threw money around and went deep into debt, then was saved at the eleventh hour by some share in commissions that buoyed my credit cards out of the red zone of termination. Sarah came along for the ride. Perhaps a childhood of poverty made her agreeable to the excess, but she was as cold and calculating as I, our eyes fixed on affluence and luxury.

Meanwhile, the bills mounted, the plans failed, the desperation loomed and regulatory corners were cut. Trouble started with a few puffs of smoke and soon the blame with its little red caboose followed. So, at some wicked, desolate platform, we went our separate ways, and Sarah was no worse for the journey.

She is hard, Sarah. She cared up to a point. It was one of the things I admired—admire—about her. That ability—no, *instinct*—when everyone else might collapse from the consequences of their actions, to liberate herself from such crushing concerns. She excelled at it: that facility for not giving the very fuck that everyone else might feel is worth giving. In that, we were also much alike. Withheld compassion has served me well. It's the cornerstone of my success. For how can you be an effective critic while looking over your shoulder? No, I have gone ahead and said what I thought. Leave it alone, laissez-faire and all that. I thought Sarah was the same. But she baffled me. The confidence collapsed. I thought she had never been interested in the long game. In those first incredible years of our marriage, we did not imagine the end of the wending road. We seemed content to wolf down what sat, gleaming, in the sun-struck dust motes of our doorway. But what got to her?

The jealousy and discord. The wild swings at love. They had their consequences. Remember Nice, France? Sarah loved the sun almost as much as we loved spending money, and we had roamed along much of Mediterranean Europe in search of both. We had booked into Le Negresco Hotel and spent several glorious days strolling Nice's Old Quarter and the Promenade des Anglais, she pointing out every specimen of dogshit in our path. It was an obsession of hers: to inform me of them. What else? She would insist on a morning swim in the sea, Georgia picking her way across the beach of flat, grey stones. She was four, fussy and head-long in her floppy beach hat and flipflops. Sarah had sold her first big houses. We felt invincible then and exercised few limits, buy-ing our way through the boutiques west of Place Masséna, ending our nights rosy-cheeked from cognac.

One night, after a long, gruelling day of doing absolutely noth-ing, I accused Sarah of flirting with some Greek businessman we had met while sitting at the Le Relais bar. He'd made a fortune in shipping, was interested in antiques, and his face was as carved, handsome and brown as the walnut of the room's original 1913 woodwork.

Since the hotel provided an in-house au pair service, we felt free to cut loose. A few rounds were purchased. Sarah was in her glory, all erudite anecdotes and low-cut bosomy laughter. When we stumbled up to our suite, after manly handshakes and frozen smiles, and Sarah with her triple air kisses, I vented.

"Fucking pompous shit," I said, tossing my shoes at the entrance baseboard.

Sarah flashed a murderous look in my direction, gesturing at Georgia's room. I slipped the door shut.

"He was nice."

Sarah's tone of dismissal enraged me even more.

"*You* fucking liked him, didn't you?" I stage-whispered.

"What are you talking about?"

"That windbag."

"I thought we were having a nice time."

"*He* certainly was. With your hand on his knee . . ."

I was cracking the seal on a bottle of Johnny Walker from the mini-bar.

"You're just pissed," Sarah said, "because of how filthy rich he is. All your fancy talk about red-figure vases and Louis the king's so-and-so porcelain-glass blah-fucking-blah. But he *buys* that shit. He *owns* that shit."

"Oh, is that what would impress you? Me strolling around with three mangy Irish bloodhounds."

"He keeps them on his yacht."

"Of course he fucking does."

"Shhhh!"

I filled a tumbler with ice and poured from the bottle until the whiskey neared the brim. Sarah had changed out of her dress and emerged from the washroom in a silk bathrobe.

"Is there money in selling yachts?" she wondered aloud. "Should we visit it tomorrow?"

"I'm not going anywhere near his ridiculous yacht. Not a chance in hell."

"Don't be a child. He was very nice to invite us."

"He was not being nice. He was trying to get into your skirt."

"That's nonsense. He asked us both."

"It doesn't matter. The super-rich are like Stalin. They think that normal principles don't mean anything to them."

"Since when did you give a shit about principles?"

"What does *that* mean?"

"Nothing."

"No, what did you mean?"

She was standing, arms folded, between the open curtains and the Empire-style armchair I had just collapsed in. Despite the late hour, many revellers still capered across the promenade two storeys below. The bass beat of a rap tune thumped away somewhere down the beach. Sarah's face had twisted into a cold reckoning.

"Oh, I don't know, Hugo," she said. "You're quite capable of cutting some corners to make a few extra bucks."

I glowered at her for two seconds, then growled, "Go fuck yourself."

She returned my sulfurous stare, but I could see her eyes casting measured glances over the hotel's bureau and coffee table.

I may have mentioned Sarah liked to throw things. Among the more notable objects Sarah has hoisted in my direction over our years together: a steel clipboard, a hand-painted decorative plate from Tunis, a pyritized ammonite fossil, pine cones, a blue vibrator, a Sachertorte (among a long list of food items) and a crystal trophy of considerable heft presented to me by the Canadian Association of Architects, which, if it had found its mark, would have meant manslaughter. Now she was scrutinizing the available objects of our suite for their portability. Between us was a floral arrangement—calla lilies in a glass vase. On the floor, to her right, was a wastepaper basket. On a side table, some antique leather books. The bureau sported a telephone, the hotel directory and a few tourist pamphlets. Over my right shoulder, on a metal stand, were two cut-glass goblets, a decanter, an empty ice bucket, a set of tongs and my recently opened bottle of Johnny Walker.

With a burst of fury, she sprinted for the liquor stand. I flung myself off the armrest of my chair and caught her by the ankle. This tipped her off-balance and she crashed into the entertainment

HUGO WALSER DURING HIS ILLNESS

console, dislodging the TV remote and a bowl of roasted almonds. We briefly paused, our attention directed toward Georgia's door. Then, with both of us prone on the carpet, Sarah repeatedly kicked at my arms and shoulders. I protected my face with my free hand while maintaining a tight grip on her leg with the other. Nevertheless, she was managing to wriggle forward and get her fingers on the door to the mini-bar fridge. With some effort, I tugged at her calf and dragged her back toward the centre of the floor. But she lashed out, grunting, with more kicks. Her heel tagged my forehead like a bludgeon. In pain, I grabbed at my scalp.

A moment later something wet and gooey was poured into my ear. We'd ordered the Sturia caviar the day we arrived. Sarah was now sitting cross-legged over me, spooning globs of it out of the tin onto my head.

"You bitch," I muttered.

I snatched at the tin and knocked it from her hand. In a fighting scramble, I got the fridge open and pulled a demi-bottle of Veuve Clicquot from the door-rack. The next minute witnessed Sarah and I half jogging, half wrestling around the room as I struggled to remove the foil and wire trap from the bottle, then popping the champers straight at her astonished eyes, her open palm deflecting the rocketing cork but unable to impede the spray of froth I shook at her outraged face. It was the tipping point of farce. We stood there, heaving from our exertions: Sarah, sodden with Veuve Clicquot, her mascara like punk graffiti, and me, my face and neck spackled with lightly salted black sturgeon eggs cultivated in the Gironde estuary. Our anger transformed into amusement as we collapsed in black laughter onto the bed, where our entwined, forgiving tongues soon attempted to forgive the two hundred euros of luxury sundries we'd just spewed over each other. And not a peep from Georgia all night.

Now, sitting in this airplane armchair, above the Atlantic on a Sunday morning, drunk or hungover, I don't know which, primed for jetlag, I discover I miss my ex-wife.

Why? We were a bit too Burton and Taylor, it's true. So how did my listing dinghy of self-respect find harbour in this sudden nostalgia? After all our arguments and petty insults, the infidelities, the betrayals, why, half-reclined, the pitch of morning turbulence churning my stomach, do I quite suddenly feel an ache for her presence? Because of who she was, as they say. No quarter was given or taken. Sarah never felt sorry for me. There was no room for pity in her heart. She accepted my fuck-ups and expected no reciprocation. Without a pinch or whine. She had her own neuroses to manage. "Pick yourself up and move on," she'd say with her scalpel stare. It gave us a kind of resilience, that contempt for each other's weaknesses, that repulsion from failure.

Oh, where is she, my formidable and merciless wife?

19

IT IS NEARING 6:30 A.M. and as we descend through cloud cover, I catch the first sight of distant coastal lights. Then, quite suddenly, we're just over the runway of the Barcelona-El Prat airport, buckled up to await the first nudge of our wheels touching down on the tarmac. I bid a cheery goodbye to the stewards while they wish their file of bedraggled passengers, some two hundred strong, the best of days. All in all, no harm done. As I step past the cleaning crew waiting with their vacuums, disinfectants and rubber gloves, I'm feeling positively lighthearted. This is often true of stepping off a plane, isn't it? No matter how exhausted you are, there's great relief of being able to stretch your legs and control the pace of your movements.

I have not been in this city for some years. We're funnelled along the thoroughfares of the arrivals area. I'm reminded that Barcelona's airport suffered for many years from lack of restructuring. Investment money needed for modernization stalled until the years leading to 1992. It was the Olympics, that great motivator of government funds, which finally inspired the Spanish muck-mucks to throw a wad of pesetas into expansion and construction costs. And a nice job, I think. Bofill designed this, if I remember correctly. Ricardo Bofill. The morning light shimmers along the polished steel and green glass of the elegant lines of his newly inaugurated Terminal 1. As we stream toward baggage claim, we can admire a central courtyard accented with red stone that frames the splendid expanse of the departure level's glass facade.

Or something like that. Sorry, I am doing it again, habitually composing a review of whatever new building I see, even though it's doubtful I'll ever write it. It used to make Sarah crazy. We'd be talking and my mind would start to wander over stylistic details of a building we were approaching.

"Hugo, are you listening to me? Georgia needs braces," she'd say.

"Sorry. Something caught my eye. What about her?"

The somnambulant airport staff are zombie-ing about the baggage carousel. I am asked a few half-hearted questions by immigration, then am nodded into the care of the arrivals concourse. There's no one to meet me. Though a colleague—my spy, my inside source—has invited me to lunch tomorrow, I have kept my itinerary empty for the onset of this sojourn. Suitcase now in hand, I'm already in a taxi and blasting downtown-ward on the near-deserted freeway. Hills, the industrial zone rising near the sea west of the old centre. Soon, we dip like a sleigh down the off-ramp and descend toward Barri Gòtic. It's Sunday morning. The white stone of the doorways and shopfronts stand deserted. My seasoned taxi driver makes good time anticipating the traffic lights, charging at the reds—with no hint of braking—a split-second before they turn green. Before long, we slow on Via Laietana and there is the Barcelona Cathedral across the square. Not Gaudí's monster further north, but the overlooked, original gothic gem.

"*Bueno, bueno,*" I tell my heavy-footed charioteer. "*Cuánto?*" I hand him the newly issued euros converted before leaving Ottawa. There is an additional tax to the charge, something I vaguely remember reading about somewhere, so I don't question the total, a quibble he looks prepared for, judging from the tone of his voice. At another time, I may have offered resistance just for the sake of ruffling him a little, but I'm exhausted. He pops the trunk for my bags and I make my way through the square. A bell signals a half hour past eight from the cathedral's tower.

HUGO WALSER DURING HIS ILLNESS

I haven't paid for an extra night, so must wait, despite protest, for eleven a.m. before I can check into my room. The concierge stores my suitcase in a nook behind the front desk. How do you say "code" in Spanish? I'm waggling my smart phone at the fellows behind the marble counter, saying "Wi-fi" and "*Número?*" One of them, sporting a friar's tonsure, jots the code down on hotel stationery and hands it to me without ceremony. With some time to kill, it might be worth checking my messages, hear from Sarah's fugitive travels, and see how the western hemisphere has adapted to my absence.

The lobby is decked out in Queen Anne chairs and sofas. A round table with cabriole legs is laid out with glasses of orange juice. Bread options. I stuff two rolls into my mouth and swill the pulpy fruit. The unadulterated sweetness jolts me. It's almost painful. In Canada we are so used to fruit being traumatized by packaging and the refrigeration of long-distance transport. When it finally touches our lips, its taste has been distilled into a cardboard neutrality. I'm reminded again that fruit is organic, not a simulated flavour we add to products. This orange juice is so healthy and fresh, it's almost aggressive. Probably squeezed ten minutes ago, picked from the tree as my plane buzzed Bilbao. I take another glass and settle into a chair, wingback and upholstered with stripes.

It takes me a few minutes to access my emails, fiddling with the code. There is nothing worthwhile in the inbox; nothing from Sarah and, typically, nothing from Georgia.

I log off from the internet and try my voicemail. There are four messages. I tap at the interface. I'm expecting a carefree message from Sarah, blithely enjoying herself and unaware of the worry she's caused for her colleagues and her daughter. But it's not her, only a man's officious grumble:

Good afternoon, Mr. Walser. This is Detective Stokehouse calling from the Ottawa Police Department. I am contacting you in connection with the disappearance of Sarah Trimble. I understand she is your ex-wife. We just have a few questions we'd like to ask you.

The police? Is this necessary? Detective Stokehouse provides a file and phone number and urges me to call at any hour and leave a message with the most convenient time to contact me. I almost believe this is some joke on Sarah's part. I would think that after thirteen years of marriage, I'd know her well enough, but she is too practical to arrange such an elaborate mind-fuck. Though she is capable of cruelty, particularly to me, after my wholesale mishandling of our future. There's only one way to find out, as they say. I must follow through and make some calls.

It's too early, or too late. Isn't that always the case? My mind pitches with a nauseous buzz of jetlag, unwilling to face time-zone conversions without proper sleep. I am certainly incapable of speaking to a police officer about my ex-wife.

What did he call it?

Her "disappearance."

A pregnant word, that. I nudge my way out the circulating glass doors of the hotel and into the cathedral square. It's a sunny, cool morning. The outdoor cafés are already half-full, tourists signalling the waiters into irritation. Being Sunday, these tables will see many orders. Nothing else is open and nothing to do but kill time. I check my map and squeeze south and west through the narrow streets toward La Rambla, where I can drag myself into exhaustion down its tree-lined *paseo* before returning for possession of my room key. More than once I get turned around, led by the false assumption that these seemingly straight avenues of the Gothic Quarter are faithful to ninety-degree angles.

I lean against the stone of an apartment entrance and study my map, setting out again, turning back, the morning light beginning to heat my neck and forehead. Beyond the next corner, I am suddenly along it, a little more north than I'd planned but here anyway. In memory, La Rambla always seemed crowded, but still

HUGO WALSER DURING HIS ILLNESS

early yet, there is hardly a soul in sight as I work my way south to the sea. The flower sellers receive deliveries. Each newspaper kiosk has thrown open its gates, their windows marked with signs announcing *Real Madrid—Barcelona: SOLD OUT*. By the time I've reached the port I am smeared in the gauze of nausea, the laser beam of a headache vivisecting my cranium. The promenade buzzes with scooters. Seagulls guffaw in begging queues above the docks. Their screeches saw at my brain, drip acid frequencies into my sinus passages.

I vomit onto a graffitied piling, the feast from Executive First reconstituted messily below a squatter's symbol. The seagulls descend to guzzle the sludge. My pan-seared cod fillet is enjoyed with pronounced gusto.

I feel better. Pausing at the roundabout below Columbus's statue, I am confident that with a thirty-minute nap, I might even settle into a regular rhythm, bypassing jetlag's curse. My stomach settled somewhat, a new pain emerges on the outside of my right foot. I am favouring it, negotiating the sidewalk with a slight limp. I should have packed walking shoes. Sneakers maybe. Returning north, there is time to sit and enjoy the sun, so I duck through some arches into the Plaça Reial and claim a chair at one of the many bar tables facing the plaza. I am desperate for caffeine, but also for something to get the edge in retreat. The waiter brings an espresso with brandy, the crema beautifully layered inside the glass cup.

I am finding my feet again.

At the next table, two women share a pastry and flip through guidebooks, travel packs tucked in their laps. The palm trees rasp against the breeze.

"A beautiful day," the blonde closest to me says, glancing at the sky. They are both in their late thirties, I'd guess. T-shirts and jean shorts.

"Starting to enjoy it," I tell them.

"Just arrived?"

"This morning. An overnight flight."

They are Americans on two-week holiday. Nurses with the US Army stationed in Crete. The blonde says they are having "a whale of a time." I tell them I'm here for a conference, which inspires less than enthusiastic reactions, so I give them the architect stuff.

The coffee and booze are buzzing away gently already.

"What do you call this?" I ask the waiter as he passes.

"*Carajillo*."

"Delicious. Another, please. Ladies?"

They laugh.

"Three," I say. We're chatting pleasantly when my buzz turns into a spin.

"Just dizzy," I assure their concerned looks. The light wobbles on the table's edge. The neoclassical facades to my left go soft-focus.

"You should get some sleep," the brunette says, citing my fatigue, the change of hemisphere and a concentrated mix of caffeine and alcohol.

"My luck to find some nurses," I say. The sarcasm gives them a laugh. White teeth in wide mouths. But I can't be a baby now, surely, so when the waiter passes a few minutes later, I order another straight brandy. "You're right. I really should avoid caffeine," I quip with a wink. The girls shake their blurry faces at me.

I have paid the bill. They are off to find a beach somewhere. They tell me the name, but for all I know it could just as well be a crater on the moon. I am standing, trying to push my chair back, but the uneven stones of the plaza force me to lift the rear legs, which actually tips it on its side, and the blonde steps over and helps me raise it off the ground. "Crater on the moon," I slur, strategizing my exit beyond the stone fountain, half mirage under the awful sun. It was nice to meet me. It was nice to meet them. Enjoy your holiday; get some sleep. Do you know your way to your

HUGO WALSER DURING HIS ILLNESS

hotel? Don't worry, I've been here before. Neoclassical. Beautiful day. Have a good time.

The shaded damp of narrow Carrer de Ferran welcomes me as I trundle east again. Scooters and smart cars squeeze through a mosey of coagulating pedestrians. It seems like five minutes have passed when I appear at the Colón's front desk, though it's past noon and I have backtracked several times in order to find the hotel and have purchased a ham and cheese sandwich somewhere in transit. They have sent my luggage up to my room, a third-floor suite facing the cathedral.

The tiny European elevator is already at capacity with two saggy retirees in straw hats, so I ascend the carpeted steps for slumber.

Bell. Bell. Bell. Bell.

A heavy gong.

A deep, heavy gong.

It's two o'clock. The cathedral belfry marks every hour, defying the advancements of wristwatches and cellphones. My cheek is rough and wet. Rolling it off the pool of saliva on my pillow, I blink into the darkness. Faint sounds of traffic. Voices pass in the hall. A fringe of daylight intensifies on the curtain's edge. It's the same afternoon. I have slept just under two hours, it seems, despite the excruciating fatigue visited on my body when I entered the hotel room. I had dropped onto the bed with the obliterating energy of a meteorite entering the atmosphere.

I am wearing my shoes.

With some urgency, I take three carpeted steps to the bathroom and find the switch. A frosted bulb reflects off the white floor tiles. Seated on the toilet, I hang my head, eyes closed, pushing the hot piss out of my bladder. I undo the laces of my dress shoes and ease them off my feet. Socks then. The pale, misshapen toes flex on the cool tile, their first oxygen in over twenty-four hours. The smallest on my right foot reveals the source of its discomfort: a chafed rash—rough and red and oozing a twinkle of liquid—has formed on its outer edge. Is this what they call a barnacle? No, that's not it. A carbuncle, then? I must go online and resolve this.

Much-needed piss done, I undress in the room, turn down the sheets and actually crawl between them for the first time. They are cool and soft. Egyptian cotton maybe. I am both dead and wide awake, the sensations eating each other. Ouroboros. I have a head-ache in my back and nausea behind my eyes. Half-eaten, the ham and cheese sandwich appears in the glow of the digital clock that, despite the cathedral belfry lurking just outside my window, has been provided for the convenience of the hotel's guest, which is me. I, the guest, ponder the sandwich until the cathedral bells strike four p.m., then, reluctant to exit the comfort of this fresh, pharaonic swaddling, I raise myself and turn my face to the wall in the hopes that just one deft move, like the decipherment of a Zen koan, will unveil the mystery of my lingering consciousness and let me fall into a deep slumber. It's not to be. Instead of lying awake, enormously exhausted, staring at the digital clock, I lie awake, enormously exhausted, staring at the wall.

With the futility of the arrhythmic tourist, I thumb the lamp switch and stew in the gloom, trying to recall if Spain is six hours ahead of or behind Canada's time zones. It is surely ahead, some-where mid to late morning in the streets of Ontario. No matter. The police don't have nine-to-five hours, do they? Not from the evidence of any of those cop shows. They are either on the street kicking the daylights out of some degenerate or trading hard-nosed theories with colleagues in the periphery of pinned-up mug shots, telephone records and bagged hair samples.

With the aid of the speed dial's archives, my cellphone buzzes another phone an ocean away.

"Ottawa Police Services. How can I help you?"

"Hi. Can you connect me with Detective Stokehouse, please?"

HUGO WALSER DURING HIS ILLNESS

I do not have the file number they provided, but I can tell them it's regarding the disappearance of Sarah Trimble. In a moment, another voice announces from the ether:

"Detective Stokehouse."

"Hi there. I'm just returning your call about Sarah Trimble. I'm in Spain, so I'm having trouble . . ."

"Who am I speaking to?"

"Hugo Walser."

He is shuffling papers, shifting files, as if there is a great amount of information to plough through to reach the significance of my identity. I wait. I can hear the shape of the room beyond his chin, another phone ringing nearby.

"Walser. You're the husband," Stokehouse says with boredom.

"Divorced," I correct him.

"Have you heard from Ms. Trimble at all?"

"No, I'm away, and—"

"How did you know she'd disappeared?"

"Your words, detective. On my phone. You said she disappeared, I believe."

There is a significant pause, or do I imagine this? Papers again.

"Where are you?"

"Barcelona, Spain," I say. Why does this satisfy me greatly? As if it were proof I'm an upstanding citizen with important things to do. As if it were an alibi.

"What are your reasons for being there, sir?"

I say, "I'm here on business," then realize this is not exactly true. "I'm attending a conference, actually. A lecture. I'm an architect and there is a lecture on . . . something that I'm interested in and I came here for it. To hear it." Am I talking too much? "I just woke up and I'm still a little fuzzy . . ."

"When did you arrive in Barcelona, Mr. Walser?"

"Early this morning. Around seven a.m."

"What was the number of your flight?"

"Oh, Christ. AC five four something . . . *Four five* something? Air Canada. The ticket is here somewhere."

Now it's his turn to hear me rummage about. I wonder what my room sounds like to his investigative ears, all echoes of curtained gloom and unpacked luggage. I find the boarding pass folded in a pocket and report my findings. I have tugged the curtains open and jabbed the latch to the balcony doors, which swing open onto white sunshine. The noise and light are dizzying and revitalizing. I gasp like Tutankhamen, prepared to crumble, parchment-like, from this forceful dose of fresh air.

"Is there anything else?" I ask, trying to sound helpful, but dead-crazed from thirst.

"Have you been in contact with anyone else since you left home?"

Several stewards, I want to quip. *A taxi driver, the hotel concierge, a couple of drunks, a sandwich vendor and two nurses from the States.* But I hold back, control my weary sarcasm, and say, "Yes, my wife's business partner. We haven't actually talked. Just a message."

"Is there a best way to reach you in the future, Mr. Walser? Can you give me the name of your hotel in case of emergency?"

Emergency? I can't help but wonder what he means by this. To contact me with good news or bad? This is all extremely silly, I want to say. I pace toward the desk in the corner for a memo pad with the letterhead of hotel information as I am having great doubts over my current circumstances, and consequently, the name for where I'm staying has slipped away. There it is, scrolled in black and gold across the paper. Detective Stokehouse thanks me for my time and pledges to be back in touch. The connection beeps to empty silence. With an absent mind, I squat on the edge of the bedcover and turn the television on for news, as if it will ground me somewhat, or distract. I can't decide which.

20

I HAVE WANDERED NORTH of my hotel to some wide, monumental streets festooned with fountains and martial statues. There is a festival atmosphere on the faces of pedestrians. The youth, in groups, loiter at every available public space. Dreadlocks and sweatshirts with the sleeves cut off. Hairy armpits and bra straps. The kids greet each other with yelps of bliss, kisses and hugs. Carefree, I guess. It reminds me of how the sun can influence an entire culture, shape the canyons of its history. I have long wanted to write some book on the architectural effect of climate. It has even affected our methods of worship. The need to either block or encourage light is responsible for the prevalence of fresco in Italy versus the use of stained glass in the north. The heat and light's year-long presence gives permission for big-heartedness, encourages sensual magnetism in its citizens. The Mediterranean world opens its arms and smiles broadly. I wonder what person I might have been if I had entered the world caressed by a Greek breeze or in the shimmering reflection of a Venetian canal.

I limp forward and wait by the traffic signal. A few cafés with plastic patio chairs are filling up. One nearby is jammed with families in Barcelona team shirts, their tables arranged in semicircles around wide-screened televisions rigged up in the open air especially for the game. A bald and beaming proprietor carries pitchers of beer from the storefront. A matronly cook works the gas grill next to the sidewalk, lovingly rotating portions of glazed octopi and beef. The street buzzes. Children dash about, kicking miniature soccer balls. A few patrons, beer in hand, have wandered to an adjacent tavern. They chat with neighbours. Ottawa paper-pushers, so orthodox with adherence to municipal bylaws, would surely be panicked to see such flagrant trespass of public property and regulations.

Though the tables are full, I spot a free bar stool through the open doors so claim it and order lager and a fiery paella dish, replete with mussels, shrimp and chorizo. Four beers later, by the time the game is over, a wonky energy has settled over the city. The match has ended in a tie, purgatory for all supporters. The Barcelona crowd are glad they didn't lose but frustrated at the missed chances for victory. It's a confusing mix of relief and dissatisfaction. Thus, the revelry becomes a compromise, some electing to call the night quits immediately, gathering up their kids and their team scarves and bundling all home in a fuzzy state of near-drunkenness pre-hangover. Others soldier on, determined to bring the interrupted state of exultation to its proper conclusion. More beer is ordered, more colourful drinks. As the supporters thin out, there's more room for arm waving and all the whinging at slow play, failure to press forward or guard the goal. Nearby, someone has burped a paella waft. Meanwhile, a stream of pedestrians flows past, deflated but still defiantly happy.

I pay my bill and amble into the street, favouring my foot with its irritating open lesion. After getting my bearings, I gather a steady pace down the sidewalk. Within a block, the pain lessens into numb discomfort. The walk's slow-going anyway; the crowd is thick and in no hurry. At the square's edge ahead of me, some breakdancers busk for the post-game multitudes. They've plugged the street with stalled onlookers at La Rambla's north access. Five of them circle and break on a section of thick cardboard. I push past, shouldering through the mix of young locals and curious tourists, the air drifting with scents of patchouli and marijuana. A sudden cheer bursts from the street audience, and I

HUGO WALSER DURING HIS ILLNESS

pause and raise myself on the balls of my feet to see two of the breakdancers hoisting a third through the air, who lands and rolls quite gracefully. Immediately, the remaining two step up and they are all stomping in unison to some rap music that thumps out of their portable stereo. The crowd is cheering with arms in the air. Though a few policemen watch from the end of the square, they seem unconcerned with this disruption in the flow of traffic. It is harmless, good recreation, a muggy night, with no hooliganism following the scoreless game.

As I turn to move on, I share smiles with the woman to my left whose been dancing drunkenly while watching the show. I'm surprised that she looks familiar and we both do a movie double take.

"Hi again," she shouts over the thundering beat of the music. It requires a moment to place her grin: the American nurse, the blonde, from the morning of my arrival. "Ha ha ha," she says. "Small world."

"Enjoying the show?"

"It's fun. Barcelona is amazing," she says unreservedly, laughing and clapping as the breakers end their routine. Each of them circulates with a plastic bucket to collect contributions. I drop a few euros into it. She adds a ten. The crowd begins funnelling into the adjoining streets, most down La Rambla. We are swept into the current together.

"Have you gotten over your jetlag?" she asks. "Or should I say hangover? You looked a bit wobbly on your feet the last I saw you."

"Well, yesterday was not one of my gold star days."

"You mean this morning."

I tap my forehead a couple of times like a radio with a loose wire. "Yes, yes, this morning. I'm a little out of sync."

"Did you sleep?"

"Only an hour or two. There's a cathedral across from my hotel . . ."

"The fucking bells!!" She starts laughing hysterically. "I can hear them too! They ring *all the time*!"

143

We pause to watch one of the locals peddling a children's toy, something you sling into the air, equipped with plastic blades that spin as it drifts back dreamily to the sidewalk. Its body is a bright LED that blinks on descent. A handful of mesmerized children stare into the cloudy stratosphere, following the gadget's return to Earth. Their eyes brim with wonder and a glazed fatigue. Normally not permitted to be conscious at such a late hour, they contribute to the night's sense of magic, their presence fantastical, like elves at a coven.

The peddler is making a steady trade of a few euros each as parents cough up for the trinket.

As we watch, I allow myself covert protracted scans of my blonde friend. She is wearing a yellow summer dress with blue stitching and spaghetti straps. Blue bra straps too. In fact, she looks very strapped, with brown leather sandals that are secured by several strands of decorative leather around her calves, something reminiscent of a Roman slave's footwear. Her hair is bound up in a topknot, amply displaying the tanned face and shoulders. Yes, late-thirties maybe, more than a decade younger than me. She looks very fit and solid, or is that the Roman slave association?

"Did you go for your swim?" I ask.

"Yes. The beach was a little rocky. The water was perfect. Sherri got a bad burn."

"Is she okay?"

"We had dinner but she was feeling pretty dehydrated. Did you watch the game?"

"An even match."

"It was a blast, wasn't it? Where were you?! My hotel recommended some ex-pat bar with a lot of English people. It got pretty rowdy."

We continue down La Rambla in the ceaseless flow of people, past restaurant patios.

"Should we have a drink," I offer. "It's still early. We can go back to Plaça Reial, if it's not too crowded."

HUGO WALSER DURING HIS ILLNESS

"Sounds good."

A block later, we witness a family struggling to get their LED whirligig into the air. The father tries to launch it as effectively as it was demonstrated, but it cannonballs weakly in a limited arc beyond them. They try again to no great effect. The children are unhappy. They can see the red and green flashes of the peddler's efforts rising three storeys and dropping into the square behind us and the contrast is frustrating their image of their father. The blonde nurse and I trade an amused look.

"The shirt always looks better on the mannequin," I say.

"Huh?"

"Marketing versus reality."

She laughs just as a drop hits my forehead. By the time we have navigated a few winding alleys of Barri Gòtic, a gentle rainfall has made the paving stones slippery as a fishmonger's causeway. We push through the foot traffic and mopeds, using what shelter a few awnings can make. Though the rain is more like a mist; something that hangs in the air, rather than falls. We abandon the patio idea for a bar farther east on Ferran. Wood tables, a white-marble bar counter, crumbling walls, a scuffed tiled floor. Oscillating fans shift the air about. She says she doesn't care what we drink, so I order two double whiskeys on ice. The bartender, a pony-tailed, rake-thin woman with Minnie Mouse tattoos, winks and slouches back to the bar.

"Did you like the breakdancers?" I ask.

"No one calls them that anymore. They're beat boys, old man."

I can't imagine the difference.

"My name is Hugo, by the way. We haven't really introduced ourselves..." I extend my hand and she takes it firmly.

"Sherri," she says. Her damp dress clings to her blue bra. There are a few freckles in her cleavage. "It's my friend's name too. We're both Sherri. Weird, huh?"

"Doesn't it get confusing?"

"Only here. At the base, everyone uses last names."

I'd forgotten they were military nurses. She looks military. Self-assured, carefree because she can depend on chain of command. She also looks like she uses a gym.

"Do you rank?" I ask her.

"Sherri's a corporal. She went ROTC. I'm civilian corps." She sips her whiskey and smacks her lips with comic satisfaction. "Sherri comes from a military family, so I think she'll stay at it. I don't think I could do it forever. A few more placements maybe and then I'll probably look for something back home. I do love the travel and seeing other places."

She tells me a story about three months she spent in Bahrain. "Very westernized," she confides. "More than home. You can have McDonald's and Burger King delivered to your hotel really cheap." She tells me she was in a four-star and a rich, very drunk Saudi asked her to be his third wife, offering her two camels and several thousand dollars to convince her. She giggles while she gulps her drink. The giggling makes her five years younger than my initial guess. I don't like her giggling but I like her shoulders.

"Give me your hand," she says.

I prop my elbow on the table and open my hand, and she takes it immediately and splays the fingers into an exposed starfish, rubbing the joints and bones beneath the skin.

"You're not going to tell my fortune, are you?"

"No, I just like hands. You have nice hands." She scrutinizes my palm a few moments longer and then drops it. "Where's the can?" she says and heads off into the recess behind the bar. I watch her back, scapulae shifting under a light tan. I should probably have packed it in by now. Tomorrow will be a big day. I will meet my "informant" at noon, hopefully to gain enough detail of Norcock's diatribe that I can plan my own obtrusive invectives to hurl at his so-called intellect.

Our server glances my way so I make a downward peace sign at our drinks.

HUGO WALSER DURING HIS ILLNESS

"I've ordered more," I say to Sherri as she returns from the bogs. She tips her highball steeply at her mouth, draining the last of her first double, sucking up a few ice cubes, which she crunches between her teeth.

"I'd say you were trying to get me drunk, except I already am."

Her hair is down. She is, as they used to say, a handsome woman. "You're an attractive woman," I say.

"Thanks. Not bad yourself. What happened to your leg?"

"My leg?"

"I noticed you were limping."

"Can't get anything past you nurses. It's my foot, actually. Nothing serious. Just a blister or something. You should see the other guy," I say.

She crunches more ice.

The bartender arrives with the second round. This time I get a better look at her tattoos and notice Minnie Mouse is holding a large knife and a gun in each hand while dancing on a royal flush.

"Disney won't be happy with you," I say to her. She gives me a confused look. "Disney," I repeat. Then louder, committing the sin of believing volume will aid translation, "Disney lawyers might be mad at you."

She smiles, not sure of my meaning, or not understanding at all. Perhaps her English is limited to bar speak.

"Oh," Sherri shrieks as she notices what I'm referring to. "I love them!" She grabs the bartender's arm and runs her fingers up and down the various details of the illustrated forearm and bicep. A highway connects a martini glass, some slot machine fruit and a skull with dice for eyes. Snake eyes, of course. It's supposed to look dangerous, I suppose, but the images look comic and ironic. Dollar signs are interspersed throughout. Obviously, her tattoo artist had as much confidence in the euro as the British government.

"Road to ruin," the bartender says to Sherri as explanation.

"I love them," Sherri repeats, and releases her arm. The bartender smiles and returns to the bar. She is unfazed by our rough interest in these permanent alterations to her body, nor caring of Sherri's unsolicited physical contact. Fondling someone's bare arm in Ottawa would not be so acceptable. A cultural thing again. I blame it on the snow.

"I wish I had the guts," Sherri says, watching her go. "Not everyone can look good with all those tattoos, y'know. You have to have the attitude."

"Or be a sailor."

"Oh, shut up, old man. *Everyone* has a tattoo these days."

"Do you?"

"A small one. But I can't show it to you right now." She winks and giggles and sips on her whiskey. "You said you were an architect, right? That's exciting. What do you build?"

"I just design. Someone else builds them."

"Same diff."

"I'm sort of retired. I *write* about buildings now."

"What do you write?"

"Articles. For newspapers and magazines."

"No, I mean, what do you write about them? What do you say?"

"I say whether they are good or not."

"So, what do you say? What makes a building good? I mean, how can you tell if one is better than another? If it stays up? If it falls down?"

I can't help but laugh. She has bitten right to the core, this one. Still, it's a good question.

"Yes, there are structural considerations, certainly. But it goes far beyond that. Many questions. What function are you building for? If it's an art gallery, it needs to be organized very differently than a courthouse, for example. Does it match the requirements that are given? Does it innovate? If not, it's not successful. Also, there are aesthetic requirements. Is it ugly? Does it enhance its environment? Is it harmonious with the existing structures in its surrounds?"

"I guess."

"As a nurse, you might understand this. The bare minimum versus more. Is design a luxury? What is life, for example? Is it only the small distinction of whether the heart is beating or not?"

"You're talking about *quality* of life."

"Yes, I suppose I am."

"That's different," she says. "I see what you're getting at. There's structure and then there's *architecture*."

"Function and form . . ."

"Yeah. And what makes the difference is pleasure. Happiness."

"Well . . ."

"Happiness," she says, impressed with herself. It immediately becomes a toast as she angles her tumbler in the air toward me. We tap our glasses and drain the Irish inside. The candied heat washes down my esophagus, and I'm momentarily grateful. For the distillation of barley and its aging in oak barrels. For the narrow streets of Barcelona. For the day's heat and the shade of trees and the sudden, gentle rain.

"You're very touchy-feely. Did you know that?" I say to Sherri, stretching out my legs beside the table.

"What do you mean?"

"I mean you like to touch people. My hands. The bartender's arm. You were grabbing people's waists while you danced in the square. You hugged a few as you left."

"I touch people all the time. I'm a nurse. Illness is very intimate."

"But this is different. I have a theory about weather and physicality."

"Don't you like to touch people?"

"Sure. I do. I will. When I need to."

She starts laughing and I join in. A man in a short-sleeved shirt is making the rounds selling foreign newspapers lifted from the unsold stacks from the kiosks outside. He dallies at our table as we laugh. I am tempted to grab a *Tribune* but when the hell would I read it? He moves silently around to each table displaying his day-old news, his eyes vigilant for any interest among the scattered tourists.

"It's good to hug people, you know. It's very therapeutic."

"Maybe you can hug my blister later."

"That's one of the least sexy things anyone has ever said to me."

21

AT THE PLAZA SANT JAUME, after a protracted tour of other Barri Gòtic bars, it's apparent we are going to sleep together and will need to decide in which hotel.

"Sherri and I are sharing a room," Sherri slurs, tipping us in my hotel's direction.

"Sherri sharing," I mumble, my hand groping her waist.

"Shut up," she says, slapping me lightly.

The hour is late. The clock on the Generalitat's facade shows just past three a.m. and the Barri Gòtic is at its most magical when there are no people in sight. The wrought iron lamps throw shadows across the stone; metal gates of the shops serve the echo effect, like a whispering wall, so someone's voice from streets away seems close to your ear. But the turns of the medieval alleys are unnerving. They hide approach. Foucault again. The panopticon. The labyrinth. Unverifiability. As you reach the end of one stone wall, you can't be certain what you will encounter at the next.

Unless you're messily drunk like Sherri and me.

In which case, you don't care.

"Shush, Sherri, shush, Sherri, Sherri, baby," I half-sing like a lullaby. We cackle at each other, our laughter clattering around the square like a flock of startled pigeons. An industrial noise hums somewhere. Within moments one of those sweeper trucks appears from a side street, its twin yellow brushes scouring the slick stone. The driver hunches over the wheel like a marionette in its glass theatre. His truck grinds past a camera shop and enters another narrow, adjoining street. The plaza looks yellow in the hazy lamp-light. I lean into the recess of a bank machine and pull Sherri a bit roughly between my open knees. She shrieks and I kiss her on the neck and she pushes at my chest and I bite at her throat. I hitch her dress up and get my thumb under the bottom of the waistband at the back of her panties.

"Let's do it right here," I mumble.

She mushes her lips around my ear. Her breath is hot. I can smell the manufactured strawberry of her lipstick. "Someone will see," she whispers, just as a portly, bald man in white shorts and stretched golf shirt stumbles into the plaza, glancing our way and continuing on. In the Italianate arch of the Generalitat, I now spot a guard. He *isn't* watching us with such determination that it's clear he *is* watching us.

"Where's your hotel?" Sherri whispers.

"Not far."

"Let's go." She tugs at my hand and I follow like a hooked trout. I feel like we may be waking the whole city with our stage whispers and laughter. I recall at least two sets of shutters being pulled shut in our vicinity. What erudite gems had the awakened citizenry been treated to? My catcalls. Sherri's screeches. At the last corner before we reach the cathedral square, she squats and pulls down her underwear and pisses on the cobblestones.

"Show me your ass!" I growl.

"Shut up. I'm trying to concentrate."

"C'mon, show me!"

"Fuck! I peed on my ankle."

I am lying flat on my bed when I open my eyes. To my right, the bathroom door illuminates the room's contours. Water is running.

"What are you doing?" I groan as my head lurches and spins.

"I peed on my new espadrilles!" From my horizontal vantage point, I watch Sherri running her sandals under the tap. "I just

HUGO WALSER DURING HIS ILLNESS

bought them yesterday. Fuck." She tamps them dry with one of my face towels and then hangs them by their straps on the bathroom doorknob. "Are you okay?" she asks. "You had a real turn there. I had to practically carry you from the elevator."

I have no recollection of this carrying, or the elevator for that matter. I prop myself upright on the lumpy bed and look around, reaching for the lamp. Switched on, its light reveals order, or at least the recent presence of some cleaning staff in the evening hours to straighten my paraphernalia of socks, ticket stubs and garbage. The ham-and-cheese has been removed. The bed linen is turned down in a dagger-crisp isosceles below the pillow. The room is stagnant with humidity. I push the switch for the ceiling fan, which activates incantatory revolutions above my head.

"Carry me?"

"Yeah, you went all pasty and by the time we'd reached the fifth floor, you'd collapsed. Still conscious though. Mumbling about stuff. George. George and the dog?"

"Georgia is my daughter," I tell her. She is drying her hands on one of the remaining white towels, a large one this time. It's possible she'll sully her way through all my hotel amenities before we couple. I assume we might still accomplish it, though Sherri's brisk movements about the bathroom are more suggestive of preparations for an imminent policy meeting than a sweaty, meaningless tryst. And given the excess of alcohol and recent impromptu bout of unconsciousness, I have doubts of my own body's operational effectiveness.

The tap has been shut. She stands, looking forward, I assume at herself, above the basin. My disclosure of offspring and potential matrimony have inspired a reluctant pause in Sherri's ministrations. The whiff of infidelity. God, not ethics and morals now.

"Divorced," I assure from my rented pulpit of mattress and linen.

"Ha ha," she says, instead of actually laughing. She pushes the door almost shut and rustles about mysteriously for a few moments before reappearing as the toilet flushes.

"How old is your daughter?"

"Early twenties. She's teaching in Korea."

"Does she have a dog?"

"She wanted one, years ago."

"She's a teacher?"

"No, she's just teaching. I don't know what she wants. She's a mystery to me. There was all kinds of trouble while she was growing up."

"Your room is nice. Nicer than ours," Sherri attests as she traverses the bedside. She pulls the curtain back and looks out at the square. "*Our* view is a bunch of garbage containers. Cheap though. Sherri found it online."

From this angle, through the armhole of her dress, I can see the sheer lace of the blue bra. Tanned shoulder blades shift again as she moves the curtain back. Below my belt, the signal of lust.

Yes, I think I could just manage this.

As she drifts past me again, I reach and slither a hand around her thigh. She seems genuinely surprised. "Oh," she says. "I was just thinking about some room service."

"You want food?"

"Well, you were barely conscious a minute ago."

"I'm fine now," I say while pulling her roughly toward me. Still gracelessly drunk, she falls like a set of bagpipes onto the mattress, and I roll across her torso to gain some purchase, both of us wheezing. Her strawberry lipstick tastes like I'm kissing a can of aerosol but I take a few mouthfuls of her tongue as my hand winches her dress up past her waistline. Her panties aren't blue, but white cotton with grey flowers. Except in lingerie ads, do women's bras and underwear ever match?

"Wait, I'm just going to . . ." She grabs the hem and flings the dress up over her shoulders, over her head and completely off in a flourish of breathless prestidigitation. I pull at my belt and shirttails. I kick my trousers to the floor. Her bra lands on my shoes. My mouth is at her nipples like swine for truffles.

We are close to butterball naked, backlit and dizzy with contact. I groan comically like a salesman in a French farce. Her stomach tastes like salt water and oily coconut. There, at the nub of her hipbone, is the promised tattoo: a trio of de-clawed cat prints ascending from her bikini line. Trio? But what's happened to the poor cat's fourth leg? Maybe bitten off by a previous lover. No, here it is, etched indelibly above her mons pubis. Meow. I fold the waistband down and edge my tongue along its untanned border. Her pubic hair is trimmed, short and tidy. I tug the panties down her thighs. Far up past the horizon of her ribcage, I hear the trill of a throaty giggle.

Then electrifying pain crackles along my side. It stilettoes into my stomach and explodes like glass shards down my leg.

"Uh," I grunt.

Sherri laughs, thinking it some kind of bawdy Casanovan groan. But I'm in the throes of a mysterious crisis. Bile floods my mouth.

Agony.

I have a moment of animal panic and then I vomit across Sherri's stomach and groin.

"EEEeaughAAeee," Sherri screams, part shock, part disgust, part existential denial. Though her wail sounds like a boggle-eyed alien as it's cut in two by a laser beam, she might be entitled to every ounce of her B-movie horror. She rockets into the bathroom (thwacking my temple with her knee in transit) and cranks the shower taps, screaming all the way, while I bear groggy witness to the trail of paella across the mattress edge, carpet and tiles.

In the paprika-red assemblage are half-digested chunks of mussels, chorizo, shrimp and boneless, skinless chicken thighs deposited of late across her pelvis and vagina. I slump against the box spring, my head reeling, a viscous drool glommed across my chin.

Sherri, still sobbing and gasping, thrashes about in the shower, angling body parts at the steaming hot spray. In her furious hurry, she has left the curtain open and water is everywhere. She is intermittently calling out phrases to what must be an Old Testament God, so emphatic and profound is her misery.

The intense pain I just felt has thankfully lessened. But I'm too reluctant to stand, afraid that some bend in my abdomen will resume its recent agony. I squat like a malevolent goblin at the foot of the bed, listening to Sherri's attempts at baptism. After a few moments, there's no sound but the spray of water. It goes for some time. Then I hear the taps squeak shut.

"Is everything," I say, quite confident of her answer, "okay in there?"

"Fuck."

"There was an awful pain."

A pause ensues. The taps gush forth again. The shower thunders. Then it all stops. Her arm appears in the mirror by the television, taking the last towel off a chrome rack. Her voice lifts from the bathroom, replaced with professional calm. "Where was the pain?" she says.

Forever the nurse.

"A really sharp one. In my stomach and down through my groin. Out of nowhere."

Through the half-open door, I can see her towelling off. Tanned, trim with the once-eager nudity. And me, crumpled on the soiled carpet, grains of regurgitated rice on my chest. My own private Satyricon.

Someone taps on the door to my room.

"Yes," I say, with a minor tone of indignation, the only way to really respond to a knock on your door at three thirty in the morning.

"Hotel security, sir," a voice with a Spanish accent announces. "We had some complaints of . . . disturbance. Is everything respectable in there?"

"Yes, respectable. Very respectable."

"Shouting was heard, sir."

Sherri shouts from the shower stall: "Everything's fine in here! There was a small accident."

This new, unmurdered voice seems to reassure the security detail, who apologizes through the door and reminds us to please keep the disturbance down as other guests are trying to sleep.

Within minutes, I hear the telephone ring in each of my adjoining rooms; mumbles, flushed toilets and injured silence.

22

AT FIVE A.M., or more precisely, a few cathedral bells after five, I wake, disoriented, feeling slightly post-coronary with a numb arm and another saliva pool on the pillow. There's been no attack, though, just the fallible massing of vice and exhaustion. My temples throb. I roll and dig my forehead into the coolness of the alternate pillow and am almost comfortable when my bladder calls for action. I fold the sheets back. The room reeks like a rotting porpoise. The outline of rooftops outside my curtain, and a shape to last night's proceedings, both dawn on me simultaneously.

Sherri is nowhere to be seen. My shoes, socks, pants and shirt are heaped at the foot of the bed like dead flies on a sill. The carpet by the washroom is stained and crusty. The washroom itself resembles a cross between an abattoir and a Turkish bathhouse, all meat lumps and slippery marble, as I tiptoe over the tiles to settle on the toilet's arctic seat. The cold's a shock, jolting me more awake than I wanted. A rain-stick of pain slinks down my abdomen and disperses. My ass groans into the basin, but parps nothing but air.

In addition to these internal grievances, the rash on my right foot has cycled from manageable scab into open wound again. It stings as I study it, my nude body crouched forward like Blake's drawing of Newton. After a few moments of me posed here, head in hands, I drape a crumpled towel across the damp floor, like a cotton duckboard, and wipe my feet dry before returning to the bedsheets. Forty-five fully conscious minutes later I turn the television on to distract me from morning light and traffic. Onscreen, a purple cartoon dog makes a sandwich. CNN speculates on the psychosis of another school shooter. For several minutes, I'm entertained by an Italian game show called *Bella e Brutte*, which pits beautiful women against ugly women in a team contest of trivia, skill and the culminating obstacle course. Only in Italy. The ugly women lose. They have been lulled into a false sense of compensatory intelligence. But nothing's fair or balanced here, only coldly cutthroat. So, it's the blonde events planner from Naples who knows there were twelve labours of Hercules. And the archeology student with adorable freckles will be the first over the inflatable climbing wall.

I must try to sleep. There is lunch at 11:30, still five hours away, with my informant. Plenty of time for rejuvenation, if I can rest. I feel dead and winched up by strings. And my brain tumbles like a clothes dryer, hot and spinning with mismatched items: Sherri, Georgia, Gaudi, Alan Norcock.

And Sarah (AWOL).

I find my cellphone and check for messages. Another one from the police in Ottawa, urging me to call. It must be midnight there. I try Sarah's phone again. The message centre is still full.

I dial Georgia's number. It should be afternoon in Korea.

No answer.

I admit I haven't the least concern about AWOL Sarah, though her disappearance has produced an effect she'd be pleased with. She likes attention, the stir of drama. She would be happy to know that her day at the spa, or whatever luxury she's self-prescribed, has inspired the attention of the constabulary. Or at least employs the use of a file folder and a few paperclips on the desk of one overworked member of Ontario's law enforcement. No doubt she is better than ever.

They have probably already talked to her, fresh from a tippling tour of Niagara wineries.

What did Sherri say I was chittering on about last night in the throes of delirium? Georgia and the dog?

The dog? Why that? There was a dog, I recall, that strutted its hour upon the stage and then was heard barking no more. Ten days it strutted, actually. Swamped with invoices and work orders one May, I surrendered to Georgia's incessant pleas to own a dog. So, I bought one, a beagle if memory serves, on my way past a pet store. I thought the animal would return me to favour in my daughter's eyes after disappearing for three weeks on a site survey, but it caused more problems than it solved. It shat all over Sarah's handwoven cream rug. Then it pissed twice on a magazine rack and began targeting a leather ottoman as a chew toy.

"Where's Peanut?" George said, emerging from the sunroom after school.

I explained to her that it wasn't a good time to have a dog and I'd returned it to the store (not easy, but I'd raised a fuss with the owner). The news didn't go down well. How old was Georgia then? Six? Seven? She started screaming and crying. I cited carpet, magazine rack, ottoman, further furniture slobber and middle-of-the-night whining. I told her she was not being responsible enough.

"I want Peanut," she wailed through tears.

Sarah was no help, going back the next day to repurchase the cursed beagle, only to be told it'd been sold to another family. I took the blame, though Sarah was the one with the fetish for hygiene and tidiness. No matter. Another strike on my low batting average and few seasons left to run. The divorce was still a few years away.

Add the scene to the string of my Greatest Flops. My mistakes bob there in memory like buoys on rippling water. If only I had learned to steer clear instead of hurtling wildly into the dangers they flagged.

But why the dog now, surfacing in my mind? Worse things have passed between me and my daughter. Guilt, no doubt, for

HUGO WALSER DURING HIS ILLNESS

the terrible shambles left of our relationship. Can't something be mended? After all, I gave life to her. I shared in that.

And didn't I also save her life too?

It's not an image I like to summon, my desperate shouting and all that blood everywhere.

My mind has started to wind its rubber band. It will be impossible to sleep. I survey the remnants of my amorous efforts. Was that woman, Sherri, even in this room? Did any of it happen? Did I dream the whole thing, a nightmare version of romantic hijinks wrought from fatigue?

Yes, there's the evidence. A curt memo scrawled on the hotel notepad: *Go see a doctor. It might be food poisoning. XO. Sherri*

How caring she is, this nurse from America. But she's left no phone number, hotel location, or any information for further contact. Just as well. I won't have much time and must shore up my focus for the task at hand. I pick up the phone and dial room service for a large *café con leche* and baguette. But once it's delivered, I find I have no appetite, joylessly lipping the coffee, breaking the ever-hardening baguette into small pieces that are mostly abandoned on the plate. Perhaps it was food poisoning, some uncooked chicken thigh slipped into the paella like a rag of smallpox. Or likely, the shadow of something far worse. The thought turns my stomach and I rush to the toilet in fresh disquiet, coughing up air and milk.

When I wake for the second time today, it's to panic. After perusing the morning TV programmes, I had just put my head down for a little shut-eye, and now I see it's eleven a.m., thirty minutes until my lunch date. I fill the basin with cold water and splash it around, dunking my head, zipping a toothbrush over my teeth for good measure. The least offensive towel I can find is a damp facecloth. I pat my head down with it. I pass the comb through my hair and lean into the mirror. Not bad. Not bad. Though a red blossom has appeared on my left cheek under the skin. A burst blood vessel. I'll wear the strain. No blemish that a blazer over a fresh Tilford shirt can't fix.

Having dressed, I breeze through the lobby, chugging a glass of complimentary orange juice, its sweetness like an attack of sunshine.

I give the taxi driver the address and he accelerates without a nod. Soon, Eixample's ordered grid begins to appear through the chaos of the Old Town's streets. It must be garbage day. Trucks block corners, tightening traffic. We trickle north to a humble square off Diagonal. As the taxi pulls to the curb, I spot Casa Sayrach on the corner of the square, a late Modernista creation, more understated than some, but reminiscent of Gaudi's curvy abandon. Squeezing through some parked mopeds, I limp into the *plaça*. It's a bright day. Perfect, really. A cool breeze in palm leaves overhead. In the middle of the square, a restaurant patio is laid out for lunch, a dozen tables set with white linen, plates and cutlery. Two waiters smile at my approach. The noon crowd is twenty minutes away so the patio is still empty. Except for one patron, who rises from under a large umbrella festooned with ads for mineral water.

Estrella Mera.

We take each other's hands and kiss cheeks. An elegant whiff of perfume dallies on my nose. "Estrella," I say. "How long has it been?" Estrella smiles, but with something held back. A stiffness in her gestures. Though it's been a few years, she looks the same. Thick black, shoulder-length hair. Black eyes below dramatically curved black eyebrows. Her earrings, silver discs, hang like brooches on each side of her tanned face. She gestures to sit.

"Years," she says, "years," as if the word is distasteful and cruel. She must be close to her late sixties now if I did the math.

"I saw the Sayrach on the corner," I say, gesturing with a look. "Was it your private joke, to choose this location? Right in the heart of Modernista."

Estrella opens her mouth in mock horror, then says wearily, "I know your feelings on this but it really was not my purpose. Frankly, I have an apartment nearby and hate the traffic, so . . ."

Her open palm sweeps the air in conclusion.

The waiter pours out mineral water and takes a wine order from Estrella. They act familiar. It must be her regular place. As she makes suggestions from the small menu, she looks me over a few times. When I glance up from the list of food options, I catch her eyes shifting. They are organizing an opinion of something.

I have always admired her. I met her many years ago, when she was a professor at the Higher Technical School in Madrid. I was red-hot to write my book and had gone there to access their extensive archives. She joined me for lunch, or drinks, a number of times over my month-long grant period, guiding me to documents on Le Corbusier's Dom-Ino House and suggesting I research bunker design. Why, with her busy schedule, she made the time for this strange student from Canada, I couldn't understand. I must have convinced her of my sincerity. I even attempted intimacy one night after two bottles of wine in a tapas joint.

"Aren't you a married man?" she'd asked, not at all ruffled. She must have dealt with that sort of thing all the time.

"We've had a fight."

"Silly boy," she said, like I'd dropped a lollipop in the sand. The disregard for my desire to drag her, an older woman, to my bed only fuelled it more. But she would have none of it, laughing at my clumsy propositions one more time before I left for Canada. Still, she took no offence, or was flattered by my reverence. We kept in touch, less and less as time passed. I would receive an occasional postcard, usually in reaction to a nasty article I'd written about a colleague's building, chiding me as if I'd never changed from the lumbering twenty-two-year-old she'd once known.

So here she sits, Estrella Mera. An architect of promising brilliance, she had switched her focus in mid-career to sustainable development, affordable housing, Utopia for the masses. Consequently, her projects are no longer grandstanders, they are exemplars of the repurposing of existing structures using local materials. Who am I to disparage? Two of her designs have received awards from the Aga Khan Foundation.

Three weeks ago, I'd opened her email, which arrived out of the blue. It mentioned she was attending the Arquitectura Cívica and guess who was the keynote? Alan Norcock. At once, I found the conference website and the event description:

TALKING THE WALK: Keynote address with Alan Norcock will revisit failures of the classical order (Serlio) and deal with topics such as organic technologies, passive systems, texture warp, "funk" design and post-structuralist approaches with case studies.

The waiter pours our wine. Estrella, lifting her glass, studies it and tries a sip, then places it very carefully back at the side of her plate. Serious and vibrant, she is as composed as the influential papers she's written. If one could brood and still be worshipped by the sun, it's Estrella Mera.

"How are you?" she asks. The question is quite sincere. She does not do small talk.

"I'm fine. Not busy. Less work than ever, actually. The magazines seem more interested in what celebrities eat for lunch."

"As it was, ever it shall be."

At this I accelerate into my usual diatribe regarding the death of culture and people's ever-shortening attention spans. I have honed this into a concise rant of three and a half minutes, almost an elevator pitch, though with the right audience and a ready bottle of spirits, it can be stretched into hours. Estrella listens patiently. She has heard this all before, or one of its variations. Complaining has always bored her. She has said so to me, in a number of her letters. *Your testy grievances are a waste of energy,* she'd once written in

HUGO WALSER DURING HIS ILLNESS

response to a negative blast I'd given to Gehry's Seattle Center. *If you think a project has been created badly, then create something better.* As I start my speech on the world wide web, she interrupts.

"What happened to your book? Perhaps it's time to finish it now."

My great book. The other subject I have bored her with over the years. My bright comet with its endless, dwindling tail. *The Labyrinth's Walls.* In those years after its inception, I've sketched chapter ideas, written pithy observations, structured grand arguments and patchworked an extensive bibliography. All of which Estrella has encouraged and been critic to. But, excepting the preface, I have never finished a single chapter.

"As it was, ever it shall be," I echo with requisite hollowness.

"Then this is the perfect moment. If your journalism is less in demand, then use the free time, Hugo. I have always told you that those ridiculous articles denied you time for real work."

"They paid."

"No matter. You must take a year. Pack your notes, go away somewhere and finish the book."

"How romantic."

"Please shut up. It is the best course for you. You can write something wonderful. You can save your rep—"

She stops herself.

The waiter sets two plates down in our midst. Estrella takes a slice of tomato bread. The patio is beginning to fill up. Business types from the neighbouring offices. The square becomes hurried, bustles with chatter. A new waiter has appeared to seat people. Estrella sits back in her chair, dabbing her fingers on her napkin.

"Hugo, why the hell did you come here?" Estrella says, her black eyes settling on my face like two crows on a stubbled field.

"For the conference, of course. Norcock's presentation."

She heaves a great world-weary sigh.

"You warned me in the email . . ." I add for context. For the touch of complicity the discussion will require.

165

Now Estrella is smiling, with all the meagre light of a crack under a door.

"I told you to amuse you," she says. "It was simply that reason. Nothing else. I just don't understand . . ."

"Norcock needs a thrashing," I clarify.

"You should not have come." She stops and lifts her chin, her gaze shifting over the canopy of some kind of tree above our umbrella. The intense light of noon, fragmented by the leaves, skitters across the stone façade of the shops opposite us. As if in a scene from a European film, a young boy marches past carrying an entire ham wrapped in plastic.

"What is your intention?" she says.

"You must understand, Estrella. It's time to call him on his bullshit. I'll go there and have a few words."

"At the conference?"

"Why not?"

"You will only look like a fool."

"What else should I do? Sit back and let him drag my name through the mud?"

"The talk has nothing to do with you."

"Did you read the description? It's exactly about me, about all we've been arguing about over the years. Who do you think his so-called case studies will be about?"

"You are paranoid."

"Norcock is a snake oil salesman. Texture warp!? What the hell is that? Sounds like brick and steel to me. It's just old fish wrapped up in today's newspapers."

"Hugo, please. If you go there uninvited and start one of your rants, it will only make you look unprofessional. A lunatic. You don't even know what Norcock is going to say. At least wait until the paper is published and then you can have your reaction."

"I'm sick of these scholarly responses," I say, hooking my fingers into quotation marks. "He needs to be called to account. In

HUGO WALSER DURING HIS ILLNESS

the flesh. He can't hide behind those snotty editorials anymore. It's time for some good old-fashioned heckling, don't you think? Some direct engagement. Everything on the table."

"It is a big mistake."

"I thought you'd be on my side," I protest. I've emptied my wine glass and pour out more from the bottle, slopping a wet stain on the linen in my agitation, adding, "I thought that you were helping me."

"I am trying to help you by keeping you away."

Estrella waits as a salad is placed in front of her. I have ordered a tastefully arranged pyramid of calamari, ringed with aioli and a drizzle of olive oil. She pushes her walnuts and spinach about grimly and looks off toward the street, where the sanitation trucks have arrived, levering and tipping the dumpster's rotting contents into their compacting container.

The air fills with the churn of engines.

"What is the name for these trees?" I shout at her through the grinding noise. I point at the knotted branches.

"Plane trees," she says. "They are English." Indifference in her voice. She is not concerned with discussing civic arbour projects. We wait until the metal bins are dropped with a dead clang onto the flagging and the truck's air brakes release it into motion. In a moment, the square is peaceful again.

As if our discussion had not been interrupted, Estrella leans toward me above her plate. "If I had known you were stupid enough to fly over here," she says, placing her fork down, "deluded with some senseless scheme, I would never have said a thing to you." Her voice is unhurried and clips along precisely like a castanet. "I have respected and supported you, Hugo. You know this. You had such energy. You asked questions, sometimes difficult ones. Your early ideas seemed so clear. Elegant, really. I defended you, you must know this, even after the gallery mistake. It was a good design but the math was wrong. I still believe it. But then you started those excessive assaults in the papers, disguised as journalism. And that television rubbish. You are emotional, passionate. I know this about you. But enough is enough. You are dried up and no one will hire you. Those articles get attention but it is a hollow thing. Do you want to become—what is the expression—a laughingstock?"

"I don't see—"

"Look at yourself. You are a disorder. You have ruined your . . . status. All of this drinking and anger, years of feeling sorry for yourself. What good is it?"

I spear a piece of battered squid and smear it through the aioli. I'm not hungry at all. The moment the calamari arrived at the table, my appetite was daunted by the smell of sea and fry-up. But I am hunting for a pause. My methodical chewing is meant to indicate I'm in no hurry to answer, or even care about, her disappointed interrogatives. I gnash the rubbery flesh between my molars and study Estrella.

What is her game? She has summoned me here, has she not? She knew of my impolite history with Norcock, our barbed dust-ups, so she must have guessed his public appearance would provide occasion for a shooting gallery. Instead, she frowns in the shade across from me, severe and immovable, with claims of neutrality, like Judgement herself.

"Estrella, I thought you despised Norcock too."

"He is a showman. A very smart amateur with dramatic ideas. But many take him seriously."

"I will change that."

Estrella's eyebrows arch. It's almost a bored look. I see the age in her face now, the wrinkles around the mouth. Perhaps the sun has found the right angle to expose them.

"I can't support you," she says.

"What does that mean?"

My stomach twists. A queasy wave floods my head, and stony, cold sweat flutters across my temples. I pull on my collar to get some air down my neck. Estrella has begun to explain herself. Something about consequences. But I'm struggling to concentrate, to remain composed. The scene around me wobbles in a set of unfocused lurches as if I'm scuba diving in a wreck. I grit my teeth, nodding and shifting in my chair, and watch Estrella's face uncomprehendingly. A minute bobs around me before I interrupt her, excusing myself to slow-march to the restaurant's washroom, doing my best to hide my painful limp and clammy faintness.

I'm momentarily blind in the dark vestibule. Leaning against an iron pillar, getting my breath and bearings, I scan the back of the dining area for any hazy apertures that might divulge a washroom entrance. A passing waiter directs me to the deep right. Step by step, I work my way to the back, knocking into one chair, but otherwise successful as the saloon-style door swings with a nudge of my hand. Splashing. A tap left on. I find the sink, pins winking across my vision, and cup some water to my face. It spills down my shirt front, but the cold liquid has steadied me. I believe the crisis has passed. I prop my palms on the edge of the counter and breathe in and out, trying to slow my heart rate, diligent should the nausea return. Reluctantly, I meet my reflected face in the mirror. Perhaps I don't look as dead-tired, ill or shaky as I feel. There are heavy lines under my eyes. The burst blood vessel is pronounced on my grey skin. Stubble. Grinning a mad clown smile, I can see the teeth are decent. A fortune in dentistry. Not bad. Not the worst. I undo my top button, yank a handful of paper towel from a dispenser and dab it into my neck. Feeling good. Better. A few minutes and I should be right as rain.

What did Estrella call me? A disorder.

That was it, wasn't it?

It's a set-up then. She is not here to help me. After all these years, I can see her true colours. The boosterisms and critical fellowship. All these mixed messages. But I need to say something, to state my version of the truth. Before it's too late. She would prefer I disappear with my uncomfortable opinions. Who can blame her? She's just protecting her stability. The state of things. Norcock is their man of the month, so he is given free rein for now. No matter how spurious his theories and opinions are. Time will vindicate my actions. I won't let them barricade me from the academic garrison. In the meantime, I can start a right nasty bonfire on their own front step.

I check my face again, push and pat my hair into order. Bent over, with the aid of the hand blower, I dry the wet splashes on my shirt. There is another moment of dizziness but hardly worth mentioning. I have never felt better. The bright sun hits my face as I step out into the square and hobble to our table.

Estrella is not there. Her plate is gone, her napkin cleared. Nothing but the remainder of the wine and my own cutlery flanking the disarranged calamari. I cast my gaze about in search of her. Most of the other patrons have also departed, back to their hidden offices. The waiters leisurely tidy the tables, wiping surfaces and folding linen. Birds peck at crumbs. A flower shop across from the patio displays an impressive collection of sunflowers, their stalks thick as arms. But there is no sign of Estrella.

"Señora Mera has left," I'm told by the waiter. "*Pagado*," he says, smiling. "It is all paid."

23

THE FACTS OF ANTONI GAUDÍ'S life can be found using any search engine: Born in 1852. Early designer of lampposts and cabinets. Eventual commissions for houses of rich industrialists. The obsessive, devotional dedication to construction of La Sagrada Familia, his great church, in his last years. His accidental death, at the age of seventy-three, struck by a passing tram.

That was 1926, and less than a quarter of the church—only the crypt, the apse walls, a portal and tower—had been completed. The project stalled. Three more towers were slowly erected, according to Gaudi's surviving plans, when in 1936, Catalan anarchists broke into the church, smashed and burned everything they could find of plans and models in the on-site workshops. Then it wasn't until 1952 that work began once again. Controversy still abounds as to the accuracy of the reconstructed designs, how faithful to "God's architect" they are. But since the turn of the twenty-first century, with the use of computer-aided technology and off-site milling machines, work has been done at a relative breakneck speed, though it must be said, it will take 140 years for the last of its structure to be complete. Perhaps Barcelona is cursed with the assembly speed of their places of worship. Critics of the Sagrada's slow progress need to be reminded that their famous Gothic Cathedral, currently banging its bells quarter-hourly outside my hotel windows, took some seven hundred years between bedrock, tower and facade.

My unsuccessful lunch had ended. Having balked on a doggy bag offer from the indifferent wait staff, and with still no sign of Estrella's return, I decided to stretch my legs through Eixample. Its wide avenues, circular intersections and connecting side streets carried me forward in the sun. For twenty walking minutes, I've been trying to decipher the subtleties of Estrella's comments, when I become aware of where my feet have led me. Rounding another line of shopfronts below wrought iron balconies, the towers of that improbable church rear its fanciful spires. La Sagrada Familia. Of course, this is its neighbourhood. With no possible location options in the old city, its ground had been broken north and east.

Looking up, surprised to see it piercing the haze of the extension's sky, I walk headfirst into a folding sign showcasing the menu of a Chinese restaurant, knocking it over onto a parked moped. The proprietor gives it a double take, assuming blame for the sign's position on the sidewalk, and offers me a metal chair to recover. He fusses about, experimenting with the sign's position, then brings me a bottle of water. Is he expecting a lawsuit? Perhaps if I groan a little, I can negotiate a free meal and a small envelope of cash.

The chair is a welcome break for my lame foot, which has continued to plague me with mounting discomfort. It's a nuisance. There is something decrepit, even untrustworthy, about a limp. No matter how well-dressed one is, a limp adds a note of hard times. The homeless are forever limping. Shuffling on corners, disappearing down alleys, they invariably limp while doing it. It causes suspicion: What led to that unsteadiness? Violence? Poor nutrition? Sleeping on concrete? In doorways? Don't get me started.

Perhaps my Chinese restaurateur has pitied me for a similar reason.

Nevertheless, there is shade here and I'm in no hurry. My one scheduled task for the day, the meeting with Estrella, though far from a success, is over. The bottled water is cool in my hand. I gaze upward at the spires of Gaudi's church, abuzz with super-cranes, and begin assembling adjectival phrases for the lampoon it deserves. Disney Modernism. Crap Nouveau. Admittedly, I have only visited La Sagrada once, back in the early nineties, when it was hardly more than a monument inside a construction site. It has doubled its presence since.

I follow a diagonal path of the tree-lined plaza to my left and approach its western façade.

Whatever else can be said of it, the church has presence. As I trundle forward past the gaggles of camera-hoisting tourists, I am reminded how perspective must have similarly awed medieval peasants when confronted by Chartres or Saint Basil's. Having never seen any other dwelling in their lives but some godforsaken village made of hovels and two-storey barns, to trudge into the shadow of some soaring arches, buttresses and limitless spires must have been proof of a greater glory than what we know. I had experienced this once as my taxi rounded a corner in Istanbul and I arrived in that magical avenue running between the Hagia Sophia and the Blue Mosque. Those inclined planes heaping up to the otherworldly domes. Is there another place like it on Earth? Not here.

Where the Hagia Sophia's terraced buttresses and heaving lines accumulate to its historical inevitability, the forced verticals of La Sagrada's spires seem superimposed on an otherwise workaday suburb. Though these towers are meant to soar, their elongated pine cone shapes, slatted with grey ventilation galleries, look more droopy than glorious.

After a few minutes of walking, I arrive in front of the Passion façade, poor old Christ pinned up there, in faux El Greco starkness amidst his struggles. The entrance to the interior is glutted by tourists, the line for tickets stretching back down the street and bending past the far end of the site. I have a press pass but linger among the shuffling penitents. Mere steps away, life goes on for the locals, as if there's no sacred, implausible building mounting into the heavens above them. At the bus stop, a few grannies are shifting fruit purchases in their net bags. Cyclists thumb their bells at the continuous stream of oblivious pedestrians in their path. Still, it's not every day you can watch a church this massive being built. Probably almost never at this scale since the nineteenth century. Those cranes and distant scaffolding reorganize the sky, carting piecemeal concrete slabs and stone into the nudged expanse.

I edge my way along the chain-link of the perimeter. Several workers in site boots chug Powerade by a delivery entrance. At the corner, where a construction trailer has been remodelled as a ticket office, I approach a security guard studying the queue from under a sweaty cap. The day is now scorching with accumulated heat. "Press," I say, and wave a business card from *Architecture Ontario*, the only status I can produce at the moment. He looks it over skeptically and points me toward a security hut. There's less enthusiasm here. It is late afternoon. After a morning of ceaseless tour groups and stupid questions in a dozen languages, the appearance of a provincial journalist is not overwhelming them with hospitable instincts. The administrator checks the card.

"*Who*?" she says in an irritated tone.

"Canada," I reply. She taps on her keyboard, with bureaucratic pauses, as if Canada itself needs to be verified. Her palm opens on the counter.

"Photo."

As she hands me back my driver's licence, she nods. I seem to be who I am. Tired of grunting, she says in perfect English, "Do you want a guide to take you around?"

I'm not here to see anything, to assess anything, to write anything, and am very much not interested in having a guide drag me around the place for the next few hours, regaling me with the extraordinary facts and figures of symbolic detail and vault heights, so I decline the offer. This visit will be strictly hit-and-run, a distraction realized by the convenience of happenstance proximity.

A thirty-minute step inside should do it. A break from the heat; just a bent neck to peek at the transept. A mortal squint into the gloom.

I'm issued a pass with a lanyard and descend the stone steps to the crypt where the great man himself is buried. It is surprisingly standard issue for the nineteenth century. Compound pillars collecting into a rotunda with side chapels. Traditional, elegant. Very un-Dr. Seussian. It is cool inside these stones and shadows. I rest for a moment on a wooden pew. Gaudi's grave is in an alcove to the left of the main altar. On a nearby table, a clipboard collects signatures for his sainthood. If I were actually commissioned to write an article on La Sagrada Familia, I would start here. I would draw attention to the simplicity of the crypt, one of the few details Gaudi saw through to completion. Did he really expect, in his seventies and with so much still to assemble, that he would live to see the church's consecration? His urgency propelled his obsession, dogged by a dearth of funding. Several dearths. Dearths upon dearths. By the truckload. No one was exempt from requests for donations. He would practically beg in the streets if it meant one more column or rose window could be paid for. But if he had lived another ten, fifteen, twenty years, would his plans have changed? Would he have altered his designs, would his ideas have evolved, the way every façade, elevated by a new era, reflects a new taste?

We can't expect to inhabit our highest aspiration. Can we?

So, we must accept a grave in the cellar.

I suppose, given the circumstances, I should try to pray.

Instead, my mind wanders.

. . . Sarah.

Can there be any purpose to dredging through memory for the great rupture that ended our marriage? It was not the fights and shouting. No, nothing that dramatic. Isn't it always the thousand cuts that do it? We can forgive the flaming rubbish lobbed over each other's parapets, but never the poison slipped past the gates and tipped discreetly into the well. It was betrayal after all that finished us. Yes, we had our infidelities, and left clues as traceable as a red dotted line on a hospital floor: suspicious phone messages, fragrances and stains, fake appointments. We assembled the whole tired cliché and chose reciprocally to look the other way, turn the other cheek, and let all the bygones get gone by and carried past into the steady, choppy water that flows under the bridge. Because we liked each other too. Because we had shared so much. We would laugh and make ourselves useful. Sarah thinks it was her tryst with Andrew the decorator, or whatever, that made me go. But it was something far more painful: her loss of faith in me.

I'll tell you what happened.

Sarah and I were on no great steady ground as it was. I had been drifting in and out of town between assignments, handing wodges of cash to taxi drivers, it seemed, dumping myself onto the study's couch at odd hours. Sarah took weekend trips too, left notes. We were always just missing each other. Her Audi would be parked in the drive when I arrived but gone when I awoke. Meanwhile, the house was transforming in increments without my participation. Foreign objects accumulated in our rooms. A new sectional appeared by the TV. A kitchen island was replaced. New tiles. There was some abstract art thing on the sideboard by the stairs.

"Did you see I changed the curtains?" she would say. Or "I had the deck redone, by the way," in the most casual tones.

I thought nothing of it. But I should have seen she was rearranging my relationship with what we owned. The old wraiths of upholstery and chrome were being exorcised. She was beautifying a new world, free from the soiled associations of our conjugal life.

"Have you heard from Leonard?" I asked Sarah one rare evening when we were both in the living room, sharing a bottle of red. Leonard Capps was a textiles magnate. Sarah had sold several houses to him and they'd once made a pretty penny flipping them after expensive renovations. Sarah would sell these too, often at double the previous price, and both of them had been very happy with the arrangement. They'd kept in touch; she'd run into him and he mentioned a 5,300-square-foot property on a bluff in Georgian Bay. The location was killer but was occupied by a drab postwar bungalow. Instead of renovating, Leonard had decided to tear it down and build a whole new structure on the site. Sarah said he was looking for an architect.

"Why don't I do it?"

Sarah looked at me, almost a double take, the first amused, the second serious. "You don't design anymore," she said.

"I've been thinking I'd like to get back into it."

"Since when?"

"Lately. I have a number of ideas. Office spaces. Cottages. That kind of thing. Baby steps. This house might be a good location to work with."

Sarah had shrugged. "If you had an idea, I could ask him."

"Just give me the specifics of the site and I can send him a few sketches. Preliminary stuff. Then I'll talk to him. If necessary, I can drive up there and have a look."

She said she would and a few months passed. "Have you heard from Leonard?" I asked in a rushed phone call. Sarah sighed. "Oh. Yes. Yes, I forgot to tell you. It sounds like he already had someone else in mind. A friend of his or something."

That was that. But I was annoyed and sniffed around. One day I was talking residential with a colleague in Toronto and mentioned Georgian Bay and Leonard's property.

"The Capps house," my esteemed colleague said. "Yeah, Rick is working on that." And he gestured to a thin guy with a red goatee and mismatched shirt-blazer combo just ten feet down the hall from us. So, I talked to Rick. It was just casual shoptalk: how long he'd been with the firm, how he liked Toronto, and I heard he was working on the Capps house . . .

"Oh, that," Rick said. "Yeah, nice property. Over the water. I've given them lots of view. Expansive windows. Cedar-clad walls. Very natural. It just fell into my hands."

When I confronted Sarah, my regret was the timing. I had planned to raise the topic in person, to see her face. But I had left Toronto directly for a week in Santa Fe, reviewing an artist retreat that had just opened. A few days after arriving, we were on the phone. She had made some joke about the weather, how the sun must be hard to take in February, and something in her sarcasm got to me. I remember thinking distinctly that I'd wait.

But my voice said, "Guess who I was talking to in Toronto?"

And I told her about Rick. Who was *not* an old friend of Leonard Capps's. And how *lucky* he was, since the commission for the house had just *fallen* into his hands.

"For Christ's sake, Hugo. I never asked Leonard. You must know that," she said. Sarah was very capable of lying, but when caught out, she was as honest as Abe. "He was my best client. I can't fuck that connection up. A million things could go wrong."

"A million things."

"Yes, a million fucking things," her voice asserted across the satellites. "Should I spell it out? Design, budget, contractors, manufacturers, materials, building delays . . ."

I hung up and, with no interest in her further demands, arguments or diatribes, turned my phone completely off. It seemed the best possible solution. It would make Sarah crazy and it would give me temporary peace. I rented a car for another week and drove to Texas, arriving in San Antonio the next day. Azure sky and the empty horizon. I wanted to stay away, disappear for a while, and the city had just appeared on my map. It is famous for the Alamo, of course, a subject I'd once considered for my dissertation. A religious mission repurposed to a military fort. What could be a more fascinating site plan for study? A structure, in its essence, is walls. Add a roof and it's a shelter. The history of fortification explores the most advantageous use of these two elements. And how we adapt under siege. It is a good exercise for thought.

What is essential, after all?

I wandered the plaza, trying to imagine Travis and Crockett scrambling to fend off Santa Anna's troops—defending the garrison walls, changing tactics, more and more desperate as their choices got smaller—but it was too hot, too bright, and the tour buses were idling their noisy engines across the street. Under the landscaped trees, I bought an ice cream and sat on a stone wall, very busily trying not to think about what I should have been thinking about. Other tourists wandered out of the chapel entrance, adjusting their backpacks and squinting into the sun. In front of me, a red SUV was blasting honkytonk through half-open windows, the approximate spot where the Mexican troops had breached the compound.

My marriage was over. Sarah did not believe in it anymore.

Matrimony can last through the worst financial straits. It can endure mistakes and tragedy. But it must believe in happiness.

On the walk back to my rental, I stopped for a few drinks in a bar. What a lovely place: all that wood and glass and darkness. It was part of the Menger Hotel, historical in those parts, I was told, purported to be the most haunted hotel in Texas. "The first public demonstration of barbed wire was done here," the bartender said. "They showed how it worked outside, then they took orders in here."

The details seemed right to me. I had needed just such a place: full of ghosts and weird heritage. I kept my tab open and went to the lobby to check in and stayed for six days, drinking at the bars on the River Walk, or there in the Menger.

When I returned to Ottawa, I rented a condo and began my life alone.

Nonsense, nonsense. It's not reverie, nor nostalgia, just sunstroke that's poisoning my thoughts. I must have drifted off there for a moment. I open my eyes. It's so quiet and still. The crypt is almost empty in La Sagrada Familia. The whispers of a few stragglers echo against the intersecting vaults. This chapel is notably spartan compared to the mad swirls and fancy of the edifice and pinnacles. The bench is hard. Not a decorative carving to be seen. Stained glass and Biblical figures. All the old stuff. I look at the time on my cellphone. Less than half an hour before they close the church. Over the PA, in Spanish and English, they are thanking us for our visit. My foot still burning, I climb the winding steps into the basilica.

There is still time to cross the transept and get a sense of scale.

Once I reach the entrance, it becomes a struggle against the opposite mass exit of the crowds, security urging them out to the exterior steps. I shoulder through gawkers, their chins tipped up in scrutiny at the sculptured doors. Once inside them, I flash my press card at persistent employees eager to empty the fathomless nave. A reverent gloom emanates from the redistribution of sunlight through windows. Pinks and greys pulse from the marble floor. I am doing it again, writing the whole thing as I walk. And I cross to the centre, amid the stone columns that Gaudi imagined as trunks and branches towering into vaults some fifty metres above the congregants. And yes, it is quite . . . what?

Tremendous.

Breathtaking.

Awesome, in the old sense: replete with awe.

Awash in it.

The apse and ambulatory have been fitted with stained glass but down the aisles the windows are still clear and dusty. The just-assembled walls void of history and time; the columns chalk-dull, plain, almost fragile-looking bones; a just-born fawn testing its legs. Here at the crossing, I look up into the ceiling: granite, basalt and porphyry stretching to the skylight medallions. Though I am standing here on the floor, I feel I'm falling. It's mesmerizing, like photos of the barrel and endcap of the Large Hadron Collider's ATLAS detector, seeming to reorder perspective. Physics and God touching.

Back in the afternoon sun, I press on toward the Old Town again, steady on, steady on, down the shopping avenues with their flagship stores. Zara and Mango bags abound. On a whim, I swing past Casa Batlló, the location for tomorrow's lecture. I understand they will hold it on the back patio, with a tent and chairs, views of the building's absurd balconies as showcase to Gaudi's achievement. Above the intersection, I spot an Arquitectura Cívica banner strung between light posts. There is only tomorrow left of this Barcelona adventure. I should be buzzing with adrenaline, measuring my steps for the running leap into redemption. But I feel deflated. Uneasy. My meeting with Estrella did not bolster me. I had been expecting full support, perhaps collaboration on my imminent skirmish. Though it's not her resistance that has rattled me. I do see her argument but refuse to understand it. She's been trapped by her position, of course. Reputations to preserve, future projects to lobby. Tenure. All the burdens status carries. The knots, pulleys and levers of institutional careers.

I have remained independent. It must grate them to see it. I have stuck my ground here on the outside, in the fitful winds, thus highlighting their sheltered compromises. And where has it left me?

My cellphone is ringing. I can hear its muffled trill from the inside of my pocket. Unknown number, but I thumb the accept button.

"Yes, hello," I say, waiting at the traffic light.

"Hugo?" a woman says with a slight time delay.

"Hello," I say again, buying a moment, trying to place the voice.

"It's me, you oaf," she says. "It's Sarah."

Sarah. Of course. Risen from the tomb, reconstituted from her vanishing act. How had my ears, my memory, failed me? That deep, precise timbre sustaining its vibrato across the years. Absent and then present.

"Where are you?" I say, swivelling without a pivot to attach myself to.

"I'm in Ottawa. Home."

Her tone sounds grey, flat, as if she'd run a race and burned through her adrenaline reserve. "What's happened to you?" I say. Indistinct noises clatter on the line behind her.

"Long story. Just listen."

"I'm *listening.*"

I have stepped out toward the traffic island and have forgotten to look back at the roundabout. A moped blats its goosy horn and swerves past me at an asteroid speed, so close I can feel its rearview brush the front flap of my blazer. The cellphone tumbles from my hand, its fall broken by the toe of my shoe. The device's plastic case rattles across the pavement and comes to rest a few feet from the curb. "Shit," I shout, lunging forward to retrieve it. More insistent horns squawk with urgency. The light has turned. Sharply retreating, I lose balance. A stabbing pain at my hip. Wheels rush past in a smear of chrome and rubber. There are people helping me up from where I must have fallen. Faces crowd out the sky. Spanish phrases, questions. "*¿Está bien?*" "*Que pasó?*" "*. . . borracho?*" I brush my palm across my trousers. Someone is handing me my phone. We are outside a perfume store, thick with scent. "Hugo? Hugo?" my ex-wife pleads through static

I station the receiver against my ear. "Yes, I'm still here."

"What's going on?"

"Nothing. Nothing."

A few concerned Samaritans still linger in front of me, watching my movements with curatorial interest. I nod and wave at them to move on, to get on their way. I cup my hand across the voice piece. "*Bueno. Very bueno. Gracias,*" I say, making an okay circle with finger and thumb. I point at myself, nodding and grinning like a happy-go-lucky idiot.

"Listen, Hugo," Sarah is saying. "We'll discuss this all later. I've just replaced my cellphone after spending all morning at the police station and I'm exhausted."

"Police station?"

"I told you it's a long story, Hugo."

What time is it there? What time is it *here*, for that matter? The evening sun, the lengthening shadows. As if through powers of suggestion, Sarah's tiredness has claimed me too. I am immeasurably tired now. My joints are filled with sleep; my gammy limbs are weight-laden. There is a new throbbing discomfort on my hip where I have fallen. The suit leg is scuffed and I can see the knee is slightly torn. If I weren't already limping, I would be limping. Maybe all the afflictions will cancel each other out. Presence, then absence. The effect is not unlike vertigo. Like the Basilica ceiling, the dizzying tug of focus against void, hurrying each element into harmony too quickly. I have been away, really away, these past days. I have been removing, piece by piece, contours of my being.

"I'm not well, Sarah," I say into the phone. "I need to talk to you."

"Later, okay? Get some sleep."

"Yes, yes. Sure," I say.

But I haven't convinced myself of anything.

"Sarah?"

Nothing. *Nada.*

She's already gone.

24

THESE WERE NOT THE LAST unsuccessful communications I was to have this day. When I struggled along the thoroughfares toward Barri Gòtic, nursing knee, hip, foot and stomach, I mentally picked away at the various nuances of my cancelled conversations.

I didn't mean to be so short with Sarah. But there are things that must be said. And time is passing. Why do I react in such ways? Why such frustration with those who could have been close to me? We had once shared our future hopes. Had we shared love? Whatever was the case, in mounting stages, she had withdrawn. Estrella too. She had nurtured my imaginative life at a crucial juncture in the past but refuses to support me further. I am alone now, and to the sundry, disengaged participants of my life, the sole beneficiary of my fate.

In one of the countless tapas bars along Carrer de Jaume, I stop for a whiskey. To "get the edge off," as they used to say. A sketchy bloke in a floppy black hat and a beard that looks like it was barbered with a machete is floating about the café tables looking for change. He proffers the reservoir of his ceramic cup at each table, waiting with an edgy stare for a few coins before moving on. He's had no luck. Maybe because he smells like a bag of corpses. With every successful tourist city comes its itinerant denizens. Not the legitimate poor saddled with job loss and children to feed, but the international parasites who arrive looking for a few wild months of parties, then descend into a cycle of addiction maintenance and petty crime. I have seen it many times.

Once, a few years back, researching for a municipal project, I spent an entire day following a vagrant around the sidewalks and service lanes of Ottawa. I nicknamed the vagrant "Fred" for his thick pioneer sideburns and his orange, cheetah-print T-shirt. I believed, romantically perhaps, that the most accurate way to understand a city was through the migration of its homeless, the authentic inheritors of long-term urban development. Their movements reveal the dynamics of pedestrian movement, not only exposing the organic interplay of the main thoroughfares but also the side streets, alleys, parking lots, niches and store entrances, leading to where they'd come to rest. Or so my theory went. I had imagined a map of coloured arrows representing the homeless, like wind currents, pouring and bending around corners and intersections to illustrate the animate relationship of humans to city spaces. The living city. But all that resulted from my idea was a wasted morning idling by a Chinatown market stall, watching Fred pilfering a daikon radish and a package of double-A batteries. By lunch we had migrated to some haggard tree-lined square where Fred sold the batteries to three youths rolling a joint on the curb. They haggled him down with threats of violence. He gave the daikon to a man feeding bits of a sugar-dusted pastry to an aggressive seagull.

I was renting in a nearby street, so I often saw Fred in those same places afterward, plowing his route from morning to eve. He was no different from me, I thought. No different than the nine-to-fivers. Even with no obligations, he kept a routine: tethered to orbit, back and forth, back and forth, around and around and around. Rootless and meaningless. It scared the hell out of me. Had I been trapped forever in comparable habitual routes?

Georgia was in her troubled late teens then, on occasion grunting at me during our infrequent phone calls. Rebellion was in the air. A full state of it. I would get reports over voicemail from Sarah. *Georgia's done this; Georgia has done that.* There were cautions from both school and police. Her grades treaded water. Her hair turned blue. A fungal pong of weed hung on her clothes. I had suspicions she was a lesbian. Someone had seen her kissing that friend of hers. I asked her about it and she just told me I didn't understand, that "the world had changed and those tags didn't exist in hers." Which wasn't an answer.

My parental interventions were not welcome, neither from wife nor daughter. Georgia had become Sarah's domain, like the furniture.

And Georgia had perfected her cynical sneer at anything I said. "You have no soul," she said to me once in the flurry of sarcasm.

That was following the "big blowout." It had started from the renewal project on some downtown bank towers in Ottawa. The city had agreed to include some anti-homeless spikes in recessed areas where there would be exposed heating vents, like any of those numerous alleys where a homeless person could camp out and keep warm. The banks and businesses wanted to discourage loitering with the placing of bumpy, sharp spikes, and generally deter the homeless presence in the downtown core. In my world, it's called "defensive architecture." Loiter-proof benches with central armrests. Anti-skate lumps of bolted metal on plaza surfaces called "pig ears." I'd been hired as a consultant.

Affordable housing and homeless advocates were up in arms. Protests were almost immediately organized. A student group occupied the peripheries of bank properties with tents, tarps, sleeping bags, even mattresses, to reclaim improvised shelters before the changes were made. The "sleepover" began along Sparks Street near the Parliament Buildings. The protesters blocked entrances. Slogans and banners. There were irate editorials regarding dehumanization versus acceptable behaviour. The protest made the evening news. Which is how I heard about it.

I went over there. And there was my daughter, thick in the throng, chanting "Property is theft." That friend—Natalie was the name—was beside her holding a *When Did Poverty Become*

HUGO WALSER DURING HIS ILLNESS

a Crime? placard, their hands defiantly interlocked as part of a human chain. All this the focus of media outlets.

Bad press. Did I get any other kind? The City consultation was a good contract. I needed the money. I had debts. So, I strode into the camp and demanded that Georgia go home. She refused. You can imagine. I believe she called me a fascist. I denounced her as a reckless, stupid cherub. The words were quoted in the papers, to our mutual mortification. The media made the family connection and ate it up. Generational social justice or some nonsense. My fault, I know. I should not have gone over there.

Eventually, an order was radioed in. Georgia and a dozen of her conspirators were dragged away by the police. I did nothing to intervene and watched them being loaded into a police van. At the station, Georgia insisted she was homeless, then later offered her mother's name as her only legal guardian.

Sarah was on business in Montreal. She called me. "I can't get back tonight. Can you get her?"

"I tried."

"Where is she?"

"Still there. In a cell. She refuses to leave. *Solidarity.*"

Behind me in the tapas joint, a couple share sardines in oil, *Pimientos de Padrón* and a roquette parmesan salad with big glasses of red. They take photos of each other with their cellphones. The poses, the faces. The laughter. A mirror lines the wall where they sit, so the whole restaurant is doubled in its reflection. The couple are laughing in stereo, quite literally beside themselves. It is a tableau of happiness.

A waiter in a black vest walks past and sets another whiskey down on the bar next to me. And there I am, perched on a spindle-backed bar chair, my eyes studying the suspicious, weary look of my other lamp-lit face, like a late Rembrandt self-portrait. My wrinkled and scarred forehead, the puffy skin. The torn knee.

I have been a trial to others. My heart is garbage.

I slug the whiskey back and push some bills toward the bartender. Out the door, the air has cooled, the evening settling in. In another dozen minutes I round the corner and see the entrance to Hotel Colón ahead of me. Progressing across the fitted stone, I notice a man gesturing at me from the closest table of the hotel's patio. The sun is dropping a line of blinding yellow across the square, like the winched edge of a solar guillotine. The man's hand is raised, but backlit. The silhouette softens as I approach and the face becomes familiar. He is wearing a white linen blazer over a powder-blue dress shirt. He is raising his sunglasses. Thick fingers with a gold wedding band. A few more steps and I can see his features clearly. I am three feet away from Alan Norcock.

He is smiling. Arrogant, self-satisfied. He sips an espresso. He has the face of an astronaut, with the shaved crop of grey hair and chiselled chin. I wonder at that chin. Has it ever been struck? I'm not a small man myself. I could give his nose a sizeable, physical jolt. I might. But for now, I'm curious.

"What the fuck are you doing here?" I say with all its rich nuance.

"Hoping I might catch you, Hugo. It's been a long time."

I am tempted to say *Not long enough*, but there is something too John Wayne about it. Instead, I just stand here, shifting my weight onto the ball of my left foot to hide the pain of my right.

"Estrella told me where you were staying. I want to talk to you," he says. His open palm indicates an empty chair next to him. His eyes stray to my scuffed and torn trousers. He looks me over again with a baleful squint, as if he'd discovered something tremendous. Something fresh to mock. I step toward the table but won't sit down. My little victory.

"So, Estrella's turned me in, has she?"

"She's concerned."

I snort and look across the square, where groups are scattered on the stone steps leading to the old cathedral. A young couple are singing a Spanish song with a straw hat set out in front of them. The man, with a spray of dreadlocks, stares at the ground, strumming a battered acoustic guitar. The woman warbles high notes that penetrate the street noise.

"What do you want, Norcock?" I say, summoning a tone of annoyance.

He shrugs but it has no conviction. Because he wants the world. And sitting there with his tireless self-assurance and well-fed, pink cheeks, he thinks he can have it. I thought I could once too. I glance down the patio held in the sun's weakening rays. There's a couple with a small child at a nearby table who are looking our way. It might seem strange to them that I'm here, talking to this other man and refusing to sit down. They have gleaned our body language.

It's started now. The conflagration I had pictured for weeks, years really, is in front of me, and I have no fuel left to feed it.

A waiter approaches with a questioning air, trying to assess the meaning of our stiff postures. Norcock sees him and smiles. "Please," he says. "Another grappa. And a whiskey for my friend."

Once the waiter has nodded and returned to the café interior, Norcock repeats the invitation for me to join him. "It *is* whiskey, isn't it? I think I remember. But I've always been a student of the grape."

I hold my ground, my features blank, though dizzy and in pain. He sighs and leans forward, gesturing to where the waiter had stood.

"He thinks you're begging for change, Hugo. Sit down, for heaven's sake. What have you done to yourself?"

I tug on the chair and sit. The blood rushes to my head. It buzzes through the arteries of my weary feet. "I got swiped by a car," I say, an embellished, abridged summary of the evolving collapse of my physical being.

Norcock actually tsks at this. The sharp, salivary clucks reduce my tribulation to mere tiresomeness.

"I could have been killed!"

"The traffic here," he says. "You have to be careful."

Patronizing prick. I should smack him right here. Lay him out flat in his stylishly wrinkled blazer. But my head's spinning. The sweat is trickling down my spine and I need to catch my breath. Maybe with a few minutes to regain my energy I can put this whole farce to rest. Bring it to its proper conclusion. With a nod, the waiter delivers our drinks. Norcock drains his espresso and pushes the cup to the side of the table. He takes the delicate stem of the grappa glass between his thick fingers, holds it under his nose and twitches his nostrils like a rabbit in dewy clover. Then he looks me up and down again.

"The grapevine tells me you are preparing to do a very stupid thing," he says. "Do you really think it would be smart for you to stand up in front of your esteemed colleagues and make some kind of scene?"

"I think—"

"Please, let me finish what I want to say. My time is limited. I've spent this whole morning preparing a few words for you when I should have been polishing tomorrow's lecture. So, you see, you've done it to me again. Your appearances in my life have the uncanny capacity for siphoning off energy that could be put toward much more important things. You are like some collapsed star, Hugo, a black hole pulling away at the available light. What happened to you? I don't know. But you've been hell-bent on demolition for so many years now. A revenge scheme against the world. Everything you touch, you turn to bitterness. You find a fresh spring in the meadow and immediately pour your poison into it. Sure. Sure. You don't like what I have to say. You don't like my taste in architecture. At one time you were even articulate about it. I respected that. But you have gone way beyond rational discourse. Take a step back and look at yourself. You haven't had a commission for years. Don't you wonder why your columns have been dropped from the *Independent*? Don't look so shocked. Everyone knows this. No one wants to go near you. The vitriol. The name-calling. All the drama and strife. And now here you are, on a flight across the ocean, to do what? Barge into a conference uninvited for the sake of some public display?"

"I'm trying to defend my name."

"I am not your enemy."

"You don't say."

"You're deluded, Hugo. In fact, I want to help you."

I drain the scotch Norcock has bought for me, though I should have saved some to spit in his face.

"*Help* me?!"

"Do you really believe that I have been plotting against you? Think back. You attacked *me*, Hugo. We had disagreements, yes. It was there in the papers. The interviews. We played each other. For the public's attention. It was fun."

It's the last word I expect from his mouth.

"I thought you were enjoying it too," he adds. "The game of it. The hyperbole. The nudges and winks. Do you think I took it all that seriously?"

He puts the grappa to his lips and scans the square. The warbling couple have finished their finale of "What a Wonderful World." They are gathering loose change and bank notes from the bottom of a guitar case. Another busker stands by, shirtless, tattooed and dreadlocked too. What wonders is he capable of?

Norcock leans toward me. I look at his shimmering expression.

"Two apprentice monks come to a river . . ." he begins to say.

"A parable, Alan? Are we really at the parable stage?"

"It's a good one. I was going to start my talk with it tomorrow."

"Spare me, Confucius."

He concedes with a wave of his hand.

"I remember your labyrinths, Hugo. It's all you talked about those many years ago. The great metaphor. It's easy to take a few wrong turns," he says. "Mistakes can be made. In the end, they constitute a life. Perspective. It's about perspective. Take a step back. Adjust. Go forward differently. Change a little. Allow yourself that. Why is it so hard?"

I grunt and fold my arms.

"Forgive yourself," he adds.

Where am I?

The older neighbourhoods of Barcelona are confusing at the best of times, but it is late now, and dark, and I've been drinking all day with very little sleep. In fact, I've slept hardly at all these last days. Ten hours? Twelve? What counts as authentic sleep anyway? Something about REM or brainwaves, if I recall. I look down the narrow street, its metal shutters tarted with graffiti. SEXO POLICIA, someone has sprayed on the concrete wall beside some pipes. I have arrived beside a line of dumpsters to take a piss. Some service lane, though it's hard to tell in these medieval quarters. Paint a few signs and fit in some wide glass and it could be a shopfront. Instead, double-locked steel doors and vents count as frontage. I drift down the alley. Two men, boys really, chat in the shadow between street lamps. They are in kitchen whites, their aprons splashed with purple and yellow smears. Nearby, a service door has been propped open with a wedge of folded cardboard. A distilled rot of fish wafts from a compost bin but does not conceal the smell of the weed they are smoking. As I approach, they look me over and seem unconcerned, hardly pausing in their tête-à-tête. I am no threat, they've silently surmised.

"*Buenas noches*," I say, shuffling up to them. One of them sports a goatee, the other is dark-skinned, of North African descent perhaps. They nod, unhurried. It must be a quiet night inside, or dinner has reached a lull. I picture the rattle of coffee cups and spoons.

HUGO WALSER DURING HIS ILLNESS

Liqueurs and pastries with rosewater. It's tempting to find the street front to see what fare they have on offer.

"Can I smoke?" I ask. I gesture to their shared joint. They immediately begin to laugh and shake their heads. They pass the smoke between them, watching me.

"C'mon guys," I say in English. "Give a man a break. I'm in pain. I got hit by a car today." I point at my torn, scuffed suit and limp a few demonstrative steps as display of my plight. "Auto," I say and growl out an engine sound, slapping my palms together for impact. They mutter something in Spanish to each other, laughing, and pass the joint between them again.

"Okay?" the North African asks me, pointing to my leg. "You okay?"

I nod and shrug.

Pinched in his fingers, he holds out the last scrap of the joint.

"*Gracias.*" I take it and press my lips around the burning paper and weed. It's been years since I smoked anything, tobacco or otherwise. It took four stern warnings from my doctor to dissuade me from my pack-a-day of yore. But my lungs receive the smoke like an old lapdog, the warm weight shifting and settling into familiar contours.

My benefactors pat me on the shoulder. "Okay," they say in turn. "Okay, okay."

They wave at me as they slouch through the back entrance, pull the cardboard away and thump the door shut.

There is enough of the joint to draw a few more lungfuls of the pungent marijuana down my throat before the paper begins to taste like ash.

I flick it onto the cobbles.

There is something attached to my shoe.

Somewhere along the way, I've stepped in dogshit.

I look up and down the passage, uncertain which direction I've come from. Where is north or south? Which way to go?

193

Unverifiability.

The secret to a labyrinth is its uniformity, the illusion of movement coupled with the conviction of stasis. The mind is lulled by dull paths and ninety-degree turns. The heart races for the same reason. You believe you're moving because nothing argues that you aren't. You keep going because if you stop you might get lost. In suburbs and prisons, we are reassured by homogeneity. It is the source of our panic too. Removed from the source of our wanderings, we are denied the sight of our goal. Inside, we are denied escape. Some have argued labyrinths are sacred spaces, and to walk them is a form of meditation. These Catalan back alleys and side streets, though quaint, reiterate the labyrinthine through their monotony. With their metal shutters lowered, in the dim street lights, the routes look identical to visitors. Bereft of grid patterns, with few right-angle turns, it is nearly impossible to plot any organized headway.

Or it might just be the weed.

Ha ha.

Ha ha ha ha ha.

By the port, there are raucous shouts along the promenade. A group of five tourists—French, I think—are stumbling up the wide *ronda*, wheeling around each other, dashing forward and back in thievish scurries, like a band of raccoons. They've found some sturdy cardboard box and are kicking it around in an improvised, drunken game of footie. Legs splayed, I squat low by a palm trunk and bounce with my weight on my knees. My arms are out, hands spread. They spot me and laugh, forming a line of forward positions, advancing on me with concentration.

The box is walloped around between them with chaotic punts. The two women watch. They shout encouragement with high-pitched squeals. One of the men, faking a pass, boots the box directly at me. I get my palm on it.

I boot it back.

The cardboard is knocked erratically about for a few more seconds. There is a goal, though no posts can truly confirm this achievement. But we are all exultant, arms raised and voices roaring into the night air.

"Goal!" "Barcelona!" "Goal!"

Just as quickly they are gone, these revellers, waving at me, their voices threading up past the Columbus statue toward La Rambla and into the night.

I stumble along past the old Customs House to Port Vell's Olympic renovations. The last time I was here, a replica of *Santa Maria* was moored by the wharf. Now a marina drawbridge, the Rambla del Mar, crosses the harbour, with two retracting decks, like the gull-wing doors of a DeLorean. The bridge is slick and modern, the walkway's undulating widths add visual drama to an otherwise mundane conveyance.

I am doing it again.

The night is funny. I find it quite funny. "Goal!" I am giggling and laughing on a park bench, in the middle of the night, thinking too of Norcock. How silly he is, that studious gravity, that false indifference. I'm finding it very funny and can't stop laughing at the whole thing.

Two men in oily blue overalls stride past, and though I try to stop laughing, the idea of stopping also seems extremely funny. I consider telling the men they are wearing blue overalls, or even telling them I like their blue overalls, which is funny and I chuckle to myself. "*Sexo Policia,*" I say out loud. I look down the boardwalk to see if they heard me, but the men are far away now, almost out of sight.

I will say it to the next people I see.

That will be funny.

I pull my cellphone from my pocket. I should call someone. I'll call Georgia. It must be morning in Korea. What do they eat for breakfast? I'll call her and ask her how she's doing. *How are you?* I'll say. *I'm in Barcelona. What are you eating for breakfast?*

But my cell's security code isn't working. I try it three times, tapping out the numbers with the same result. I'm confused. My head is not clear. I reverse the numbers. The phone is dead in my hand. The battery is dead. The screen flashes a little heart with an X crossed through it and then goes blank.

The pleasure boats are lined up at their moorings. I walk along the pier and read the names of the boats.

"*Brezza Estiva.*" "*Gabrijela.*" "*Utferdstrang.*"

Summer families from Italy, Norway, Germany and Croatia.

We learned how to sail, Sarah and I. Once. It was a brief passion of ours. We even talked of buying a boat, but it came to nothing.

Very pleasant here, the inner harbour arrayed with ordered piers, like the street grids of cities.

It is the simplest, logical thing: space and access.

I can hear the banging of steel across at the dockyards, but otherwise it's very quiet. The prows dip and lift in the jewelled water. The masts and rigging, with their lowered sails, cut a fine picture against the lights of El Raval.

Part 3
SARAH TRIMBLE
IN THE WILDERNESS

25

WHAT WOULD BE NICE is if they had a decent coffee place on the drive up here. It wouldn't be hard. Worth trying. An old-timey sign with an attractive graphic of a steaming coffee cup. Warm interior. Potted plants or something. Ice cream once the summer arrives, some patio umbrellas out front.

Must be a herd of cottagers who would die for something like that.

Instead, greasy donuts and dirty gas stations.

Would be nice if they could pave these roads properly too. Or leave some decent signage prior to the exits, so you're not constantly jamming on the brake pedal at the last minute, in danger of getting back-ended or pitching into a ditch.

Potholes, crumbling shoulders. The pavement is garbage. Where's the infrastructure?

I'll have to write a letter of complaint. I'm a taxpayer etc. Blown tire fib maybe. Danger of injury or death, threats of litigation. Costs. Wear and tear on the vehicle etc. Property values affected. This is certainly no way to stage a sale, with a future of a daily jolting commute.

What would be nice is if it stopped raining.

I've got the wipers at full blast, slapping back and forth through the Biblical deluge bucketing into my windshield. I need a shovel rather than wiper blades. I had to pull over for a few minutes at the 307 turnoff. Terrifying. Couldn't see the median. Tires touching rumble strips. Like driving through a car wash without soap. I should've turned back. Should've. Stupid day. But my schedule's limited. I've got a meeting on Friday, then something in Toronto this weekend and my creditors have been calling for . . . what is it they are calling for?

Guidance?

Clarity?

I'll just drive up and take a look. A quick glance around. Home by dinner. No harm.

Had breakfast, at least. Get my stomach into gear to work through the calories. What I like to do now is mix stuff. A bit of bran with yogourt for the brain and bowels. Some walnuts. Dried apricots. Cranberries. Surprises the taste buds. Dates and almonds. Sweet, soft, crunchy. I bolted it down and tried to get on the road in a sweet spot between morning rush hour and those who wait to avoid morning rush hour. A little window there. Like how it's good at Starbucks a few minutes before nine. When everyone's left empty seats to get to work. I've made a science of not standing in line. Waiting is exhausting.

I shouldn't remember this drive. It's been years and years and I've only made the effort a few times. And not to stay; only a hurried look to confirm the cabin is still intact. It's got its charms. A dramatic landscape. Granite rock-cuts and Group of Seven pines, little sudden lakes glimpsed through valley drops. I'll make a note of that. I'll showcase it in the telling. "Scenic, country escape." Get their minds off the pavement as they drive this empty highway.

Another note: bring clients in summer.

Better: October when the leaves are an autumnal, crimson-bronze mosaic. *Ooh, so beautiful.* Find a perfect day. A crisp, blue sky and gentle breeze. Sells itself.

But I wonder what the cabin looks like now. More than a few years. I'd forgotten the property, actually. Easy to forget, tucked away up there in the woods, at the end of a difficult road and a short hike. I've been told the road is better now. Widened and resurfaced several times. Layers of repair. The small lake at the bottom has attracted cottagers these past decades. There's been some development, though the cabin is useless where it is, too far up the mountain and too rustic for a comfortable weekend stay at the lake. Leave it to my relatives to build on a steep hill instead of grabbing something lakeside that could sell considerably higher years later. Maybe that's why I've forgotten the place existed. Never really mine anyway. My aunt and uncle owned it. Kathleen and Gerry. They even had their names wood-burned into a square of cedar, then lacquered and nailed above the door, as if anyone was ever likely to pass by and need to know the names of the owners. But when Aunt Kathleen died, predeceased by Gerry, and there was no one else, the property was released into my name, their only living relative. I remember getting the notification in the mail, suspicious of the attorney's stamp. I tore the envelope open, bracing for a lawsuit. Instead, I said to Hugo, "I've inherited property!" He looked at me with his own suspicion, hearing the sarcasm in my voice.

Laughing at me. "You have an Uncle Gerry and Aunt Kathleen?" Correcting him: "Had."

I never talk about family, parents, all that. The *past* etc. Hugo, my ex-husband, would ask occasionally. But it was not a point of discussion on my part and he didn't press me. *Don't press me*: he learned my look for that. I'm told I have several looks, many subtexts. I could fill the room with cold air by disliking something. One way of handling indecision: unpredictability. My sales have always been good.

The "property" is a few acres of wood lot and a one-room cabin of pine logs and barn boards built on a rise not quite a kilometre above Lac Henri. Legend has it my aunt and uncle purchased it from a conscientious objector in the late forties. What he probably objected to was getting mortared in the South Pacific, from what I understand. So, he'd followed the Adirondack ridges to the Laurentians and slipped across the New York–Quebec border one night and managed to buy the land with the help of a fake birth certificate and a no-questions-asked supply of cash. The municipality was happy to sell it; he was happy to pay their inflated price. That kind of mutual concord clears a lot of paths in my business. He'd come from a family of moonshiners and Appalachian trappers and knew a thing or two about living off the land, clearing trees and keeping his head down. The story dries up there. How the place ended in my relatives' possession, I don't know.

I went there when I was a child. Three, four summers. For what? What do I remember? Mosquitos. The forest path to the lake. My friend Daniel and I spent an evening salting a slug in a plastic cup, then torturing it over the fire. Maybe there's no magic in childhood, just cruelty disguised as boredom. At the end of my teens, I stopped my visits and never went back. Uncle Gerry rented it each summer to god knows who would need it—serial killers or recluse alcoholics or suicidal poets—until just a few years before he died. The lawyer told me he'd gone peacefully in his sleep, but I'd missed the funeral by two years. I had lost touch with all of them. Gerry and Kathleen and little Danny. I was busy with clients and the housing boom. At the time it was 24/7 for me. If I blinked, I'd lose a thousand dollars.

In the heavy rain, the twists and turns are daunting smears of progress. I jam the ball of my foot down on the brake pedal as a truck's high headlights kaleidoscope my view. Shattered gems of glare. I actually put on my seatbelt. Hate them, but. Had the shop disengage the warning light. Clicking the thing into the belt, I lose track of the centre line and thunder over rumble strips again. Fuck. Around yet another bend there's a roadside rest stop and I pull in, not to eat any disgusting highway food, but for a break from the downpour. No one around anyway. A fluorescent strip light fills the interior of a chip truck but there's nobody there. *Onions Ring and Pop: $2.50* says a misspelled, handwritten poster in the sliding service window. Three picnic tables under collapsed patio umbrellas attest to what should be a bustling Sunday trade of local potatoes in lethally hot grease. It's not a day for overweight cottagers. Unless they are building an ark. Maybe Noah was just building some picnic tables and the project got out of control.

Something sad about a picnic table in the rain.

This has to let up at some point.

Makes me wonder what kind of shape the cabin might be in. Abandoned for those many years. Who knows how much abuse it's taken from big old Time. Or Gerry's anti-social tenants. The elements. Rain and snow and wildlife.

Preparing myself for: rotting wood, a collapsed roof, infested crawlspaces. Raccoons and swarms of squirrels. Bird-shit carpet. I'm ready to write the whole thing off, sell the land for firewood. Won't go below fifteen, but I'll ask for twenty thousand. Even start at forty, fight for fifteen. I can finesse this.

Cozy cabin on hiking trail, with private access to lakeshore.

Idyllic private location on 1.8 acres of matured trees.

Hillside oasis.

Beautiful.

Better to give the place a name. Give the dump some posh. Push another few grand into the price. *Warburton Regency Estate?* Too much. *Warburton Acres.* Well, there's barely two acres, but it's close to plural. Canadiana instead of British snobbery?

Warburton Beaver Lodge?

No.

Okay: *Warburton Acres Lodge: Ninety years young with private access to secluded lake. This charming rustic log cottage is perfect for owners who love to swim, hike, listen to the resident loons, sit by an original cut-fieldstone fireplace and soak in a claw-foot bathtub in the midst of a peaceful six-hundred-acre hardwood forest. Hillside oasis!*

Exclamation mark?

Exclamation mark.

The description is inviting enough. And technically true. Well, no fireplace but an old woodstove. Doesn't sound terrifying at all. *I almost want to buy it.* But better add *within forty-five-minute drive to Ottawa.*

Better offer the chance of escape.

I will also need to find a claw-foot bathtub. And some charm.

But I'm getting ahead of myself.

How I ended up on the road driving north into western Quebec, just south of the Laurentian Mountains, desperate for money, hoping to assess and prepare an abandoned forest cabin for a quick sale, isn't a complicated story. Even if you gather up all the complicated threads of bad investments, it comes down to the combination of dumb trust and a bent investor. A classic Ponzi scheme, actually. Threw a whole lot of my money, a *lot* of savings, into a pot with a big hole in it, though I kept being told there was something significant cooking. Not too complicated after all. The scoundrel Trevor Brent, my "investment advisor" came on strong with talk of percentages, high returns and minimum risk. When I asked for quarterly reports, he gave me charts and showed me numbers. He even cautioned me to go slow at times, wait a bit and keep some money back. Did I keep some back? Not really. Not much. Then two weeks ago, I got the call from Douglas, my associate at the realtors, sounding deathly and weird. Telling me: "I've got bad news." Douglas had recommended Brent. They'd gone to school together. He cited consistent profits. So, we both threw money at Brent.

And Brent fucked us.

Never trust someone with two first names.

"I thought you'd gone to school with him?" I said to Douglas, still in disbelief. As if that would guarantee some ethical failsafe.

Douglas saying: "I did. High school. It was a long time ago."

A long time ago. Long enough for anything, or nothing, Douglas seemed to imply. Long enough to chuck simple decency. Long enough for a person to change into a greedy, life-destroying, shit-headed, shit-for-a-soul piece of shit.

The money was gone. And so was Brent. As soon as the Ponzi scheme started to show its holes, he had slithered through one of them. His message centre had filled up. His office cleared out. Police went around to his condo and learned it had been sold years ago, the money pulled from a now-closed account. They tracked his address to an extended-stay hotel on Cooper Street, where he'd lived for the past nine months, but he was gone from there also, with three outstanding months left on the year lease. He'd already prepared to be a ghost if he needed to.

"We'll catch him," the police told me. "He's sloppy."

I'd kill for that coffee right now. I've been good. I've cut the tobacco forever, but some caffeine would help. Staring at the service window of the chip truck, hoping for movement. Someone in there? Please see me out here, stranded in the rain. And put a pot on!

Lots of land. Satellite town of the future. With the right development. What they need is an attraction, a getaway, like a winery. The climate and soil are garbage for grapes though. Maybe a spa. A yoga centre in the woods. *Serenity on the Canadian Shield.* Hmm. Pictures of an open-concept pavilion with jigsaw white-pine flooring, fit and happy twenty-somethings blissing out in lotus position on multi-coloured mats while evergreens thrive in the background. That hot Bikram stuff in the winter would draw. Yes. Yes, it would.

Winter tranquility.

You could build a little town around the concept. This is destination stuff. These static properties. Stuff you could buy and resell. Hotcakes, if the timing's right. I have to remember I'm still good at this. I may have been taken by a number-crunching weasel named Trevor Brent but I'm still good at *this.* I check my cellphone but of course there's no service in this godforsaken wilderness.

Hugo must never hear about Trevor and my great financial mess. Oh, how he'd love to rub it in. I can see his face now, all self-satisfied and superior and mock-exasperated with concern. With "You should have checked this guy out a little" and "Why did you invest so much?" With "What can I do to help?" Hugo, who thinks he's the master of finance even after his wild schemes and fuck-ups and mansplaining clarifications. He won't hear a thing about any of this if I can help it. Since our divorce, we have successfully tiptoed around sharing anything of real significance in our lives, while gaining points through the art of humble brags. It's chess by voicemail. "Hugo. Need to be in Boston for some brownstone sales. Can you check on Georgia?" I'd say, implying bountiful dollar signs in my accounts. Hugo grunting, "Must be off to Rio for an article," blithely evoking exquisite locations with lavish perks. We were competitive, no doubt. We didn't want to be equal, but better. Better than the other firms; better than each other. We bickered. We got petty. We amassed nitty details. And when Hugo's façade started to slip and he got desperate, he didn't ask for help. He just made a bigger mess.

Almost from the moment I met him, Hugo talked big. It was a vocation. He even got in a fist fight over me in a crap bar in Montreal, if I recall. I was their high priestess in a ceremony of male testosterone. The Aztecs sacrificed virgins to appease the gods. Modern man sacrifices his dignity.

Such high promise. We worked though. *I* worked. As he made his way through final courses of architecture school, I interviewed at some big realtors in Montreal. They were impressed by my bombast over room composition and aesthetic proportion, the art-speak of property turnover. I'd read enough of those books at the Centre for Architecture—my part-time job while studying design at LaSalle—to raise the discourse above bedroom numbers and nice views. Sure, the engineer report assures a client, but it's the access-to-sunlight that signs the papers. Hugo and I were red-hot with plans those first lightning years. I finished my articling period and joined a real estate agency. Once graduated (barely), Hugo worked on designs at a gateway firm, a few conventional office towers mostly, while pursuing private commissions for wealthy acquaintances he'd met in school. He extended bedrooms and remodelled family areas, all the while handing out business cards for his own future firm. That didn't sit well with his employers. Once they'd got wind of it, he was *persona non grata* and promptly invited to box up his personal belongings on St. Marc.

He didn't blink. We were throwing shit at the walls and some of it stuck. Wasn't long before he was co-designing a major renovation of a river-view embassy in Ottawa's Rockcliffe Park. Meanwhile, back in Montreal, I had assisted in the turnover of a few houses in NDG, with decent percentages, and the higher-ups considered giving me a Westmount.

I remember that. The day before the showing, I dropped fifteen hundred on a Dolce & Gabbana stretch-wool jacket and pants. It was sleek. I looked like a knife with peak lapels and four-button cuffs. I rented a silver BMW for its spectacle. Its smell of success.

The front grill filleted the sunlight down Edgehill Road's stately trees. Joseph was waiting for me in the driveway. A partner in the realty firm, he'd been nervous about the collective decision to "let me have a go" at this one. It was a beautiful four-bedroom residence sitting on a 547-square-metre lot but overpriced at three million. Listed all summer, they wanted it sold before October or they'd have to drop the price. Letting it sit there all winter sent out an unpleasant signal. Dropping the price, even worse. Joseph agreed to let me try the sale, but would step in if needed, which meant he would find *something* to step in about. I knew his kind. He'd find a way to take the credit. If I got something to grow, he'd rake around the dirt so everyone could see the lines he made. But I knew he couldn't move this house. He was tired and had mumbled through the same patter for too many months, too many years.

He was stuck on the wrong details. Rumpled suits. Saying the client's name too often; pushing the process too quickly.

But he was happy to hold onto the leases so he could co-sign with his ridiculous Bic roller.

Joseph checked his watch while I put the car into park.

"Yes, I'm on fucking time," I grunted to myself as I plucked the portfolio from the passenger seat. We had fifteen minutes before the client arrived.

Joseph handed me the keys. We started a walk-through.

I'd studied the house meticulously through the previous week, from its side-entrance columned porch to the chef's kitchen lined with glass-panelled cabinetry. The buyer's name was Barry Monclerc. I'd met him a few weeks prior to determine his house range, show him some options and go through some listing sheets. There was very little information available about Barry himself, online or anywhere. Some property development connections. Hints of importing through consortiums. I would have liked to know more, what personality to sell to, what features to spotlight.

While we waited for him, Joseph settled into another unsolicited tutorial on property sales.

"If you're happy drawing a paycheque, or commission, it could take up to two years to start making money," he was rabbiting on. "Really depends where you are in your life. I know a guy, did only residential work. He was an animal: first in the office at seven every day, way ahead of the curve, pulling salary and getting a licence, which will take a few months if you're full-time at it. Hardest things of working on all these deals is prospecting, finding more deals or you're dried up. The legends, the few guys in the real estate market who are legends, they just keep pumping it out . . ."

I was putting little effort into understanding the point.

"Fuck, there he is," Joseph said.

Outside the sink window, a navy-blue KIA had parked flush beside my car on the double drive. Barry Monclerc, with a rugby-sized chest, dressed in a golf shirt, chinos and aviation shades, surfaced and strode along the manicured stone path toward the main entrance.

Joseph was prancing into the vestibule.

"Joseph," I warned before he reached the door. He looked at me. "I thought *I* was doing this."

He raised his hands in mock surrender and then flourished them, with a sneer, at the entrance. I tugged on the door handle. The frame separated from the weather-stripping in a gentle suck of air.

"Hello Barry. Welcome to Westmount," I said, extending my hand. "You remember Joseph, my associate?" They nodded heads and shook hands.

Joseph said, "You're early."

"Is he?" I said, breezy and skeptical. Thanks, Joseph. Thanks for chiding our client for schedule mismanagement. Thanks for proposing we're inconvenienced. Thanks for suggesting we're checking, or even care about, the time. And thanks for wearing your fat, mismatched tie two inches too ridiculously long.

Barry gestured to the BMW. "Your rental is nicer than mine," he said to me.

"Oh, that," I laughed. "All they had left in the lot."

Smiling.

"Do you know the neighbourhood?" I asked. He knew very little. So, I ran down a short history of Westmount, noting its French colony origins in the mid-seventeenth century. "Not far from here there's a house from that period: Hurtubise House. A fifteen-minute walk from here," I said. "It was built in 1739. You should have a look if you get a chance. It's very beautiful. Three storeys, gable roof, two-foot-thick stone walls. The windows are framed by flat stones, very rare in those days. The family must have been very wealthy. They set an example for the neighbourhood. You could say it all started with them."

Joseph furrowed his brows at me, doubtless wondering why I was talking up a property we weren't standing in and couldn't sell. But you don't just sell the house, you sell the neighbourhood. Not just conveniences and location, but history. This place had pedigree and Barry was going to know about it. I was not just inviting him to take possession of herringbone flooring and bay windows but also to inherit his rightful place in a long tradition of affluent, proud pioneers.

In any case, something worked. After an inspection and engineer's report, and discussions over a few finer points with the listing agent, Barry signed for ownership under the recessed skylight of the private study.

That night I stumbled through the door of the walk-up near the Atwater Market. Hugo and I were still renting, eager to own but without solving the anxious question of where we meant to settle. I wanted to stay near the better housing markets. This was years before the Vancouver/Toronto bubble and though Montreal's prices were low, properties were moving steadily. But Hugo was getting more commissions in Ottawa. After many years of humble office buildings, the government was finally investing in architecture worthy of a capital.

"I sold it!" I shouted as I tossed the BMW keys onto the hall table. Hugo's head appeared from the kitchen door at the far end of the hall.

"The Westmount?"

"Three. Million. Dollars," I said, dancing toward him, throwing my hips side to side until I crashed into his arms.

"We should celebrate."

I pulled him hard against my pelvis and plunged a victory kiss into his open lips like a clumsy diver cannonballing a swimming hole. I was hungry not only for food. Triumph had fuelled my sex drive. When I get something, I want everything.

26

THE RAIN IS STILL viciously falling. Monsoon deluge. The field next to the parking lot is more pool than earth. If you tried walking through it, they'd never find you. I should have stayed in the city. I'm not even sure if I'll find the cabin now. It's probably all changed. A few trees here, a bend in the road there. Easy to get lost or miss it. I'll wait a few more minutes and then I'll head back into town, have a glass of wine and decompress. If there was any service up here, I'd click and scroll and swipe. The icons on my phone swarm and glower. There's a lot of stuff I should uninstall. But I'm a sucker for the bait; algorithms can't keep up with me. Though when was the last time a dating site did me any good? Another useless hobby.

Two years ago, someone in my running club told me about an app that identifies birdsong. I downloaded it onto my phone and then forgot about it for weeks. But out on a run along the canal, I had stopped to get my breath. The trees were raucous with song. How many birds were up there? Sounded like thousands. I held my phone in the air. Ping. The names started coming. Red-winged blackbird. House sparrow. White-throated sparrow. Northern cardinal. Gray catbird. Dark-eyed junco. American goldfinch. Chestnut-sided warbler. In just one hour in September, I identified twenty-three types. My phone did, anyway. It was all twittery static to me. But it got addictive, collecting names and replaying the songs and flight calls from an archive.

Where do birds hide in this rain?

Perhaps, when I get back, there'll be a call regarding Trevor Brent, dragged out of some narco party, held in some squalid interrogation room while the police confirm his identity and charge the little fucker with money laundering etc. There's no hope of getting any of my invested money back, but there'll be some justice in watching him squirm in court. I wonder how many years he'd get. The police said the amount of money he stole was "significant." My personal nest egg was over one hundred and twenty thousand. A pittance for some but an achievement after the disaster Hugo dragged us through.

Is this why he's on my mind lately?

We had moved to Ottawa. The property market in Montreal was a mess. Volatile and unreliable. Whole retail sections of Sainte-Catherine were closing down. Post-Lévesque separation fears still lingered and businesses were nervous about investing in Quebec. So, people also moved but with no one buying. We went with the current. Hugo and I agreed Ottawa was temporary. He would establish himself and then pull in some international commissions. Build in Spain or Brazil or Indonesia, wherever the work went. The Old World, the New World, it didn't matter. Somewhere else. We agreed I'd develop my portfolio, maybe work toward my broker certificate, take the provincial exams etc. Meanwhile, we travelled, sometimes for pleasure, sometimes to inspect a client's proposed office plan or a memorial pavilion. France, Germany, India, the States. I was eyeing some hires with Sotheby's International Realty, taking notes on the market. For those plum positions you have to know your geography too. And I wanted it.

After a few more uninteresting commissions, Hugo got his break on a new municipal art gallery in Trois Rivières. He convinced the gallery board, trustees and developer with whimsical line drawings. He argued for structural clarity. He proposed long, uninterrupted, low-ceilinged rooms with indirect skylights and sunken seating areas where Zen-like gravel was pooled around contemplative study areas. There was a glass curtain façade designed to envelope the foyer, which could double as an events space. The plan beat out five other firms. And the trustees insisted Hugo was named chief architect on the project. He threw himself into the planning with fanatical energy, working out endless discrepancies, reshaping technical challenges, consulting with contractors and engineers. Did he sleep? I don't remember. Did I? We were both crazy to succeed. We drifted around each other with our files and summaries, our property descriptions and blueprints, our lists of building materials and inventory.

We'd been married barely two years.

When I learned I was pregnant, I sprung the fact on Hugo as if it was no news at all.

"Anyway, it's the wrong time," I said, dropping some tenderloins into the cast iron as the oil was just starting to smoke.

He'd popped in for dinner before a meeting with a manufacturer who was trying to sell him on pre-treated zinc cladding. Hugo sat at the table, chin in palms, weighing our unwanted discussion, uncomfortably trying to not look at the clock. My pregnancy test with its terrifying double pink lines lay on a napkin in front of him, evidence that one of Hugo's inconsiderate sperm successfully nudged a path up my uterus to plant its chromosome-ridden semen into my ovum. There should have been precautions. We did not take them. So, I told him we'd need to do something now. But what? He'd said something as unexceptional as "Oh, okay" when I'd given him the news. He'd put his briefcase down; he'd unbuttoned his blazer and poured himself a glass of wine. He was rolling the bowl between the fingers of both his hands as he digested my monologue regarding children and careers.

Me, rambling: "We've never even talked about this before. Maybe we should have talked about it, the idea, the idea anyway, but I thought we were agreed we'd wait. Or wouldn't. It didn't get discussed, right? Is a wait, a time for a pause, good? I'm in the middle of a housing frenzy right now. The tech boom and all these geeks with money to burn. There's a stream of fresh and desperate clients gnawing at the listings, Hugo. I'm juggling offers. I've got three deals in escrow at the moment and just waiting on the percentages. The market's going to flatten. It can't last. I've got great work, we're busy, making money, buying our own house ... it just doesn't make sense to loosen a wheel when everything is rolling along so nicely."

He was letting me talk. Rare for him. I turned the steaks over. The new side of flesh hissed into the hot metal.

Hugo saying: "Can we talk this over later?"

"But we're talking about it," I said. He was letting me talk because if he actually started to talk, offering full opinions on the subject, it would constitute a conversation and we'd be "talking," something he didn't want to happen right now. According to this logic we were outside the fringes of dialogue, uncommitted still. We were near the field of play, certainly, but still milling about, tying our shoelaces, stretching our legs and sizing up the other competitor before the run.

I added sprigs of rosemary and a clove of garlic to the cast iron and turned the steaks once more with the tongs.

"I've got twenty minutes," Hugo warned.

"This is important."

"Exactly. Do we need to do this now?"

"Can't you cancel your meeting?"

"He's flown from New Jersey, Sarah."

I pressed my fingertips into the beef to check the cook. The surface had charred nicely, but the inside was a guess. What you want is that perfect balance of resistance and tenderness.

"Do you want a baby?" I said without looking at him.

"We hadn't planned on it."

"Not what I was asking."

I turned around and leaned back against the counter. I looked him over, that husband of mine, and wondered maybe not for the first time about the unconditional love we'd pledged to each other in front of churchgoers, drunken friends and important colleagues. I needed honesty. Crouched above the toilet, peeing on the absorbent strip that morning, I'd consciously willed a negative result, it's true. I did not want a baby with attendant baby poop, baby crying, baby carriages and further baby luggage-train at this point in my career, but when the two pink lines conspired against me, my heart starting to armlock my head. What I realized I needed most of all at that very moment was a considerate opinion. Support and information. From my husband. At this windy crossroads, in good times and bad, as they say, I was dying to know if my life's partner thought about this, and if so, would he care to share some of this very thinking.

"Is this the right time?" Hugo said. He filled his glass again.

"For what? The baby or the discussion?"

"Maybe both."

I lifted the bottle by the neck and took a swig directly from it, a couple of full gulps, and set it down.

"Should you be doing that?" Hugo said.

"What does it matter?" I said, remembering the steaks, which were scorched now beside the smoking rosemary and blackened garlic. I pinched one tenderloin between the metal tongs, carried it to the table and dropped it on Hugo's lap. He shouted some obscenities and knocked it to the floor, a greasy stain left on the ruined fabric of his Canali trousers.

"Enjoy your dinner."

I signal a left turn and the tires bump off the highway's blacktop onto a cracked, grey version of the same, a side road once paved but never maintained, low on the list of this municipality's priorities, if ever there at all. The road immediately begins an ascending slope into the forest, lined by wire fences and thick green clover. Going by guess now. Used to be a barn across from the turnoff. Used to be a sign. But the distance seems right, the slope seems right, and I'm getting impatient. When the heavy rain finally let up back at the empty rest stop, I eased the wheels toward the highway, pointing them south, then changed my mind, continued on, duped by a hopeful disruption of cloud cover. The showers have renewed their energy, slashing down in a mix of water and wind. Over the next hump of the road, the broken paving disappears altogether and becomes wet mud, gloopy but still driveable from the compression of decades of logging trucks and fishing trips. It's also wider than I remembered, though ridden with teeth-chattering washboards every hundred feet. Absolute garbage. I'll need to address this, possibly pop for a few truckloads of raked gravel in the roughest places before any showing. Draw attention to the trees and sky. The Laurentians are ancient, some of the oldest mountains in the world, worn down and gradual, the opposite of the dramatic Himalayas, those infants of geology. I drive over each gradient, dipping into mini valleys, keeping to the centre, through kilometres of hardwood, wipers on high, pushing the cloudburst back and forth out of my view. Every few minutes, there's a sign, usually handmade, nailed to a tree beside the merest hint of a forest road. *No Trespassing.* One is store-bought, the front silhouette of a car crossed out in red. Someone's shot at it a few times over the years, dinted with bullet marks. As I drive farther, I'm fighting a growing sense of dread: that the property is worthless, that I'll have trouble even giving it away unless I can find a survivalist whose looking for a site to raise a garrison when the government comes for their tax money.

It's just at this point when (flash) a deer appears over the next rise, twists its neck to identify the source of this unexpected disturbance in the rain-soaked woods, and (zing) a split-second after my appearance, throws its limber, beautiful, muscular form, with a graceful leap through the air, into the path of my oncoming car.

They do say these things are felt in slow motion. The brain slowing reality down. A crawl through the terrifying selections of memory. I have a nanosecond to jam on the brake and watch the deer's tufted tail and hind quarters clear some brush and disappear (swish) unhurt into the woods on the opposite side of the road. The car jumps to the right, slides a little, but avoids disaster as the tires gather and ride a ridge of softened earth chunky enough to drag my trajectory to a halt.

Thunk.

Shit.

Hands clutch the steering wheel; my silver bracelets have jangled down my arm, resting near my elbows. Everything sits still, as if I'd slipped through a rift in time where nothing has yet happened or will. I look toward the entry point of the deer's escape into the forest to confirm it was not some imagined being I'd conjured from my boredom. But it's long gone, confused as I am of the chance encounter.

The rain hangs thick in the light like a heavy drape.

My wipers bang back and forth, clearing a brief view, in one-second intervals, of the saturated ditch kissing my front bumper.

Fuck.

Without thinking, I put the gears in reverse and ease down on the accelerator. It's not much of a ditch. I'm not technically *in* it, just shoved up against clumps of displaced clover that fill a hollow on the roadside. But there's mud, and the tires have plowed deep into it during my sudden deceleration. I push the gas. One of the tires starts to spin and spit globs of brown earth into the air. Don't want to start digging a hole, do I? I rock my body in my seat, hoping to encourage grab. The engine strains.

But I chance a serious push on the gas and the wheels do dig in, rolling the car backwards.

Okay. This is good.

I twist my head from side to side, checking to affirm my reclaimed and rightful location in the centre of the road. Out through my right, rain-filled window, I note the muddy troughs excavated by my front wheels. When I shift again into drive, the engine whirrs, its tone a slightly lower register, reassuringly robust for all the water and trauma I've exposed it to. This should be great. I'm certainly giving thanks in the briefest way, my relief already transforming into a home investment story at some future convention-drinks session.

Except my foot is still on the brake and the car seems to be moving.

No, not the car. The road. Or something.

In the last few seconds, the old post I'd faced near the ditch has inched past my rear-view and repositioned itself into being an object in my *front* windshield. The wire fence is travelling forward very slowly, an automated walkway speed, carrying the trees and grass with it. Plus, I'm turning. I've rotated so I'm no longer pointed in the much-desired direction I'd intended to continue on but am now back to an angle and still revolving. But that's not quite right either. Looking out the window, I can confirm it's the car that is sliding back-sideward toward the ditch again, though I'm also able to determine that the ditch is now part of the road, or more accurately, the road has deteriorated into a fast-growing river. Panicked, I look to see a few feet of brown water rushing along the tire rims and I realize that I am experiencing a flash flood.

The car is sliding sideways, buoyed and weightless. And no matter how many times I turn the steering wheel or push at the brakes, I am no longer in control of my course.

An involuntary high-pitched grunt rises from my throat, much like how a dog might indicate stress, as the left side of the car then rises and dips and the whole chassis wiggles over several feet in a fluid motion, a roller coaster readying for a significant "thrill" for the ticket holder.

I'm not thrilled.

Not very much.

Instead, I'm feeling disordered and uneasy and actually downright ill with fear as the car rocks to a standstill against the former right bank of the shallow ditch that is maintaining its recognizable shape only with the aid of a granite outcrop now anchoring the increasingly undefined distinction between road and waterway.

What do you do while trapped in a vehicle during a flash flood? I'm pretty sure there's sage advice in a manual somewhere. It might even be a common student drill in one of those regions prone to this form of disaster. Along the Red River maybe, or mountainous areas of India. As I examine, with alarmed attention, the chutes of water jetting across my driver's window, I try to recall the most prudent option in this fucked-up situation. It's there in one of those cute bathroom readers I'm always loathe to include in a staging. Those emergency situation booklets, with for-and-against research by experts. Answers being either "trust your instincts" or just as likely "don't follow your instincts." There is a certain variety of bear you should play dead with, for example, if you want to survive an encounter in the woods. But there is another variety you must "make yourself big" with, poke in the eye or punch in the nose. The likelihood of remembering which is which in the moment of crisis (I think the species is black versus brown) is pretty low unless you are a specialized forest ranger with steely calm.

I'm balancing two such options and fate is not very generous with time. Mainly, do I stay in the car or get out? If I get out, I might get washed away with the current. If I stay inside, the *car* could get washed away in the current. I might also be trapped, whereas at least outside the car there's a chance I could swim or grab hold of a tree trunk and get to safety. But I feel safe in *here*. I'm dry and who knows what's going to happen once I open that door?

Just as I'm fretting alternatives to my survival, the car shakes and rearranges itself a few unstable feet farther toward the edge of the washed-out road. Its torrent hooks the right rear bumper, sending up a forceful spray, tugging at the machine's weight.

Fuck it. I need to get out. Dumb instinct or not, I don't plan to drown, trapped and helpless in a car.

The driver's door faces the worst of the stream rushing and bucking against my window. Grabbing the opposite armrest, I drag myself over the gearshift into the passenger seat and tug on the handle.

Noise. Terror.

It takes four tries to heave the door wide and hold it ajar with an outstretched foot. The right side of the vehicle has been jammed into the muddy bank, moored with comparative calm to the gushing crevice on the left.

I'm two metres away from the granite outcrop. I test a sneakered foot on the sodden slope, launching forward off the door. It isn't elegant. I fall twice, scrape an elbow, dragged forward in the dirty sluice, am slathered in mud, but then scrabble onto the rock. Now what?

27

I'VE HIKED A FEW HILLS IN THE PAST. I try to keep in good shape. The gym etc. Summers, I run along the canal to a few upbeat eighties mixes on my iPhone. But I'm not going to stress out if I get lazy. In the winter I'm unmotivated for months but I won't feel guilty and then view exercise as punishment. I'll just push out a few gruelling weeks on the elliptical in March and regain the upper hand over the onset of middle age. *Early* middle age, thank you very much. I even joined a running club, briefly, a few years back. Maybe I'm a loner but it failed to motivate me. Maybe I don't like people with the same goals. I had a few tumbles in bed with, uh, Leaf, that was his name. He'd changed it from Matt because he was part of a bigger organism and wanted to be free. Something like that. He owned a Subway franchise and was resident alpha male in the club. He had hairy shoulders and obsessed over his personal best and almost convinced me to enter the Death Valley Marathon before he got weird and coachy with me and I changed my phone number as the unsubtlest prelude to a restraining order. Longer story that I don't have time for.

Anyway, who wants to run through a landscape with the word "death" in its name?

And what is it with my choice in men?

Preachy, know-it-all but brain-dead Leaf. Leaf, whose goal in life was to eventually own *two* Subways and clock the Boston Marathon qualifying time, though he mentioned no plans to actually run it.

Then my yoga phase. I missed having an activity, something that opened me to broader interests. A Bikram yoga ad popped up on my phone one day. A shirtless guru stood on a woman's back, like a cat kneading a cushion. I remembered there was some kind of hot room above a shawarma restaurant near my office, but when I eventually participated it was catastrophically hot and smelled like garlic, which made me feel like pressed chicken on a roti every time I swayed there, perspiring in my eagle pose. I tried the chanting yoga at another place. I kind of liked it. Dude with Art Garfunkel hair strummed an acoustic guitar to maintain the rhythm. But I wasn't getting anywhere. Where *was* I supposed to get? I couldn't tell if I was good at it. What are the signs? I was told more serenity would be attainable with the less I cared. I started to care so much about not caring. I got increasingly neurotic about my lack of tranquillity. Everyone was better at this than me, with their smug beatific gazes and angelic seed words. It made me feel like I wasn't being grateful enough.

I persevered with the birding app though. It was a weird thrill to detect unusual appearances of purple finches, or swamp sparrows. Cedar waxwings. Their song's a sort of flutey stutter, high and nasal. I sometimes play recordings of a dawn chorus when I'm stressed. I find it's soothing. Or hopeful or something. Migration routes astonish. I fixate on a live migration map of the arctic tern when I can't sleep. They're the record holders for global flight. They breed in the far north and then fly to Antarctica and back. The "birdcast" follows terns tagged with geo-locators. You can replay a bird's journey from Baffin Island to the Weddell Sea. Or track real time, a yellow dot stalled within immense distances. I fall asleep and dream of it high above the Atlantic Ocean, dropping, lifting, carried over the lonely turquoise currents ribboned by waves.

I'm certainly grateful to *something* now as I face, cold and soaked to the bone, the door to my destination on this unpromising day:

Warburton Acres Lodge. The hyperbole seems particularly stark and desperate in the present circumstances, but so it goes. Twenty minutes after my escape from the doomed car, a few familiar contours have led me to the cabin I'd lost hope of finding, its unreachableness a size-and-distance distortion from childhood perhaps.

But there it is, the entrance of slate flagstones encroached by weeds.

The cabin looks humbler than I remember, one decent-sized window on the front and a roofed lean-to attached to the west side where remnants of stacked firewood remain. Can't help but think Adirondack chairs. I'll bring two of them, brand new, one painted red, the other blue, and park them out front, all postcard cottagey to mask the dreary isolation of the place. A strong first impression more than ever. It's a sodden sight today but seems solid enough. No broken windows, no porcupine nests in the rotted shingle. Two large nails pierce the centre of the gable, once the mount for a set of antlers, I think, now gone. Find some new antlers? Could be a quaint touch.

The outer door is missing sections of mosquito screen. It creaks open on its hinges. The second is more substantial, barred by a deeply rusted padlock, one which I thankfully have a key for, and more thankfully, one of the things inside my pocket during that emergency jettison back down the road. It takes a frustrating minute to free the slippery thing from my tight, soaked linen. It actually fits the lock, but before I twist with much force, the whole pin drops out from the brass casing onto the slate below. A bright "ding" as it connects, strikingly exotic in the washy-wash shush of the rain. I pick it up, the steel coated in rust, set it down with the casing on the outside sill, pull the stiff hasp off the staple screwed to the frame (also rusted) and push open the door.

Musty darkness.

I stand there, two steps inside, not getting rained on but dripping onto a grey rag rug. I leave the door open for light. The reaches of the room expand as they become clearer. A counter along one wall, a bucket and white plastic tub placed on top. Table and four chairs. Metal-framed bed with slat springs and no mattress. A wooden daybed with drawers for bedding storage. Again, no mattress. A rattan chair with curving arms, probably the most comfortable-looking item in the room. At the back, a metal flue runs down from the roof into a cast iron stove. Most importantly, there's a rack with dry sticks and, collected in a beer Koozie, an assortment of venerable Bic lighters. I flick their little wheels with a mounting sense of defeat. But the fourth one produces a flame. Within minutes, with the flue adjusted, I coax a humble fire from branches and a dusty L.L. Bean catalogue in the belly of the stove. I learned something from those cottage days, at least. On the east-facing wall above the table are two windows. I step toward them and pull the cream drapes aside. The fabric is ancient, plastic-feeling and greasy, and could tear apart with no effort. Dozens of dead flies are clustered on the sill. The yellow light swims with dust. It's all suffocating. I tug on a latch; the sash pops loose and the stale air seems to rush through the opening, inhaling the exterior breeze. I drop onto one of the chairs at the table and plan to think this all through.

My eye can't help but reorganize. In the early evening the details of the room show themselves: a bamboo screen lined up against the wall. A badminton racket (stringless) hanging on a nail. On the counter, a handmade spice rack, with nothing on its two shelves but a faded Tylenol container.

I scan the room for those personal touches I'm always refereeing with clients. Some home stagers claim their job is like theatre. That is only partly true. Mostly misleading. The stage of a theatre seeks to form an image of a specific world, something distinctive and unrepeatable, that the audience will remember for months or years after the performance. Interior decorating does this too, stamping the personality of the homeowner onto the visitor's mind. But home staging is the opposite. It tries to remove signs of personality, to neutralize a space, so potential buyers can imagine making it their own. It removes obstructions of style while retaining possibilities of character. No one wants to look at photographs of someone else's family in their future home; they want to imagine themselves as the first inhabitants. And just as a crime scene detective looks for anything that tells a story, a home stager does the opposite. Stories in a room complicate decision-making. So, on any working day, I will remove the table tennis trophy and starfish husks on the mantelpiece, the bamboo wind chime outside the door. If it weren't so faded, I might keep this waterfall painting above the daybed. Its associations are vague. But the African mask will go. Too specifically cultural.

Unintentionally, I begin to circle the cabin. It's become clear that I'll need to sleep here tonight. The amplified warmth of the cast iron is heartening. My delusions that it may be animal-free are put to the test by discovery of a mousetrap under the counter, complete with mummified remains of its last victim. But otherwise, the cabin seems miraculously shipshape, dusty but not decaying, cobwebbed but not infested. Some long-scentless air fresheners have been left on shelves and counters, further evidence of caretaking by Gerry or Kathleen.

My memories of this place are vague. We would take the path down to the lake, which seemed like hours, but was likely only fifteen minutes. There was a small, wooden dock there. We'd make a picnic. There was A&W root beer in jugs. I'd dangle my feet in the water. I never brought Georgia here. She was a fussy child. I hated the sand and pine needles and the graceless outhouse procedures, so I imagined she'd hate it too. Hugo? Ha. I can just see his face at the suggestion: "A cabin? Where? And why would we go there?"

In the end we did have the baby, didn't we? Georgia. Though a formal decision was never really made. We just put off discussing the subject. Then we had no choice. And then Hugo went off to Spain to do research for that book he was planning. What was he going to call it? *The Labyrinth: Access and Escape*, or some such nonsense. A book on prison architecture. He was going to dedicate it to me; he claimed I'd given him the idea the first time we met. He was gone for a month, drinking wine, exploring Madrid and Catalonia, living a romantic scholar's life while I dealt with nausea, weight gain, swollen ankles and a uterus growing to the size of a small planet. It was Hugo's last window for research before the pitter-patter we'd soon hear. I didn't want him regretting the opportunity. I didn't want him holding it against me for the rest of his life.

I've never told Georgia this, the reluctance for, and inconvenience of, her birth. I wonder if she sensed it from the womb. She was born with a frown and has exuded negative energy since. God, she was a terror. She fought the very socks we'd try to put on her. She screamed with particular finesse from the bars of her crib. Her rage at confinement was total. While nursing, she'd squirm in my arms, bruising my breasts with bites and pinches so I eventually switched to a formula. Likewise, she witnessed all the enmity between Hugo and me. Arguments and cold shoulders. It couldn't have helped, the sarcasm and disappointment that all came to a head with the Trois Rivières Art Gallery and its collapsing wall.

At the time of its construction, there had been some taxpayer controversy. Cultural relevance versus cost. Hospital upgrades were needed. Proper roads etc. Why build an expensive showcase to some regional Canadian artists? I can't think of one of their names to this day. But Hugo promised to keep the cost low and to source materials, ha, from competitive suppliers. The building rose, austere in both budget and aesthetics. On completion, it was loved and hated.

A beautiful gathering of lines and volume, one reviewer proclaimed.

Ugly, others said.

Then, a few years later, the gallery wall fell. Technically, it only cracked in a few critical places, but the glass ceiling attached to it shattered and the gallery was closed until further structural assessments could be submitted. There'd been a minor earthquake the week before, and for a short time, Hugo had worked this into a scapegoat. But an overzealous reporter started digging into details about Hugo's subsequent projects and depicted a string of problems for her exposé in the weekend *Globe and Mail*. She interviewed some of his residential clients who complained of roof leaks and dissatisfaction with contract specifics. An atrium fountain had drainage issues. The board of governors of a downtown office building reported design errors and grossly inaccurate cost estimates. A war of words ensued. Hugo claimed they were out of touch with the cost of a modern building, that it was all a witch hunt, that the job was rushed by the board's unmanageable deadlines. Then the reporter found a tradesman who was willing to admit they'd been bullied into forcing inferior metal girders at foundation levels, which had warped and led to "load-bearing compromises." By the time a contractor's name was linked to the Montreal mafia, Hugo's career was over.

He was unbowed, took all interviews to make his case, challenged his detractors to produce "one shred of proof."

It just looked desperate.

A week later, Sotheby's called me. They'd hired me on probation less than a year earlier but had hardly acknowledged my existence. Now they wanted to meet. Could I come up to their office in Montreal? I did, business class on VIA Rail, walking straight from the station into the firm's art deco lobby. Buzzed through Nigel Oldham's door. Nigel. He was a senior partner at the firm. He wasn't smiling.

And there was a security guard inside the office.

I'm no dummy.

"What's going on, Nigel?" I said.

Him starting, his thumb resting on a prepared statement: "I regret to inform you . . ."

"Inform me?"

"That we are terminating your services as of today."

"The fuck you are."

"As of today, and you will be properly compensated according to the contract particulars."

"Why?"

He looked me in the eye for the first time. "The reasons are outlined in your termination documents." He handed me a manila envelope tied off with a red string. I pushed it away with my fingertips and leaned across his desk. The security guard stepped forward. I was livid.

"This is fucking ridiculous and you know it. It's garbage. Is this about Hugo? Is it? You at least owe me an explanation."

"They are outlined—"

"Tell me why, Nigel! To my face. You piece of shit," I growled.

On my first visit inside his office months earlier, two precious silver-framed photos had occupied the left corner of Nigel's desk. I had always admired the understated elegance of the design. With silver it's not necessary to overload with decoration. I had always meant to ask him where he'd bought them.

I backhanded one toward the wall.

It crashed to the floor and bounced, turning over face-up: some people crowded on a mountaintop, their thumbs raised in victory against a snow-dotted abyss.

Nigel gave a look to the guard, who took a position beside the chair.

"Ma'am," he said and raised an open, ushering hand.

"Security will escort you out," the piece of shit prompted.

After my pregnancy with Georgia, a woman I knew from the gym mentioned she'd been taking hapkido lessons to get back in shape. It was self-defence, a lot of blocks and throws. She was having a blast and I should come along. There was a space in Little Italy where we'd go every Tuesday night to pitch the other participants, substitute rapists and burglars, to the mat. Then go for cocktails.

So, at that moment in the office, when the security guard took a firm hold of my bicep, I considered breaking his grip and trying an attack move. The guard was significantly bigger than me.

"Don't fucking touch me," I said instead, glaring at Nigel. I snapped the dismissal envelope from the desktop and walked out alone.

Georgia wanted to be bounced on my knee at the kitchen table that evening as I looked through the items of dismissal. They were suitably vague, citing "conflicting philosophies" for the direction of the company. Absolute horseshit. It was wrongful dismissal and wouldn't hold up. Unfortunately, the destruction of personal property in the form of a silver photo frame might make a more convincing justification.

I heard the key rattling in the lock.

Entering, his suit jacket slung over his shoulder, Hugo dropped two plastic bags of groceries from the Italian deli onto the floor, folded and placed his jacket over the hall bench and walked into the kitchen.

"Shoes," I said.

Without a word, he bent his knee and pulled one dress shoe off, then the other. They were brown and had been re-shined the day before. I told him regularly to stay off the ceramic tiles. Hugo was ceaselessly leaving scuff marks.

"I got fired," I said next.

"What do you mean?"

"They fired me. Occupation terminated. Finito. Here are the dismissal papers."

I looked down at them spread out in front of Georgia, who was humming some indecipherable tune of her own composition. In my general irritation, I increased the frequency of my knee bounces. She responded with a kind of sick laughter.

Hugo glanced at the papers with all the energy of a wounded ape and said, "What did you do?"

"I didn't *do* anything. I didn't *say* anything. I did nothing but help sell their overpriced properties in Hampstead and Nuns' Island, took my cut and handed them a sum for theirs. All for the honour of being part of their 'team.' Being part of their 'good name,'" I said, air-quoting. "Anyway, it's your fault."

Hugo was unpacking the grocery bags. He set two packages of espresso on the counter, some biscotti, a bottle of aged Modena balsamic. They were things I'd asked him to pick up, so he placed them there like a rebuke: *I've taken care of your wishes and this is how you treat me.* We were at the stage where gestures of affection were played like chess pieces. He went to the fridge and put a wedge of parmesan into the cheese holder. He shut the door and I could almost see his scowl reflected in the brushed stainless steel.

"My fault?"

I was bouncing Georgia furiously on my knee.

"Don't act stupid, Hugo. This is about reputation and association. The gallery mess, the newspaper takedown. You sticking your head in front of every camera looking for a self-justifying quote. Take your lumps. There's not much we can do. But advertising yourself as a desperate loser is not going to help. You can't win that game. Defending yourself in front of the media is wrestling with pigs, you know. *You* get dirty and *they* just have fun."

"It's a witch hunt." He liked saying that lately. It had a ring to it, but it didn't pardon the accusations. The design errors, budget failures and mafia connections were still there, like a priest turned into a newt.

"Whatever it is," I said, "*I'm* part of it. I'm *in* this. *My* name's in those reports. This is us. Sotheby's doesn't want that kind of garbage connected to one of their salespeople, do they? It's why I'm sitting here—unemployed."

"Find something else. With your sales record. Not a problem."

He was wishing the problem away by saying it wasn't one. But word would get around. Tainted couple equals bad news. We were bad news now. Only big money could ignore the scent of scandal. And we didn't have that kind of wealth yet. We were methodically making sure of that.

Georgia made a cartoon gurgle. Hugo was unnaturally silent. I looked at him. His face was red, defeated, almost a husk. The bluster was gone. His failures had squeezed it out of him. The wax had melted and he'd plunged into the sea, mortal in his bespoke dress shirt. I ushered Georgia over to him and he took her. "We'll be okay," I said. And I wrapped my arms around them both.

28

CHECKING OUTSIDE, I find a blue plastic bucket around the corner of the cabin. It's upright, full of rainwater: clear, cool and spilling over the sides. There is one green leaf floating on the water's surface, so crisp it must have dropped from a nearby tree only seconds before my arrival. Slipping my shoes off, I tip half of the bucket over my shins and feet, washing away the mud and dirt as best I can, then centre it again beside the stone flagging. Above me, clogged grey swirls promise more rain, though the sky has softened briefly. There are even scrapings of blue beyond the clouds.

There is Hugo again. I resent his intrusions into my existence. Desolate conditions seem to summon him. I can go months without a thought of what he's doing and then stress drags me back into his orbit. He attaches to my misery. He smells it and comes loping toward me, like a retriever for a stick. He'll be off again, on Saturday, on a flight for Barcelona. Some conference he swore is absolutely necessary to attend. He'd given me a courtesy call to say he'll be gone, should anything come up. "I need to straighten some things out," he'd said. I held my tongue on that. Deliberation would do no good. Sometimes our marriage counsellor's words, when we were briefly serious about saving the thing, come back to me. She criticized my sniping, those hurtful attempts to get empty points without aiding growth.

Hugo waited on the other end of the line.

"Then you should do that," I answered eventually.

"Everything okay with you?" he added. (No, I'm divorced, a serial first-dater, and I've just royally fucked up my finances due to some third-rate weasel with two first names.)

"Everything's super," I said. "Hope your conference goes well."

"I'll call you."

"Please don't. I'll be busy the next few days. Drop me an email when you get back. Okay?"

"We had some good years, didn't we?" he said.

Oh no. Nothing worse than the sentimental Hugo. The remorseful Hugo. I wish it wouldn't happen. I can't go back. The energy it subtracts from my dwindling supply. What is he playing at?

"I should go."

"I'll call you."

I think I sighed. "Okay. Yes, sure."

Hugo likes to claim that I cheated on him first, but that's hardly verifiable. It's true I was hitting it off with Andrew, a businessman who owned some upholstery and paint stores in Ottawa. Having been rejected from the realty community, I was a few years into my switch to a private home-staging business and Andrew was helpful. He'd agreed to offer deals to my clients who followed my advice about organizing light renos before calling in the realtors. First impressions, all that. I argued for a pressure-wash of siding and driveways. Oiled hinges. A fresh coat of paint on the front door. Studies show you have less than ten minutes to grab the viewer's attention. Andrew was pleasant, divorced, a diplomat's son whose boutique renovation stores were doing reasonably well but needed a boost in client base. We worked over several colour systems to brighten rooms. We created illusions of depth by painting one "feature wall" a slightly different shade. There was no great depth to his personality, true, but he was handsome, with well-groomed salt-and-pepper hair and a penchant for skinny-fit suits and subtle aftershave. I was not having sex with him.

One night, at home, I climbed out of bed and went downstairs for a pee and a sip of water. It was shortly past two a.m. and I found Hugo in our study pouring over a thick book in the glow of his desk lamp. Hugo looked up at me, the early sag of middle age in his neck accentuated in the moody light. "What's that chair called again?" he said, consistent in his annoying custom of assuming everyone was obsessed with whatever he was thinking about. Noticing my blank look, he added: "The one with the metal tubes, the leather . . ." Gesturing helplessly in the air as if his hands were rescuing a collapsed sandcastle.

"Wassily?" I guessed.

He nodded, just barely. "By Loos."

"No, Marcel Breuer."

"Yes, yes . . ."

He folded the book closed, one of several about design that I owned.

I glanced around the room. An open bottle of Maker's Mark. Dirty tumblers. A Hudson's Bay blanket was jumbled across the sofa. He had been sleeping on it regularly for months.

"Just this article I'm trying to write," he said without affirming anything in particular. Then: "Was Andrew here?"

I think I might have looked alarmed, but only because I thought he'd meant the study itself, that Andrew had come into it and taken something, or left something—what, I couldn't imagine. My eyes searched the various surfaces again, ready for an obvious sign of some oddity that could be explained or wondered at.

"To drop off some quotes. Why?" I said.

"He left his watch in the kitchen."

His what? Oh yes. Andrew's watch. He'd forgotten it. The Seiko with those unfortunate glow-in-the-dark hands. I'd offered him a cup of tea, then bumped his elbow while handing it over, sending a wide splash down his arm. He'd taken the watch off to clean up, wiping the wristband dry. He went to the sink, ran his forearm under the tap while I dabbed some drips off the table. The soiled paper towels, the cups and teapot on the dishrack: the real unsullied story was all there for Hugo to see. If he just looked. Even the stain of Earl Grey on Andrew's shirt sleeve could be verified, if Hugo was willing to drive over to Westboro to check.

But surely none of this would be necessary. Reason would triumph. I was about to explain the whole misunderstanding. Except it was actually sounding like one of those frantic, contrived stories that are the stock invention in every affair.

Meanwhile, Hugo persevered. "Is something going on?"

"For heaven's sake, Hugo. Don't be an idiot."

"Are you fucking him?"

Me laughing. "He's not my type."

"Otherwise, you would."

"I'm not talking about this now. It's the middle of the night."

"So, you are fucking him . . ."

"I spilled tea," I started.

Yes, it was already sounding absurd. But I finished the story, under Hugo's dull, skeptical glare, wherein we entered into the nasty labyrinth of accusation and defence that was a hallmark of our squabbling sessions over the years. The argument lasted an hour. The rage. Like sex, it hotly jabbed and rubbed at the tenderest places, confused as much as cleared the mind, and dissolved in the light of morning.

And, uh, there's that word again. "Labyrinth." If I had a nickel. There was a year or two where it's all Hugo talked about. His book. His prisons. His restricted means of dwelling. His entries and escapes. What did it have to do with putting up a building? He got Georgia involved, getting her worked up on the topic for a section on mythology in her history class. They even built a miniature one out of Styrofoam, the spiralling passageways and hidden ends modelled on a mosaic at Knossos.

"Most directions are wrong," he said. "But you need to make each corner appear like the right one."

She brought it to school for a display.

Anyway, poor Andrew. Hugo wouldn't let it go, insisting I stop using his paint and textiles. I refused. He'd done nothing wrong. I'd done nothing wrong. What is it they say about an irresistible force and an immoveable object? Hugo claimed he trusted me but the marriage was over if I didn't stop working with Andrew. I told him if he *did* trust me he'd stop talking all this paranoid garbage. I had no intention of changing a very productive and profitable business relationship.

Then I fucked Andrew.

It wasn't much fun, actually. I'd met him for a glass of wine in a little neighbourhood bistro near his place. It had been weeks since Hugo's ultimatum. But I'd continued to work with Andrew on a few upgrade collaborations. You can imagine the tension at home, Hugo arriving late in the evening usually, hibernating in the study, grunting a few essential points of domestic information over the kitchen island in the morning. Georgia observed it all, mismatched pyjamas, dark bangs in her eyes, perched glumly above her granola like a fallen angel condemned to dwell among men. She was disappearing more and more as the months passed, withdrawing her personality from our presence, becoming as invisible as possible in order to fly under our parental radar.

I'd been restricting my meetings with Andrew to the daytime, my one concession to Hugo's martial law. But a realtor had just called to say a house I'd staged in Rockcliffe—one tarted up by Andrew's boutique glosses and drapery—had been sold in under two days, initiating a sizeable contractual bonus and, fuck it, I felt like celebrating.

After another argument, Hugo decided on a trip to San Francisco. I don't know why I called Andrew—there were several girlfriends that would have enjoyed a bottle of wine with me—but I dialled his number and said I was in the neighbourhood.

No.

I do know why, don't I?

Because Hugo had forbidden it.

That was one thing.

Because I'd done nothing wrong was another, certainly. After all, hadn't I dragged myself out of the mess he'd made of my career? Perhaps Hugo had unintentionally planted the illicit seed of adultery, an image I couldn't escape while reviewing order forms, Andrew's hairy arm brushing my elbow. I really wasn't attracted in the slightest, but I was angry, hurt and vengeful, and yes, most probably clouded in judgement. But sometimes you clear the weeds with a rake and sometimes you use some gasoline and a match. Whatever was my motive, there I squatted in the darkness, naked and parched beside Andrew's bed, collecting my bra and tights from the hardwood and preparing a soundless exit.

On the bedside table, glowing off the hands of Andrew's Seiko, the time showed 2:43 a.m.

Meanwhile, ever since the gallery scandal, Hugo was flourishing. Having wrestled with the pigs, Hugo then got hired by them. They must have liked how he got dirty. Some media boss was impressed and Hugo was soon writing architectural reviews for magazines and papers. They didn't care about scandal. The more the better. Tainted and defiant, Hugo was reinvented as the bad boy of urban renewal and architectural design. He even had that thirty-minute television panel for a couple of years. It was late at night but it had a following before the era of YouTube. A season was picked up by PBS. He had discovered the perfect job to satisfy his long-winded need to offer critical judgement while avoiding any practical work. They flew him everywhere. Dinners and drinks and chauffeured viewings. I would get phone calls every few days from Johannesburg, Kagoshima, Brussels . . . Wherever the next exciting building was being raised.

"Not too early, I hope," he'd say from Helsinki.

"It's not even dawn. The ringing woke Georgia," I reprimanded. She was seven or eight then, the age when one first suspects that adults are denying you some hidden excitement. It was hard to get her into bed at a decent hour, and once woken, she was wired.

"Sorry, it's the first chance I've had. Just got back to the hotel and I couldn't have called in the morning." The line hiccupped through the distance. His voice, with a delayed, overlapped effect, repeated itself: "In the morning," the tinny double said.

"She wants to say hi."

"Do you think it's a good idea? She'll get worked up and won't go back to sleep. (To sleep)."

"She's up now. She's right here."

"Okay (okay)," he sighed. "Put her on. (On)."

I gave the receiver to Georgia. She said hello and curled up on the sofa with the cordless, as if the phone were just another stuffed toy. She was still hazy with sleep. I watched her propped in the half world of dawn, groping for comfort in the bodiless voice of her father. She grunted and nodded, said "yes" and "no" to whatever small talk Hugo was directing from the desk of some boutique hotel room across the Atlantic, innocent of the increasing remoteness of his emotional life. A characteristic frown wiggled across her forehead. Her personality was materializing with every passing day, combative like Hugo, the parental legacies less than gifts. But stop for a second—let me look at her there now. Let time hold her, briefly, and preserve something. Innocent, unaware, her harmless childhood about to fade into the pain of each adolescent year. If I could give it back to her, I would.

When they'd finished their exchange, I took the phone back from her, confirmed Hugo's return flight number and promised I'd let him know if I could pick him up.

"Daddy is far away," Georgia mumbled when I lifted her off the sofa.

Georgia was ten when I kicked him out, or he left, one or the other. It's hard to see where the thickening fog of bickering and separation really starts. Georgia seemed lost. She watched the wandering pantomime. Hugo continued to make appearances. The house was a ghost limb that niggled at his pain. When he dropped by, it was unpleasant. He grumbled. He pronounced. The further he got from a daily connection to our lives, the more it seemed he wanted to control it. I found Hugo pathetic and annoying but to Georgia he became the enemy. Hugo blamed it on me. He blamed it on travel. He blamed many things.

For a while, he blamed Natalie.

Natalie, the alien life who landed on Georgia's planet in her teens, brought additional adventures. They started several punk bands. They went topless on family beaches. If someone questioned them, they'd point out all the men doing the same. I was conflicted; Natalie created chaos but she was what Georgia needed. Now Georgia had an accomplice for her rebellion. Because Georgia was an alien too.

"What the hell are you wearing?" Hugo said for the umpteenth time to Georgia during one of his drop-ins. There she and Natalie stood, dressed in camisoles and pleather jeans, half their bangs dyed green.

Once, the two girls were delivered soaking wet by police after a late-night exploit in a car wash. They'd driven my car inside, then got out and danced in the spray of the automated arms. Hugo showed up more drunk than they were. He was livid. He claimed I was letting them run wild.

DAVID O'MEARA

"Calm down, dude," Natalie said.

This didn't help things.

"Get out of my house," Hugo said.

Georgia: "It's not your house."

Later, she stewed. After Hugo and Natalie's departure, we sat on stools, drinking carbonated water. She was unpeeling a third tangerine from the bowl on the counter. It was three a.m. I was exhausted and wide awake.

"Where are you getting your drugs?"

"What?"

"I'm not stupid, George."

"It's just weed."

"You stink of it."

"Thanks."

"It's not good for you. It messes with your brain patterns."

In silence she chewed and swallowed a few of the citrus segments, pretending I wasn't there. In the glass door to the back deck, our reflections tried to outwait each other.

"I guess this is not the time to discuss your grades," I resumed.

"No," she said. "I'm way too high."

29

I WAKE TO A SHARP STING, discomfort in my left rib and a rock stadium clamour of birdsong. European starlings. Black-capped chickadees. Opening my eyes, I see my filthy shoes discarded on the floor near the woodstove. I tug them on. The air smells like a wet dog, light fuzzily glowing around the curtain. I groan and sigh and sit up on the creaking side bed where I'd fallen asleep, improbably, last night in the pitch-black cabin. I'm alive in a weird crossroad, the remote details of a childhood place mixed with the disastrous past that led me eventually here via Trevor Brent. And the notable image of my Audi floating off a dirt road into the ditch. Obsessions I entertained before surrendering to exhaustion here in the arse-end of nowhere.

Surprised I slept at all.

I'm not much of a camper. Not one to drift off on a pine bench with the threat of rodents scuttling across my face. I treasure my comforts, my Australian wool duvet and Turkish cotton bathrobe. But I've done okay here, under the circumstances. The fire is down to ashes but I'm relatively dry now. The pain in my side is more a consequence of a bloated bladder than hard, unyielding surfaces. Might even say I feel rested. I rub at my cheeks. Could use a mirror—basic luxury usually taken for granted—though I'm distanced from any reason to look presentable. Why this desire to check my face? To see I'm intact, I suppose. To confirm something. To verify. That it's the same self that I brought here yesterday.

Don't we shed our whole epidermis every thirty days? Isn't dust mostly human skin?

Could I be gone, essentially unrecognizable, in the course of a night?

Raising the hook, I push the door open. The clouds, having dumped their heavy wet cargo all through yesterday, sit grey and grainy still, hoicking the occasional spray over the landscape. Denied a confirmation of my identity, I'm deprived of time too, guessing it must be mid-morning, though the cloud cover blurs the sun's position. The bird chorus stutters as the screen door bangs shut, then twitters back to white noise. I look into the bucket, full to the brim again, there by the stoop. I glimpse a reflection, the watery outline of my dishevelled hair, and squint into the unclear squint that must be looking back, just as uncertain. Skimming off the top of the rainwater, I cup some into my mouth. Christ, I'm so fucking thirsty. I pick the bucket up and drink a few extended gulps from the rim. Then my bladder chimes. I walk around the cabin, squatting near the wall. I'm pissing and to my surprise, giggling! Modesty and/or convention has led me to the back, out of sight of what?

Where was the outhouse? Along a path off to my right, but there's no sign of it. Collapsed, the shit and piss returned to the earth.

Almost finished. My Capri pants around my shins. A deep rumble in my stomach. I feel exhausted again. And hungry. It's been eighteen hours since my sushi lunch off Elgin Street. I need to start thinking about what I'm going to do. There's little choice.

I have to start walking.

I have to get to the road and get out, hike to the highway and hope to see a car or a cottage. No one is going to just find me. I've said nothing about coming here. I'll miss this morning's meeting and my working lunch with Doug. He'll think I ditched him. Though I'm skeptical of Douglas's judgement now. He hadn't lost as much to Trevor's criminal scheme, and he's promised to rebuild the business with whatever we have. I'm not holding my breath. I told him exactly that. I was quite murderous. If he's tried to call, he may think I'm screening him.

It can't be more than four hours on foot to the highway, right?

I haul up my pants and fasten the buttons and take another swig of water from the bucket. After a quick glance inside the cabin (for what?) I pull the door closed. There's no lock for the latch but fuck it, the raccoons can have the whole cabin if they want. I think I'm done with this place. Who would spend a cent on this hellhole? The birds can shit on it until it sinks into the ground.

I'll raise a toast to them as the water jets pulse across my shoulders in my Jacuzzi bath tonight.

Everyone needs a goal.

Trudging through the undergrowth, my sneakers are soaked through again, doubling their weight within minutes. There's a section of a tree-root fence on a ridge that leads down to the road, gapped and collapsing where time scattered it. I imagine some pioneers dragging these roots up, horses roped to each girth, more likely clearing the land than attempting to fence it in. I fall once, flat on my ass, into the wet leaves, and slide a few feet before gaining my footing again. For a moment I've lost direction, uncertain if I'm pointed east, where I believe I left the road in the storm. What time is it? A whole wall of the road embankment has collapsed from the rain. Gripping handfuls of grass, I lower myself down the slope where the washed-out gravel appears beyond a break in the trees.

And there, a little further on, is my car, abandoned, elevated at the front, grille jammed into the ditch bed, but still upright.

The road is clawed-up by the force of flooding, fissures still rippling with rivulets, but easily stepped over, my treads leaving a hieroglyphic trail in the mud. Approaching the car, my heart sinks. I'd held to some hope the thing could be excavated and driven away, maybe even salvaged with a tune-up and a vigorous vacuuming.

I circle and inspect the ruins. The front section of the chassis is a foot deep in mud. In my hurry to get away, I'd clambered through the right passenger door, which is wedged, still ajar, against the outcrop. I had also left the keys in the ignition, the engine running and the headlights on. The Audi is dead, a desiccated husk. Looks like the flood had poured into the interior, swamping the front leather seats, depositing sediment in the cup holders and on the floor mats. It's a writeoff. Surely the insurance will cover this. Acts of God.

There is my cellphone, like an arrested Pompeian figure, tucked in the sludge. Useless to me with no signal up here. I take it anyway, slipping it into my back pocket, a stubborn hope something will ring, or rev, with a magical reserve of power and summon some roadside miracle. I snap open the glove compartment and remove the registration, then pull the keys from the ignition. The rain has started again, light and cool. The air looks artificial, like a stage set of a gloomy day. Popping the trunk, I find the floor mats are slightly damp but have survived the worst of the deluge. Under the promotional banners— *Trimble Staging: We Show Your Home to the World*—and my pink traffic cones (certain clients *love* these) are jumper cables, a snow brush and a spare tire. Remembering my gym bag, I lift it out. Next to it, inside a yellow "deluxe carrying case" is the auto emergency kit. I sort through the contents and find candles, a wind-up flashlight, two road flares, a whistle and a packaged Mylar blanket, which I pop into a side pocket of my gym bag for safekeeping.

Then I remember the protein bars stashed in the other pocket. There are three: two a chocolate peanut butter medley, one caffe mocha.

I tear a wrapper off and gobble down half of one just as I see the animal come out of the brush about a hundred and fifty metres down the road.

It's black, squatting on its haunches, nose pointed into the air, harvesting a deep, proprietorial sniff of its surroundings. I stop chewing. Frozen in place, staring. Every single part of me wants to turn and run but I'm too petrified by the noise I'll make, too hopeful my presence will be overlooked. Or oversniffed. I watch its head bob as it steps into the middle of the road. The whole shaggy silhouette shifts until it's clearly moving leisurely up the gravel toward me. I step backwards to the other side of the car and then bolt through the ditch, scramble up the slippery incline to the fence and then charge along the undergrowth before I dare a look back down from the ridge where I can see the thing has just reached the spot I hastily vacated not two minutes ago. It finds the car interesting. It props paws on the back bumper and peers into the open trunk. This lasts a few seconds before it drops down to the ground again, nosing its bulk forward, and squatting, having found the remains of my protein bar, which it licks and smells, polishing off the leftovers in one maw-wide gulp. I don't wait to see what happens next. Maybe it will smell me, maybe follow, but it knows there's food now and I remember enough rules from summer camp to know that's not good. I race for the cabin, tripping on roots, my gym bag tucked close for minimum jostling noise.

It must take ten minutes.

Inside the cabin, I'm all business. Tossing the gym bag onto the bench, pushing the thick, inner door shut, I drag the bedframe into position across the entrance. Then I get the wood table and chairs and stack them over the sagging springs. There's something bedroom farce about the whole thing, or horror movie. The genres share much in common. The wrong place at the wrong time. Doesn't that sum the crux up essentially? What am I doing here? Why is this happening? That kind of thing. At the moment, viewing my thin barricade versus the whims of a two-tonne animal with lethal claws and teeth, I can't help feeling peripheral to luck. It has been a banner week for bad decisions.

Options?

Where is my bathroom reader now? It's a bear, right? If it wants, it can knock everything aside like a pile of sticks in a tornado. Then

what? Do I play dead? Hide in the cupboard? Throw a bucket at it?
Test my hapkido training? I have that whistle from the roadside kit.
I zip open my bag and remember the road flares.

I'll dazzle the thing.

I'll whistle the bejeezus out of it.

Then nothing happens. For hours. Trickle of rain, birdsong, the
rising temperature and mugginess. Stressed out on the wooden
daybed, my knees tucked against my chest, I'm fine-tuned for
noise, a radar dish reading the slightest rustle of leaf or branch. For
the first hour I barely move; the flares, beside me, are ready to be
uncapped. I've read over the instructions fifteen times, though it's
simple as lighting a match. Hold away from the body and strike.
Obsessing over the scenario of the animal's arrival, I imagine any
number of grisly results. Grizzly results? Ha.

Okay. Calm the fuck down.

Remembering my stomach, I eat another protein bar and a
banana I'd put in a lunch bag for my potassium fix yesterday. Wasn't
that the plan, after seeing the cabin, to drop by the club for an
afternoon workout? I could almost cry to be at the gym right now,
tormented by squats, persecuted by multiple reps assigned on the
torturer's multi-station, but at least out of danger, in sight of a hot
shower.

I make all kinds of silent promises if I should get out of this.
Gratefulness shall follow me all the days of my life etc.

Inside the gym bag are my spandex running shorts, a black
sports bra, a T-shirt and a change of panties. A small towel. There's
hair gel, face cream, a deodorant stick, a combination lock in a
Velcro pouch, an old pair of Coach sunglasses (with cracked lens),
and oh yes, a twist of paper in a Ziploc bag.

Forgot about this too. I have a little business relationship with
Roberto, the hipster barista at the gelato joint on Preston, who
provides me with a few grams of powder when I'm in need of a
boost. After chewing out Douglas over the Ponzi crap, I rushed

over there, barking expletives at my windshield, calling on all varieties of indignities to be visited on Trevor Brent's body and soul.

Roberto was behind the counter, just topping off a customer's waffle cone with chocolate sprinkles and candied ginger. He gave me a wink, mimed two fingers against his mouth to his co-worker, then went out the service door. I retreated through the front entrance and found Roberto smoking near the *Private—Reserved* sign. His uncle owned the business. Usually a black Fiat Spider was parked there.

"That was subtle," I said.

He squinted at me in the bright sun. "Doesn't know, doesn't care," he said, referring to the rosy-cheeked part-time student at the cash.

He glanced over at the sidewalk.

The lunch crowd were exiting the trattoria across the street.

"You want the same?" he mumbled.

"Double, if you can."

He nodded, smiling, pulling out a cigarette pack from the pocket of his apron, where BELLISSIMO GELATO was stencilled into the fabric.

"*Someone's on a holiday,*" he drawled.

"Hardly."

I lifted out two of the paper twists mixed among the smokes. Took a cigarette too, put it into my mouth as we walked to my car.

"How's that beautiful daughter of yours?" Roberto said. He liked flirting inappropriately. It was a game. Too young for me, too old for Georgia, he hit on us both with a ghoulish wink. He was creepy-charming, one of those men who hugs you for too long. I put up with it because he was my coke source, a reliable connection I'd discovered through my friend who owned a popular club in town.

Beautiful was not the word I would conjure for Georgia. She was pretty, I guess. But who could tell with the hacksaw haircuts, black lipstick and shreds of clothing so in fashion with her vampire friends those days.

"She's in Korea," I told Roberto. "For almost a year now."

He raised his eyebrows, either from surprise at the length of her absence or the existence of this "Korea" thing. My Audi responded with two exclamatory beeps from an electronic key and I jerked the passenger door open. Little did I know it would soon be an escape hatch from disaster.

"That's cool," Roberto said.

"She's teaching," I added.

"She's a smart girl."

"Sure."

How would you know? I was thinking. I suppose we needed to make small talk, but I wasn't interested in discussing the level of my daughter's intellect with slippery Roberto. I just wanted a little bump to shake off my own disappointment and despair. I was pulling some twenties from my wallet, trying not to look like I was doing a drug deal with a high school drop-out from a rich family, mid-afternoon in front of a gelateria. I stuffed the cash in my hand and shook Roberto's, transferring the sum. We had prepared a story, if ever caught: I had stopped for directions and I was thanking him for a cigarette. Not very original, I guess. But our relationship had never been about imagination. It was what he had and I needed. Supply and demand. Only sporadically recreational on my part; I wasn't his biggest customer by far, but he also knew I wouldn't show up shaking and frothing at the mouth for a fix and with no money to cover it.

That night I snorted a line, did two more the next day. Then I took a step back, stuffing the second sample into my gym bag for later consumption. A simple rule with me: not three days in a row. Three days meant routine, meant dependence, meant the high could take control. The high's purpose was to manufacture invincibility for an hour. A chemical vacation, that's all. It said, *Conquer the fuckheads* and *Climb over the garbage pit, you are awesome.*

I am going to admit that I'm not entirely awesome at the moment.

I'm penniless. I'm disillusioned. I'm mud-stained, smelly and one protein bar away from the need to eat grass and pine cones. It's late afternoon now, too late to make the highway before dark. Even with the wind-up flashlight, I do not want to be trudging through the forest at night, easy dinner for any number of dangers. Pulling back the grimy curtain, I check the front perimeter of the cabin, then do the same at the side. Nothing but cheeping birds and wet foliage. I watch, wait and listen. After fifteen more minutes, I drag the bed away from the door just a squeezable foot and listen again before popping the hook. As my hand nudges the screenless door open, my heart rate is around a quazillion trillion. Sluggish light. The air seems drugged. I grab the water bucket, full again, and carry it carefully inside, then reverse everything: re-close, re-hook, re-barricade and re-scan the landscape through the window. A country silence. Thirsty, I cup some rainwater into my mouth, then recall a water bottle in my gym bag. I fill it and drink. Things could be worse, though they could be infinitely better.

Restored by protein bars and hydration, I dunk the towel in the bucket and wipe my face down. That feels good. I strip off my Capri pants, shirt and underwear and run the towel around my neck, over my arms and pits, between my legs, across thighs and shins, everywhere where sweat has collected in the last twenty-four hours. Cool on the skin, the water drips onto the floor, leaving a Rorschach of rinse on the wood grain. Needing to ration what water's left, I pull a dry brush through my greasy hair and tie the lengths back, then dress with the bra and fresh panties, running shorts and T-shirt. The T-shirt's lime green. On it, in yellow letters, a rat's head snarls with sharp teeth, three drops of spit arrayed around its snout. And the words *Worst Vermin* in a horror-show font. The Vermin were one of my daughter's high school bands during the "musical years" in her teens. Another excuse to make a lot of noise, those anti-social peers and her, banging away on their poor instruments like they were trying to wake the dead. She had a few different groups, different versions, but always Georgia and her poor friend Natalie at the centre of the maelstrom. If I remember correctly, I paid for most of the T-shirts. They'd ordered twenty-five for some "all ages" show in a Centretown warehouse but their online fundraiser fell through. At least that was what she told me. Her stories were chaos to decipher. All her plans were chaos. I think that was the goal.

I just gave her the money and told her to weed the flower bed in return. A week later, there was a sprig of cosmos and a T-shirt on my nightstand.

"What's this?" I said to her, carrying it into the kitchen, where she was stirring up quinoa during her vegetarian phase.

"It's yours," she said. "The band shirts. We got them today."

I unfolded it and looked it over. A chemical smell lifted off the yellow lettering. The whole thing was repulsive: the smell, the image, the colour combination.

"I'll never wear this."

"Why not? What's wrong with it?"

"It's terrifying."

"It's a T-shirt. Lighten up. You just don't like my band."

"I've never heard your band, Georgia."

She turned and pointed at me with the wooden spoon. "No, you haven't."

Hoisting the spoon high, like a conductor's baton, she dramatically hurled it into the pot, a habit for projectiles she may have inherited from me. Specks of quinoa scattered. Then she stormed out, that appropriate verb with its dark clouds and lightning. I tried not to worry. Our eruptions had patterns. We are a familiar system, daughter and Mama. Her hot mass and my cold fronts. Georgia's squalls build quickly from the blue nowhere and I wait them out. She'll be gone for days, in a tidy fit about something, and then she's here again, polishing off an artisan baguette in the kitchen. The phone calls too. From school and the police. They'd lectured us both before I'd drive her home in monastic silence. What good was talking to her? But then after what happened to Natalie. And Georgia's breakdown. The counsellor's lecture: "You need to listen . . ."

Maybe I needed to. I thought I was trying.

After this past Christmas, I managed to reach her on a friend's phone in Korea.

"Is that Becky?"

"It's Becca."

"Is Georgia there? She gave me this number."

"One second."

Mumbling voice, then Georgia's: "Hi, Mom."

"Was that Becky?"

"Becca."

"Is it snowing there?"

"A little. Not much. I'm in the south. We just got back from surfing."

"Surfing? In water?"

"Yeah, you know. Surfing. Surfboards. I'm just learning."

"Is it safe?"

"It's fine. We have wetsuits. It's fun."

"That's good."

"What is?"

"That you're having fun."

"Yes," Georgia said. "I think I am."

A few hours later, I thought of that word again.

Fun.

Was I having any fun? I used to. On Friday I had gone through invoices, matching the deliveries for our inventory (a whole box of bamboo venetian shades unaccounted for). The business was steady. I thought my investments were growing. I had a few glasses of wine. I folded some laundry. Then phone calls on Saturday. Emails. I puttered in the grocery aisles. What was I forgetting? Milk?

I had forgotten fun. I used to go dancing. I used to "hang out" with people. There was a time Hugo and I would just read in the sheets for half a day. That frivolity. Those unproductive hours with indefinite goals, where did they go? It's all maintenance now. Maybe we envied Georgia for that. She and her friends and their talent for doing nothing, smoking on the fire escape, tromping through the park in housecoats and sandals, like rumpled circus clowns making a mockery of all our vain ambitions. It drove Hugo to distraction. Our stabs at success, our catastrophic bungles, and we seemed worse off. And there she was, sailing along, penniless, oblivious and having all the fun. Until the accident. Until the reality we had been warning her about, almost wishing on her, raised up its viperous head.

Freshly washed, I feel baptized, de-degraded, retrieved from my private abyss of helplessness. From the gym bag, I produce a stick of deodorant and run it across my itchy pits, as if everything were normal. If I had a few more hours of light, I might even consider a mad dash for the highway. But I pace the cabin floor, sensing dusk's burnish through the gauzy curtain, agonizing between the urge to run and the prudence to wait.

The truth is I'm terrified. Or it's just intense boredom that's gnawing at me. What do they yammer on about in yoga class? Chakra this, your prana that. I wish I could channel all those energies as easily as it's professed, rid my life of the stress, but I'm afraid I thrive on it. It provides structure to my days. The loss of tension would leave me in a soft general collapse.

After pacing some more, I zip my gym bag open and remove the twist of paper with the coke inside. I carefully tear off one end, unfold the creases, like a flower's snug petals, and tap a gram of white dust onto the countertop.

With my car registration, I cut up two very fine lines.

Just a bump each; I don't want to be out of my head, just on the bright electric side of it.

I take my time with the powder, tapping and dragging, first one direction, then another, chopping as thoroughly as possible. My nose is delicate and easily agitated. Besides, there's no need to hurry. I'm here all evening and night.

The two emergency candles are packaged in brown wrap. I use the paper, roll a tube and bend down, snort a line into each nostril, fuse the remnants into a third one, snort that and rub the excess powder onto my gums, not wasting a particle. That done, I wait until the buzz starts, the intervening boredom sizeably more tolerable with a lift in sight, the way a lineup is less annoying when you're nearing the front. I look around, uncertain what I'll do with the impending euphoria. Needless to say, I've never been coked up alone in a forest cabin. The warp is magic for a club thumping with dance music, or mad talk at a dinner party, but in the total solitude of my present circumstances, I'm in uncharted territory. A shade of paranoia darkens my thoughts, but just as I'm dismissing it the chemicals kick in. Or the chemicals are dismissing it. It's hard to tell, here on the verge. Where does the wrist become the hand, that kind of thing? Soon it's unmistakeable though. The boost. The humming tremor.

I'm going to get through this. I'll walk to the highway tomorrow morning and be in my bath by lunch. Ha. The coke is filtering out all the dirty water sloshing through my head. Sparkling clarity. Why did I let that rat, Trevor, Bent Brent, whatever ha ha, fucking shithole rat-soul for a fucking soul, why did I let him get to me? I'll recover and live my life and he'll squirrel away in his rathole somewhere, comfortable, no doubt, the little shit, in Cozumel or

Argentina, but I don't care, I can't waste my time, life is just the wind shaking the barley, or something something, isn't it?

Okay, this is good. I'm happy. I could stay here for days.

Then the door shakes.

Something knocks heavily against it.

Rattle, scratch, thump.

The front door bangs open an inch against my barricade of flimsy bed frame and pine furniture, which it turns out isn't really hard to move at all. They are almost weightless, in fact, these objects, if you're a hungry bear who happens to weigh several tonnes. All you have to do is push your big, meaty paws against these pesky things and they will move quite handily in front of you. I'm frozen over here by the stove. The flares and whistle are on the daybed, over there near the entrance. Out of reach, of course. These details are sharply defined, chemically enhanced, like an extremely slowed-down film of lightning crawling its skeletal way to the ground. I look around. For what? A magic door to a storybook kingdom guarded by elves? The mind, I think, is going to invent hope out of nothing as long as it can.

There's an iron poker miraculously resting by the base of the stove, its tip grey with ash, its handle blacksmithed into a curled, artful grip. I take it in my hand and feel strong. It would hurt, even be lethal, on something smaller than a bear, I imagine. Better than the flare or whistle? I liked the idea of those flares. It would be effective to stick one down the animal's throat. I think that would help. But I have the poker and I can attempt to bring it down very hard against the bear's nose—*surprisingly hard*, the bear might record in its increasingly enraged brain, and possibly be distracted, possibly intimidated, I'd like to fancy, for the alarmingly short future I'm imagining of the next tragic minute or so of a very, very bad week.

"Hello," a voice calls out. "Is someone in there?"

A human voice. A male human voice.

I manage, "Hello? Hello. I'm in here. I'm *in here*." Maybe I say, "Who's there? I'm in here. There's someone here. Oh god oh god oh god."

Things like that.

The barricade is knocked against, shoved, more resistant it seems, now that human voices are involved. I should help but I'm struggling here with comprehension. The disaster is being transformed. I'm not entirely going to believe anything just yet.

"Are you okay?" the voice calls out, and the door butts against the bed frame. I step forward and tug on the foot of it and it slides back enough for this voice to wedge its face through the entrance and blink into the haze of the cabin's interior.

"Yes, I'm fine. I'm fine," I answer.

Why do I keep repeating everything?

"I saw the car and the footprints so I thought I'd come and take a look."

He steps into the room. He's thickset, about my age, not bearded but unshaven with a few days' growth. He is wearing a light-blue golf shirt, the collar darker with a geometric design in yellow around the neck. His Expos cap looks like it may have been purchased when they were actually a team, not only sports nostalgia. His jeans are very undesigner, one of those shapeless, warehouse brands that are cut to fit anyone. Everything is just a little dirty and faded.

"Did you see the bear?" I ask.

"Bear?"

I tell him the whole story of the flooded road, the car, the night of rain. He listens, clucking his tongue.

Then he's laughing. "That was no bear," he says. "What you saw was a dog."

"It wasn't a dog. It was a bear. The thing was gigantic."

"Yeah, well, Karen, the neighbour, a few properties that way," he gestures, "keeps a Newfoundland out here. They're good in water. Webbed feet. They're really big dogs. That's the truth."

He squints toward the forest off to the east.

Me saying, "A dog?"

Him nodding, slapping his thigh. "Really big one. I saw the tracks. His name is Harold if you want to meet him. He's got a tongue the size of your face."

My barricade looks comical now. My whole existence for the last day or two. A new sense of scale.

"It's all good," he says. And we laugh together. "What brings you up here?"

"I'm selling this property. I just drove up to have a quick look."

He looks me over again with a new, skeptical gaze, studying my face while his own shifts expressions like a shadow has passed over it. Then he glances further inside the cabin. I look too, at the disarray, the dislocated bed and chairs, my scattered garrison of road flares and gym bag. A discarded pile of yesterday's clothes— Capris and underwear—mark where I'd stripped off and changed.

I realize I am still holding the metal poker.

"Selling it," he says, glancing around once more.

"I know. Way out here in god knows where. Bears and bugs and no toilet. Who'd want it?"

He clucks his tongue again. "You probably need a ride back to town," he says.

"You can't imagine," I say and immediately start collecting my things and stuffing them into the gym bag. Outside the light is nearly gone. The sky ripples with an orange glow, casting the tree-tops in silhouette. We pick our way along the collapsed fenceline and descend the slope. His truck is parked just beyond my car in the washed-out roadbed. I describe the flood again, the chaos, the car lifting into the ditch. He grunts and shakes his head, scrabbling down to the passenger side, and with a few heaves, he frees the open door from where it's jammed into the slope and slams it shut. Walking around, he inspects the front. "Brand new model. What a shame. Not sure if you'll drive it again, but there's plenty of good parts to sell. I know someone who can tow it if you're interested."

Then we walk to the truck, a four-wheel drive, practically gleaming with polish above the tire wells.

"I can't thank you enough for this," I say as we climb in. I'm still purring from the coke, babbling how grateful I am, how crazy the whole situation is, how desperately I want to get home and shower. He settles into his seat and slips the key into the ignition as he turns and gives me a strange smile.

"You don't know who I am, do you?" he says.

The ignition keeps beeping. But he hasn't turned the key.

"What do you mean?" I say. "Should I?"

He pulls the key back out and the beeps stop. All the little lights on the dash go black again. The man studies the cluster of keys in his palm and then looks over with a grin.

"Daniel," he says. Then, as I stare at him questioningly, "Danny."

30

DANIEL—DANNY—MULVIHILL! My childhood friend, my summer playmate, when my parents sent me to the cabin to stay with Uncle Gerry and Aunt Kathleen, sits beside me in his truck.

"You're not going to lie on that couch all summer," my mother used to say, packing my swimsuit and jeans with the bug spray and towels. Gerry and Kathleen had no kids and were happy to have me for a few weeks in July. So were Danny's parents, since he otherwise spent his vacation in lonely conversation with imaginary friends, prone to bleak boredom by evening. For my part, I was shoved kicking and screaming into the car every start of July, denied the urban pleasures of shopping malls and TV binges with my regular school friends. Then I'd be dropped off at the Quebec–Ontario border a rustic week later like a prisoner in an amnesty exchange.

Maybe once up there, after a bonfire meal and a dead-to-the-world sleep in the canvas cot under army-issue blankets, I enjoyed myself. Sometimes. I find it hard to imagine me liking the inconveniences and discomfort. Maybe "like," maybe *pleasure,* is not the right category. Maybe my memory is failing. I won't entertain nostalgia. Please. Childhood is such a cloak-and-dagger existence: disowned from power, forced to construct a shadow reality in earshot of authority, trying to work the edges of influence for a little gain. Why would anyone pine for exile once you'd escaped it? Is that why Georgia's gone to Korea? Is she trying to erase me, or her father, even Natalie from her existence?

Danny's family owned the adjacent property, just to the west of our lot, where the path led downhill to the lake. To access any water, we had to cross a section of their land. The arrangement was good on all counts. My aunt and uncle and Danny's parents were fine cottage friends. Games of horseshoes or euchre, cold drinks on the deck. Those evening activities occurred most often at Danny's cottage, since they had a generator, therefore refrigeration, ice and emergency electricity. I was always slightly ashamed of our inferior state up the hill, backwards cousins to the relative luxury of the Mulvihills' cottage. We had an outhouse, a charcoal grill and a Frisbee. They had running water, a gas barbeque, a dock, a canoe and a cupboard full of board games. To Danny's credit, he never lorded this status over me, but the contrast was inevitable when it came to entertaining ourselves.

"Let's go to my place," he'd say. "We can go swimming. We can skip rocks from the dock. I've got Trouble. I can beat you this time. Or we can set up the badminton net."

What did I have to compete with that? Collecting pine cones and tossing them at the wood pile? Was that fun?

I haven't thought about any of this for years. Now, in the dashboard glow of the pickup, my brain reels, connects, and excavates hard-to-reach niches of memory.

"Danny," I say. "Danny *Mulvihill*. Oh my god."

It *is* him, inside that stubble and middle-aged attire. Gone are the dorky shorts. Gone the feathered, sandy-blond hair, now clipped and grey-flecked beneath the ball cap. But it is that distant child I once was close to. We're so rinsed of doubts and disappointments at that age, it's hard to believe we'd learned to recognize intimacy. Maybe that's the point. Maybe the boundaries haven't settled on us yet and we're as near as we'll ever be to each other.

"Aren't you chums," Aunt Kathleen would say as we appeared from an adventure in the woods, tapered branches in our hands to be used later as swords in battle or spears for marshmallows.

You could wiggle the powdery nuggets near the edge of the flames until they slowly browned, or just stick them right in the fire so they'd burst to a charred sweetness.

When I look Danny over, his face surfaces into the essential details of what I still recognize: grey eyes in two wrinkled cavities and the Adam's apple in his slightly saggy neck. He puts the truck into gear, turns around and starts down the gravel road (hallelujah!) as I start babbling away about how long it's been and what a crazy coincidence and miracle it is he found me out here.

"I come here a few times every summer," he says. "Just to have a look around, check on things. Sometimes I'll snowshoe up in the winter. You don't want the place left alone for too long. Might fall apart. I've done a few repairs. Hope you don't mind. Funny. I wasn't sure if anyone owned the place anymore. Since your uncle died."

"I kind of lost track of it."

"Sure." He laughs. "Isn't hard to do around here. Out in the woods. But I wasn't sure. I didn't see you at your uncle's funeral so I thought maybe you'd gone somewhere else."

"No, I was busy. I might've been overseas," I say, not remembering at all.

Is that a little bit of guilt Danny's inflicting on me? The coke is starting to wear off and I'm feeling like one of those marshmallows, burnt out and gooey and shapeless. The sharp crests on the dirt road are making me nauseous too. There's a cranky smidge of headache needling my temples. And my stomach growls like a cornered mutt.

"Anyways," says Danny. "I got worried about the cabin with that big rain we just had and decided I'd better drive over for a gander. Then I saw your car and the tracks. Quite an ordeal for you. Not soon forgotten."

We drive through the night, stars winking above our side mirrors. I keep talking, terrified of silence, grateful for any sentence that comes to mind, some of which I say out loud, diatribes regarding brunch as overrated or the virtue of buying a quality umbrella. How did I remember this? My thoughts are coming fast, crystalline and translucent as an ice cavern.

We attempt to catch up on the long past. He got his electrical training, did a stint on a cruise ship of all places, looping through the Caribbean and back up along the eastern seaboard for a couple of years. But he got tired of it. "Sounds romantic, I bet. But it was just a lot of changing light bulbs and patching cords. Pretty boring stuff. Good feed though. Buffets and all that. But now I do some contracting mostly."

He'd been married too. A woman named Patricia. Trish. She was from Nova Scotia. A nature nut. Sustainable ecology etc. She convinced him to try going off the grid, moving to a repurposed container in some bay I don't recognize the name of.

"I cut out windows, insulated it and built a deck for the summer." Danny details the daily composting, the greenhouse, the organic garden, the kit for wind power they bought online and had shipped to them that fall. They even had a sun oven. He explains how it operated: external mirrors and internal double glass that collects heat in a "thermal absorber plate." The way he describes it sounds both primitive and science fiction at once. He talks about the winter and trying to keep warm. He uses the word "wind" like I'd never heard of the thing. I watch his thick fingers grip the steering wheel as he describes the whole domestic adventure, which ended in sadness.

"I think we went a little crazy out there," Danny concludes, giving the windshield a defeated look. As if I'm not really there at the moment. "Took things out on each other. Didn't really work out."

"No shame in that," I tell him.

We have reached the highway. Real pavement. Real road signs. He turns right and accelerates. Compared to the vomit-inducing curves and washboard gravel of the side road, the main highway feels like a ride on a silk cloud.

DAVID O'MEARA

"Divorced too?" Danny deduces from his end of the seat.

I nod.

"It's a wild world," is his response.

I mumble how I'm glad the marriage didn't work out, that I'm better off, and the real question is how much time I've wasted with everything. We are onto the topic of my career and I explain the whole home-staging biz in a nutshell, which leads to renovation talk and the messy electrical jobs he's found in old walls. I nod and grunt in agreement, feeling fuzzy as we lurch past a tractor trailer on the first straight stretch of highway I've seen since we started. Compost bins mark the driveways beside the mailboxes.

"You okay?" Danny says. "You're looking a bit green."

"I might pass out," I say, my voice trailing. "I haven't really eaten anything and . . ."

And what? And I'm fighting a major bummer comedown right now. The coke's worn off. This re-entry into reality is not looking as attractive as it promised.

Danny gives my pallor a glance.

"I'd be happy to drive you straight to Ottawa," he says. "But you should eat. There's a spot that's not far from here. Let's get something in your stomach."

Thirty minutes later, I've regained some poise. The dizziness has let up. The need to vomit is almost gone. A half-eaten BLT, my second, rests on the off-white plate in front of me.

Coleslaw and a dill pickle beckon.

The truck stop is almost deserted, brightly lit, clean and inviting. Our server, Jeanette, is wearing a blue apron and pours my third coffee into the cup, one of those diner versions designed to hold two mouthfuls before needing a refill. I don't usually use sugar, but I'm using sugar. I'm a vacuum of crave right now. The excess is a reward for being alive. And compared to what I was facing two hours ago, this Quebecois diner is the banquet hall at Versailles.

Danny has been telling me that he sold the family house near Wakefield, plus the cottage by the lake, when he and Trish made the decision to up stakes to their experiment on the bay. They needed money for the move, with renovations to the container shell.

"I regret it, believe me," he says, hunched over his grilled cheese and baked potato.

But I don't hear much bitterness in his voice. It's an emotion he identifies but refuses to display, a descendant of the practicality of blue-collar forebears. The face of a silly child I knew is mostly gone, replaced by a serious adult; required pragmatism fashioned by grownup decisions and missteps. Lost dreams. Failed marriages. Ha. He could follow my own trials through credit card statements. Sitting here with Danny, I can't help but indulge another version of myself, an alternate me who didn't run, at her first opportunity, from a poor childhood in the townships to a design college in Montreal, then a too-hurried marriage and divorce.

Instead, what if I'd stayed, worked the minimum-wage job trail through Tim Hortons to Walmart, met a guy like Danny who is good with his hands and settled into a two-bedroom bungalow with a decent mortgage and room enough out back for an addition once the kids outgrew their bedrooms?

Would I have been happy?

Happy?

No.

No. I don't think so. Not me.

"So where are you living?"

"Still in Wakefield. I rent an apartment. Not that far from the house. I might buy again. Who knows? Maybe the old home will go up for sale one day."

"Why not move somewhere else?"

"Don't know. I didn't like the bay. And I know my way around here. I can find work easy. No surprises. You look like the travelling type. But I like to stay where I am."

I tell him about the birdsong app and the arctic tern. In a lifetime, they fly the equivalent of three trips to the moon and back. I think he finds this interesting, nodding and smiling and sipping his water.

I'm feeling nauseous again. Too much food, caffeine and sugar much too quickly. I push the plate away.

"If you want to finish my sandwich, go ahead," I say.

"Thanks, but I'm vegetarian."

"Really?"

"Yep. Trish got me to cut meat and I've never gone back."

"You don't look like one."

"What does a vegetarian look like?"

"I don't know. Not . . . like you. A hippie, I guess. My daughter is one."

Danny lifts his coffee to his mouth in his big paw hand. "Your daughter's a hippie?"

"A vegetarian. She was, anyway. She's been everything, week to week, it seems. I can't keep track."

"Sounds like she's just trying to find herself."

"Or escape."

I tell him about her mood swings. The blowouts with her father, the brushes with the law, the stupid escapades and the roof accident when Georgia and two friends climbed up a half-finished building, drunk or high, and fell through some scaffolding; one ended up with a concussion, but everyone lived. They were lucky. Mostly. Georgia wasn't there when Natalie died but she blamed herself. She took it hard. We had her with a therapist for a while, I tell him. Counsellors.

But I don't tell him everything.

Danny sighing. "Immortality and youth."

"It's maddening. She keeps it all inside."

"She in university?"

"Teaching. In Korea. She went over last fall. Heaven knows why. I tried to talk her out of it." My fingers tap the white ceramic of the coffee cup. "She's *surfing*."

Outside, I stand in the cool air, waiting for Danny to use the washroom. A padlocked ice machine hums beside a cage of propane tanks, also padlocked. There's an old codger smoking a roll-your-own at a picnic table on the edge of the parking area. He's wearing a train engineer's hat, the grey and white stripes having seen cleaner days. Dirty jeans and a blue T-shirt. He squints at me through a few folds of wrinkles. I nod at him.

"Hello," I say.

"You know Jimmy Howard?"

"No, I don't."

"He's doing okay," the man informs me anyway, a lyrical slur in his voice suggesting a Valley Irish heritage. "He's had a few hard knocks. Been in trouble. Poor Jimmy. But don't worry. He's doing okay. I just saw him and he looks good. Come up here for the fishing and saw him two nights ago. A new man. He loves the fishing. The fishing calms him."

Danny exits the diner and gives me an inquisitive look.

We walk to his truck.

"Say hi to Jimmy!" I shout back to the man.

"I will."

The highway widens and the roadkill increases in frequency. A skunk, knocked dead by the blunt force of someone's bumper, is now smeared over the width of one lane, reeking considerably for the good part of a kilometre. Increasingly urban, the road signs warn of lower speeding limits and advertise exits to downtown Ottawa or east to Montreal. We pass a flea market, then a car dealership, klieg-bright with banks of lights and red-and-white tasseled carnival flags. A Canadian Tire's red triangle looms in the gloom. A "Salon de Coiffure." A depanneur where three teenagers smoke cigarettes on a lowered tailgate.

Danny and I have run out of topics.

"Which way are we going?" he asks when we approach the Macdonald-Cartier Bridge spanning the river from Quebec to Ontario. The horizon flickers with embassy and government office lights. Several green exit signs whip past. I point him to Sussex and we skirt Lowertown.

"Oh shit, I don't have a car," I think out loud; a million things to do tomorrow and my wheels are back there in a muddy ditch. I'll have to rent in the morning, schlep down to the Market and hope the tourists haven't booked everything. And no cellphone. The whole idea exhausts me. I need control now, after so much disorder.

"Would you do me one more favour?"

I borrow Danny's cellphone and call Avis Rentals at the airport. Their office is the only location open past eight p.m. Months ago, they had mixed up a reservation so gave me a code for a future discount. I demand a luxury vehicle, and Danny has now agreed to drop me off there, bless his soul. It would be so very good to go to sleep without expecting any hassle in the morning. We are driving south again when I float another thought: "Are you at all interested in the property, Danny?"

"Property," he repeats.

"The cabin. You did say you were looking."

Danny, who had been driving with his right thumb at five o'clock, moves both hands up to the ten-and-two position like they instruct you and squints into the oncoming headlights.

"Hmm."

Then he doesn't say anything.

A minute passes.

"You could fix the cabin up. It's still in good shape, thanks to you. Ha. Or just tear it down and build something else if you want," I say.

"Didn't you say *Who'd want it?* a little earlier?"

I hate being quoted. Hugo had this awful habit of repeating things I'd just said to annoy me. It did. It infuriated me.

"Yes," I say to Danny. "That was just me venting. Talking garbage. Listen, I'm going to be very honest. I need to sell it. I have to. I messed up my finances. Royally. I took some financial risks that didn't pay off. It's a long story. I was stupid and I got burned. I could lose my business. But listen to me. If you want the property, it's yours. For a song. I mean it. No nonsense. You can look it over and decide on a price. We can work something out."

It's not a convincing pitch. I'm exhausted and my voice is empty. My enthusiastic words sound scraped and dragged from the bottom of a burned-out gulch. But he knows the property better than me anyway, its relative value and potential, and the fact that I've left it abandoned for years.

I look at his profile in the dash glow.

"I'd need to think about that," he says.

The truck enters the concrete ramp toward the airport's rental area. He slows to avoid a family of holiday makers leading their luggage on plastic wheels toward the long-term parking. We pass through a series of concrete pillars until our destination's in sight. Signs with Avis, Hertz and Budget appear, each company's drop-off points. Danny eyes the tight space between barriers and executes a three-point turn worthy of Euclid. The truck's in park. He thumbs the steering wheel again. Danny turns to me.

He says, "You weren't very nice to me. Do you know that?"

"What?"

"When we were kids. You weren't very nice." He expands in detail. That I always tried to belittle him. He uses that word: *belittle*. Then he uses the word "humiliate." The sentences tumble out, sudden and unrehearsed. I start to say something, to argue, but he gives me a look and he continues, this time through specific anecdotal evidence, describing a series of terrible, nasty little episodes—throwing his toys in the lake, stealing things—that I faintly recall, though I affect ignorance. He keeps using that word: *nice*. That I wasn't nice.

I wasn't a nice person.

"I used to go home crying," this burly middle-aged man is saying. "Because I thought we were friends. And then there would be those abrupt betrayals. I couldn't understand it. I found it very confusing. My parents tried to explain. They said you had a troubled family. They said you didn't mean anything by it and I shouldn't let it bother me. I understood that eventually. I did. But it hurt then. It felt," he paused for the right word, "very lonely."

Reeling, I push the truck door closed and Danny drives off like the Ghost of Summers Past. I step into the rental office. The two employees behind the desk look like college students who have pulled too many all-nighters, grey rings under their eyes, their skin a moon pallor. Do they get any oxygen down here? Sunlight? I'm informed the car I requested is not here but they are retrieving it from a subsidiary lot. It will only take a few minutes. I grind a fatigued look into them. I tell them I'll be back in twenty when I hope they'll have it parked and ready for me to go. I march through the parking lot, across the roadway where the shuttles and taxis line the arrivals section, half-deserted at this late hour, and glide through automated revolving doors to an ATM, then down the hall to a washroom where I dump my gym bag on the counter, pull out the remaining coke, cut it up and snort it through a twenty-dollar bill.

Thumbing my nostrils, patting my cheeks, my eyes settle on my own ineradicable image: running shorts and green punk-rock T-shirt, a dry crown of hair gathered into a bristly topknot, flecks of mud still spattered on the right side of my neck. I run the tap. The lukewarm water splashes across the exposed skin, which receives the drops like the Gobi after years of drought.

I let myself have a little cry, ha ha, just two plump tears that gather near the lower lashes before I can clear them with a scrap of paper towel. Crying is garbage. I am falling low but the chemicals will be my parachute. Across from the domestic baggage claim, I order a large double-double and watch a member of the airport staff operate an industrial buffer across a section of the floor while the Tim Hortons employee bangs a roll of quarters over the edge of the counter to make change. She is not practised at this. She strikes it a fourth time and the paper wrapper splits and spills half the coins onto the floor. She releases a service-industry sigh and squats to gather them. Across the baggage hall the escalators begin to fill up with arriving passengers, returning from where? A quick scan of the rolling schedule suggests Toronto. Though Washington is also in the queue. Some arrivals are being greeted. Hugs. Kisses. There are cries of delight, even surprise, that someone is waiting at the end of their long journey to take them into care and carry them home. There will be a late-night tea or a glass of wine. They will talk over the success of some trip, the difficulties, the sights . . .

I wasn't nice?

I'm struggling here. What was he talking about? I always wanted to be strong. I'd wanted a beautiful life, or a successful one. Can these states co-exist? Without the expense of greed and cruelty? Danny and I have agreed to meet up, for a drink maybe, in the weeks to come, and talk the thing over. The sale, I mean. But there's more that I need to talk about. My mind is running swiftly through the leaf-shadowed paths of my childhood, trying to catch an unguarded look into my youthful face. I feel like a big mirror has shattered in front of me, but I can still see my reflection in the pieces.

I take a large gulp of coffee and set off back to the parking garage. Reaching the entrance, I tap the door open with my hip. On each side of the vestibule there are elevators and a long wheelchair ramp to access the lower levels. Straight ahead, a man is struggling with two suitcases and a duffel bag as he wedges himself through the next set of doors. I walk across and pull the handle, holding the door wide so he can drag his luggage through.

"Great," he grunts, giving me a nod while he continues toward an elevator, tapping the ascent button to take him to departure level.

Odd.

He looks familiar.

Everything looks radiated and half-real in this concrete-and-steel jungle gym of an airport, all striped crosswalk and highlighted LED. Which might also be the coke starting to bend my brain. I shift the strap of my gym bag across my shoulder and turn for the ramp.

Then it comes together.

I do know him.

The man, his back to me, is dressed in a tight blazer and jeans. Designer jeans, Japanese selvedge maybe. They shimmer with a buffed newness. He pushes at the elevator button again and again, though its neon blue circle is already alight with recognition of its summons. No one can resist doing this, tapping that thing repeatedly, dramatizing our urgency.

"Hey," I grunt in the man's direction. He turns. His eyes, the set of his jaw, show more annoyance than curiosity as he studies my T-shirt and jogging attire.

"Trevor Brent," I say.

What he does next is he sucks in some air and puffs his chest out. A malicious gleam fills his bloodshot eyes. A little disbelief in there too.

Him saying, "What the fuck do you want?"

Yes, it's definitely him.

The chinless asshole.

The fucking pirate.

He's even got a gold loop in one ear. My head revs with a destructive energy, a kind of adrenaline hum, part rage, part fear. I take a step toward him, grinding my teeth.

"I want my savings back, you piece of shit. You stole my money. You fucking ruined my life."

"Are you crazy?" he says. "I don't know what you're talking about."

He sneers a bit, arrogant and guarded. There is just a nanosecond when I feel doubt. That maybe I've identified the wrong person. That this is not Trevor Brent at all, but some poor sap off to a conference in Detroit. Maybe I'm losing it. Maybe anxiety and fatigue and disgrace and, let's face it, the cocaine, has gotten to me, has warped my perception past clarity, and I have transformed into a raving lunatic in a sports bra and Worst Vermin T-shirt.

The elevator dings and its steel doors slide open and the man practically pitches his suitcases inside. It's a little too rushed, a little too desperate, and I lunge forward and block the door. He's trying to tap another button. I slap his hand. When he shoves me, I reach and get hold of his carry-on, the duffel bag slung over his shoulder, and he loses balance and falls back against the rear of the elevator.

"Shit," he says.

He gets up and pushes at my face, rubbing it into an advertisement for the airport pub, Darcy McGee's, on the elevator wall.

"Fuck," I say. "Fuck."

He's kicking at my legs, which hurts, and I'm clutching the strap of his bag for dear life. We see-saw back and forth, a shoving match, the door banging half-closed and open, blocked by the edge of Brent's suitcase. He's hissing obscene syllables at my face but I'm not listening, concentrating on keeping my grip on the duffel strap. After a moment it breaks and I go tumbling out, backwards, onto the floor outside the elevator.

And the sliding doors close behind me.

I'm winded.

Battered.

My face hurts.

There's hardly a sound but the fluid movement of the elevator ascending to the third level. A minute passes as I lie there, gasping for air. Outside the glass, in the near distance, a KLM flight descends into view.

The silence is broken by the bell of the returning elevator.

The doors open again. And there is Trevor Brent, red-faced and murderous. The stitching on a front pocket of his blazer is ripped and he too is gasping.

On a happiness scale, he's reading deficit.

He leans through the doorway.

"Give me my fucking bag," he says.

I glance to the side of me, where the rumpled duffel lies, torn from his arm in the tussle. Getting to my feet, I kick it farther away.

Me: "You're going to jail."

A very ugly look crosses his face. He's got to get out of here, but the flight he's likely booked is out of the question now that I've identified him. He'll have to leave the airport, retreat to whatever bolthole he came from and regroup for another day. Or do something, I don't know what, to keep me very quiet for the next few hours. Trevor steps toward me. The elevator doors slip shut.

I drop my arms, bounce a few times on the balls of my feet. I still can't remember which type of bear you should play dead with.

Trevor starts chuckling. "What are you? Some fucking karate master?"

Part 4
CHANDELIER

31

IN THE BREAK BETWEEN TERMS, the school sent Georgia to a two-day teaching seminar. Mrs. Kim picked her up at their school gate at eight a.m. Since the first day they met, when she'd helped find furniture for Georgia, Mrs. Kim had always been kind. Motherly. Georgia could talk to her, make jokes. Most importantly, she understood sarcasm, vital for Georgia, who dwelt on the indirect side of communication.

She was going to miss Mrs. Kim, who would transfer to another school. Everyone got moved around every four years, even the top principals. As they drove to the conference centre, she prepared Georgia for the two days ahead. "I'm sorry. I don't know why they are sending you to this seminar. It's all in Korean." It was a refrain between them. "Board policy," Mrs. Kim would sigh. Every Monday at the school there was a staff meeting that Georgia was expected to attend, though she understood nothing. Mrs. Kim would spend fifteen minutes of her free period giving Georgia the highlights afterward. They'd have persimmon tea. She'd ask how her apartment was, what she was doing in her free time.

Finite time shaded these chats now. Mrs. Kim was going soon. Georgia asked her where she would be transferred.

"It's a country school. Not far." She sighed. Some teachers liked the rural jobs, she explained. They were quiet and much easier. You had less students and could focus on them. But many students were from farm families and didn't see the benefit of learning English. So, her job would be difficult. She would be frustrated. She loved the puzzle of language.

When they'd stopped at a red light, she glanced at Georgia with a funny grin. "Anyway," she said, "I won't be there for long. Can I tell you something?"

Georgia looked at her. She'd seen Mrs. Kim giggle before, but never blush.

"It's a secret for now, but I can tell you." Her right hand rested on her stomach. "I will have a baby."

"Oh my god," Georgia gasped. She lunged toward Mrs. Kim and they shared an awkward hug, restrained by their seat belts. A car was honking behind them. The light had changed.

"Sorry," Mrs. Kim said to no one, and waved her hand in the air between the seats, then shifted the car into gear through the intersection. The soft mountains, as ever, piled up above the city's edge. Georgia congratulated her again and they started laughing. The morning fatigue in Mrs. Kim's face had transformed into a glow. She'd been married last summer and was anxious to start a family. She was waiting for the school term to end before she announced the news. "I'm so happy to tell someone."

In an auditorium, they claimed their lanyards for the teaching seminar. Rows of theatre seats and a small stage. A bigwig from the education ministry dispensed a somber, hour-long speech. "What's he saying?" Georgia asked Mrs. Kim. "Only an introduction. He is welcoming us and wants us to be dedicated." After thirty minutes, she leaned toward Georgia and said with exasperation, "No content." Through the opening PowerPoint presentation, Georgia sat there pretending to listen, her eyes wandering between the floral arrangements on each side of the podium, distracted by the incomprehensible screen graphics, and, eventually, the glutinous scent of cooked rice. Lunch was provided in the centre's adjacent cafeteria. They were given vouchers to trade for compartmentalized metal trays, like prison. Rice, kimchi, seaweed, pieces of fish. Then more lectures, PowerPoint, a coffee and tea break. Not soon enough they were back in Mrs. Kim's car.

CHANDELIER

"Will you go back to teaching after the baby?" Georgia asked her, picking up the subject as if it hadn't been interrupted by seven hours of seminars.

"I want to. I like the students," she said. "But I don't know. I will be happy with a family," she added, almost apologetically. They'd had discussions over the difference between western and Korean attitudes. Mrs. Kim was in the first generation of Korean women who really wanted careers but patriarchy still asserted itself. Georgia told her the pressures were more subtle in Canada, but they still existed.

"You're a great teacher," Georgia told her now. "The students love you."

"You're kind," Mrs. Kim said.

It was nice to hear but Georgia didn't feel kind. It didn't seem like the right word. As much as she liked the students, she felt resentful if she had to discipline them, but annoyed if they didn't respond. She was having trouble assuming authority. *I'm on your side, I'm one of you,* she kept thinking when they acted up. Though only five or six years older than many of them, she wasn't a student anymore. She smelled like an adult now. The pack was rejecting her.

Brake lights glowed ahead of them where the road branched. Mrs. Kim slowed and shifted down.

"Here we are," she said.

They were in the lane outside their school.

"I'll just walk from the gate," Georgia said. She picked up her papers and conference files. The bag was heavy now. Everyone had been given an award—a thick plaque with the school board's crest—for attending. Thanking Mrs. Kim, she started to walk down the lane toward home.

She heard a shout and turned.

The school caretaker was running down the muddy road, waving his arms.

32

THE ANXIOUS CARETAKER spoke to Mrs. Kim. He'd been getting calls in English. The next time it rang, Mrs. Kim answered. It was Georgia's mother.

Mrs. Kim brought Georgia to the phone.

"What's going on?" Georgia asked.

"It's about your father," her mother droned from the other side of the world, sounding annoyed, shaken and tired.

He was dead.

Through an embroidery of stops and starts, her mother shared the skeletal details. Hugo had flown to Barcelona for a conference. At some point, he'd fallen off a dock and drowned. Georgia listened, skeptical and vacant. His body was, according to a Canadian consular source, in a morgue. The rest was mystery. He'd been in Spain only a few days. The hotel staff said he kept *horas erráticas*. On Tuesday, a jogger, at dawn, saw something in the water by the port. A Spanish newspaper reported the jogger had thought: *Was that a body?* So, he'd turned around and gone back. He ran past and looked again. Yes. The slack bulk of a torso. Then he called the police.

"Erratic hours," Georgia's mother repeated. She kept talking. She said she'd spoken to Hugo the day he'd died. She'd been exhausted and he was irritable. It wasn't a long conversation. "I just needed to get some sleep," she said several times. And "a jogger found the body." She didn't have any more information. There was still an autopsy. They kept talking in circles. Georgia kept asking what happened to him, as if each time the information would change, the circumstances would expand and become clearer, comprehended like the identifying jogger. She would say autopsy. It was her mother's new word. Someone would have to get back in touch with more details. She would call Georgia then.

"Are you going to be okay?" her mother added guardedly.

Georgia looked out at the glare on the hard ground. A crisp, limitless sky. Birds flickered in the bare branches of a tree. Blurry silhouettes gathered and detached beyond the frosted glass to the hallway.

"Georgia?"

"I don't know. I didn't . . . I wasn't . . . Don't freak out. It's okay. I just . . ."

"Please, Georgia. You know what I mean. You're not going to put me through that again, are you?"

"I was putting myself through it."

Her mother sighed assertively. Before hanging up, she blurted, as if it was totally incredible, "I was listed as next-of-kin."

Tea was brought by a discomfited secretary. Mrs. Kim fussed, offered to go to Georgia's apartment with her. "You shouldn't be alone," she said. But that's exactly what Georgia wanted. A hard wall, detached, no entry. She toddled in a daze down the road. There was nothing to do. She washed a sheet. Something was expected of her, she supposed. She couldn't sit still. She scrubbed some plates, a pot and cutlery. She dried them and put them away. Then, with the coming of dusk and darkness, she felt boxed in. A gauze of rain brushed over the rooftops and pavement. She took the bus downtown and wandered the underground shopping mall. Back and forth. She climbed the steps. It was dinner time. People passed. She stood and watched them spilling from the stairwells. The buses sped by, rocking the dirty puddles toward the drains. At the crosswalk, shoppers stepped daintily through the wet ruts. She bought a cheap cellphone and an overseas charge card. She opened the packaging. In the Lotteria Burger, she sat staring at her little heap of debris. The twist-ties. The moulded plastic shells. Information in several languages. Korean, English, French, German, Chinese, Russian. All repeating the same verifiable instructions.

Word had gone around. When she got back to her apartment, her landlady was there by the gate, talking to her, bowing and leading her upstairs where trays of food had been left. Fish, rice, sautéed vegetables. She sat Georgia down at the table. A minute later she returned with a bowl of bean and seaweed soup.

Mr. Yung arrived. Then Mr. Choi. Mr. Yung said he was very sorry a number of times and explained that the food had been brought over by other teachers and he wanted her to know that the principal and vice principal were very sorry for her loss. Her landlady was talking. Mr. Yung explained she was saying how sad she was. Georgia's reservoirs were exhausted, tapped by tributaries of sympathy and inwardness. She said she needed to sleep and that Becca was coming by later.

Just as Mr. Yung was going out the door, Mr. Choi slipped two bottles of soju onto her table, winked and bowed.

She needed to get high.

An hour later, her mother called back on the new cell number. She'd talked with police, who had been working with Foreign Affairs and the authorities in Barcelona, hoping to resolve her ex-husband's status. He'd had no travel insurance, she told Georgia. Nothing was covered, she said, rattling something around, cutlery or keys, in the background. There was still the question of the autopsy. Toxicology reports. They had to rule everything out.

"What's *everything*?" Georgia said.

"I don't know. When are you flying back?"

"Back?"

"Aren't you coming home?"

"Do I need to?"

CHANDELIER

Again, an hour later, the phone buzzed. Her mother was spilling with news and concern, fascinated with Hugo's death. The details obsessed her. She listed them off like she was reading a detective novel and wanted to solve it before the author could reveal the true killer. Everything in emergency tones. She researched the conference, where, it turned out, Georgia's father had not been registered. She'd even Googled the jogger's name. He owned a bakery not far from Hugo's hotel.

"They haven't done the autopsy," she said. "Some bureaucratic nonsense. We have to wait."

33

GEORGIA STOPPED AT A PC BANG. She needed a printer. Internet cafés were popular. On screens, gamers were saving galaxies, decapitating zombies with eerie discretion, the shriek of gunfire contained by noise-cancelling headphones. She typed her father's name into a search bar. The obit in Toronto read *Controversial Architect Found Dead*. A picture, dated by twenty years, presented the newly deceased gesturing behind a microphone. She scanned the summary: *Promising start. Career mired by allegations of corruption. Vocal critic of major architects. Brief fame as TV commentator. The jogger in Barcelona. Foul play not ruled out.*

She printed the link for Ray. They were meeting at a tea house. An elevator led to the third floor of an office block. Inside a door, past tapestries, the unexpected room opened to trickling water, tiles and traditional wooden panelling. Branches from miniature potted pines clasped the sills. Despite the wires and satellite dish bolted to the wall, the view to the mountains was peaceful.

As Ray's eyes tracked the obit, Georgia waited, rescued from its effect by hunching over her shifting shoes, absorbing the laments of a Bach fugue playing over the speakers. The circling musical phrases appealed for harmony amid the wasteful chaos. While he read, Georgia floated in anesthetized abstraction, staring emptily at floor tiles and table legs. When Ray finished, he folded the paper in two. "Christ," he said. "I'm sorry."

Three pine nuts bobbed in her tea. Flavours of persimmon and cinnamon revived her, like smelling salts.

"I don't know what to say. It's terrible, George."

She shrugged.

"Can I do anything?" Ray said. "This must be a shock."

He reached across the table and took her hand, guarding against any pithy consolations. The pressure of his palm substituted for the words that lacked repair.

"I'll stay with you."

After the tearoom, they wandered Kumnam-ro's disordered arcades and side alleys, seafood stalls advertising the morning catch on the coast. Georgia's face registered hectic mood swings. Distractions of lanterns, masks and celadon pottery were displayed in windows. They barely spoke in those unhurrying hours, Georgia picking through clothes racks positioned outside the shops on Art Street or grinding her drained face against Ray's shoulder. When she did speak, she doubted the reality of her grief, mocking herself for self-indulgence, cackling and irritated, then gasping with tearless weeping. "Ridiculous," she'd mumble. "Why should I care? We didn't get along. I guess I thought there'd be a day, y'know. Sometime in the future, where we could just laugh at everything . . ." I have to grow up, she kept thinking. Patient, Ray pivoted around the layers of damage she radiated.

Her mother was venting. The autopsy, the delay, the disagreeable vapour trails of Hugo's demise. "I cheated on him, you know."

Georgia didn't even pause. "I know."

"You're not shocked."

"I knew."

"You *knew*?"

"Yes."

"*How*?"

"He told me."

"Bastard." Georgia held the phone away from her face. When it rang, she'd been dreaming there was a thunderstorm. She seemed to be in a museum and couldn't find her way out. Now she was fully awake, though they'd been talking for twenty minutes. The cell display said 4:47 a.m. Her nose was cold. She rubbed at it and then tucked her arm back beneath the covers.

"Of course, he told you. The fuck. But it was over already, George. We were done. He cheated on *me* too."

"I know."

"There's been nothing from Foreign Affairs," Sarah pivoted. She was freaking out about the procedures and money. How much it costs to transport a body across the ocean without insurance. The onus he instigated. The husband that was not the husband.

"We could've worked it out. We did countless times. Countless. We disappointed each other. That's what it was."

"You're kidding me."

"Don't hate him."

"Why do you say that?"

"I know things were difficult. You didn't see eye to eye. You're too much alike. Stubborn. Both of you."

"It's not even five here, Mom."

Georgia could hear the birds already.

"I'm broke, George," she said. "I made some mistakes."

"Broke?"

Sarah told her about the Ponzi scheme. Georgia listened. She held the phone to her ear and pulled herself out of bed, spooning some crystals of instant coffee into a cup. The water started to boil on the element, windows fogging.

Trevor Brent was in jail. He'd been caught with a ticket to Mexico. Her mother had knocked him against a drink machine. Security intervened.

Georgia watched the birds frisking in the bare quince tree, the new light in the sky. "Uh-huh," she said. Or "What?" Evidence of her attention. The bitter coffee coated her lips.

CHANDELIER

Sarah continued: "I know I'm not easy to live with. I had this picture of my life. A clear picture. Was that unreasonable? Can I ask you something?" She didn't wait for Georgia to respond. "Do you think I'm . . . nice?"

"Nice?"

"Yes."

"What do you mean?"

"You know. Pleasant. Kind. Friendly."

"You're fine, Mom."

"I didn't ask you if I'm fine. What's fine? It's nothing. Fine isn't nice. Fine is something else. I'm asking you a different question. Am I good to be around?"

"You're a basket case."

"Don't say that."

"Why are you asking me this then?"

"I've been thinking about my life, George."

"Uh-huh."

"About everything. The mistakes. The wrong turns. I don't feel good."

"You're a strong person," Georgia said. "You've got guts. You raised me practically alone."

The gratefulness was sudden. It sapped her. Georgia saw how messed up everything was all the time. The contradictions were dizzying, a circle, some limitless merry-go-round.

"Georgia, are you listening to me?"

"What?"

A long pause.

"George," her mother said. "I need help with this."

34

HER SCHOOL GAVE HER the rest of the week off. Becca came to her apartment frequently. She wouldn't leave Georgia alone. She hovered around like her friend was an injured bird. If she'd found some twigs, she would have built a nest and sat on her.

On Thursday, Georgia went back to the Lotteria Burger for lunch. It was near the bus stop. At the shopping mall she took the escalator to the bookstore and browsed through the Penguin titles for distraction. Such misery, such helplessness. *Oliver Twist. Little Dorrit.* Destitute children and debtor's prison; you could be saved occasionally by a secret benefactor.

She went to a bar.

The old feeling rippled through her. Dead energy. The tunnel of everything. It had been safer to stop caring. Mrs. Kim was right: she was tired. Anxious again. Dissolving at her edges. Yet everything strange seemed so normal. The school, Becca, Mick, Ji-Tae, Ray. This was her life. If she could just stay still, perfectly still, without a past or a future, then she would be safe.

At some point she called Ray, who was finishing work. Mick and Becca showed up. Ji-Tae arrived and they drained thick mixes of vodka, pineapple, jackfruit and tangerines through straws. The cautious, unspoken consensus was to let Georgia let off some supervised steam. They called two cabs and headed off to the Rock 'n' Globe, a bar Ji-Tae wanted to try. Georgia climbed into the back seat and folded herself against Ray's side. Downtown, a door led to a narrow set of steps to a one-room square of thumping tunes.

CHANDELIER

The entrance was draped with loose plastic strips, like a butcher's freezer. There were six high tables with stools, a bar counter. The rest was a dance floor. The walls were painted black and flashing lights washed across them in sync to the beat. Georgia hung back by the door, watching people and getting drunk. Ray came over to check on her.

"I fucking hate the westerners here," Georgia said.

Ray looked at her.

Georgia shrugged. Her chin bobbed. She'd been drinking all day. A dark cavity was chewing through her. She could feel something letting go, releasing. What had her therapist said about impulsive decisions? False passageways; they would sap her momentum. Each reckless turn would only make her more lost.

In the washroom, she wagged her fingers through the tap water. Some shithole bar, she thought, and I'm drunk, though I shouldn't do this, drunk, shouldn't be this way. She was mugging at the mirror, straightening her face, spilling her drink. The world had become small, precise and rounded at its edges. Like watching life through a sniper hole.

She'd had a moment of dizziness, disorientation, at the door and swayed there in a philosophical pause. But the thoughts weren't coming cleanly, clawing at the crumbling verge. She scowled again at the mirror. The water was rippling around the drain. She'd pressed a wet palm against her cheek, rubbing it across her forehead, pushing her hair back. "Georgia," she said to the unprepared shape of her own face.

When she stepped back into the bar, she was surprised by her surroundings. It was not what she was expecting. She looked around. Confused contours loomed up. The furniture looked like someone's apartment: metal chairs, a table, blue blinds covering a window at the back. A fat couch against one wall. She rubbed the tumbler's rim against her lip.

"Where were you?" Becca said.

Becca tried to drag her onto the dance floor, but she wasn't interested.

They were under the strobe lights. Mick, Ji-Tae and Ray were stomping along to AC/DC.

Someone pulled a stool up beside Georgia.

"Hi," he said.

He was a tall, pale westerner she'd never seen before. *Oh god,* she thought, *I do not want to make conversation.* She nodded at him. Kept her head hung down, remote with drink. He was talking. A name in the thunder of bass notes. He told her he was from Iowa. He was teaching in a hagwon.

Surprise, surprise.

"Didn't think you were working in Starbucks," she mumbled. He genuinely thought that her sarcasm was hilarious, laughing too much to seem sincere. Georgia could see Becca's eyes looking in her direction.

Iowa was talking away. A job in Itaewon that didn't work out. His first airplane flight ever. The ground disappearing off his wing.

She stretched her fingers across the tabletop, flexing them in the strobe flashes, a blotto stop-motion display. She was trying to transform her fist into an open palm, her open palm into a fist, between each stuttered interval of light. It was like her hand went somewhere for a second and then reappeared. Like her body was a skipping stone, connected to the surface of her existence, briefly, in its flight.

She was telling Iowa that she'd been in a lot of planes. Her parents travelled a lot. They'd gone to Rome when she was a toddler. But it was exhausting to talk. Hard to get the words moving. It was like skating through snow.

"What was Rome like?"

"I was super young. Don't remember much."

"Nothing?"

"It was really hot and we were under some big trees and my father was dipping my feet in a fountain. He would take me to the bakery every day. I liked to watch them dipping the dough in sesame seeds. I remember the lobby of our apartment. Always dark and cool. It was covered in marble tiles that had drawings of fish on them. And I had shiny yellow boots for the rain."

"That could have been anywhere."

"It was Rome."

But maybe it wasn't Rome. Maybe it was just a day somewhere. Childhood memories are fugitive. Fuzzy tales decoded by adult spectators, modified by analysis. They're like the dancing strobe, theatrical in its bursts of light.

She recognized someone slouched over at the bar, tipping a beer bottle into his mouth between two fingers, his head tilted back. Pompadour, the Korean drug buddy of Brad. She hadn't seen any of them for ages.

She marched over.

"Hey," she said.

Pompadour looked her over slowly but said nothing.

"Remember? We met before. At the pool hall," she shouted.

He leaned back and barked something at the bartender, a Korean woman with black lipstick, glittered cheekbones and a tight, fake black leather dress. She was scooping ice into tumblers but stopped and shouted at Georgia: "He doesn't know you."

Georgia ignored her and positioned her mouth near the side of Pompadour's head. "Just want a bit of weed, man. Okay? Just a little dime bag."

He wouldn't look at her. He watched the mirror behind the bar.

"Hey! He said he doesn't know you," the chick insisted. She'd left two customers waiting by the other end of the counter and had come over to give Georgia her full attention. She stood, leaning forward from the service area, front arms planted, like a bulldog at the end of its chain. There were three tiny tattooed stars on her clavicle.

Iowa was suddenly there saying something.

"Get lost," Georgia shouted.

"What's your problem?"

"Fuck off, hayseed!" She shoved him hard in the chest and there was another guy—his friend, she guessed—who was throwing his arms in Georgia's direction while Becca was pulling Georgia by the waist away from the counter. Mick was holding Iowa back, all "C'mon, mate. C'mon, mate," voice of reason and glitter-chick screaming, "Get the fuck out of here" while the other bartender had come out from the back, glancing back and forth, trying to figure out what was going on. Becca had grabbed Iowa's buddy. They were shouting and shoving each other, and Georgia was screaming, "Asshole!"

"Shut up," Becca roared at her.

Georgia noticed Ji-tae at the end of the bar, wild-eyed and in the midst of a screaming match with Pompadour. Ray, with extended arms, was attempting to herd his friends out of the bar. A lot of pushing, hands grabbing at shirt collars, bar stools on the ground. It was a travelling mosh pit.

Something smacked against the side of Georgia's head.

Iowa's buddy, snarling.

Georgia whipped around and threw a punch, connecting with his forehead. He grabbed her hair but Becca jostled him and he went tumbling back against one of the high-top tables. Georgia lunged toward him. Ray grabbed her. He shouted, "No!" while pulling Georgia toward the door.

"What? So, you're saving me now?!"

"Fuck, Georgia," he said, and gave her an exhausted, pitying look.

Georgia could feel the cold air on her face and arms. They'd practically fallen up the stairs and were now standing outside. Mick was trying to catch his breath, huffing clouds into the cold street. A second later Ji-tae and Becca charged out the door, carrying all their coats, glitter-chick lecturing Ji-tae in Korean before

CHANDELIER

shouting, "Don't fucking come here ever again" at the rest of them. She slammed the door.

"Fuck you," Georgia snarled at the blocked entrance.

"George," Ray warned. "No more."

They panted in silence.

A cold breeze drifted down from the black sky. Ji-tae started handing out coats.

"It's not good," he said.

Blood was all over his face.

35

THE FOLLOWING FRIDAY, after work, they drove. The roads east were jammed, their progress slow-going. It was tight in the car with all five of them, plus their gear, bags and knapsacks. Intermittent rain fell with wind, Ji-tae studying the sky, skeptical that a good storm might bring out the waves. Ray was marking a student quiz in the passenger seat. Along the coast, the scratchy radio went in and out of signal range. A ritual now, Ji-tae translated Korean pop lyrics for them: "She is sad and doesn't want to be alone tonight."

His cheekbone was still yellow with the fading bruise.

Mick renewed the subject of the past Thursday's events: "Nice work there, George. You were a total monster. Destruction on legs."

Though Georgia had blacked out after they left the club, she remembered eating at another all-night Lotteria Burger, then puking her fries all over a plastic tray. It took her forever. She gagged up a few lumps, then swayed there with her head buckled into her chest.

Mick quoted her. "Why does fast food take so *long* to throw up?"

Georgia flinched and groaned.

"It was like a bloody revolution. Banshee league . . ."

"Enough, okay?" Becca said.

But Becca saw the banter was lifting the emotional weight off Georgia, who was smiling. She didn't care. She knew Mick was just taking the piss. Raising the mood. They'd all agreed, in solidarity, to take a weekend and get her away for distraction.

"No harm done, right?" Mick said.

CHANDELIER

Ji-tae cleared his throat.

"Sorry!" Georgia shouted from the back seat.

It was past nine when they reached the townhouse they'd rented in Busan.

They unloaded the cargo of duffel bags and groceries, then continued to Sharkey's, a bar with a Mexican-themed menu overlooking the beach. The place was booming, high-top tables surrounded by ex-pats and Korean students draining plastic pitchers of lager under a ceiling festooned with flags from Australia, New Zealand, the US, England, and yes, there it was above a giant projection-screen TV, the big, red, pointy maple leaf of Canada. Orange ring buoys hung on the wall. A dartboard. A cartoon poster of Sharkey himself, a Great White in Hawaiian shirt and sunglasses, grinned toward a bottle of Corona clutched in his left fin. The place was frat vibe, western and popular. Everyone seemed to be filming something with their phone. Ji-tae set off to find his buddy who had agreed to lend two boards for the surfing weekend. They spotted him shaking someone's hand and bowing. Moments later they both came over with two pitchers of flat beer. Handshakes all around, Mick offering to get a round of shooters, the ubiquitous Jack Daniel's poured into mini plastic shot glasses. The night proceeded from there. More beer, more bad western behaviour, drunken ex-pats screeching out cover songs at the start of the open mic portion of the evening, culminating with a pack of Brits in a chorus of rugby favourites involving knickers and sausages and cheap lubrication.

Georgia found the toilet and on the way back, checked her phone messages. The bar music was deafening. She stepped outside. A desolate patio overlooked the dark beach. Slippery blue and white tiling. Stacked chairs tied together with cables. A few smokers were hunched in the cold air.

There was another call from her mother. Then another. She had never been clingy before. Now she was nervous for news, worried about Georgia and money. No results. More delays. All that. The authorities were trying to wrap up their investigation. Who knew how long they'd keep Hugo's body? But they'd found CCTV footage of Hugo on the dock the night of his death. Clear footage. The police were reviewing it. They'd interviewed some tourists who were there the night he died. They identified him, but claimed they barely exchanged a word, just knocking around a soccer ball for a few minutes. A woman came forward too. Another architect. She'd spotted an article in the Spanish papers. They'd had lunch that day. And she said he seemed normal. The police wanted to know what was normal for Hugo. Her mother laughed. But the video was sent to her as an attachment, the police wanting to know if she noticed anything strange. "Do you want to see it?" her mother said on the message.

Georgia looked up and saw Ray standing there. She saved the message.

"What's up?"

Laughing darkly, Georgia waggled her phone. "There's a video of my father the night he died."

"Jesus. Do you know what's on it?"

She twisted her mouth but said nothing. A tuneless version of Chumbawamba's "Tubthumping" erupted behind them. The window glass rattled. Ray waited, watching her, displaying an available tenderness that opened her pain and the tears came.

"He called me a few times. Last week. But I didn't answer. Turns out he had cancer. In the stomach. I didn't know. No one knew. The police just told my mother this morning. The doctor had told him months ago. And, ugh, that was his typical solution. Instead of telling his family, he just went off and died somewhere. He was such a dick."

But she stopped and, turning her back to Ray, moved to a railing that looked out over the beach. The coast was outlined with apartment blocks and street lights. In the darkness, she could hear the heave and gust of air, like a giant sail filled to its limit. Georgia imagined cold sand, the wind over water. Her thoughts too were oceanic and, just as likely, advancing in a squall.

"He saved my life once," she said.

Ray waited.

"I'd been stupid, messed up and angry," she said. "I drank a lot. Drugs. My grades were shit. They suspended me. And I stopped caring. About anything. After Natalie, I felt completely abandoned by the purpose of things. I went white-hot, crazy, quit school and tried to wreck the universe. I was fucked up on more pills. Just . . . empty. One day, there I was, at home. I saw the kitchen knife, one of those expensive Japanese ones."

She dragged her finger, like the knifepoint, down one length of the healed gash on her wrist, to demonstrate. Ray's face went naked and numb. He pulled her close and hugged her as she breathed in great gulps.

After a minute, they leaned on the railing.

"Everyone thinks the shorter scar is the second attempt," Georgia said. "But it was the first. It didn't seem real. I thought I'd be afraid. That the fear would stop me. But I wasn't capable of feeling anything then. Not fear. Or hope. The first try was a tester, an experiment, like how you paint a small patch of wall to try the colour out. The pain wasn't there. I was outside myself. I felt nothing. So, I just thought . . . *Fuck it.*"

Her timing was lucky. Just chance, she told Ray. Her father had returned to the condo for his mail. He heard her fumbling around and found her by the landing to the back door. He blocked the bleeding as best as he could before screaming into his phone for an ambulance. He kept repeating "No, George, no, George" over and over as he held her arm. She remembered being very warm and tired. There was a dazed housefly hammering against the window of the door, getting caught in the curtain, circling the landing, and slamming back into the glass again. She remembered it vividly. In the middle of the panic, just before the paramedics arrived, she watched her father very calmly reach over and grab it in mid-air.

"I still don't know if that part's true. Or my mind, or my adrenalin, made it up. But when we got into the ambulance and they were locking the gurney into place, I asked my father what he did with the fly. He didn't understand. He looked at the paramedic. They looked at each other. *The fly*, I said. *In your hand*. He opened it but there was nothing there."

36

SHE WOKE TO A SOFT KNOCKING on her door and Ji-tae whispering he was ready to leave for the beach. Checking the clock, she did the math. Only three hours since she'd flopped into bed. Lifting her head from the pillow, Georgia grunted through phlegm. She dizzily scanned the room. Faint indigo between the shutters. Ji-tae was squatting by the bed, fully dressed in sporty Lycra, assessing the unlikeliness of a quick departure.

"Here is the coffee," he said.

He gently handed her a steaming traveller cup, tip-off that it was not going to be a leisurely rise-and-shine with unhurried breakfast and some contemplative dallying.

"Oh god, Ji-tae," she groaned. "I don't think I can do it."

"There is no option," he said. "I need help to carry things."

"Take someone else. Take Becca."

"Everyone is in a coma. Vegetable state, like a potato. You are the man."

"I'm the potato," she protested.

"You are better. You are the surfing potato."

"Give me five minutes," she said, though she felt like she needed five years. Wrapping a blanket around her shoulders, she dragged herself into the bathroom and threw water on her face, took a pee and gave herself what Becca called a "Pommy shower": a few vigorous swipes of deodorant as a substitute for washing.

Back in the bedroom, she dressed in a one-piece swimsuit, pulled her jeans on and grabbed her jacket.

No one else stirred as they went through the door.

Bastards.

Outside it was cold. If there'd been any wind, it would have felt like tundra. The weak light glittered on dewed edges of buildings and street signs. Dull silver to the east. A tin radiance. Ji-tae drove several blocks, retracing the route to downtown where they stopped in an alley with lock-ups behind metal shutters. With a few spins of the dial, Ji-tae freed the combination lock and waved Georgia over. A strip light winked awake, its garish LED glow revealing a jumble of boxes and paint cans, a work bench, circular saw, dirt bike (back tire missing), numerous empty Budweiser cans and a dusty shop vac. The morning felt illegal as they laboured to avoid thumping or rattling anything while they transferred a set of surfboards and three wetsuits Ji-tae's friend had arranged for pickup by the entrance.

Down by the beach, the shops were still closed but lights were coming on. As Ji-tae laid the boards out and waxed them up on the sand past the parking lot barriers, Georgia heard her cellphone buzz. Ignoring it, she shimmied into her wetsuit. She tugged the neoprene legs on, then the arms, and zipped it closed. In the reflection of the car window, her hair tilted in a mad bulge: half Medusa, half Pisa. A cold wind whisked the coast. Ji-tae handed her a pair of swimming gloves.

"The water is not . . . nice," he said.

She made a face.

"Go," she said. "I'll catch up."

Ji-tae beamed. Without a pause, he turned toward the shore, jogging with his board across the wet sand.

"Are you anywhere?" he shouted.

She watched him leap through the morning tide, pulling comic faces at her as his body adjusted to the temperature. The gloom lifted and became a cloudless day. Early dog-walkers tossed sticks down the sodden beach or into the close plunge of a wave. The dogs would dash and snatch, shake themselves dry. Only a half-dozen people were out in the water, swimmers limbering up. Georgia saw no boards until the silhouette of one popped up from a timid breaker farther out. Ji-tae was already paddling to a set of white crests reflecting the sun on the southern end of the bay. He shouted something and waved. She tucked her board into her armpit and reluctantly plodded down the sand to the froth of the chilly, retreating tide. It would have been very nice to get in the car and go back to bed.

The surf didn't cooperate. It wasn't happening, whatever made the sea shove, turn and lift. It looked like nothing to Georgia; it seemed impossible to guess how the conditions could change. She'd been learning through the winter months that surfers are part-meteorologists too, obsessively studying the changes on the water's surface, assessing each swell with eye and feel. They had come to expect, even value, inevitable variation. No surfer will champion any one beach, since they change over time. Every location reorders itself. The sun's energy heats the Earth's surface unevenly; the atmosphere shifts, rearranging the air from areas of high to low pressure, so over time, the winds kick up in places while they flatten in others, the sea in constant renewal. The land waits to receive the tide, to lift it up into shelves. She understood that once ripples formed, the wind had something to push against. Thousands and thousands of separate random waves were surging against each other out there. Their origins, their destinations, were barely predictable. Some waves that plunged against California's coast started as a current in the Indian Ocean. She liked to imagine it, a distant storm, days away, gathering the ocean to a swell, gusting over the endless fetch.

But here, the scarce currents moved toward the shore. The water was still quiet, but it looked darker, more brooding. Ji-tae and Georgia surfed for less than two hours. Often, she'd get up, play the flow until it petered out, stepping off the board like stepping down off a bus. Haeundae was really a beginner's beach for surfers. It had been a perfect place for Georgia to start back in the fall, to get some practice in, enough quieter tides to test balance and technique, with some decent breakers if she needed a challenge. But Ji-tae was disappointed. He wanted height: six-, seven-, eight-foot waves, big rollers with a high face where you could catch real speed and adrenaline. So, when he'd heard there'd been some drama in the latest tides, barrels even, these last few days, he'd been keen to find them. One day they would come.

No such luck now. Someone had been exaggerating. Or the weather had calmed, the water had lost its defined momentum, the surf disorganized, sloppy and meek.

Georgia watched him paddling to lineup for the next surge, checking the horizon, determined that something would collect into a proper set. She admired the hope and enthusiasm. It was dedication, wasn't it? Obsession. The dream of something better. All these ridiculous mornings and evenings chasing a circumstance you don't control but can only prepare for. Learning your balance, testing and refining your skill for when the good chances come. So here they still were, splashing about and climbing on their boards, boogying through the slovenly sub-par surf for a golden instant of rush. The small waves were hard work too, but without the exhilaration. You have to hustle for speed, carve out any drama and wiggle around on the lip to keep momentum. She persisted in this swoon, scissor-kicking the tide, creating momentum, jumping up and balancing out, finding a gentle lip to ride here and there along the jumbled surface. By lunch, she was exhausted and starving.

"I could eat the arse off a skunk," she said to Ji-tae as he slipped off the beach break into the waist-high ripples. There were more swimmers now, more surfboards, but the water was still limp and lifeless. He laughed and nodded, studying the horizon again, as if the promised waves were tantalizingly just beyond, ever on the verge of rising into something momentous. Reluctantly, he

CHANDELIER

unclipped his leash and they carried their boards up to a stretch of restaurants near the beach that made monster profits in the summer months. In the glass windows, photos of bibimbap and beer competed for their attention. They found a group table in a brunch place they'd frequented a few times before.

Ji-tae texted Becca with their location. Warming up with some barley tea, they talked about the surf, Ji-tae analyzing the lack of spectacle in the water, checking his app for the promised swells.

"Yeah, I'd love to try one of those big barrels," Georgia said.

Ji-tae told her about Noosa in Australia and how terrifying it looked in his novice summer. Even to get in the lineup was impossible, so he'd stayed on the fringes. The water moved fast, it hit hard and there was a lot of egos among the surfers. The pack was viciously competitive, and when there were superior swells, an accepted hierarchy was enforced.

"They are very serious," Ji-tae said. "They paddle past you. Push you out. You can't join the club unless you have a special talent."

A gust of wind went down the sidewalk. Some traffic cones tipped over, skittering a few feet farther. Ji-tae poured more tea into their ceramic cups. Georgia told him the details of her mother's calls, everything she had said, Ji-tae's face half shock, half empathy. Then he said, "What will you do?"

"Me?"

"About your family?"

"My mother wants me to come home."

"Will you go?"

Georgia watched the sea. The waves tugged and shoved, but had order, a rhythm. Not like each day, the days before, and the ones that follow. When she left Canada, she thought she would escape something. All the stupidity and hurt feelings and pain and regret. Anger. The aura of her mother's neuroses. She could feel, even here, even now, her father's reproach.

What had she once said to him from the hospital bed?

I lost my way and I hate being alive.

A delivery truck backed through a sloppy parallel park. Georgia and Ji-tae watched. A light rain had started. Hurriedly, the driver hopped down from the cab and dropped the tailgate, untying a tarp. A teenager in a rubber apron helped him unload several blue plastic crates.

"Maybe," Ji-tae said, "your mother needs you."

The gang arrived. The restaurant was jammed but they squeezed past the waiting area to find the table. Enormous glasses of juice were ordered. Orange, mango, grapefruit, variations with kiwi and passionfruit. The restaurant was mad for juice. It was some kind of thing. Three employees toiled away behind an industrial juicer, peeling, cutting up fruit and feeding the machine with sections of citrus colours. Their aprons were spattered with the spray of their labour like war surgeons. More crates were hefted through a doorway. A bin of peelings and pits were lugged out. The background music cycling through the speakers was interrupted continually with the snarl of the juicer's hidden mechanisms reducing fruit to liquid, like a chainsaw sectioning firewood, then chipping it to pulp.

On laminated pages, there were photos of select breakfast plates: quinoa and tofu cakes, granola bowls, seaweed salads, all served with side plates of kimchi. Mick flipped through the menu. "Where's the meat section?"

"Hold on to your arteries, Mick," Becca said. "They serve something called vegetables here."

"The what?"

"Veg. Uh. Ta. Bulls."

"Sounds depressing. Can they wrap it in a sausage?"

"This place is very healthy and popular," Ji-tae said.

Every few minutes, Georgia could see him checking the weather beyond the door.

CHANDELIER

"I feel like a scratching post," Mick said. He looked exhausted, hungover. Ray and Becca too. They scanned the menus.

The food arrived. The rain began to drop in wind-blown sheets. The waiter refilled their coffees. Ji-tae introduced the idea of staying an extra night. He'd been transfixed on the horizon where dark clouds scuttled low over the waves. An offshore storm was coming. It could mean good surf. They could test the waves in the morning and surf all day. The townhouse was rented until nine a.m. They could load the car, then drive back late Sunday evening.

"I can stay," Becca said.

Mick declined. "Sounds like exercise," he said. "I'm allergic, mate. Exercise makes me sweaty and short of breath."

Ray had to back out too. He had work to prepare for Monday and was already committed to being home in Gwangju the next morning.

"Don't let us stop you though," he said. "We'll find a bus or train tonight."

"Last chance," Becca said.

"If the waves are good," Ji-tae said, "we'll try right after lunch."

"After lunch?" Ray said. "Doesn't your side stitch up? Or your head pop off or something like that?"

"I think your penis shrivels," Becca offered.

"Not mine. Rock hard. All the time. Like a tree branch," Mick said.

"One of them little twigs, y'mean?" Becca said.

Ji-tae said, "Very small tree. Like a Japanese bonsai."

37

THE STORM CAME as they finished lunch. Wind worked hard and heavy down the western channel of the strait, rattling windows, popping awnings, postboxes knocked over. They listened to the downpour roaring against the roof. The building shuddered. Something metal collapsed outside. No one left the restaurant. In an aquarium light, they drained more tea. Mick ordered a beer. A server pulled the thin curtain back; the windows were steamed up; nothing could be seen beyond the thick ripples of water pulsing down the glass. The floor was a puddle. One of the staff kept a mop going, continuously, over the soaked tiles.

Georgia stood in line for the washroom. Restless, she checked the time, and thought about returning her mother's last call. It would be evening there, she imagined. Her mother would be up doing what? Fussing, no doubt. Bouncing off the walls over something. She should call her, but Georgia needed to delay the fretting, the constant pressure to pledge her emotional state to some source of happiness that never existed, like an Eden they'd been cast from.

When she returned to the table, Mick and Ray were at the entrance, paying the bill.

"The forecast is heavy tonight," Becca said. "There's an express bus in an hour. Mick and Ray are getting out of Dodge while they can. Ji-tae's going to drive them to the station. You still want to stay?"

Georgia looked at Ji-tae.

"Can we get in the water?"

He shook his head. "Not tonight. Too dangerous." He'd seen the live webcam of Haeundae. Hurricane winds, maybe. Red flags everywhere. Totally off-limits. "But it's expected to peak after midnight. This is good. It might be ideal in the morning. Maybe barrels!" He smiled extravagantly.

Georgia waited under an awning while Ji-tae dashed through the downpour for the car. After they packed their things, he'd drive Mick and Ray to the station. Everyone else was lined up for the washroom inside the restaurant. While she waited, Georgia studied the sky. Water spilled in chaotic rivulets over the awning's fringe. Potted trees knocked back and forth, their branches wildly gesticulating. Curtains of rain fragmented down through the spaces between the high-rises near the sea. She tried to imagine the beach out there. The scattered plastic chairs on the wet sand. The stacked waves. The dark, cold tide; the sea's animate violence with its loss of structure.

She closed her eyes.

This is where I am, she thought.

Wind and rain bashed at the nylon awning.

Ray came out onto the steps. She stood there smiling at him.

"What?" he said.

"Nothing. I'm sorry. I'm an idiot."

"How do you mean?"

"I just can't seem to appreciate it. I always feel like I'm doing it wrong."

"Doing what?"

"I don't know. One of my unfinished lives."

Ray said, "Shut up, please. You're amazing."

They hugged. The others appeared. Ji-tae pulled up in the car and the boys climbed in. Their wheels threw water onto the curb.

"You go ahead. I'm going to walk back," Georgia said to Becca.

"It's bucketing, mate."

"I need some air."

Downtown, under a beleaguered umbrella, she roamed the still-shut kiosks of a small covered market, looking at window displays of kimchi, vegetables, scarves and slippers. She'd swayed in front of a shop that featured ginseng roots displayed in glass urns like science fiction aliens waiting to come to life. It was next to an internet café that sold coffee. To dry off, Georgia bought one and because she was there, decided to check her emails. There were three tables near the window. Two rows of computers filled the rest of the room. She paid for half an hour on a corner terminal and set her cup down beside the mouse.

Bunching her pack near the hard drive, she logged into a server and punched in the café's I.D. code. A little timer appeared on the bottom right of the screen, counting down from thirty.

Her mother's email was there. Titled "Hugo" in the subject box with an attachment. In her mother's characteristic expediency, there was no other comment.

Georgia clicked on the attachment and enlarged the screen.

The footage was not quite four minutes long. Starting as wasteland, a boardwalk emerged under street lights. More objects became clear. The trunk of a tree and the end of a park bench. The overhead angle, black-and-white texture, were surprisingly defined for closed circuit.

A few seconds into the download several people appeared. A couple of guys, a woman, all young, thin, looking dressed-up a little, as if they'd just had a nice dinner somewhere. Another woman came into view. Her legs dipped into the top of the screen and moved toward the bench. The men kicked a box around, back and forth, jabbing at each other's ankles, trying to steal it. On the screen they were fast but clumsy, likely drunk. She could see that they were laughing. But there was no sound. Only a dream-like rub of movement.

Then, there he was. Georgia's father.

Hugo Walser. Unmistakable. He stepped into the right of the screen and stumbled forward, saying something, shouting, waving his hand, bent down and, moving crab-like, backwards a few feet, the men forming a staggered line, tapping the box between them. Her father limped slightly. The leg of his suit looked scuffed or torn. An impromptu soccer game ensued for the next few minutes, the tourists making several attempts to get the box past Hugo. He caught it in his hand. He blocked it with his outstretched leg. But finally, they poked it past him and threw their arms in the air and ran around as if it was the final in the World Cup and nothing less. Her father too was exultant, sharing in their ecstasy. He jumped up and down, his mouth popping open in a theatrical oval. The players tapped the box between each other a half dozen more times, but their makeshift ball had crumpled, its sides collapsed now by the abuse of play. It fluttered loosely along the ground.

The tourists waved at Georgia's father, then slipped across the bottom of the screen.

In the last twenty seconds of the footage, her father is bent over catching his breath, his big palms on his knees. He's exhausted. He's all alone now, no one else there, as far as she could see. There's the edge of the park bench, a curved trunk of the tree. He stands up straight and looks around. He looks up at the CCTV camera, the first time he's even aware of it, Georgia thought. He seems amused, it looks like. She thought he might be laughing. For a second, he hunches forward. For someone's benefit, he lifts his arms in victory again, looking straight at the camera. Then, Hugo, the failed architect, father and husband, bows, just like an actor, and stumbles out of sight.

That's where it stops. Where he stops, Georgia thought, forever.

38

RAIN. ABSOLUTE HEAVY cascades of rain. After gulping down doses of warm rice, kimchi and coffee, they packed gear and hustled the bags into the car through the sluicing gusts before sun-up. Ji-tae locked the townhouse, dropped the keys into the mail slot, dashing to get into the car. In the murk, wipers brushed the street in and out of focus. Georgia looked at Becca, skeptical of any hopeful forecasts. Ji-tae stayed focused on the road. In the parking lot, they hydro-foiled through a monster puddle before the car rolled to a stop beside a set of guardrails. They sat listening to the deluge thumping the car's roof until it seemed to ease off. Ji-tae had rechecked the weather radar, which showed the last edge of the storm.

"Let's look at the water," Ji-tae said.

"C'mon, mate. We're here, right? Let's just do this," Becca said.

She tugged on the handle and pushed the door open. They unstrapped their boards from the rack. Before they even saw the water, they could hear the ocean, like cannon shots as each wave collapsed onto the shore. They jogged down the wet sand. Ahead of them, in the lifting dark, were shaggy lines of foam surging toward the beach. There was no one in the water. No one in sight. Without a context it was hard to estimate size, but the waves had height. Definite height. Ji-tae was cackling with delight.

"This looks nuts," Georgia said.

Seagulls ganged over their heads. Ji-tae looked at Georgia, smiling wildly, reaching down to strap his leash to his ankle and tucking his board into his armpit. She didn't know if he'd ever seen

CHANDELIER

waves this high at Haeundae, but he began to look serious as he studied the horizon, assessing the whole shoreline as he sized up the direction of the tide for where they should launch out. The marbled water, brown with mixed sand, pulled at their heels from a backwash. They jogged north up the beach for a few hundred metres, then waded in. The swells were messy, shotguns of force, not moving in clean lines but with short, overlapping hashmarks of curling crests. Before they could get waist deep, they were all knocked flat on their asses.

"It's better farther out," Ji-tae said. He pointed to a new set breaking south toward land. "It's okay. But be careful."

They climbed onto their boards and started paddling hard, digging with deep scoops through the smaller waves before the big ones came. The sea was icy. Becca and Georgia were both side-winded by tide, breath knocked out of them. Up ahead, Ji-tae looked back, anxious to test the swell. He had stopped paddling and waited. "Maybe it's too high," he warned. Georgia and Becca pushed past him, signalling their decision and responsibility.

The beach break was a crescent-shaped inlet, the headland protected from the storm surge. Here, the surf was calmer, leaving a channel relatively navigable. Knee-paddling now, the three of them fought for deeper water and found a takeoff area where the swell started to lift and break south. Watching where the lines formed, Ji-tae paddled for open ocean to merge with the current's momentum. Matching it, he popped up for a few seconds before getting walloped by a churning linebacker of foam. Instead of disappointment, his eyes flashed with elation in the challenge he'd been hunting for. The waves curled and rounded up into beautiful shapes. But for Georgia and Becca, the whitewater was choppy, unpredictable, and time after time they were pitched into a trough and battered around before corking to the surface.

Georgia was struggling, flustered. The water was breaking left and she paddled toward a set that was sketching out ruffled white lines in the distance. But she hadn't waited to get her breath back. So, when she stood up, anxious, already winded and off-balance, she was too slow, too behind the break. And the wave collapsed.

There wasn't even time to strategically bail.

The heavy wall banged her off her board and drove her straight under. Instinctively, she got her arms down. How close to the shore? If she went down too hard, the waves could smash her into the seafloor, break several bones, knock her out.

As the foam hit her, she'd been breathing out.

Her lungs were empty.

She thrashed, managing to boil to the surface. But as she emerged the second wedge of the wave train shoved her down again before she could take some air. The surfers call it getting rag-dolled, when you're pushed underwater, no up or down, tossed and dragged this way and that, lifted toward air then sucked back toward the bottom. Ji-tae had talked to her about keeping calm in a wipeout. But this was more complicated. It was a terrifying loss of control coupled with panic.

It was drowning.

She had resisted the tragic impulse to inhale. Rising, she got battered once more by a brick load of water. Then her head broke a trough's surface. Long enough for a lungful of oxygen. A moment later she was washed clear of the set, gasping and grateful her leash hadn't snapped nor her board had bashed her skull in. Ji-tae and Becca shouting. She raised her hand, too winded to shout back.

They paddled with her back to shore.

She told them she was fine, they should go back out, the waves wouldn't wait. "I'll join you in a second."

She watched Ji-tae carving his board across the face of the wave, almost disappearing behind the curtain of surf before emerging at the foaming edge of the tube. She was happy for him; happy they'd stayed and gambled on the conditions. Becca was taking a beating but kept at it. The barrels were coming along consistently

CHANDELIER

now, lifting and curling in sets of three or four. They were beautiful, exciting, so full of potential, but as Georgia tried to paddle back out, she was fighting hurdles of alarm. She couldn't steady her breathing. Fear. Closing in on the tremendous breakers detonating at the impact zone, she was spooked. Positioned for another wave, her nerve failed and she let the surge pass. She was done. Defeated.

A nearby crest started to peak.

What do I have left? she thought.

Ji-tae was shouting. She checked for him. He was near shore, untangling his leash before launching out again. He raised his hand.

She turned her head to see what he was pointing at.

Below the horizon, three thick lines of white crests were scrolling toward her, the water beneath a glassy, cobalt blue. They were a long way off, and could just as easily flatten out, shift and swallow themselves and become something benign.

Georgia wasn't far from the takeoff zone and started paddling hard. Pushing up and planting her feet on her board, she crouched loosely as she slid along the shallow, fast line. She was too tired, wrung out, her arms stretched, her gut wobbly. The fear returned. She couldn't help but think that if she got held down underwater this time, she wouldn't have the strength to resist panic. She'd do something stupid, decide faultily and pay for it. Glancing back toward the beachfront, she located herself. They'd chosen a mid-rise office tower as a marker for the lineup. She was just south of it. She checked the incoming waves. Small breaks swished past, until the darker, deeper energy of the ocean thrust up, and a blue wall rose.

A first peak blew past. She swayed in the trough and for a moment the surface grew peaceful and she thought she'd missed her last chance. The shore had disappeared, still hidden beyond the crashing foam of the last wave. And when she turned her head to inspect the horizon, it also had been swallowed by the returning swell, the second wave of the set bulking toward the sky. She turned her board. She didn't overthink. The spontaneity bypassed her anxiety. She dug her arms past her elbows in deep strokes, then hesitated, thinking, *Fuck, stop,* then paddling again, even faster, as the lip began to break. She could see the white foam crackle and sizzle along the crest's top, feathering, like a spark moving down the fuse of a cartoon dynamite stick.

Then it started to curl. She pushed forward with harder plunging strokes. She had stopped too early before and dropped too late. This time she got ahead of the curtain of water that was bending over her head. She ripped like a shot inside the barrel. It had height, but wasn't monstrous, so she kept low, crouched and bouncing lightly on the board to pump herself forward. Ji-tae had told her that if she got inside, it was best to stay in the middle and let the force of the wave carry her out. If she grazed the top, or got caught in the plunging foam below, she'd get ricocheted and pummelled. How long was she in there? Five seconds? Ten? Time paused as she slid across a rising wall of the ocean's journey coming to its culmination, swirling around her in a shrug of green and azure. She could feel the water detonating at her heels while she focused on her escape in the tunnel ahead as the wave shimmered in an ongoing oval collapse. Surfers call it the chandelier, that breaking fringe of foam that frames the barrel's exit. There is a grace area between panic and calm. You can't stay there forever. But you need to try even as you plan a way to exit. The magic, she understood, was to balance between the tumbling edges as long as possible before the walls crumple and close you in.

Gratitude

To the City of Ottawa and the Ontario Arts Council (and their juries) for financial assistance during the writing of this book.

To Silas White for believing in this book, and to Cecilia Chan, Rebecca Hendry, Luke Inglis, Corina Eberle, Rafael Chimicatti and everyone at Nightwood Editions for your meticulous attention and support.

To Janine Young. It's a gift to have an editor who is on the same wavelength, values and encourages nuance, character and the shape of a phrase. Much appreciation.

For crucial direct feedback at various stages on the manuscript, I am deeply indebted to Dorothy Jeffreys, Marisa Gallemit, Kevin Hersak, Harold Hoefle, Missy Marston and Andrew Steinmetz.

To my parents, whom I miss dearly, and to cherished family and friends.

Photo credit: Rémi Thériault

About the Author

DAVID O'MEARA is the award-winning author of five collections of poetry, most recently *Masses on Radar* (Coach House Books). His books have been shortlisted for the Gerald Lampert Award, the ReLit Award, the Trillium Book Award and the K.M. Hunter Award, and have won the Archibald Lampman Award four times. His poetry has been nominated for a National Magazine Award, quoted in a Tragically Hip song and used as libretto for a pastoral cantata for unaccompanied chorus, written by composer Scott Tresham. He is the director of the Plan 99 Reading Series and he was the founding Artistic Director for the VERSeFest Poetry Festival. He lives in Ottawa.